Compassion in the 4 Dharmic Traditions

Hinduism, Buddhism, Jainism, and Sikhism

Compassion in the 4 Dharmic Traditions

Hinduism, Buddhism, Jainism, and Sikhism

Editor

Ved P. Nanda

PRABHAT
PRAKASHAN

Published by
PRABHAT PRAKASHAN PVT. LTD.
4/19 Asaf Ali Road,
New Delhi-110 002 (INDIA)
e-mail: prabhatbooks@gmail.com

ISBN 978-93-5186-736-4
COMPASSION IN THE
4 DHARMIC TRADITIONS
Ed. by Ved. P. Nanda

Edition
2025

Price
₹ 800.00 (Rupees Eight Hundred only)

Printed at
R-Tech Offset Printers, Delhi

Preface

Students of comparative religion will find that the Dharmic traditions share much in common, despite a number of variations and divergences among them, both in theory and practice. The papers in this unique collection attest to this reality. Uberoi Foundation for Religious Studies gathered a number of experts in the autumn of 2014 at Naropa University in beautiful Boulder, Colorado. They deliberated on the common features among these traditions, especially addressing how the religious and spiritual aspects of these traditions relate to compassion. The authors shed light for the reader on selected aspects of this special trait termed compassion, a virtue that ennobles life and brings happiness to those practicing it. The editor and the contributors are indeed grateful to the Uberoi Foundation.

Denver, Colorado
January 2016

—Ved P. Nanda

Acknowledgments

The Uberoi Foundation owes a deep debt of gratitude to the Naropa University and its president, Dr. Charles Lief, for hosting the meeting of the Foundation's Experts in September 2014. Professor Judith Simmer-Brown was most helpful with the arrangements that led to the lively two-day deliberations—keynotes, panel sessions, presentations, reports, informal gatherings and discussions, and insightful conversations—and eventually to this unique collection of selected papers presented at Naropa. I am especially grateful to Katharine Nanda, Esq., for her invaluable help in the editing process and especially to Shri Prabhat Kumar who most graciously encouraged and shepherded this publication. I express my deep gratitude to Prabhat Prakashan for enthusiastically and painstakingly ensuring a most attractive final product.

—Ved P. Nanda

Contributors

Ved P. Nanda is John Evans University Professor, Thompson G. Marsh Professor of Law, founder of the International Legal Studies Program, and Director, Ved Nanda Center for International and Comparative Law, University of Denver Sturm College of Law. He is Chair of the Uberoi Foundation for Religious Studies.

Evan Finkelstein is professor of Comparative Religion and Maharishi Vedic Science at Maharishi University of Management, Fairfield, Iowa.

Yashwant K. Malaiya, a scholar of Jainism, is a professor in the Computer Science Department at Colorado State University, Fort Collins.

Henry John ('Harry') Walker, a Lecturer in Classical and Medieval Studies at Bates College, is currently studying Sanskrit.

Bal Ram Singh, a former professor of Biophysical Chemistry at the University of Massachusetts, Dartmouth, is currently Director of the Institute of Advanced Sciences, Dartmouth, and is leading an initiative on Ayurvedic Science and Technology.

Radhey Shyam Dwivedi is a cell biologist, Emeritus Professor of Biology at Howard University, Washington, D.C., and immediate past President of the International Center for Cultural Studies, USA.

Christopher Key Chapple is Doshi Professor of Indic and Comparative Theology; Founder and Director, Master of Arts in Yoga Studies, Loyola Marymount University, Los Angeles,

California; and Editor, *Worldviews: Global Religions, Culture, and Ecology*.

Veena R. Howard is Assistant Professor of Asian Religions at California State University, Fresno.

Judith Simmer-Brown, an Acharya (senior *dharma* teacher) of the Shambhala Buddhist lineage, is a professor of Religious Studies at Naropa University in Boulder, Colorado.

Rita Gross is a Buddhist scholar-practitioner who retired as a university professor at the University of Wisconsin, Eau Claire, and is a senior *Dharma* teacher at the Mindrolling Lotus Garden Meditation Center in Virginia.

Samir Kalra, an attorney, is Director and Senior Human Rights Fellow for the Hindu-American Foundation, Washington, D.C.

Subhash Kak, a *Dharma* scholar, is Regents Professor and Head of Computer Science Department at Oklahoma State University in Stillwater.

Dilpreet Singh Jammu is a prominent businessman in Colorado, a co-director of the Khalsa School Denver, and co-President of the Board of Directors of the Interfaith Alliance of Colorado.

Frank Tedesco, Founding President and Director of True Dharma Buddhist Mission, has taught at several universities and international organizations, including the University of South Florida and University of Maryland, and UNESCO Korea.

Contents

PART III
Compassion from the Perspective of *Dharma* Traditions

Introduction

The Dharmic Traditions Share Compassion as a Common Feature

—Ved P. Nanda

I

The four Indic traditions—Hinduism, Buddhism, Jainism, and Sikhism—have *Dharma* as their source. Although *Dharma* is hard to translate into English, in essence it encompasses foundational principles and laws that are universal in nature and uphold our very existence. To name a few selected common features of these traditions, they all agree that there is an Ultimate Reality and that we as human beings are capable of experiencing it in our daily lives. They have the common goal for humankind to attain the state of enlightenment and total liberation. Toward this end, they all recommend the practice of some form of meditation. One aspect of *Dharma* to which all these traditions subscribe is the principle of *ahimsa* (non-violence). Another principle held by all four is that they do not believe in their superiority over others, nor in exclusivity in the sense that their faith is the only way to liberation of the individual, and hence they do not engage in proselytization, which sets these four traditions apart from the Abrahamic religions. Another integral part of these traditions is the virtue of compassion.

II

The opening set of papers collected here addresses the common features of these Dharmic traditions and interactions among them.

The three essays are by Professors Evan Finkelstein, Yashwant Malaiya, and Henry Walker.

Evan Finkelstein, a professor of Comparative Religion and Maharishi Vedic Science at Maharishi University of Management, Fairfield, Iowa, notes in his essay, "The Dharma Traditions of Hinduism, Buddhism, Jainism and Sikhism in Light of their Universal, Common Ground," that in these traditions "to do no harm is not limited to causing physical harm, but also includes not hurting any being mentally, emotionally, financially, or socially." He adds that "it is not deemed sufficient by these traditions to only refrain from doing harm, but rather everyone is strongly encouraged to be helpful, empathetic, compassionate and loving to all beings: to provide selfless service, or *Seva*, to uplift and improve the life conditions of all beings." He cites authorities from all these traditions to illustrate this aspect.

Professor Finkelstein studies extensively what he calls "the central and foundational knowledge" in each of these traditions, quoting scriptures and teachings "in light of fundamental principles of what has been called the 'Perennial Philosophy.'"

Yashwant K. Malaiya, professor of Computer Science at Colorado State University, Fort Collins, Colorado, and a noted author of Jain history, examines historical records to study the relationships among the Dharmic traditions in "Interactions Among the Dharmic Traditions." He "acknowledges the need for each tradition to assert its uniqueness, while acknowledging the shared background and the mutual influence." Malaiya asserts that while it is taken for granted that all these traditions are mutually incompatible and that "choosing one necessitates rejection of everything" that the others offer, "this view does not reflect the realities of either Indian history or contemporary society." After an extensive study of the literature and historical evidence, he concludes:

> As Indians interact with people in the rest of the world, they find the need to explain their views using the perspective of Abrahamic religions.... The followers of the dharmic traditions are thus compelled to take an exclusivist view. Devout activists

> in the four traditions increasingly reject what is shared.... However, a careful look at all the sources of Indian history brings out the fact that there has been a remarkable degree of mutual acceptance among different traditions.... This paper shows that the four traditions share much more than what is often thought, and have influenced each other sometimes in ways that have not been noticed.

Henry Walker, a professor of Classical and Medieval Studies at Bates College, is a student of Sanskrit, with special interest in the interaction between India and the ancient Greco-Roman world, which is the focus of his essay, "Inter-Religious Dialogue in the Greco-Roman World". He considers compassion "an essential element of any real religious dialogue, any genuine interaction among different religions." Thus, he says, "[W]e must accept the fact that people are diverse and religions are different, but we must join in their experience both because of this difference and in spite of it." He calls for the adoption of "a compassionate internationalism that bases interaction on the existence of different nations, and on respect for that diversity."

Walker discusses inter-religious dialogue by citing the case of Pythagoras and Hinduism, suggesting that "[i]f two religious systems are very open, if they can enter into a free discussion with each other, they can have a very rich and productive relationship." He next considers the topic of the dialogue between Greco-Roman paganism and Hinduism by relating the story of Appollonius of Tyana, a Greek follower of Pythagoras, who visited India in the first century from what is now Turkey. He visited India and learned that "India is the source of the teaching of Pythagoras and that it was also brought to Egypt by the Ethiopians, who had originally lived in India." By the time he returned to Greece, Appollonius regarded himself as an Indian thinker.

Walker concludes with this caution:

> We cannot manipulate other people's minds and cause them mental harm so that they will abandon their religion. We cannot calculate ways of obliterating a religion from the face

of the earth. We must therefore accept the polytheistic view that there is more than one path to God, there is more than one road to the Great Mystery, because if we continue to pursue the monotheistic path of mutual destruction, we will inevitably come to a point when there will be nobody left on this earth to worship God in the 'right' way or the 'wrong' way.

III

The next set of essays is by Professors Bal Ram Singh, Radheyshyam Dwivedi, Christopher Key Chapple, and Veena Howard. They discuss compassion from the following perspectives: relationship with the natural world and environment; selfless service; nature connection in the *Yogavāshiṣh-ha*; and the treatment of animals respectively.

Bal Ram Singh, a former professor of Biophysical Chemistry at the University of Massachusetts, Dartmouth, is currently director of the Institute of Advanced Sciences, Dartmouth, and is leading an initiative on Ayurvedic Science and Technology to complement and advance current knowledge and practice of health and allied sciences. His essay, entitled "Compassion in the Four Dharmic Traditions: Relationship with the Natural World and Our Environment", opens with his thesis: "Dharmic traditions and nature are almost synonymous in their philosophies and practices, both outwardly and inwardly. *Dharma* by definition is the nature and, by derivation, is the source of all that exists. Thus, nature and environment are corollary to *dharma*, and people following *dharma* traditions compassionately embrace the nature and environment."

After studying *Karma* as the basis of diversity; current theory of evolution and its limitations; Darwin on diversity; evolutionary superiority of bacteria and plants; and Dharmic traditions, joint family system and environmental preservation, Singh concludes:

> Going back several millennia, the dharmic traditions contain robust philosophical, scientific, cultural, and ritualistic practices of respecting nature and protecting the environment for sustainable progress of humans materially, intellectually, and

spiritually. These practices need to be modernized and presented to the world as complementary and alternative approaches to the current scientific and technological efforts being employed for sustainability.

Radheyshyam Dwivedi, a former professor of Biology at Howard University, Washington DC, and a noted scholar of the Dharmic traditions, provides a comprehensive study of compassion related to *seva* in his essay, entitled "Compassion and Selfless Service". He notes that there is no consensus how compassion, a rather controversial topic, evolved, as he states, "Within evolutionists opinions differ whether compassion and sympathy are the products of evolution, as Darwin assumed, or it cannot be so because it is generally too costly to the individual." He addresses psychology and physiology of compassion and related behaviors, neurologic bases of compassion, and the genetics of compassion before studying compassion in the Indic religions, which consider "compassionate acts of kindness...as the observance of the *Dharma*." He illustrates this observation with several stories from these traditions.

Next, Dwivedi addresses the glory of human birth and *Yama* and *Niyama* before addressing the practice of compassion as '*Seva*, the selfless service', which in the Indian literature is considered a Dharmic duty. He asks the question, "Is selfless service really possible?" and responds:

> Selfless service is an ideal of Seva, and while serving in a selfless manner may be difficult, it is not impossible, and it is not only for the selected few. It can be learned by anyone at any age, and any selfless service to the deserving/needy in any shape or form, by itself, is an ennobling experience. It is an invitation to sublimate the all-too-common egoistic selfish human nature. In Swami Vivekanand's words, it is for "*Atmanomokshartham, jagathitaya cha*—for one's own salvation and for the good of the world at large."

Dwivedi further studies selfless service as moral duty and a 'wholesome humanitarian activity', and concludes that compassion has "survived because it is so natural and healthy for the personal and collective welfare of all."

Christopher Key Chapple, professor of Indic and Comparative Theology at Loyola Marymount University, Los Angeles, writes on "Nature Connection in the *Yogavāshiṣh-ha*". He divides the essay in two parts: *Elements* and *Sorrow, Birth, and Rebirth*. He states that there is celebration of nature and its elements in Indian thought from the *Rg Veda* on to the *Atharva Veda*, the *Upaniṣads* and the *Markandeya Purāna*. To illustrate, the *Rg Veda*

> celebrates Agni as the god of heat and light, Indra as the deity of the thunderstorm who releases the waters of each year's monsoons, and Soma, the creator of a special herbal elixir. The Vedas also extol Dyaus, the Lord of the heavens (referred to by the Greeks later as Zeus), and Pṛthivī, the goddess of the earth.

Chapple cites numerous verses by Vasistha extolling the Earth, the waters, fire, and air, wind, and space, as the sage "describes the planet with great precision and emotion." In his words, "nature speaks to and moves Vasistha to a place of deep connection." After discussing sorrow, birth, and rebirth in part 2, Chapple concludes:

> The scientific process of observation may be seen as kin to the *pañca mahābhūta dhāraṇā*, the sustained observance of the five great elements, with similar results. Just as Vasistha saw the myriad connections between earth, water, fire, and air and was drawn into a state of elation, so also the research scientist comes to recognize a plethora of connections, seeing that plant life, insect life, reptiles, mammals and more live in a web of mutual dependence. From this realization arises an ethic of care, a sense that one must act responsibly for the whole rather than seeing all nature as merely instrumental for human comfort. Becoming larger than ourselves, making the move from anthropocentrism to anthropocosm, from self-centered

concern to an embrace of the largest of the large, the universe itself: such is the calling of meditation, a meditation that connects the individual through elevated consciousness with the cosmos.

Veena Howard, who teaches Asian Religions at California State University at Fresno and is currently involved with a project of developing pedagogical tools for the study of Indian traditions, has entitled her essay, "'Animals are Persons Too': Ancient Indian Narratives and the Contemporary Question of the Animal Compassion." The animal narratives found in the Ramayana and the Mahabharata, she says, "argue not merely for the sameness of all beings, nor 'speciesism,' but set up a more complex framework that allows the reader to experience a world in which animals, humans, and gods co-exist and often share their existence on equal footing, even to the point of interchanging their bodies through disguises." Thus, "the portrayal of animals and the relationship between nature and humans take a form that invokes ethical questions regarding the treatment of animals."

Howard asserts that "[t]he sacred Hindu tales present a framework with which eco-critics, eco-psychologists, and eco-philosophers may investigate questions regarding the relationship between the humans and the natural world."

IV

Each of the six papers comprising the final set addresses compassion from the perspective of one of these Dharmic traditions. The authors are Professor Judith Simmer-Brown, Professor Rita Gross, Samir Kalra, Esq., Professor Subhash Kak, Mr. Dilpreet Singh Jammu, and Professor Frank Tedesco.

Judith Simmer-Brown, a distinguished professor of Contemplative and Religious Studies at Naropa University, studies the Shambhala Buddhist tradition, the founding tradition of Naropa University, in her essay, "Creating Enlightened Society: Compassion in the Shambhala Tradition". She notes that this tradition is "rooted in the contemplative teachings of Buddhism, yet is a fresh expression of the spiritual journey of our time. It teaches us to live in a secular world with courage and compassion."

After narrating Shambhala's history and lineage, especially warriorship in this tradition, she focuses on the practice of meditation for warriors. She further explains Shambhala's core teachings, with their emphasis on societal happiness and the creation of an enlightened society. Finally she concludes:

> The Shambhala tradition has provided the basis for a powerful transformation of the motivation that seeks the welfare of the world, and asks its citizens to step in and find a tangible, enduring way to help. Some Shambhala warriors have become activists; many have become leaders and visionaries in their fields. Most have become inspired by the dignity and beauty of everyday human life, and have found a way to contribute to the long-term goal of enlightened society. Through the transmissions of the Shambhala lineage, warriors have resilience and stamina and an ancient optimism about human potential.

Rita M. Gross, a Buddhist scholar-practitioner in the Tibetan tradition who retired as a professor of Comparative Studies in Religion at the University of Wisconsin, Eau Claire, and is a *dharma* teacher, writes in her essay, "Compassion and Religious Diversity—Some Buddhist Perspectives", that the link between religious diversity and compassion is obvious, "though some might not recognize that link immediately."

After discussing the following four points about Buddhism and diversity—"recognizing the need for detachment from views and ideologies; the need for tools to develop a flexible, pliable state of mind; the interdependence of self and other; and our hyphenated identities"—Gross addresses the issue of compassion and religious diversity from a Buddhist point of view. She proffers the thesis that,

> while religious diversity does cause discomfort, that discomfort is due, not to the presence of different religions co-existing within the same geographic area or on our one small planet,

> but to our own discomfort with diversity and our preference for uniformity and conformity. Those are the problems we must cope with and diffuse, rather than seeking for religious uniformity, sameness, or agreement. What needs to change is not the existence of religious others but our own discomfort with difference. We have to learn the spiritual and psychological skills to be willing to let others be different.

Samir Kalra, an attorney and Director and Senior Human Rights Fellow for the Hindu-American Foundation, asserts in his essay, "Compassion in Hinduism through the Preservation of Human Rights", that in Hinduism the concept of compassion, "in its broadest sense, can be viewed as an extension of *ahimsa* and applies to all living beings, not just humans. *Ahimsa* is 'the Hindu belief that symbolizes love, genuine care, and compassion towards all living beings....'" Compassion, he says, is similarly based on "notions of *atman* and the ability to feel for others as we feel for ourselves."

After citing several Hindu scriptures that expound on the importance of compassion, Kalra discusses international human rights law for conceptualizing compassion as well as spiritual and scriptural foundations for human rights in Hinduism. He explains that compassion is manifested through the preservation of human rights and suggests that "human rights in the modern era is a vehicle to carry out acts of compassion for the benefit of universal brotherhood."

Subhash Kak, an award-winning scientist and a scholar of Indic studies, is Regents Professor and Head of the Computer Science Department at Oklahoma State University in Stillwater. In his essay, "Morality and Compassion in Hinduism", he explains *Dharma* and the very name by which Hinduism is known, *Sanatana Dharma* or Vedic *Dharma*, and observes that the earliest Hindu texts stress the centrality of ethical life. After a detailed and meticulous exposition of several topics such as Virtue and Social Welfare, Varna and Jati, Circles of Morality and Freedom, Vedic Cosmology, and

Medical Ethics through the Lens of the Vedic Scriptures, Kak suggests that the theme of moral and compassionate conduct runs through most Hindu teachings.

Kak aptly concludes:

> The Hindu belief is that science and technology must be harnessed in a manner that furthers man's inherent quest for self-knowledge. Since an individual is defined not in isolation, but through his interactions with other persons, this quest of knowledge cannot ignore the larger good of the society, and it requires ethical preparation on the part of the individual. In the Upaniṣads this is addressed as the coming together of both *vidyā* (spiritual knowledge) and *avidyā* (material knowledge).... The Hindu ideal is to embrace life and its challenges without losing sight of the larger world and remaining compassionate in dealings with others.

Dilpreet Singh Jammu, a co-director of the Khalsa School of Denver, co-President of the Interfaith Alliance of Colorado, and a prominent businessman, analyzes the text of the Sri Guru Granth Sahib Ji and examines compassion within the Sikh faith. In addition to nearly 3,000 references to synonyms of compassion, he finds the word 'Compassionate' and 'Compassion' in the translation of Sri Guru Granth Sahib Ji 115 and 75 times, respectively, which, he says, "speaks to the importance of compassion within the Sikh scriptures and for practitioners of the Sikh faith."

After examining these 190 references for context, he finds that these references fit one of the following three major categories: 1. A description of the Divine or exemplifying an attribute or quality of the Divine; 2. A supplication to the Divine; or 3. A description of the State of Human Existence or the State of Being. He explains these further and narrates the three values of Sikhism and its traditions and history: Remembering and meditating upon God; Living and working honestly; and Sharing with others. He provides several examples of compassion in the Sikh traditions and history and concludes that "[c]ompassion is central to the human experience."

Frank Tedesco, a Buddhist chaplain and Founding President and Director of True Dharma Buddhist Mission, has taught at several universities and international organizations, including the University of South Florida and University of Maryland, and UNESCO Korea. In his paper, "Compassion and Service in Buddhism", Tedesco calls compassion "an impetus for selfless service to others in the Dharmic tradition of Buddhism." The focus of his paper is on 'socially engaged Buddhism', which, in his words, is 'compassionate service' in contemporary Buddhism.

After a detailed and insightful review of 'socially-engaged Buddhism', he describes his study and writing about death and dying, formerly in South Korea. He discusses 'Christian aggression in Korea':

> Random attacks on Buddhist temples in Korea continue today. It is not enough that Buddhists continue to live in fear of attacks, burying their heads in the sand, praying and hoping for the best, forgiving their tormentors.
>
> They must act. They have to engage the perpetrators or their controllers vigorously by means of continuous communication, break down walls of suspicion, changing minds and changing society.

Next he relates his experience as a Buddhist chaplain and meditation teacher in the county jail, and enumerates a number of compassionate service activities initiated by True Dharma International Buddhist Mission, "to encourage other Buddhist organizations in the area by example."

V

This collection of essays by some of the leading scholars of the *Dharma* traditions should help the reader to understand and appreciate how scriptures, writings, and action in these traditions hold compassion as an integral part and a supreme virtue.

PART I
Common Features of the Dharmic Traditions and Interactions among Them

1

The Dharma Traditions of Hinduism, Buddhism, Jainism and Sikhism in Light of their Universal, Common Ground

—*Evan Finkelstein*

Introduction

This chapter is intended as a resource aimed at promoting a deeper understanding and appreciation of the Dharmic wisdom traditions—Hinduism, Buddhism, Jainism, and Sikhism (Sikhi)—and their common ties.

The Perennial Philosophy: The Universal, Common Ground of Diverse Traditions

In his famous text *The Perennial Philosophy,* Aldous Huxley concisely explained the essence of this term:

> PHILOSOPHIA PERENNIS—the phrase was coined by Leibniz; but the thing—the metaphysic that recognizes a divine Reality substantial to the world of things and lives and minds; the psychology that finds in the soul something similar to, or even identical to, divine Reality; the ethic that places man's final end in the knowledge of the immanent and transcendent Ground of all being—the thing is immemorial and universal. (1970, p. vii)

In order to understand how it is possible for various religious traditions to have a common ground in spite of differences among them in both theory and practice, it is vital to note that all of these traditions agree that there is a divine reality, an Ultimate Reality. Of course, the names these traditions give to this higher reality differ, but it is foundational to them all that there *is* an Ultimate Reality and also that this Reality can be experienced and lived in daily life. In addition, these traditions all agree that the main purpose of human life is to align with and fully attune oneself to the nature of this Ultimate Reality; and, when one accomplishes this, one has attained peace, fulfillment and freedom of a permanent nature that is not diminished by the time-space-bound limitations of the continuous ebb and flow, loss and gain, of the ever-changing aspects of life.

These traditions also concur that the central aim of all their principles of knowledge, high moral and ethical values of behavior, study, prayers, worship and rituals is to accomplish the full liberation or enlightenment of the individual and, eventually, society as a whole. They all teach that without the full realization of this highest reality human life will continue to be filled with an endless array of suffering, conflicts and problems; and that the ultimate solution to the seemingly never-ending problems of humanity is to be found in the achievement of the state of enlightenment—the full knowledge of and direct conscious attunement and unity with this Ultimate Reality.

In each of these traditions, the regular practice of meditation is recommended as a key means through which this direct realization of this higher reality can take place. An effective technique of meditation is said to enable an individual's awareness to transcend all the time-space boundaries of the ever-changing temporal and finite world and bring one to the direct experience of this reality. All agree that this supreme reality is limitless and eternal, unborn and undying, formless in its essential nature, and is the infinite abode of all knowledge of everything in the cosmos, and the substratum of all energy, love, compassion, and creative power. To become fully awakened to this ultimate value of existence and to spontaneously live it in life for oneself and for all others is the shared highest aspiration of these traditions. Also, this daily practice of meditation is said to put one in harmony with the universal force of *Dharma*.

The term 'Dharmic source' expresses the vision that the 'common ties' of all these traditions could be found in 'the Dharmic source'. *Dharma* is commonly understood to be the foundational, universal principles or laws that promote and sustain order in the universe, and individuals are supposed to conduct their lives so they are always in harmony with the *Dharma* of universal nature, the ways of that nature. *Dharma* is always associated with fairness, justice and righteousness, the highest standards of moral and ethical behavior. It is a shared principle of these traditions that all behavior that is opposed to *Dharma* is not conducive to the health and well-being of the individual or society; nor is such Adharmic (non-Dharmic) behavior supportive of an individual's or society's spiritual development towards achieving a state of enlightenment. "*Dharma* is that invincible power of nature which upholds existence. It maintains evolution and forms the very basis of cosmic life. It supports all that is helpful for evolution and discourages all that is opposed to it" (Maharishi Mahesh Yogi, 1990, p. 26). One central aspect of *Dharma* shared by all these traditions is the principle of *Ahimsa*.

Ahimsa or non-violence is the vital duty to never be an aggressor, to never initiate, promote or even encourage harm to any being or the ecology in any way: to do no harm is not limited to causing physical harm, but also includes not hurting any being mentally, emotionally, financially, or socially. In addition, it is not deemed sufficient by these traditions to only refrain from doing harm, but rather everyone is strongly encouraged to be helpful, empathetic, compassionate and loving to all beings: to provide selfless service, or *Seva*, to uplift and improve the life conditions of all beings. All the traditions proclaim that all individuals should see it as their duty to provide assistance to others in every way they can without the expectation of receiving anything in return for their service. The underlying common-ground understanding here is that all beings are expressions of that Ultimate Reality and therefore deserve our sincere respect, love and attention: in the deepest sense, because all equally share the same Ultimate Source, all are most intimately connected to one another at the very core of their being. In other words, to help another individual is to help a form of one's own Being. This unifying vision is the basis of the 'Golden Rule': to treat others as you would like to be treated.

In his excellent text *Oneness: Great Principles Shared by All Religions,* Jeffery Moses (2002) demonstrates how the 'Golden Rule' (as well as many other basic principles) is a central value shared by *all* Dharmic traditions:

"Hurt not others with that which pains yourself." (Buddhism)

"This is the sum of all true righteousness—treat others, as thou would thyself be treated. Do nothing to thy neighbor, which hereafter thou would not have thy neighbor do to thee." (Hinduism)

"Treat others as thou would be treated thyself." (Sikhism)

"A man should wander about treating all creatures, as he himself would be treated." (Jainism)

Among these traditions, let us begin with Hinduism.

Hinduism

To consider some of the central and foundational knowledge expressed in the great tradition known in the world today as Hinduism, it is commonly agreed among most scholars of religion that Hinduism, with the ancient Vedas at its core, is the world's oldest living religion (Klostermaier, 1998, p. 7). Hinduism does not have any one founder, rather it is based on the cognitions into the nature of reality by the ancient Rishis or seers.

It says in the Rig-Veda, "He who is awake, the *richas* (the verses of the Veda), seek him out" (Rig-Veda, 5.44.14). Meaning that if a person is truly wide awake, if he or she is in a fully expanded and enlightened state of awareness or consciousness, such a person will be able to spontaneously gain profound insights into the nature of all existence. The Rig-Veda explains:

> The verses of the Veda exist in the collapse of fullness (the *Kshara* of 'A') in the transcendental field, the Self,
> In which reside all the *Devas*, the impulses of creative intelligence, the laws of nature responsible for the whole manifest universe.
> He whose awareness is not open to this field, what can the verses accomplish for him?
> Those who know this level of reality are established in evenness, wholeness of life.
> Rig-Veda, 1.164.39 (Maharishi, 1997, pp. 52-53)

The key point is that to clearly understand the nature of life one first needs to gain direct experience of the absolute transcendental field, the Self. The word Self, when written with a capital 'S', refers to the universal and infinite field of existence, the Wholeness of life that is said to be the ultimate foundation and source of everything and everyone in the cosmos. This infinite Self is referred to by the word 'That' in the well-known Creation Hymn of the Rig-Veda, part of which is presented here:

> Neither mortal was there
> nor immortal then;
> Not of night, of day was there distinction:
> *That* alone breathed windless
> through inherent power.
> Other than *That* there was naught else.
> Rig-Veda 10:129 (Maurer, 1975, p. 234)

This central theme of knowing *That,* realizing the infinite value of Self, which is also referred to as *Brahman*, the Great, the Totality of all existence, is also clearly evident in the *Mahavakyas*, the 'Great Sayings' of the Upanishads. The Upanishads are said to provide the highest level of the Vedic teachings; they are also referred to as the Vedanta, the end or supreme culmination of the Vedic knowledge. These four Great Sayings are:

Aham Brahmasmi—I am Brahman (The Totality, the Wholeness of all life).

Tat tvam as I—You are That.
Ayamatma Brahma—This Self is Brahman.
Pragyanam Brahma—Brahman is supreme knowledge, supreme consciousness or intelligence.
"The most important message of the Vedas is that everything and every being is divine." (Sarvam Khalv-idam Brahma—"All, indeed, is Brahman (God)").
(Adapted from Swami Bhaskarananda, 2002, pp. 13-14)

And the highest aspiration to realize these truths has also been expressed in the Upanishads; for example, the *Brhadaranyaka* Upanishad, I. 3.28 states: "O Brahman, lead us from the unreal to the real. Lead us from darkness to light. Lead us from death to immortality" (Brown, 1990, p. 18). According to this Vedic tradition, these four great sayings express the highest level of Self-knowledge, or Self-realization that can be achieved by any human being. And, traditionally, the essential means for gaining this realization was through the regular practice of meditation. It is through effective meditation practice that the individual was able to consciously transcend, all the boundaries and limitations of the environment, the body, behavior, senses, speech, mind, intellect, emotions and the sense of a limited individual 'I' or ego. Having transcended the entire relative realm of time and space the individual directly experiences the existence of unbounded awareness, infinite pure consciousness, the Self, which is one's own essential nature.

This Self is said to be of the nature of Ananda, bliss. There is a Brahma Sutra, also referred to as Vedanta Sutra that declares: *Anandamayo 'bhyasat'*—"Brahman, the Self, becomes blissful through practice" 1.1.12 (Egenes, 2001, p. 16). It is understood that through the daily practice of meditation one can realize and stabilize the bliss of the Ultimate Reality into one's daily life. However, it is not considered sufficient to experience this Ultimate Reality only in terms of one's own inner reality; one should grow to experience all levels and aspects of life, everyone and everything, in terms of this infinity and bliss. There is a beautiful example of this knowledge and experience expressed in the *Taittiriya* Upanishad:

> Bhrigu, the bright one, approached his father, Varuna, the lord of the waters, and said: "Sir, teach me about Brahman."
> Varuna taught him of matter, life, sight, hearing, mind and speech. Then he added:
> "Seek to know that from which all these are born, by which they are sustained and into which they return."
> Bhrigu retired and meditated, and through meditation he saw that matter is Brahman. For, indeed, from matter all beings are born, by matter they are sustained and into matter they again return.
>
> Having realized this he again approached his father, and said: "Noble Sir, teach me of Brahman."
> Varuna replied: "Seek to know Brahman through meditation, for Brahman is meditation."
> Bhrigu retired and meditated, and through meditation he saw that Life [Prana or vital energy/life force of the body] is Brahman. For, indeed, from Life [vital energy that maintains the body] all beings are born, by life they are sustained, and into Life they again return....

Bhrigu continued his meditation and, over time, began to understand and experience increasingly more subtle values of existence as being deeper aspects of Brahman. For example, "through meditation he saw that mind is Brahman," and then "that intelligence [or intellect] is Brahman." Then, the Upanishad states:

> Bhrigu retired and meditated and through meditation he saw that Brahman is bliss, for truly:
>
> From Bliss all being are born,
> By bliss they are sustained,
> And into bliss they again return.

Lastly, the Upanishad concludes with the following verses:

> This wisdom that Varuna taught Bhrigu is the Highest. He who know it becomes established in the Highest. He becomes the possessor and enjoyer of riches, great in fame, great in offspring, great in cattle and great in the splendor of the sacred wisdom. (Shearer and Russell, 1978, p. 90)

This highest knowledge is not only meant to give one the direct experience of the unboundedness of one's own Being, but also to make one successful and comfortable in the material world, as well. A fullness of life is to be created and permanently established both spiritually and materially based on the understanding and application of this knowledge. This highest knowledge was intended to not only create enlightened individuals, but enlightened societies and nations, as well.

One vital aspect of this highest knowledge of the Universal Self or Brahman is that It is all that there is in existence: It is simultaneously both Absolute and relative, unmanifest and manifest, formless and all forms, unmoving silence and moving dynamism, individual and universal. It is the one core Self of all and It is all. The all-encompassing nature of this Ultimate Reality is beautifully expressed in the *Shvetashvatara* Upanishad:

> Brahman, Thou art One. Though formless, through Thine own power and for Thine own unfathomable purpose, Thou givest rise to the many forms.
> Thou createst the whole Universe from Thyself. O Brahman, give us clear understanding.
>
> Thou art Agni, the fire. Thou art Aditya, the sun. Thou art Vayu, the wind. Thou art Chandrama, the moon. Thou art the Brilliant stars. Thou art Hiranyagarbha, the golden womb of creation. Thou art the cosmic waters. Thou art Prajapati, the Lord of all creation. (4.1) (Shearer and Russell, 1978, p. 95)

It is clear from this deep Upanishadic understanding of the nature of Brahman that there is only One Ultimate Reality:

Ekamevadvitiyam, "One without a second," and this same exact principle is also expressed in the *Chhandogya* Upanishad (6.2.1). Also, in the Rig-Veda it states: *Ekam Sat Vipra Bahhudha Vadanti* (1.164.46), "That which exists is One: sages call It by various names" (Vivekananda, 1989, p. 20). This brings to light a vital point regarding the Vedic tradition of India—contrary to what many may think, at its core, as expressed by its own highest knowledge, it is not a religion that believes in many gods—it believes in many forms or manifestations of only One Ultimate Reality.

This is a theme that often comes up in the Upanishads; for example, in the *Brihadaranyaka* Upanishad (3.9.1-3.9.9), there is a conversation recorded between the great sage Yajnavalkya and one of his students. The student asks him, "How many gods are there?" And the sage first replies, "Three and three hundred, three and three thousand." The student senses that the great sage is testing him, so he asks the same question a number of times; each time, the sage reduces the number until he declares, 'One!' The student then asks "Who is that one God?" And, the sage replies, "The life-breath, which they call Brahman, or THAT." It becomes clear that all the many cosmic creative powers, or devas, are just the many names, forms and functions of that One Ultimate Reality.

Not only is Brahman all the divine, cosmic creative powers of life, but the *Shvetashvatara* Upanishad also states that Brahman expresses Itself as all specific forms of existence and is also the ultimate source of all knowledge—the Vedas:

> Thou art woman, Thou art man. Thou art the youth, thou are the maiden. Thou are the old man tottering along with his stick. Having taken form, Thou facest in every direction.
>
> Thou art the deep blue butterfly, Thou art the parrot, green with red eyes. Thou art the father of lightning. Thou art the seasons and the seas.
> Unborn [in Your unmanifest, formless state], Thou art everywhere, and all that is, is born from Thee.

> Of what use are the Vedas to those who have not experienced that supreme eternal Being, from whom the Vedas come, and in whom the devas dwell? Only those whose being flows with Thee find eternal joy....
>
> By knowing Him, who is subtler than the subtlest, the still center of all activity, the fashioner of all forms, enfolding the universe in His embrace, by knowing Him as Love, we find eternal peace 4.3-4.14. (Shearer and Russell, 1978, pp. 95-96)

Direct personal experience of this Reality is a central value of Hinduism. Swami Vivekananda expressed this aspiration in the following manner:

> The Hindu does not want to live upon words and theories. If there are existences beyond the ordinary sensuous existence, he wants to come face to face with them. If there is a soul in him which is not matter, if there is an all-merciful universal Soul, he will go to Him direct. He must see Him, and that alone can destroy all doubt. So the best proof a Hindu sage gives about the soul, about God, is: "I have seen the soul; I have seen God." And that is the only condition of perfection. The Hindu religion does not consist in struggles and attempts to believe a certain doctrine or dogma, but in realizing—not in believing, but in being and becoming. (Swami Vivekananda, 1989, pp. 7-8)

The question of how can one know Him "who is subtler than the subtlest, the still center of all activity" is answered very directly in the famous text, the *Bhagavad Gita*. Traditionally, the *Bhagavad Gita* is known as '*Yoga Shastra*', the scripture of how to attain yoga or union with the Ultimate Reality. It is understood to be the record of the dialogue that took place between Lord Krishna, who is traditionally taken to be the incarnation or full embodiment of the Supreme Reality, and Arjuna, the most famous archer and warrior of his time. Arjuna desperately needed to gain that highest knowledge and experience that would enable him to fulfill his duties as a warrior successfully, but without incurring any sin for himself, his family or his society. The dialogue took place just before a major war was about to begin. Lord Krishna gave him the following wisdom:

> The Vedas' concern is with the three *gunas*. Be without the three *gunas*,
> O Arjuna, freed from duality, ever firm in purity, independent of possessions,
> Possessed of the Self.2.45
>
> You have control over action alone, never over its fruits.
> Live not for the fruits of action, nor attach yourself to inaction. 2.47
>
> Established in Yoga, O winner of wealth,
> Perform actions having abandoned attachment and having become
> Balanced in success and failure, for balance of mind is called Yoga. 2.48 —(Maharishi, 1990, p. 126)

Traditionally, the three *gunas– sattva, rajas,* and *tamas*—are understood to be the fundamental constituents of *Prakriti,* or Nature, out of which the entire creation arises. They are said to be responsible for all activity in the entire field of creation. In the *Bhagavad Gita*, Lord Krishna is telling Arjuna that in order to fulfill his duty properly and to remain without sin, the primary need is to "be without the three *gunas*," which will allow him to be free of all duality and will give him the direct experience of the Self, the unbounded field of pure universal Being, pure consciousness.

In his commentary to verse 45 of chapter two, Maharishi Mahesh Yogi explains the process of how one can "be without the three *gunas*":

> There are gross planes of creation and there are subtle planes. When the Lord says: "Be without the three gunas," He means

> that Arjuna should bring his attention from the gross planes of experience, through the subtle planes and thus to the subtlest plane of experience; transcending even the subtlest plane, he will be completely out of the relative field of life, out of the three *gunas*. So the Lord's words, "Be without the three *gunas*" reveal the secret of arriving at the state of pure consciousness. (Maharishi, 1990, p. 129)

This process of allowing one's awareness to travel from the gross to the subtlest and then to the transcendental pure consciousness is the process of gaining the state of yoga, or union with the Self; it is the traditional, natural process referred to as meditation. Traditionally, a guru would teach his students how to meditate. However, after this process of transcending during meditation, Lord Krishna explains that one must then perform action. But the action that one performs, *after* becoming established in yoga, will be without attachment to possessions, or to the results or 'fruits' of action. Because of the state of yoga gained, one is now capable of being "balanced in success and failure, for balance of mind is called Yoga."

In a classic text on yoga written by Maharishi Patanjali, his *Yoga Sutras* states: "Yoga is the complete settling of the activity of the mind" (1.2). And, once this settling or transcending of all mental activity has occurred, he states: "Then the observer is established in the Self" (1.3) (Egenes, 2010, pp. 11-12) meaning that the actual state of yoga has been gained. Maharishi Patanjali also made it clear that the state of yoga is basic to success in all the ethical virtues such as: *ahimsa*, non-violence; *satya*, truthfulness; *asteya*, non-stealing or non-covetousness; and *aparigraha*, absence of greed or possessiveness.

It is the state of yoga, the full realization of the Self, that also enables genuine appreciation, compassion and love of others, no matter how different these others may be from oneself. In the context of the Hindu tradition, it is understood that Self-realized persons, experiencing the bliss and contentment of unbounded pure consciousness in themselves and also experiencing it permeating everyone and everything, are capable of universal love, of recognizing the truth of *Vasudhaiva Kutumbakam* "The whole world is my family" (Mahopanishad, 71-73)—they see the whole world as their family and they appreciate that all, regardless of race, caste or religion are divine at their core, whether they are currently aware of it or not, and that all are moving towards that realization of the divine Ultimate Reality. This enlightened vision is beautifully expressed in the words of the saint Ramakrishna (1836-86):

> I see people who talk about religion constantly quarreling with one another. Hindus, Mussulmans [Muslims], Brahmos, Shaktas, Vaisnavas, Shaivas [different Hindu religious communities] all quarrel with one another. They haven't the intelligence to understand that He who is called Krishna is also Shiva and the Primal Shakti [infinite creative power seen as Mother Divine], and that He, again, is called Jesus and Allah. "There is only one Rama and he has a thousand names."
>
> Truth is one; only It is called by different names. All people are seeking the same Truth; the variance is due to climate, temperament, and name. A lake has many *ghats*. From one *ghat* the Hindus take water in jars and call it *jal*. From another *ghat* the Mussulmans [Muslims] take water in leather bags and call it *pani*. From a third the Christians take the same thing and call it 'water'. Suppose someone says that the thing is not *jal* but *pani*, or that it is not *pani* but water, or that it is not water but *jal*. It would indeed be ridiculous. But this very thing is at the root of the friction among sects, their misunderstandings and quarrels. This is why people injure and kill one another, and shed blood, in the name of religion. But this is not good. Everyone is going toward God. They will realize Him if they have sincerity and longing of heart. (Harvey, 2001, pp. 96-97)

Ramakrishna's words reveal the very heart of the Perennial Philosophy that provides the underlying unity, the common ground at the basis of all these traditions of wisdom. The understanding and, most importantly, the call for the direct experience of that One Ultimate Reality that is the source, course and goal of all life both individual and universal.

Let us now explore how the profound tradition of Buddhism expresses this universal understanding and experience.

Buddhism

The founder of Buddhism was said to have lived approximately between 560 and 480 BCE, as the exact dates are unknown. His given name was Siddhartha Gautama and he was also called *Shakyamuni*, meaning the wise one from the tribe of the Shakyas. However, he would be the first to point out that the details of one's personal life are not what is significant. What was significant to the Buddha is the full and permanent end to all human sufferings and the living of life with constant deep wisdom, tranquility, loving-kindness and compassion for all beings.

It is commonly known through Buddhist traditional lore that the Buddha, meaning the 'awakened one' or 'enlightened one', was born into a royal family. His parents tried to protect the young prince from experiencing any type of misfortune or suffering. He was to be shielded from any sight of death, sickness or old age. However, despite the best efforts of the king and queen the young prince did come to experience all these human sufferings and they affected him deeply. From the Buddhist text *Majjhima Nikaya,* we have the following summative description of the Buddha's insight into nature:

> When I was a young man, at the beginning of my life, I looked at nature and saw that all things are subject to decay and death and thus to sorrow. The thought came to me that I myself was of such a nature. I was the same as all created things. I too would be subject to disease, decay, death, and sorrow. But what if I were to search for that which underlies all becoming, for the unsurpassed perfect security which is *nirvana*, the perfect freedom of the unconditioned state? (Bancroft, 2001, p. 1)

The Buddha decided that it is most vital to dedicate one's life to realizing the unconditioned, unborn and undying state known as *Nirvana*. The word *Nirvana* actually means 'to extinguish', to 'put out' and it refers to extinguishing the human 'fires' of craving for things that cannot possibly bring one permanent contentment or happiness. The Buddha realized that all of manifest life is causally interdependent (*paticca-samuppada*) and, therefore, made up of various components; as such, all things share three fundamental features: "Impermanent (*annicca*) are all component things," "Involved in suffering (*dukkha*) are all component things," "Unsubstantial (*anatta*) are all component things." *Magga-vagga* (Klostermaier, 1999, p. 70)

However, the Buddha also realized that there is a state of existence that can, in time, be achieved by every individual who is dedicated to an effective path of enlightenment. This unique state of existence is not bound, dependent or conditioned and is, therefore, not impermanent, involved in suffering or insubstantial. It is this state that he refers to as *Nirvana*; it is in this Reality of unconditioned awareness or unbounded wakefulness that these three limiting features of life have been totally and permanently extinguished. In his text, *Buddhism: Its Essence and Development*, Professor Edward Conze has summarized various descriptions that the Buddha has given to *Nirvana*:

> But on the other hand, we are told that *Nirvana* is permanent, stable, imperishable, immovable, ageless, deathless, unborn and unbecome, that it is power, bliss and happiness, the secure refuge, the shelter, and the place of unassailable safety; that it is the real Truth and the supreme Reality; that it is the *Good*, the supreme goal and the one and only consummation of our life, the eternal, hidden and incomprehensible Peace. (Conze, 2003, p. 40)

Overall, what becomes clear is that the Buddha, based on his direct experiences, gained penetrating insight into the full range of existence both conditioned and unconditioned, ever-changing and never-changing, limited awareness and unbounded awareness (unbounded Wakefulness), ignorance and Truth, suffering and Bliss. What resulted from the Buddha's experiences and insights are his teachings, his *Dharma*, as concisely expressed in The Four Noble Truths and the Eightfold Path. Because these are so central to the Buddha's teachings that it would be important to present them in some detail and in what Buddhist tradition accepts as being Buddha's own words. It is commonly understood that the Buddha spoke of four central noble truths. The lists and explanations below have, for the most part, been taken from the text *Teachings of the Buddha,* edited by Jack Kornfield (1999, pp. 28-31).

Buddha's Four Noble Truths

1. The first noble truth is the existence of suffering.
2. The second noble truth is the origin of suffering.
3. The third noble truth is the extinction of suffering.
4. The fourth noble truth is the eightfold path that leads to the extinction of suffering.

What is the Noble Truth of Suffering?

Birth is suffering; decay is suffering; death is suffering; sorrow, lamentation, pain, grief, and despair are suffering; not to get what one desires is suffering *(Samyutta Nikaya)*.

What is the Noble Truth of the Origin of Suffering?

It is the craving, which gives rise to fresh rebirth, and, bound up with pleasure and lust, now here, now there, finds ever-fresh delight. But where does this craving arise and take root? Wherever in the world there are delightful and pleasurable things, there this craving rises and takes root. Visual objects, sounds, smells, tastes, bodily impressions, and mind objects are delightful and pleasurable: there this craving arises and takes root...will, desiring, thinking and reflection are delightful and pleasurable: there this craving arises and takes root *(Samyutta Nikaya)*.

What is the Noble Truth of the Extinction of Suffering?

It is the complete fading away and extinction of this craving, its forsaking and abandonment, liberation and detachment from it. The extinction of greed, the extinction of hate, the extinction of delusion: this indeed is called *Nirvana*. And for a disciple thus freed, in whose heart dwells peace, there is nothing to be added to what has been done, and naught more remains to do...the Peaceful One, freed from rage, from sorrow, and from longing, has passed beyond birth and death *(Samyutta Nikaya)*.

What is the Noble Truth of the Path that Leads to the Extinction of Suffering?

To give oneself up to over indulgence in sensual pleasure, or to indulgence in the base, vulgar, unholy, unprofitable; or to give oneself up to self-mortification, the painful, unholy, unprofitable: both these two extremes the Perfect One has avoided and has discovered the Middle Path, which makes one see and know, which leads to peace, to discernment, to *Nirvana*. *(Samyutta Nikaya)*.

The Noble Eightfold Path of the Buddha that Leads to the Extinction of Suffering

1. Right Understanding (right views)
2. Right Thought (right aspirations, purpose)
3. Right Speech
4. Right Action (right conduct)
5. Right Livelihood
6. Right Effort
7. Right Mindfulness (right thoughts)
8. Right Meditation (right concentration) (*Samyutta Nikaya)*

Transcending the sense of an individual 'I' or ego is one of the foundational principles of Buddhism—it is the concept of *anatta,* which is usually translated as 'no self'. This concept has often been misunderstood to mean that the state of *Nirvana* itself is absolutely nothing—that it has no positive existence at all, but this is not accurate. *Nirvana*, as was already explained above, is a positive state of bliss, peace, contentment and the highest happiness. Some other examples of this (from Bancroft's text) follow: "Meditate, and in your wisdom realize *nirvana*, the highest happiness" (*Dhammapada*). And, "The highest happiness is indeed *Nirvana*, which has been taught by him who has perfectly understood the sorrow-less, stainless security where suffering is dissolved" (*Theragatha*).

It is recorded in the *Mahaparinirvana Sutra* that Buddha's disciples were also unclear about this doctrine of *anatta*:

> The monks were taken aback. They said, "Honored One, according to all you have taught and spoken, we have been asked to cultivate selflessness, leading to the dropping of the idea of a self. But now you tell us we should cultivate the idea of a self—what is the meaning of this?"
>
> "Good," replied the Buddha. "You are now asking about meaning. You should know that, like a doctor, you should find the right medicine for an illness. It is as a doctor that I observed the ailments of the world. I saw that ordinary people believe they have a self and that whoever they meet has a self. They think of the self as within the body. But it is not like that.
>
> "Because it is not like that, I have shown the fallacy of all the ideas of self and shown that the self is not there in the way it is thought to be. In everything I have said I have shown that the self is not as people think of it, for this is expedient means, the right medicine.
>
> "But that does not mean that there is no self. What is the self? If something is true, is real, is constant, is a foundation of a nature that is unchanging, this can be called the Self. For the sake of sentient beings, in all the truths I have taught, there is such a Self. This, monks, is for you to cultivate." (*Ibid.*, pp. 195-96)

It is important to note that when Buddha spoke about the true nature of Self, the unconditioned existence, he was speaking of that which cannot be known directly through spoken language or mental concepts. It is a Reality that can only be known by *being it*, not by thinking about it.

Professors Huston Smith and Philip Novak in their text, *Buddhism: A Concise Introduction*, observe that there are a number of main forms of Buddhism currently practiced: *Theravada* (The way of the Elders), *Mahayana* (The Great Raft or Way), Zen Buddhism, *Vajrayana* (The Diamond Vehicle or Thunderbolt Vehicle, which is also known as Tibetan Buddhism), and the Pure Land Tradition of Buddhism. However, regardless of the differences that exist among these various systems of Buddhism, the Four Noble Truths and the Noble Eightfold Path are accepted by all as being central to the Buddha's teaching.

In addition to this, there is general agreement on the ethical virtues that need to be developed—the *Dasa-sila* rules. Professor Klostermaier, in his text *Buddhism: A Short Introduction* refers to them as "the ten components of good character." He presents a traditional organization of these rules in terms of *ducarita*, 'tenfold misconduct' that are to be avoided and *sucarita*, 'tenfold wholesome behavior', which should be cultured. The *ducarita* are categorized into verbal, bodily and mental values:

Verbal:

1. Lying
2. Slander
3. Rudeness
4. Gossip, idle chatter

Bodily:

5. Taking of life
6. Taking what is not given
7. Promiscuity

Mental:

8. Covetousness
9. Malevolence
10. False views

The *sucarita*, or positive values are:

1. Giving

2. Morality
3. Meditation
4. Honoring
5. Giving service
6. Surrendering what was given
7. Reflecting with delight on the attainment of merit
8. Listening to the *Dhamma* (Buddha's teachings)
9. Preaching *Dhamma*
10. Setting one's views straight

The Buddha's view on the cultivation of ethical values is concisely expressed in the following quotation:

> Abandon wrongdoing. It can be done. If there were no likelihood, I would not ask you to do it. But since it is possible and since it brings about blessing and happiness, I do ask of you: abandon wrongdoing.
> Cultivate doing good. It can be done. If it brought deprivation and sorrow, I would not ask you to do it. But since it brings blessing and happiness, I do ask of you: cultivate doing good. (*Anguttara Nikaya*) (Bancroft, 2001)

The regular practice of meditation was considered to be necessary and very helpful to enable every person to fully develop all of the needed ethical virtues. Buddha clearly understood from his own experience that it was the highest bliss and peace, which came from the fully awakened state of *Nirvana* that made it possible for people to be genuinely loving, generous, forgiving and compassionate. A few examples of the Buddha's teaching on love, compassion and generosity, also taken from Bancroft's text, are as follows:

> Putting down all barriers, let your mind be full of love. Let it pervade all the quarters of the world so that the whole wide world, above, below, and around, is pervaded with love. Let it be sublime and beyond measure so that it abounds everywhere. (*Digha Nikaya*)

> Arouse your will, supreme and great,
> Practice love, give joy and protection;
> Let your giving be like space,
> Without discrimination or limitation.
>
> Do good things, not for your own sake [for selfish reasons]
> But for all the beings in the universe;
> Save and make free everyone you
> Encounter,
> Help them attain the wisdom of the way. (*Prajnaparamita*)
>
> Friends, now the monk remains pervading one quarter, then a second, then a third and a fourth with a mind filled with friendliness, compassion, tenderness and equanimity. Up, down, horizontally: in all directions, everywhere, he goes on pervading the whole world with a mind filled with friendliness, compassion, tenderness and equanimity, extensive, expanded, boundless, and free from hate and malevolence. (*Dirga Nikaya*)
> "Never retaliate in kind," the Buddha told his followers. "Hatred does not come to an end through hatred but can only cease through generosity." (*Jataka* Tale)

Another major theme of the Buddha's teachings regards what can be referred to as 'Perfect Wisdom'. Like the state of *Nirvana,* its Reality is beyond all conditioned, impermanent states of existence, including the thinking of the mind or any emotional mood or attitude. Perfect Wisdom is the ability to completely penetrate into the Truth of life and to know it and to *be* it in its totality and its essence. Perfect Wisdom is the result of achieving *Nirvana*, the state of the unconditioned and fully awakened awareness. It can be lived but never fully described due to limitations of thought and language.

Next, we will examine the ancient tradition of Jainism.

Jainism

As it is traditionally understood by Jains, Jainism did not actually have a beginning in time. Its principles of knowledge are considered eternal in the same way that the Jains consider the soul, *Jiva*, and the universe to be without beginning or end. There are endless cycles of time that the universe goes through and in the cycle in which we are presently, about 2,500 years ago a man named Vardhamana (599-527 BCE) was born into a royal family. In similar fashion to the Buddha, who lived during that same era, Prince Vardhamana realized that nothing on the ever-changing sensorial, mental or emotional levels of existence was capable of providing him or anyone with a permanent state of peace, freedom, contentment and the ability to be fully compassionate and helpful to all beings. As it states in the text *Bhagavati Aradhana,* 1143: "Just as fire is not quenched by the fuel and the ocean by thousands of rivers, similarly no living being is satisfied even with all the wealth of the three worlds." (Tulsi, 1985, p. 93) He realized that suffering and dissatisfaction is experienced in every person's life because the true nature of the soul is covered up and bound by all the *Karmas*, all the activities of life and the inevitable consequences that arise from these activities. As it is expressed in the Jain text *Uttaradhyayana,* 6.1: "All unenlightened persons produce sufferings. Having become deluded, they produce and reproduce sufferings in this endless world." (Tulsi, 1985, p. 87)

Vardhamana knew from the traditional Jain teachings that were taught by Tirthankar Parshvanath and the other Tirthankars before him (a Tirthankar is known as a 'ford-maker', an enlightened being "who creates a path to liberation for beings trapped in the realm of *samsara* [the cycles of suffering, birth, death and rebirth]; 24 tirthankaras appear in each cosmic cycle; Mahavira [Prince Vardhamana] is the 24th tirthankara of our current cosmic cycle." (Long, 2011, p. 205) Prince Vardhamana, who after he gained enlightenment was called Lord Mahavira, knew that there was a way to directly realize the true nature of the soul. What is this path to enlightenment and liberation?

Acharya Tulsi, a well-known Jain monk and scholar (1919-97), explained the fundamental elements of this path in his text *Bhagavan [Lord] Mahavira*:

> After he attained *kaivalya* [pure, total knowledge] Bhagavan Mahavira in the first sermon explained the fourfold path of self-realization:
>
> 1. Samyak Darsana—Spiritual experience of Reality or Faith in Truth,
> 2. Samyak Jnana—Knowledge of Reality,
> 3. Samyak Caritra—Spiritual Discipline [also known as Right Conduct], and
> 4. Samyak Tapa— the washing off of the effects of accumulated *karmas* through right austerities [activities that help purify the body and mind].
>
> The world consists of two types of basic substances: the soul and the non-soul. A soul or *atma* bound by a body is called *jiva* or an embodied soul. A free or disembodied soul is called *Paramatma* (Perfect Soul). That which causes transformation of the soul into the perfect soul is called *dharma* or religion. (1985, p. 39)

In Jainism, a perfect soul, also known as a *Siddha*, is a completely pure soul that no longer has a human form nor resides in the human world; however, it is important to note that Lord Mahavira and all the others who became fully enlightened, a *Kevalin*, those who have achieved total knowledge of life, also referred to as *Arihanta* (those who have destroyed all of their inner enemies such as anger, lust, hatred, greed, fear, egoism, etc., and know the true nature of the soul through constant direct experience) are fully awakened human beings living in the world. In other words, human demise is not thought to be a prerequisite for enlightenment. Pravin K. Shah in his text *Jainism: Religion of Compassion and Ecology* explains this value of enlightenment:

> Lord Mahavir said that, "A living body is not merely an integration of limbs and flesh but it is the abode of the soul

> which potentially has infinite perception (*Anant Darshan*), infinite knowledge (*Anant Jnan*), infinite energy and power (*Anant Virya*), and total bliss (*Anant Sukha*)." Mahavir's message reflects the freedom and spiritual joy of the living being. (2009, p. 17)

Pravin Shah also reflects on the main purpose of all of Lord Mahavir's teachings:

> The ultimate objective of his teaching is how one can attain total freedom from the cycle of birth, life, pain, misery, and death, and achieve the permanent blissful state of one's self. This state is also known as liberation, *Nirvana*, absolute freedom, or *Moksha*. (2009, p. 17)

In Jainism, this state of freedom and enlightenment is achieved through following the abovementioned "fourfold path of realization." In some Jain texts, it is referred to not as the four, but as the 'Three Jewels' or 'Three Gems', 'The *Ratna*'; in this description of the path to enlightenment *Samyak Tapa* is not listed separately, but is closely related to the category of *Samyak Caritra*. The first of the aspects of the path, *Samyak Darsana,* which Acharya Tulsi defined as "Spiritual experience of Reality or Faith in Truth," can be seen from various perspectives. One main view is that one knows the essential truth of the nature of the soul (*Jiva*), that which possess consciousness and is considered a living substance, and also knows the non-soul (*Ajiva*), those aspects of life that are said to not possess consciousness and are classified as non-living substances, through one's *direct experience* and thereby gains clear conviction about the nature of these fundamental aspects of life. The other main view is that before one has clear personal experience of *Jiva* and *Ajiva*, one develops a strong faith in all the teachings of those who, according to Jain tradition, have had clear direct experience of these aspects of life and who are considered to be enlightened souls. It is interesting to note in this context that the word Jain is derived from the word *Jina*, which is defined as "victor, spiritual conqueror; one who has attained *kevalajnana* [pure, total knowledge]." (Long, 2011, p. 197)

What are the characteristics of person who has *Samyak Darsana*? (This term can also be translated as 'Right Vision'.) In their on-line article titled *"The Three Jewels—The Ratna"*, Sancheti Lal and Bhandari Mal provide the following list of qualities:

> There are five distinctive marks of one who possesses the Right Vision noted below:
> 1. Spiritual calmness (*Prasanna*),
> 2. Desire for liberation (*Samvega*),
> 3. Non-attachment to the world (*Nirveda*),
> 4. Kindness (*Anukampa*), and
> 5. Belief in the fundamentals (*Astikya*).
>
> Similarly, the person with Right Vision is free from the following eight types of pride:
> 1. Pride of family,
> 2. Pride of strength,
> 3. Pride of beauty,
> 4. Pride of knowledge,
> 5. Pride of wealth,
> 6. Pride of authority,
> 7. Pride of worldly connections, and
> 8. Pride of spiritual advancement.
>
> (Jainworld website, Section on *Right Vision*, para 6)

In my view, it is clear that possession of many of these qualities indicates that a person already has achieved a significant degree of spiritual advancement. Otherwise, this list could be viewed as a 'wish list' for those aspiring to achieve these qualities. In terms of gaining direct vision or experience of the true nature of the soul, the practice of meditation has always been a part of the Jain path to liberation. This fact is evident from the following Jain *sutras* taken from the text *Saman Suttam* that speak of the value of meditation and the true nature of the soul. These selections are from *Saman Suttam*, from the text compiled by Sri Jinendra Varni, 1993.

> He who has gained victory over his senses and meditates on the very nature of soul, is not bound by *karmas*; how can the *prana* [life force] which is made of Karmic matter follow [bind or become attached to] such a being? (*Saman Suttam* 63, pp. 33-35)
>
> Just as a tortoise protects itself by withdrawing all its limbs within its own body, similarly a wise man protects himself from evil by withdrawing himself from extrovertness [by going within himself through meditation]. (*Saman Suttam* 137, p. 69)
>
> Know for certain that the soul is the home of excellent virtues, the best among the substances and the highest among the realities. (*Saman Suttam* 177, p. 87)
>
> The soul has no color; no taste, no smell, no touch, no gender like male or female or neuter; no bodily form and no bone structure. (*Saman Suttam* 183, p. 89)

From the above discussion and these Jain *sutras,* it is clear that the true nature of the soul is not bound by the limitations of body, mind, individual ego or activities, rather the soul is unbounded in its essential nature and composed of infinite knowledge, bliss, and energy. The regular practice of meditation is essential to unfold and actualize this truth. What knowledge is available to these enlightened *Jinas* is revealed in their teachings about the nature of both human and cosmic existence—it is the *Samyak Jnana*—Knowledge of Reality aspect of the Jain path to liberation. However, before we delve into some specific Jain teachings about the nature of life, it would be valuable to point out the essential foundation upon which *Samyak Jana* is centered; it is called *Anekantavada* and its related principles of *Nayavada* and *Syavada*. I think Dr. Jeffery Long in his text *Jainism: An Introduction* explains these approaches to knowledge clearly:

> The first of these doctrines, *anekantavada*, claims reality is complex, or *anekanta* (literally 'non-one-sided'). This is a claim about the intrinsic nature of existence: that entities cannot be reduced to a single characteristic or concept, reality being irreducibly complex.
>
> The second doctrine, *nayavada*, the 'doctrine of perspectives', is an epistemic corollary of the first.... Given the complex nature of reality, anything can be known from a variety of *nayas*, or perspectives, that correspond to its many aspects.
>
> This implies, finally, the third doctrine, *syadvada*, or the doctrine of conditional predication (literally, the 'maybe doctrine'), according to which the truth of any claim that one makes about a particular topic is dependent about the perspective, or *naya*, from which the claim is made.... (Long, 2011, p 117)

The main practical value about the Jain approach to knowledge of reality is that it encourages a non-absolutist outlook on knowledge. It creates a ground for mutual respect of the doctrines and opinions of others. It reminds us that unless one has gained full enlightenment, our perceptions and understandings can only reveal partial aspects of the total truth. That we are like the blind men (in that famous analogy), who touch only one part of an elephant and based on the limited part we know we draw our conclusions about the nature of the elephant. The key to gaining total knowledge is in the full development of one's consciousness by gaining direct experience of the full and true nature of the soul.

The Jain scriptures are replete with teachings on what the tradition views as the proper approach to gaining knowledge—below are some examples from these scriptures:

> Those who treat one portion or aspect of a thing as a whole thing have wrong understanding like those blind persons who treated some one particular part of an elephant as a whole elephant. Those who take together all the stand-points and

thus grasp all the aspects of a thing have a right understanding just as those with eyes are able to grasp an elephant as a whole. (*Saman Suttam* 731-732, pp. 375-77)

What is said from the substantial viewpoint appears, as a rule, unreal from the modal [transformative/changing] viewpoint. Similarly what is said from the modal viewpoint appears unreal from the substantial viewpoint. From the modal viewpoint, things necessarily originate and perish. But from the substantial viewpoint, there is neither origination nor destruction. From the substantial view, everything is of the form of substance (always remaining the same), but from the modal viewpoint everything differs from time to time. From each particular standpoint, a thing appears to its corresponding form [value or aspect of being]. (*Saman Suttam* 694-696, p. 355)

There is no substance without the modes, nor are the modes without substance. The characteristics of substance are origination, permanence and destruction. (*Saman Suttam* 662, p. 335)

The mode of a substance which emerges is one and that which vanishes is other than it, while the substance neither emerges nor vanishes. The individual [*Jiva* or substance of consciousness] remains the same person from his birth till the time of death, though he assumes the various states of childhood, etc. (*Saman Suttam* 666-667, p. 337)

The cognitions of a substance are universal and particular and are uncontradicted. This is the right cognition whereas the contrary to it is not. One and the same person assumes the relationship of father, son, grandson, nephew and brother, but he is the father of one who he is [the father of] and not of the rest (so is the case with all the things). A person is certainly possessed of alternative relationships and also assumes single relationship.... (*Saman Suttam* 669-671, pp. 339-41)

> The particular qualities (of a substance) are mixed together just like milk and water, so it is not justifiable to exclusively distinguish them as 'this' or 'that' quality. (*Saman Suttam* 672, p. 341)

Now, we can begin to explore some of the specific Jain teachings about the overall nature of life. As mentioned previously, the universe is said to be an eternal reality and this uncreated existence is explained as consisting of six fundamental substances:

Jiva—Soul or consciousness
Pudgal—Matter
Dharma—Medium of motion
Adharma—Medium of rest
Akasha—Space
Kal—Time

After providing the above list, Shah (2009) also explains that the "Soul or *Jiva* is the only living substance, while the other five substances are non-living substances and they are collectively known as *Ajiva*." (p. 34) It is the soul that brings the element of consciousness to the human body. And it is in the body that the soul, through its actions, attracts the *Karma* Particles known as *Karman Vargana*. Jainism holds that a person's good and bad actions both attract *Karman Vargana*, which is said to be made up of "extremely minute particles." (*Ibid.*) In other words, the effects of one's actions create a very fine covering of matter, invisible to the human eye, that obscures the true nature of the soul; consequently, one cannot perceive its true reality. By way of analogy, one would not be able to perceive the true nature of water after it has been mixed with mud. The only way to know the water in its purity would be to fully remove the mud and to ensure that no additional mud will be added to it. Jainism explores the nature of *Karma* and its effects on the soul in great detail and depth—it is central to the teachings of the *Jinas* and is included in its various aspects in the list that enumerates the Nine *Tattvas*, fundamental principles or elements. *Jiva* and *Ajiva* are also included in this list:

Jiva—Soul or living being (Consciousness)
Ajiva—Non-living substances [in terms of *Karma*, this includes the minute *Karma* particles that are an aspect of *Pudgal* (matter).]
Asrava—Causes of the bondage of *Karma*
Bandha—Characteristics of bondage of *Karma*
**Punya*—Merit or Karma of good deeds
**Pap*—Sin or Transgression or *Karma* of bad deeds
Samvar—Stoppage of attachment of new *Karma*
Nirjara—Exhaustion of the accumulated *Karma*
Moksha—State of total liberation from all *Karma*.

*Some literatures define *Punya* (merit) and *Pap* (sin) as separate *Tattvas* while others include them in *Asrava*. In reality, *Punya* and *Pap* are the result of *Asrava*. Hence, truly there are only seven *Tattvas*. (Shah, 2009, p. 39)

The *Tattva* of *Asrava* is of great significance as it explains the specific natures of the main types of *Karmas* that obscure the reality of the soul. The essence of the soul is said to be limitless pure consciousness, it is the Knower of all sensorial, mental and emotional experiences and activities, yet somehow its absolute, pure and infinite status gets overshadowed by it becoming mixed with these varying modes of limited and changing experiences. It is like a pure colorless crystal taking on the color of the paper that it is placed upon. There are five types of *Asrava* enumerated as follows:

Mithyatva—A person's illusion, which includes wrong conviction and wrong knowledge of reality
Avirati—Lack of self-restraint or vowlessness [no taking of personal vows: no specific attempt to meet higher standards of behavior]
Pramada—Spiritual laziness or unawareness
Kashaya—Passions like anger, ego, deceit, greed, and lust
Yoga—Activities of body, speech and mind. ['Yoga' in this

> specific context refers to the 'union' or 'mixing together' of these various modes of activity with the pure nature of the soul.]
>
> These causes convert the *Karma* particles or *Karma Vargana* into *Karma* attaching to the soul. *Asrava* is in fact defined as any vibration in the soul caused by the activities of body, speech and thought which attract *Karma* particles. (Shah, 2009, p. 40)

In addition, Dr. Bimla Churn Law in his text *Mahavira: His Life and Teachings* writes of four main obstructive *Karmas*, which are obviously related to the *Tattva* of *Asrava*:

> There are four *ghatiya* or obstructive *Karmas*: (1) Knowledge-obscuring *Karma*; (2) faith-obscuring or perception-obscuring *Karma*; (3) that which obstructs the progress or success of the soul; (4) that which infatuates or deludes the soul. All these destructive *Karmas* retain the soul in mundane existence. (2002, p. 105)

In addition to the above destructive *Karmas*, there are also what are known as *Aghati Karma*, meaning 'non-destructive *Karmas*', which include the types of *Karma* that determine one's favorable or unfavorable environmental conditions and physical level of health or sickness, particular type of physique, social status and lifespan. (Shah, 2009, pp. 42-45) However, the ultimate goal is to permanently transcend all these causes and effects of every type of bondage, resulting from either positive or negative *Karmas* that trap the soul in ignorance of its pure and infinite nature. How can this be fully achieved? In the tradition of Jainism, in addition to *Samyak Jnana* (Knowledge of Reality) and *Samyak Darsana* (Spiritual Experience of Reality or Faith in Truth), there are other aspects to the Jain path that serve as supplementary and complimentary to these other Jewels of the path—as mentioned above they are: *Samyak Caritra*—Spiritual Discipline [also known as Right Conduct] and *Samyak Tapa*—the washing off of the effects of accumulated *Karmas* through right austerities [activities that help purify the body and mind].

All of these aspects of the Jain path are interdependent and as mentioned previously *Samyak Charita* and *Samyak Tapa* are often put together into one category usually translated as Right Conduct. According to Pravin K. Shah, there are "three cardinal principles of conduct": *Ahimsa* (non-violence), *Anekantavada* (multiplicity of views) and *Aparigraha* (non-possessiveness [being without greed]). (2009, p. 60)

It can be said that *Ahimsa*, non-violence, is the core teaching of Jainism. *Ahimsa* is the natural and spontaneous conduct of an enlightened being because such an individual knows from direct experience that the inner life of all living beings is the unbounded pure soul. That on the level of the ultimate reality of life we are all equally worthy and equally perfect and, therefore, all beings should be equally loved, respected, honored, protected. None, at the very least, should ever be harmed through wrong thought, speech or action.

> *Ahimsa* is the principle that Jains teach and strive to practice not only towards human beings, but also towards all other living beings, including [the] environment. The scriptures tell us: "Do not injure, abuse, oppress, enslave, insult, torment, torture, or kill any living being including plants, vegetables, water, air, and earth." The teaching of *Ahimsa* refers not only to the avoidance of physical acts of violence but also to the avoidance of violence in the hearts and minds of human beings. *Ahimsa* also refers to an active concern and compassion for fellow humans and other beings. Ancient Jain texts explain that the intention to harm and the absence of compassion is what makes actions violent.
>
> *Ahimsa* also has a deeper meaning in the context of one's spiritual advancement. Violence imposed upon others in any form by our body, mind or speech leads to the bondage of new bad *karma*, which hinders the soul's spiritual progress. In other words, violence towards others is violence towards one's

> own soul because one acquires bad *karma* which impedes one's spiritual progress. (Shah, 2009, p. 60)

The Jain scriptures very often place great emphasis on the vital necessity for *Ahimsa*. Some examples are offered below:

> It is the essential trait of a wise man that he does not kill any living being. Certainly, one has to understand just two principles namely non-violence and equanimity (of all living beings). (*Saman Suttam* 147, p. 73)

> Just as pain is not agreeable to you, it is so with others. Knowing this principle of equality treat others with respect and compassion. (*Saman Suttam* 150, p. 75)

> Even an intention of killing is the cause of the bondage of *Karma*, whether you actually kill or not; from the real point of view, this is the nature of the bondage of *Karma*. (*Saman Suttam* 154, p. 77)

> No mountain is higher than Meru; nothing is more expansive than the sky; similarly know that there is no religion [*dharma*] equal to the religion of *Ahimsa* [non-violence] in this world. (*Saman Suttam* 158, p. 79)

> Oh Mortal being! Be free from fear and you let others be free from fear. In this transitory world, why do you indulge in *himsa* [violence]? (*Saman Suttam* 159, p. 79)

In terms of the three cardinal principles of conduct on the Jain path mentioned above, we have already examined *Anekantavada* (multiplicity of views). Lastly, let us explore the principle of *Aparigraha* (non-possessiveness [to be without greed]). *Aparigraha* is one of the five vows that ascetics (Jain monks and nuns) and many lay male and female Jains (known as *Shravaks* and *Shravikas*, "listeners to the teachings of the *Jinas*") take to help themselves on their journey towards enlightenment and liberation. The goal of the ascetics is to follow these vows absolutely in their strictest application, but the lay Jains are allowed to follow them less strictly, but to the best of their current capabilities. These five vows are enumerated by Bharat S. Shah (2002) in his text *An Introduction to Jainism* as follows: 1. Non-violence (*Ahinsa*), 2. Truth (*Satya*) 3. Non-stealing (*Asteya*), 4. Celibacy (*Brahmacharya*—for the Jain laity this means being fully faithful to one's spouse and being moderate in sexual activity with one's spouse), and 5. Non-hoarding (*Aparigraha*). (pp. 29-40) He defines the fifth vow, in the context of the Jain laity, simply as "...not accumulating wealth, possessions, power, etc. beyond the minimum that is absolutely essential." And, he further explains that the act of hoarding polarizes society into rich and poor leading to tension and "the seeds of violence." (p. 39)

Sometimes the term *Aparigraha* is defined as "the vow of non-attachment for possessions." Drs. Rajendra Muni and Mahesh Jain in their text *Lord Mahavira: Life and Philosophy* write: "The vow of non-attachment for possessions compels a man to lead a life with limited means and substances essential for necessary needs." (2013, p. 71) The key idea indicated here is that the central goal of human life should be to gain full enlightenment and liberation from all ignorance, egotism, suffering, and behaviors that are harmful to oneself, to any living being, or to the environment as a whole, and *not* to have one's main goal be the mass accumulation of various possessions. In the Jain scriptures, it states: "Attachment binds the soul (with *Karmas*); a soul which is free from attachments becomes liberated from *Karmas*. Know that this surely is briefly (the nature of) the Karmic bondage of souls." (*Saman Suttam* 596, p. 301)

Of course, actual 'non-attachment' to possessions directly implies that one is, at least to some significant extent, not controlled or overshadowed by strong inner cravings and needs for the accumulation of many possessions. The question then is what can free people from such powerful attachments, needs and cravings? The key answer is centered on the vital necessity for the direct experience of the true nature of the soul. Mainly, it is the experience of the bliss and unbounded freedom of the soul that frees one from attachment to anything of a changing and limited nature; the Jain sutras make this very clear: "The valiant does not tolerate indulgence, nor does he tolerate abhorrence. As he is pleased with his own [true] self, he is not attached to anything" (*Acaranga*, 2.6. 160). Also, the *Pravacanasara sutra* states: "If one's vision is capable of expelling the darkness, he would not need a lamp. Likewise, the soul itself being blissful, there is no need of external object for bliss" (1.67). Lastly, in his text *Bhagavan Mahavira*, Acharya Tulsi (1985) also offers the following *sutras* from the *Niyamasara* text:

> A monk engrossed in meditation renounces all evils. Meditation is therefore the best way of regression from all transgressions. (63)
>
> The monk who is absorbed in meditation achieves victory over attachment and aversion and the senses. His fear vanishes and his passions are shattered. Finally, he extirpates his indulgence, abhorrence and delusion.
>
> One who meditates on the soul, attains the supreme *Samadhi*. (129)

In Jain tradition, the inward journey to the realization of the vastness, brilliance and bliss of the soul is meant for all people of every race and creed and regardless of social position. It is for monks and nuns, as well as for the men and women living and working in the worldly professions. It is for all those who dedicate themselves to the realization of the supreme nature of their own souls.

Our last inquiry is on Sikhism, or Sikhi, the most recent of these four traditions.

Sikhism

In terms of the nature of the Ultimate Reality, Guru Nanak, the founder of Sikhism, refers to this Supreme Reality as God. He expresses his vision in the following description, which is the first sentence of the holy scripture of the Sikhs, the *Guru Granth Sahib:*

There is but one God
He is the Eternal Truth
The Creator, All-Pervading Divine Spirit
Unfearful, without hate and enmity
Immortal Entity, Unborn, Self-existent, and
He is realized by the Grace of the True Guru.
Meditate upon Who was True before the creation
Who was True in the beginning of creation
Who is True now, and O Nanak,
Who shall be True for ever.
(*Mool-Mantar*, Preamble of *Japji*)

(Sikh Missionary Center, 1990, p. 273)

According to some Sikh scholars, the entire Guru Granth Sahib is a detailed elaboration and explanation of these above words. It is clearly stated by Guru Nanak that there is but one God who is the immortal truth or reality, which is the Creator of all and at the same time completely pervades all of His creation with his own Being or Spirit. This ultimate existence is without any dread or hatred and is unborn, undying and is 'Self-existent', meaning that God is not dependent upon any other existence for His Being.

In addition, Guru Nanak states that "He is realized by the Grace of the True Guru." For Guru Nanak, in the context of the above verses, the 'True Guru' is actually God. This understanding is supported by the following verses:

The Guru is Almighty,
Guru is Formless, High, Inaccessible and Infinite
Ineffable is His praise; what can a sayer say? (Sri Rag Mohalla 5, p. 52)

The Guru is Himself the Transcendent Lord, the Supreme God,
Saith Nanak: meditate thou on that Guru. (As a Mohalla 5, p. 387)

(Sikh Missionary Center, 1990, p. 7)

According to Guru Nanak, God is realized by human beings through God's grace. The finite human being cannot achieve Divine realization unless God decides to reveal Himself. Divine experience cannot be taken by any person, but it can be given by God to anyone God decides is worthy of receiving it. However, human beings are encouraged to engage in certain types of behavior that can help to create the conditions that can make it more likely for God's grace to dawn. All of these behaviors are for the purpose of increasing the purity of the mind, heart and body. Guru Nanak tells his students to:

> Meditate upon Who was True before the creation
> Who was True in the beginning of creation
> Who is True now, and O Nanak,
> Who shall be True forever.

In Sikhism, the terms related to the process of meditation are *Nam Simran* and *Nam Japna* (Cole, 2004, p. 72). It is beyond the scope of this paper to go into the details of these practices, but the core idea is that if one properly engages in daily meditation, one will be able to bring greater purity to one's mind, heart and physiology, which will result in making one more capable and open to receive the enlightenment and liberation that comes from God's grace.

In addition to regular daily meditation, one is encouraged to earn one's livelihood by honest means (*Kirat Karo*): one should never engage in deceit in one's business activities or in one's personal life. Guru Nanak emphasized that "Truth is high but higher still is truthful living" (Sri Raag Moh. 1, p. 62). One should strive to be financially independent and to not rely on the charity of others unless it is impossible to do otherwise. After earning in this honest manner, one should be mindful to compassionately share the fruits of one's labor with others, especially those that are most needy (*Vand Chhako*; also known as *Dan* or charity). Guru Nanak said "They who eat the fruit of their labor and bestow something in the name of their Lord, O Nanak, recognize the right way" (The Sikh Missionary Center, 1990, pp. 65, 271). Guru Nanak also taught the importance of fidelity in marriage and that one should never attempt to harm anyone through misrepresenting the truth. The Sikh gurus in general upheld that one should keep oneself healthy by refraining from smoking, alcohol and the use of non-prescribed drugs.

All the abovementioned guides for proper behavior have one main purpose for a Sikh: to become fully united with the Ultimate Reality, with God. The human being is considered to be that special being created by God who has the God-given capacity to realize his or her Maker. It is thought that the other species have not been granted that capacity. Consequently, human life is an immense opportunity that should be cherished and never wasted. In Sikhism, as well as in the other Dharmic traditions, the inner consciousness or soul can be placed in numerous and varied kinds of life forms:

> In how many births wert thou a worm or a moth!
> In how many births an elephant, a fish, or a deer!
> In how many births a bird or a serpent!
> In how many births wert thou yoked as a horse or an ox!
> Meet the Lord of the world, this is the time to meet Him
> After a long period of time hast thou attained a human body.
> (Gauri Guareri Mohalla 5, p. 176)

When a human body has been gained, it is thought that every moment is precious and that one should not waste one's time in matters that are not mainly centered on the realization of the Supreme. However, it is considered perfectly acceptable to live and work in the world; in fact, in Sikhism, one is strongly discouraged from leaving the world and living the life of a monk or nun. The ideal of Sikhism is to be a family person actively, honestly, and charitably engaged in the work of the world, while at the same time enjoying the fulfillment of being fully united with God. Nevertheless, one should be careful to not make material gains or achieving a high social or professional status the main focus of one's attention and efforts. If one forgets one's highest purpose of God Realization, one can become totally lost in comparatively superficial and trivial matters:

This time having been born as a human being
This is thy turn to meet the Supreme Lord.
Thy other activities will be of no avail at the end,
Seek the company of holy men
And contemplate on God.
Set thy mind on crossing the sea of life,
For life is being wasted away
In pursuits of pleasures of the world.

(As a Mohalla 5, p. 12)

O man, thou comest to earn merit (spiritual)
But how vainly art thou engaged
While the night of life passeth away.

(Sri Rag Mohalla 5, p. 43)

Sleeping through, man wasteth the night,
Eating, he wasteth the day away
And lo, the Jewel of life [God Realization] is bartered away for a trite.

(Gauri Bairagan Mohalla 1, p. 156)

Having wondered through eighty-four lakhs of species
Thou hast obtained the very precious human life,
Nanak, remember thou then the *Nam* [the glory of God's name]
For thy days are numbered.

(Sri Rag Mohalla 5, p. 50)
(Sikh Missionary Center, 1990, pp. 271-72)

Lastly, it would be important to mention that Sikhism believes in social equality for all men and women and the concept of the spiritual unity of humankind. For example, Guru Nanak rejected the caste system as it was applied and understood in the India of his day. He emphasized that "God is concealed in every heart; His light is in every heart." And that "All hearts are illuminated by the Light of the Lord...." (Sorath Mohalla 1, p. 597)

The Sikh scriptures also state that "Whoever contemplates on God, caste or no caste, he becomes a blessed devotee of God" (Basant Mohalla 4, p. 1178). And, "The man who knoweth God, looketh on all men as equal, as the wind bloweth on the commoner and the king alike." (Gaurie Sukhmani Mohalla, p. 272)

In terms of the principle, the spiritual unity of humankind, Guru Gobind Singh explained:

> As out of a single stream, countless waves rise up and being water, fall back in water again. So from God's being emerge alive and inanimate things, and since they arise from Him, they fall in Him again. (Akal Ustat)

And, Guru Arjan wrote:

> You are the loving God, the Protector,
> You are the Master of us all
> I remember you every moment.
> We are the children looking up to you for support.... (Sorath)
> (Duggal, 1993, p. 135)

All beings are seen as coming from the same one divine Source and then all return to It. Differences in caste, creed, culture, religion or economic status, are not significant as all are equally expressions or manifestations of the same one divine Unity of life, which is God. In Maj Mohalla, it states, "Thou are the Father of us all... all are partners, Thou art alien to none" (5, p. 97). And again, in Sorath Mohalla, "There is one Father of us all, and we are children of the same Father." (5, p. 611)

Also, given this unified vision of life, it is not considered significant that the Supreme Being is called by different names by different faiths. God is the same one Being regardless of differences in culture, religion and language: "I am neither a Hindu nor a Muslim; the soul and body belong to God whether He be called Allah or Raam" (Bhairo Mohalla 5, p. 1136); and, the result of this vision of life's ultimate Oneness in terms of how one perceives all others, has been beautifully expressed in the following verse:

"There is no enemy, none is 'other', a sense of universal brotherhood has come to me." (Kanra Mohalla 5, p. 1299)

At the conclusion of Sikhs' morning and evening prayers, there is a request made of God for the entire human race: "By thy Grace, may everyone be blessed in the world." (Sikh Missionary Center, 1990, p. 308)

It is clear that Sikhism, in its philosophy and practice, eloquently and powerfully expresses the essence of the perennial philosophy, the universal common ground of the Dharmic traditions.

Conclusion

In conclusion, this paper has explored some of the features of the common ground existing among the traditions of Hinduism, Buddhism, Jainism and Sikhism in light of fundamental principles of what has been called the 'Perennial Philosophy'. This paper examined how divergent religious traditions have significant common characteristics despite differences among them in theory and praxis. It argued that these traditions all concur on the following points: (1) There is a higher reality, an Ultimate Reality, even though the nomenclature used to refer to it may differ. (2) This supreme Reality is limitless and eternal, formless in its essential nature, omniscient, and the substratum of all energy, intelligence, love, compassion, and creative power. (3) This higher Reality can be directly experienced by human beings and lived in life. (4) The central purpose of human life is to identify with and fully attune oneself to the unique nature of this Reality. (5) Full integration with this Reality brings permanent peace, fulfillment and freedom that is not diminished by limitations of the ever-changing aspects of existence. (6) Without the full realization of this highest reality, human life will continue to be filled with an endless array of suffering, conflicts and problems. (7) The practice of meditation is recommended as a key and necessary means through which direct realization of Ultimate Reality can be attained. (8) To become fully awakened to this supreme value of existence and to spontaneously live it for oneself and all others is the shared highest aspiration of these traditions.

REFERENCES

Bancroft, A. (2001). *The Pocket Buddha Reader.* Boston, Massachusetts: Shambala Publications Inc.

Bhaskarananda, S. (2002). *The Essentials of Hinduism: A Comprehensive Overview of the World's Oldest Religion.* Seattle, Washington: Viveka Press.

Brown, K. (1990). *The Essential Teachings of Hinduism.* London: Arrow Books Limited.

Cole, W.O. (2008). *Understanding Sikhism.* Edinburg, Scotland: Dunedin Academic Press Ltd.

Conze, E. (2003). *Buddhism: Its Essence and Development.* New York, NY: Dover Publications Inc.

Duggal, K.S. (1993). *Sikh Gurus: Their Lives and Teachings.* New Delhi, India: UBS Publishers' Distributers Pvt. Ltd.

Egenes, T. (2001). *Vedic Words and Expressions Used in Maharishi Vedic Science.* Self-published document.

Egenes, T. (2010). *Maharishi Patanjali: Yoga Sutra.* Fairfield, Iowa: 1st World Publishing.

Harvey, A. (Ed.) (2001). *Teachings of the Hindu Mystics.* Boston, Massachusetts: Shambala Publications Inc.

Huxley, A. (1970). *The Perennial Philosophy.* New York, NY: Harper Colophon Books.

Johansson, R.E.A. (1998). *Pāli Buddhists Texts: An Introductory Reader and Grammar.* Richmond, United Kingdom: Curzon Press.

Klostermaier, K.K. (1998). *Hinduism: A Short Introduction.* Oxon, England: Oneworld Publications.

Kornfield, J. (1999). *Teachings of the Buddha.* New York, NY: Barnes and Noble Books.

Lal, A.S. and Mal, B.M. (n.d.). *The Three Jewels (The Ratna).* Retrieved from http://www.jainworld.com/jainbooks/firstep-1/ratna.htm

Law, B.C. (2002). *Mahavira: His life and Teachings.* Kolkata, India: D.L.S. Jayawardana Maha Bodhi Book Agency.

Long, J.D. (2011). *Jainism: An introduction.* London: I.B. Tauris and Co. Ltd.

Maharishi Mahesh Yogi (1990). Maharishi Mahesh Yogi on the Bhagavad Gita: A Translation and Commentary, Chapters 1-6. London: Arkana/Penguin. (Original work published in 1967.)

Maharishi Mahesh Yogi (1997). *Celebrating Perfection in Education.* India: Age of Enlightenment Publications (Printers) 2nd Edition.

Maurer, W.H. (1975). "A Re-examination of Rgved X.129, the Nasadiya hymn". *Indo-European Studies*, Vol. 3, No. 3, p. 234.

Moses, J. (2002). *Oneness: Great Principles Shared by All Religions.* New York, NY: Ballantine Books.

Muni, R. and Jain, M. (2013). *Lord Mahavira: Life and Philosophy.* New Delhi, India: Shree Publishers and Distributors.

Shah, P.K. (2009). *Jainism: Religion of Compassion and Ecology.* India: JAINA Education Committee.

Shah, B.S. (2002). *An Introduction to Jainism* (2nd ed.). New York: The Setubandh Publications.

Shearer, A. and Russel, P. (1978). *The Upanishads.* Great Britain: Wildwood House Ltd. Reprinted by Unwin Hyman Limited in 1989.

Sikh Missionary Center (1990). *Sikh Religion.* Ann Arbor, Michigan: Sheridan Books Inc.

Smith, H. and Novak, P. (2003). *Buddhism: A Concise Introduction.* New York, NY: Harper Collins.

Tulsi, A. (1985). *Bhagavan Mahavira.* Landun (Rajasthan), India: Jain Vishva Bharati Press.

Uberoi Foundation Website (2013). *Vision and Mission Statement.* Retrieved from http://www.uberoireligiousstudies.org/vision.html

Varni, J. (Compiler) (1993). *Saman Suttam.* Varanasi, India: Sarva Seva Sang Prakashan.

Vivekananda, S. (1989). *Hinduism.* India, Mylapore: Sri Ramakrishna Math Printing.

□

2

Interactions Among the Dharmic Traditions

—*Yashwant K. Malaiya*

ABSTRACT

In this paper, I examine the interrelationships and the interactions among the dharmic traditions (Hinduism, Jainism, Buddhism, and Sikhism). Generally, such relationships have been examined from a tradition-centric perspective that prevails in modern sectarian literature. This paper presents a perspective that relies on historical perspectives, some of which have not previously been brought together. The paper acknowledges the need for each tradition to assert its uniqueness, while acknowledging the shared background and the mutual influences. The paper points out that some of the widely held beliefs regarding the interrelationships among the four dharmic traditions are misleading.

Introduction

In India, there has always been religious diversity. The native traditions, which are sometimes termed Dharmic traditions (in contrast with the Abrahamic traditions), include Hinduism, Jainism, Buddhism and Sikhism. Each of them in turn, includes multiple sects. It is now often taken for granted that each religion is mutually incompatible with all the others, and choosing one necessitates rejection of everything that the other religions offer. As the discussion below shows, this view does not reflect the realities of either Indian history or contemporary society.

The four traditions are not easy to demarcate. Hinduism encompasses both Vedic and Puranic texts and practices as well as the new philosophies and *sampradayas* that emerge time-to-time. The two *shramanic* faiths are Jainism and Buddhism. Their modern forms are based on the teachings of Lord Mahavira and Gautam Buddha, respectively, however both traditions view them as the last of a series of teachers. While Sikhism is based on the teachings of the ten gurus, the Adi Granth includes the work of non-Sikh authors who lived before the Gurus.

The perspective taken here may be termed Jain centric, but it differs from the common perspective found in contemporary Jain writings. The paper brings out what is often ignored or avoided, that is, that many of the perceived or purported dividing lines between these traditions do not actually exist.

We first examine a difficult question: Are the four traditions just variations of Hinduism, or are they distinct religions? We next consider the rulers in India who belonged to the Jain or Buddhist traditions. We examine the role of Brahmins, who are widely portrayed in the other three traditions as being the guardians (and exploiters) of orthodox Hinduism. We examine historical evidence to see if the prevailing academic view that Buddhism was exterminated by the Brahmin is correct.

Question of Identity—Are Jains Hindu?

This paper focusses on Jainism and its relationship with other traditions, especially the Hindu tradition. The relationship between Jainism and Hinduism has been widely debated in the form of the question "Are Jains Hindus?"[1]

The answer to the question hinges on how the term Hindu is defined. Tilak's oft-quoted definition, from his 1915 *Gita Rahasya*, "Acceptance of the Vedas with reverence; recognition of the fact that the means or ways to salvation are diverse; and realization of the truth that the number of Gods to be worshiped is large" was cited in a 1966 Indian Supreme Court judgment, and appears to be the common connotation of the term Hinduism today. It would exclude Jainism, Buddhism and Sikhism.

However, historically 'Hindu' was an ethnic term and not until the 1881 census were the terms Hindu and Jain used mutually exclusively. The Jain Poet Banarasidas (1586-1643) used the terms Hindi and Turk to imply ethnicity.[2] Jain Acharya Mahavirkirti in his 1945 *Dharmananda Shravakachar*, regarded Jains to be ideal Hindus.[3] The dedicatory inscription of 1439 at the famous Jain temple at Ranakpur terms Rana Kumbha as 'Hindu Surtrana', in contrast with the Turk Sultans Allauddin and Muhammad Khalji.[4]

The term Hindu did not occur in Jain or Buddhist literature until recent times. In the Buddhist Tamil classic *Manimekalai*, datable to about the 4th century CE, Indra is mentioned as a popular non-sectarian deity, and the philosophies discussed are Nyaya and Vaiseshika, Saiva, Brahmavadi, Vaishnava, Vedavadi, Ajivakas, Nirgrantha (Jain), Sankhya, Vaiseshika, Bhutavadi and Buddhist.[5] The 14th century *Sarva-darsana-sangraha* of Madhavacharya discusses Charvaka, Buddhism, Jainism, Ramanuja sect, Purnaprajna sect, Pashupat, Shaiva, Pratyabhijna, Raseshwar, Vaisheshika, Naiyayika, Jaimini, Mimansa, Vaiyakarana, Samkhya and Advaita. The 10th century Jain Acharya Devasena in his *Darshanasara* mentions ten philosophies, including Buddhism, Ajivaka, and Vaidika, composite and universalistic philosophies; the other philosophies are several Jain sects.

In the past, the Jains have termed themselves Hindu (and non-Jain Hindus as *ajain* or Vaishnava). In modern times, some Jains still accept the term Hindu,[6] but others reject it.[7] There is an organized movement in India[8] to have the Jains recognized as a minority.[9] Some Jains maintain that socially they may be termed Hindu, but not in the religious sense. Clearly, it depends on whether the term is used in its historic sense as an ethnic term, or in the modern sense as a religious identity. Rashtriya Swayamsevak Sangh (RSS), an Indian nationalistic organization, uses the term Hindu in its historic sense. Some of the RSS-affiliated political leaders such as Amit Shah, the Bhartiya Janta Party (BJP) president, are Jain.

Social Interaction between Jains and Hindus

Marriage is the closest form of social interaction. Even deeply religious Jain and Hindu Agarwal families intermarry. For example, Vishnu Hari Dalmiya, the former Vishwa Hindu Parishad (VHP) president, is closely related to the late Sahu Shanti Prasad Jain, the noted Jain philanthropist who was accorded the Jain title 'Shravak Shiromani', as the convention has been that a girl follows the faith of her husband after her marriage. A few merchant communities, most notably the Agarwals, can be either Jain or Hindu (Vaishnava or Arya Samaji), as Jain and Vaishnava Agarwals from the same regions appear to have intermarried traditionally since the 19th[10] and early 20th centuries.[11] Historical sources attest to the existence of Jain Agarwals since 1132 CE[12] and the joint presence of Jain and Hindu Agarwals since 1338.[13] The number of Jains among Agrawals is now about only 6-8 percent.[14] However, some 17-19th century texts mention about half of them to be Jain.[15]

Mahatma Gandhi, a devout Vaishnava, was significantly influenced by Jain philosophy. His parents, who belonged to the Modh community,[16] often invited Jain monks to their home. When Gandhi wanted to go to England, his other invited Becharji Swami, a Jain monk born in the Modh community, who made Gandhi take the three famous vows—not to touch wine, women or meat, while in England.

Rajput Kings, Jainism and Buddhism

Chittoregarh is the most storied of the Indian castles, home of the Sisodia clan and the legendary queen Padmavati, whose fictionalized account has been narrated in Malik Muhammad Jayasi's Padmavat. It is notable that majority of the temples at Chittoregarh are of Jain affiliation; this is not an exception, as Jain temples stood within all Rajput bastions. The Jains served as councilors, financiers, administrators, and sometimes even as generals.

Some of the Rajput rulers had an affinity to Jainism to such a degree that they are termed as having been Jain. Chaulukya Kumarpal was a major ruler of Gujarat, whose leanings towards

Jainism are well known, although he also undertook a major project to rebuild the Somanath temple. Gonk, a Shilahar ruler is also known to have built many Jain temples. Several of the Rashtrakuta rulers, including the best known of them, Amoghvarsha, were devout Jain. The Rashtrakuta princes where conquests took them to both northern and southern borders of India had a long association with Jainism. Even after the fall of the imperial Rashtrakutas at Manyakhet, one of their branches at Hastikundi, near Jodhpur in Rajasthan, continued to patronize Jainism. The Gahadwal ruler Jayachand (who has been vilified in Prathviraj Raso, written in praise of his opponent) was a major supporter of Buddhism.[17]

Table 1 gives a few of the notable Buddhist and Jain rulers of India. It should be noted that in many cases it can be quite hard to judge if the king belonged to one specific faith. In fact, as we note from Ashoka's Rock Edict 7 and the Kharvela's Hathigumpha inscription, the kings in India were generally expected to support all the traditions.

Jainism and Buddhism are correctly termed pacifist systems. However they have been favored by some of the strongest rulers including some notable conquerors. Lalitadidya Muktipad is the only Indian ruler who conquered central Asia in addition to a large section of India.

Buddhism, Jainism, Sikhism, and Brahmins

Ambedkarite Buddhist activists have widely promoted the view that Brahmins were opposed to Buddhism and were responsible for the disappearance of Buddhism in India.[18] However, historical facts suggest a completely contrary view.

Brahmins were always prominent in the Buddhist Sangha even during the lifetime of Gautam Buddha himself. 40 percent of the Buddhist monks whose caste is recorded in the texts, were Brahmin.[19] Practically all famous Brahmin Acharyas were Brahmin – Sariputra, Maudgalyayana, Mahakashyapa, Nagarjuna, Asvaghosha, Padmasambhava, Shantarakshita, and Shantideva, for example. The Mahabodhi temple at Gaya was built by two Brahmin

Table 1: Some Notable Jain and Buddhist Rulers of India

Ruler	*Leaning*	*Clan*	*Preceptor*	*Duration*
Kharvela	Jainism	Chedi		193-170 BCE
Harshavardhana	Hindu/Buddhist	Pushyabhuti		607-647 CE
Lalitadisya Muktipada	Hindu/Buddhist	Karkota	Sarvajnamitra, Cankuna	724-760 CE
Amoghavarsha	Jainism	Rashtrakuta	Jinasena-Gunabhadra	800-878 CE
Kumarpal	Jainism	Chalukya (Solanki)	Hemachandra	1143-1172 CE
Jayachandra	Buddhism	Gahadaval	Srimitra	12th cent CE
Gonk	Jainism	Shilahara	Maghanadi	1020-1050

brothers. And the Tibetan monk Dhamaswamin reports that the last teacher of Nalanda was supported by a local Brahmin. Further evidence follows.

Evidence from *Dhammapada:*

Dhammapada, a collection of sayings by Gautam Buddha himself, contains a section entitled Brahmanavaggo with verses relating to Brahmins and Brahminhood.[20] Here is a selection that illustrates what the Buddha thought:

> Who is meditating, stainless, settled, has done his duty, is without taints,
> has reached the highest attainment—him do I call a Brahmin. (386)
>
> During the day shines the sun, at night shines the moon.
> The Kshatriya shines when armed, the Brahmin shines when meditating.
> And the Buddha shines with splendor all day and night. (387)
>
> One is called 'a Brahmin' because he keeps away from evil.
> One is called 'a recluse' (*samano*) because he lives in tranquility.
> If one has renounced one's own impurities, then one is called 'a monk' (*pabbajito*). (388)
>
> Who does not perform any evil deeds by body, speech or mind,
> who is restrained in three ways—him do I call a Brahmin. (391)
>
> Who is like a moon, spotless, clean, bright and undisturbed,
> who has destroyed the existence of pleasure—him do I call a Brahmin. (413)

Evidence from *Jataka Mala*:

The influential text *Jataka Mala* of Arya Shura is thought to have been composed in the 4th century CE, arguably at the peak of Buddhist influence in India. It narrates 34 Jataka stories and has the unique distinction of having been quoted at Ajanta. Jataka scenes are inscribed with quotes from Arya Shura, depicting

Kshanivada Jataka (ch. 28, verses 4, 15, 19, 56), and Maitribala Jataka (ch. 8, verse 44) in Cave II, which has been dated to the latter half of the 5th century. It had already been translated into Chinese in 434 CE. It thus apparently represents the Buddhist perspective at the peak of Buddhist influence in India.

It is instructive also to look at the Buddhist view of Brahmins. Here are some excerpts.

In many of the Jatakas, the *Bodhisattva* (Gautam Buddha in his former lives) was born as a Brahmin. In some others, he treats Brahmins with reverence.

Shibi Jataka: The *Bodhisattva* Shibi gives one of his own eyes to a blind Brahmin (actually Indra disguised as one):

केनानुशिष्टस्त्वमिहाङ्गयुपेतोमांयाचितुंब्राह्मणमुख्यचक्षुः ।
सुदुस्त्यजंचक्षुरितिप्रवादःसंभावनाकस्यमयिव्यतीता ॥२.११ ॥

"Who has instructed thee, illustrious Brāhman, to come here and to ask from me one eye? No one, it is said, will easily part with his eye. Who is he that thinks the contrary of me?"

Agastya Jataka and Brahmana Jataka (7th and 12th Jatakas in *Jatak Mala*, respectively). Bodhisatva was born in a Brahmin family:

बोधिसत्त्वभूतःकिलायंभवांल्लोकहितार्थंसंसाराध्वनिवर्तमानशचरित्रगुणविशुद्ध्यभिल क्षितंक्षितितलतिलकभूतमन्यतमंमहद्ब्राह्मणकुलंगगनतलमिवशरदमलपरिपूर्णमण्डलशचन्द्रमाः समुत्पन्नेवाभ्यलंचकारासयथाक्रमंश्रुतिस्मृतिविहितानवाप्यजातकर्मादीन्संस्कारानधीत्य साङ्गान्वेदान्कृत्स्नंचकल्पंव्याप्यविद्यायशसामनुष्यलोकंगुणप्रियैर्दातृभिरभ्यर्थ्यप्रतिगृह्यमाण विभवत्वात्परांधनसमृद्धिमभिजगाम।

"In the time, when our Lord, still being a *Bodhisattva*, was moving on his road through Saṅsāra for the good of the world, he was born of an illustrious family of Brāhmans, which being distinguished by great purity of conduct might pass for an ornament of the earth. His birth enhanced the lustre of this family in the same way as the moon rising in autumn with full and spotless orb, beautifies the firmament. He had in due order obtained the different sacraments ordained by the sacred texts and the tradition: jātakarma and the rest; he had studied the Vedas with their Aṅgas and the whole ritual, and the fame of his learning filled the world of men."

Vishvantara Jataka (9th)

अयंमांब्राह्मणस्तातलतयाहन्तिनिर्दय: ।
नचांयब्राह्मणोव्यक्तंधार्मिकाब्रह्मणा:किल ॥९.६५ ॥
यक्षोऽयंब्रह्मणच्छद्मानूनंहरतिखादितुम् ।
नीयमानौपिशचेनतातकिंनावुपेक्षसे ॥९.६६ ॥

"This cruel Brahman, father, hurts me with a creeper. No, it is no Brahman, to be sure. Brahmans are righteous, they say. It is an ogre under the guise of a Brahman. Certainly he carries us off to eat us. Why do you suffer us, father, to be led away by this ogre?"

Brahmana Jataka (12th)

बोधिसत्त्व:किलकस्मिंश्चिदनुपक्रुष्टगोत्रचारित्रेस्वधर्मानुवृत्तिप्रकाशयशसिविनयाचारश्लाघिनिमहतिब्रह्मणकुलेजन्मपरिग्रहंचकारासयथक्रमंगर्भाधनपुंसवनसीमन्तोन्नयनजातकर्मादिभि: कृतसंस्कारक्रमोवेदाध्ययननिमित्तंश्रुताभिजनाचारसम्पन्नेगुरौप्रतिवसतिस्म ।

"Once the Bodhisattva, it is told, came to life in an illustrious family of Brāhmans, well-reputed both on account of their ancestry and their conduct. They were highly esteemed and renowned, observing their traditional customs and setting a high value on good education and good manners. Having received in due order the different sacraments: garbhādhāna, puṁsavana, sīmantonnayana, jātakarma, and the rest, he dwelt at his teacher's, who was a Brāhman distinguished by the superiority of his learning, by his birth, and by his practice of the customary conduct, with the object of studying the Veda."

Buddhism in Kashmir

William Dalrymple in a review of "The Buddha and the Sahibs" by Charles Allen, published in *The Guardian* (Saturday September 28, 2002), writes:

> It was because of this persecution, several centuries before the arrival of Islam, that the philosophy of the Buddha, once a serious rival to Hinduism, virtually disappeared from India: Harsha Deva, a single Kashmiri raja, for example boasted that he had destroyed no less than 4,000 Buddhist shrines.

Dalrymple's claim is incorrect. Harsha (r. 1089-1111) started out as a capable and noble king, then ran into financial trouble because of his spending habits and became an evil person. For the gold he started raiding temples and started destroying statues.

Kalhana's *Rajatarangini* gives an interesting account of Harsha. Note that Kalhana's father, Champaka, was a minister of Harsha. Harsha wrote during the time of Jayasimha (1127-59 AD).

Harsha destroyed both Hindu and Buddhist temples. He created an office of 'devotpaatana-nayaka', destroyer of gods.

Note that in Kalhana's time, Buddhism was flourishing in Kashmir, and it was not distinct from 'Hinduism'. He refers to Buddhist deities just like Brahmanical ones. Kalhana was very familiar with Buddhism, and mentions Buddhist concepts accurately.

King Harsha appears to have become insane. Here is the account from *Rajatarangini*. Taranaga VII (Stein's translation):

> 1128: Other parasites plundered him by showing an old woman and saying, "There, we have brought your mother Bappika from heaven."
>
> 1129: Others brought slave girls before him and said they were goddesses. He worshipped them, and abandoning his exalted position and wealth was laughed at by people.
>
> 1148: He had carnal intercourse with his sisters, and angered by a harsh word he punished and violated Naga, the daughter of his father's sister.

It has been suggested that he had been influenced by Turushkas:

> 1149: While continually supporting the Turushka captains-of-hundreds with money, this perverse-minded [king] ate domesticated pigs until his death.

Here Kalhana appears to be stating that Harsha did not even follow the religion of people he was favoring. He however does call Kalhana 'that Turushka':

> 1095. There was not one temple in a village, town or in the city which was not despoiled of its images by that turushka, king Harsha.

1096. Only two chief divine images were respected by him, the illustrious Ranaswamin in the City, and Marthada [among the images] in townships.

1097-97. Among colossal images, two statues of Buddha were saved through requests addressed by chance to the king at a time when he was free with his favors, namely the one a Parihasapura by the singer Kanaka, who was born there, and other in the City by Sramana (monk) Kusalsri.

The statue at Parihaspura was built by Lalitaditya-Muktapida. IV. 203:... he made the glorious [statue of] the Great Buddha which reached up to the sky.

Abul-fazl mentions that the temples of Parihasapura were finally destroyed by Sikandar 'Butshikast' (1389-1413).

There was a great fire in Srinagar during the reign of Sussla. All the buildings were burnt except the colossal Buddha:

VIII 1184: In the City, which was reduced to a heap of earth, there remained visible and aloft only the great Buddha, which blackened by smoke, and without its abode, resembled a burned tree.

That reminds one of the great Buddha of Kamakura, the wooden temple of which was destroyed by a tidal wave. The temple of the Great Buddha of Nara was similarly destroyed by fire, but was later rebuilt. Note that a colossal copper image of Buddha once stood in Nalanda, said by Hsuan-Tsang to have been 80 feet tall. The great Buddhas of Kashmir may have been similar.

Here are some quotes from Nilamat Purana from Kashmir (trans. by Dr. Ved Kumari). It correctly represents the religious spirit of ancient India.

709-710a. O Brahman, the god Visnu, the lord of the world, shall be (born as) the preceptor of the world, Buddha by name, at the time when the Pusya is joined with the moon, in the month of Vaisaksha, in twenty eighth Kali Age.

710b-12. Listen as to how his worship should be performed in

the bright-half, from that period onwards, in future. The image of Buddha should be bathed (with water rendered holy) with all medicinal herbs, all jewels and all scents, in accordance with the sayings of the Sakyas. The dwellings of the Sakyas (i.e. Viharas) should be whitewashed with care.
713. Here and there, the Caityas—the abodes of the god—should be provided with paintings. The festival, swarming with the actors and the dancers, should be celebrated.
714. The Sakyas should be honoured with Civara (the dress of a Buddhist mendicant), food and books. All this should be done till the advent of Magha.
715. O twice-born, eatable offerings should be made for three days. Worship with flowers, clothes etc. and charity for the poor (should continue for three days).

Buddhism appears to have survived in Kashmir for a long time. At Baramulla a Buddhist monk was present until the 14th century. Abul-Fazl, author of Aine-i-Akbari was able to locate Buddhists in Kashmir.

Shankaracharya and Buddhism

It is widely believed that Shankaracharya (788-820 CE) was responsible for having defeated Buddhism and for having destroyed Buddhist institutions by force, aided by the army of a King Sudhanva. The story forms the basis for several articles claiming that Buddhism was destroyed by force by the Brahmins. However, facts do not support the hypothesis.

1. Buddhism peaked during the Gupta dynasty (320-550 CE). It had already peaked by the time of Xuanzang (Hsüan-tsang; c. 602-664) who visited during Harshavardhan's rule.[21] He found that Hinduism dominated at Thaneshwar, Kanyakubja, Prayaga, Kosambi, Shravasti, Varanasi; and Jains flourished in Vaishali, Pundravardha, Samatata, Cola, Dravida. It had become weak by the 12th century, but still had major centers like Nalanda and Sanchi, and following in many regions of India at noted by findings of 10-12th

century Buddhist images. It survived in several regions until the 15th century. Two isolated Indian communities, the Baruas of Chittagone and Newars of Kathmandu are still largely Buddhist. Shankaracharya may have contributed to the long and gradual decline, but there is no evidence that Buddhism suffered a major reversal in the-8th century.

2. Shringeri, the oldest center founded by Shankaracharya, is quite close to the Jain centers of Humcha (81 km) that dates back to the 8th century (possibly established before Shringeri) and the later Mudabidri (72 km) that still flourish today. They would not have existed if there was violent destruction of rival faiths.
3. The account of destruction first occurs in *Shankara Vijaya* written by Madhava in 14th century, six centuries later.
4. A Shravanabelgoa inscription of 1128 mentions the 8th century. Jain Acharya Akalanka defeated the Buddhist scholar Dharmakirti, and as a result Buddhism was banished to Srilanka. However in South India Buddhism survived as late as 16th century, as attested by Buddhist bronzes found at Nagapattinam.

Sena Kings of Bengal

The Pala kings of Bengal (8-12th cent) were enthusiastic supporters of Buddhism. They were followed by Sena rulers (1070-1230) who had migrated from Karnataka. In 1203-04, the Turkic general Bakhtiyar Khilji, who is famous for having destroyed the great vihara at Nalanda, attacked and conquered a large part of the Sena domain.

In both West Bengal and Bangaldesh, the academic history texts state that Buddhism was persecuted by the Sena dynasty which caused Buddhism to decline there. There is however no archaeological or textual evidence to suggest that there was any persecution under the Sena rulers. Lama Taranath (1575-1634) gives a detailed account of Buddhism, especially in Eastern India, on the Four Sena Kings:[22]

> During their period, the Law was nourished by many scholars and siddhas like Subhakaragupta, Ravisrijnana, Nayakapasri, Dasabalasri and, shortly after them, by Dharmakarasanti, Sri Vikhyatadevabharmakaragupta and many other followers of Abhayakara.
>
> There also came many Persian followers of the mleccha view. To protect Odantapuri and Vikramasila, the king even converted these partially into fortresses and stationed some soldiers there.
>
> While the other centres for the Doctrine became practically extinct, though it is said that the number of monks both in Vikramasila and Odantapuri remained as it was during the time of Abhayakara. After the death of Rathikasena, the few years of Labalmasena's reign were peaceful. Then came the Turushka king called the Moon to the region of Antaravedi in-between the Ganga and the Yamuna. Some of the monks acted as messengers for this king. As a result, the petty rulers of Bhamgala and other places united, ran over the whole of Magadha and massacred many ordained monks in Odantapuri. They destroyed this and also Vikramasila.

Archaeological evidence suggests that while Buddhism continued to weaken during the Sena rule, it continued to be practiced.

The noted scholar of both Buddhism and Jainism Padmanabh Jaini has critically examined the seven factors that lead to the virtual disappearance of Buddhism suggested by R.C. Mitra. One of them is Brahmanical persecution. Jaini did not find this to be a valid explanation.[23]

Surviving Indian Buddhist Communities

The surviving Indian Buddhist communities, the Baruas of Chittagone and Newars of Kathmandu valley[24] apparently also worship Hindu gods.

The Shared Background of the Dharmic Faiths

It is quite easy to spot the shared concepts, symbols and practices among the four traditions. What is hard is identifying who came up with the innovation and who followed.

Indra was the most invoked deity in the Rigveda, with 289 verses compared with 28 for Mitra, six for Vishnu and one for Purusha. He was a very popular God as seen from Tamil classics and his Yatra is still a major celebration in Nepal. However, today he plays a more prominent role in Buddhism (as Shakra) and Jainism. It is common for Jain shravakas to dress up as Indras during major Jain functions. In modern Hinduism, Brahma worship is rare except at a few sites like Pushkar. Brahma however is a very popular God in Buddhist Thailand where worship of Hindu gods is common.

Buddhist activists often regard worship of *devas* (Hindu gods) as an aberration, something that was introduced when Buddhism had become weak. However, this is contradicted by the excavated remains at Bharhut. The Bharhut stupa, dating back to the 2nd or 3rd century BCE, the early period of Buddhism, had numerous panels that represented not only events from the Buddha's life and the Jatakas, but also many *yakshas*, *yakshis*, *nagas*, etc. Bharhut is unique among the Buddhist sites in that most panels have a brief text that makes identification ambiguous. The deities include Kubera *yaksha* and mother Goddess Shri.[25] These deities represent folk religion that was a part of Buddhism and Jainism, as well as Hinduism.

Swami Dayananda Saraswati had a major influence on modern Hinduism. He identified that the Vedic tradition did not have idol worship. It is indeed supported by textual evidence. Manusmriti was critical of Devalaka Brahmins who performed worship of gods in temples.[26] Swami Dayananda blames Jainism for having started idol worship.[27] While as a Jain, I don't necessarily agree with his criticism, he may be right. While the Buddhists developed the craft of creating Buddha images on a much wider scale, some of the earliest Jina images, from Lohanipur (which may date back to Maurya period) and Mathura are thought be older than the oldest

Buddha images. It is interesting to note that the oldest Saraswati image is of Jain origin and the oldest Lakshmi (Shri) image is of Buddhist origin. While the Jain *shasan devis* are thought to have been influenced by Hinduism, however archeologically the worship of mother goddesses appears to have developed in all three traditions around the same time.

The use of Sanskrit for Buddhist and Jain texts came later. However, Ashvaghosha's *Buddhacharita* is thought to have influenced Kalidasa. Still widely used *Amarakosha* was composed by a Buddhist. The *Subhashita Ratna Kosha* was compiled at Jagaddala vihara in Bengal. The earliest Jain Ramayana mentions the text by Valmiki. The Shaiva Siddhanta text *Periya Puranam* was inspired by Jain Jivaka Chintamani and Mahapurana.

It is interesting to note that Lord Rama of Ikshvaku clan is significant in all of the dharmic traditions. In Hinduism, he is an avatara of Lord Vishnu, and *Ramcharitmanas* of Goswami Tulsidas has been a very popular religious text for the past several centuries. In Jainism, he is a *siddha* (the highest state of being) and is invoked in the *Nirvanakanda*. Buddhist texts mention him and his father Dasharath as progenitor of the Shakyas, who are a branch of the Ikshvakus. The Bachitranatak of Guru Gobind Singh mention both Bedis and Sodhis (eight of the ten Sikh Gurus were born in these two clans) are descendants of the two sons of Lord Rama.

Conclusion

As Indians interact with people in the rest of the world, they find the need to explain their views using the perspective of Abrahamic religions, which form the majority. The followers of the dharmic traditions are thus compelled to take an exclusivist view. Devout activists in the four traditions increasingly reject what is shared. Several scholars of religions in India feel compelled to counterbalance intolerance encountered by the Indian traditions by emphasizing isolated incidents of intolerance among the dharmic traditions. However, a careful look at all the sources of Indian history brings out the fact that there has been a remarkable degree of mutual acceptance among different traditions. This provides a fertile ground for the emergence of new sects and philosophies (such as Arya Samaj, Swaminarayan, or Sai Baba movements). There have been attempts to cleanse a specific tradition by removing what has been perceived to have come from outside. This paper shows that the four traditions share much more than is often thought, and have sometimes influenced each other in ways that have not been noticed.

While this chapter is generally focused on Hinduism, Jainism, and Buddhism, many of the observations are also applicable to Sikhism[28] and its relationship with Hinduism and Jainism as well. And while Zoroastrianism is technically not a dharmic tradition, it has interacted with Hinduism, Buddhism and even Jainism.[29] The interaction of other traditions with Sikhism and Zoroastrianism needs to be studied in detail.

Dharmic Traditions: Brief Chronology

Remote antiquity: (Universally agreed dating is not feasible)
Composition of Vedas and sections of Avesta
Shramana traditions develop
Mahavira (last of the Jinas) and early Jain texts (traditionally 540-468 BCE)
Gautam Buddha (last of the Buddhas) and early Buddhist texts
Panini's Sanskrit Grammar Ashtadhyayi (4th c BCE)
Maurya Empire: spread of Buddhism and Jainism (540-468 BCE)
Mahabharata and Ramayana finalized
Kumarajiva translated Buddhist texts in China (334-413 CE)
Sankhyakarika of Ishvarkrishna (4-5th c CE)
Gupta Dynasty, Kalidasa, emergence of temple architecture (320-550 CE)
Hunas conquer western India (5-6th c CE)
Appar (610-91), Sambandar, Saiva Siddhanta
Sankaracharya (788-820 CE)
Rashtrakutas in North India, Rajputs (8-9th c CE)
Rajatarangini (1148-49) of Kalhana
Basavanna (1134-96), Lingayat movement

Turkish conquest, end of Nalanda, Sanchi (1193, 1233)
Sikh Gurus (1539-1708), Adi and Dasham Granth
Lama Taranath (1575-1634 CE) History of Buddhism in India
Jain movements (15th century)
Chaitanya (1486-1534)
Swaminarayan sect (1826)
Several Hindu, Sikh, Jain and Buddhist reform movements (1875-1955)

NOTES

1. Koenraad Elst, Are Jains Hindus?, in Who is a Hindu?: Hindu revivalist views of Animism, Buddhism, Sikhism, and other offshoots of Hinduism, Voice of India, New Delhi, November 2, 2001.
2. Kavivar Banarasidas, in Jain Kaviyon Ka Itihas, Mulachandra Vatsal, 1937, p. 122.
3. Sachche Hindu ka Kartvya, Dharmanand Shravakachar, Acharya Mahavirkirti, 2003 (Original in 1945), Ch. 1, Verse 24, p. 72.
4. R.V. Somani, Jain Inscriptions of Rajasthan, Rajasthan Prakrit Bharati Sansthan, Jaipur, 1982, pp. 34-36.
5. Alain Daniélou and Iyer, Manimekhalai, the Dancer with the Magic Bowl by Shattan, New York, 1989, Ch. 17.
6. "Resist ploy to divide in the name of Hindu, Jain and Buddhist" (Interview with Jain Muni Acharya Vijay Ratnasunder Surishwar Maharaj, Organiser), October 8, 2006.
7. Jains Dispute Legislation Including Them as 'Hindus', *Hinduism Today*, October 3, 2006.
8. Is Jain Minority Right in India Receiving A Fair Deal?, Bal Patil, November 27, 2006, Countercurrents.org
9. Gujarat Conversion Law Amended To Suit Jains!, Adnan Alavi, September 19, 2006, IndianMuslims.in
10. Denzil Ibbetson, *A Glossary of the Tribes and Castes of the Punjab and North-West Frontier Province,* Volume 1, 1911, p. 100.
11. Chetandas, Vaishya Jati ke jainiyon men Parasparik Vivah, Jain Hitaishi, August 1903, pp. 539-43.
12. Vaddhamana Cariu, Edited/translated by Prof. Dr. Rajaram Jain, Bharatiya Jnanapitha, New Delhi, 1975.
13. Parmeshwari Lal Gupt, *Agrawal Jati Ka Vikas,* Kashi paper Stores, Kashi, 1942.
14. According to 1911 Census, there were 1,019,698 Agrawals and in 1914 there were 67,121 Agrawal Jains, i.e. 6.5% were Jain.

15. Navalsah Chanderia, in his Vardhaman Purana of 1768 states that half of the Agrawals are Jain.
16. There have been several notable Jain monks of Modh origin, most notably the great Jain Acharya Hemachandra Suri (1089-1172).
17. It should be noted that the Gahadawals intermarried with the Pala rulers of Bengal who were devout Buddhists.
18. Dr. K. Jamanadas, *Decline and Fall of Buddhism: A Tragedy in Ancient India,* Bluemoon Books, Essel Mansion, 2286 87, Arya Samaj Road, Karol Baug, New Delhi 110 005.
19. Richard Gombrich, Recovering the Buddha's message, in Earliest Buddhism: Madhyamaka, David Seyfort Ruegged, Lambert Schmithausen, BRILL, 1990, p. 13.
20. Readings in Pāli Texts—*Dhammapada*—Chapter 26: The Brahmin.
21. For Hsuan-tsang's travel narrative, see the translation by Samuel Beal, Si-Yu Ki: *Buddhist Records of the Western World* (London: Trubner and Co., 1884; reprint ed., Delhi: Oriental Books Reprint Corporation).
22. Alaka Chattopadhyaya and Lama Chimpa, *Taranatha's History of Buddhism in India*, Debiprasad Chattopadhyaya, ed., Motilal Banarsidass; 2nd edition (February 17, 2010).
23. Padmanabh S. Jaini, "The Disappearance of Buddhism and the Survival of Jainism: A Study in Contrast," in *Studies in History of Buddhism,* A.K. Narain, ed. (Delhi: B.R. Publishing Co., 1980), pp. 181-91.
24. David N. Gellner, *Monk, Householder, and Tantric Priest: Newar Buddhism and its Hierarchy of Ritual*, Cambridge Studies in Social and Cultural Anthropology, July 31, 1992.
25. Sir Alexander Cunningham, The Stūpa of Bharhut: A Buddhist monument ornamented with numerous sculptures illustrative of Buddhist legend and history in the third century B.C., London: W.H. Allen, 1879.
26. *Manusmriti*, 3-150-152, 3-180.
27. Satryartha Prakash, Swamidayananda Saraswati, 1882, Chapter XI.
28. For some related discussion see Harjot Oberoi, *The Construction of Religious Boundaries: Culture, Identity, and Diversity in the Sikh Tradition*, University of Chicago Press, 1994.
29. For example, the Bhojak priests in the Jain temple have an obscure connection with the Zoroastrian priesthood. See S.R. Kakshi and Pathak, Rashmi, *Punjab Through the Ages: Studies in Contemporary Indian History,* Sarup and Sons, 2007, p. 61.

□

3

Inter-Religious Dialogue in the Greco-Roman World

—Henry Walker

Compassion and Inter-religious Dialogue

Compassion is a Latin word that was created to translate the Greek word *sumpatheia*, sympathy. It literally means to feel or experience something (*passio, pathos*) along with (*com, sun*) someone else, to share in their experience. The normal meaning of 'sympathy' is pity, but it can describe how metal objects will vibrate together,[1] the irresistible way in which we will yawn if we see someone else yawning,[2] the connection that Babylonian astrologers see between the stars and events on earth,[3] the relationship between the body and the soul.[4] Sympathy is therefore a force that unites things that are different. You can of course feel sorry for yourself, but then you are looking at yourself from a distance. In a famous play by Euripides, the hero says:

> If only I could stand opposite and see myself:
> I would weep at the misfortunes I am suffering.[5]

He cannot feel real sympathy for himself unless he stands away from himself, unless he sees himself as a different person. If everyone in an orchestra is playing the same note on the same type of instrument, there can be no harmony or sympathy or symphony. The essence of sympathy is difference and diversity:

you are sharing an emotion or experience with someone who is distant and different from yourself.

Compassion is therefore an essential element of any real religious dialogue, any genuine interaction among different religions. It means we must accept the fact that people are diverse and religions are different, but we must join in their experience both because of this difference and in spite of it. We must reject the globalizing tendency of monotheism, a globalization which either demands that everyone should become the same, or claims that everyone is already the same.[6] We must adopt instead a compassionate internationalism that bases interaction on the existence of different nations, and on respect for that diversity. If inter-religious dialogue is going to work, we must remember that the word *inter* means 'between' and the world *dia* means 'across', so there must be a gap and a difference between religions, and we must speak across that gap.

This is very difficult for monotheists. If there is only one true God, if there is only one correct way of experiencing the divine, how can I share the experience of someone who is not a monotheist, who does not believe in my one true God? Monotheism forces me to believe that their experience is either empty or wrong, zero or negative, and how could I want to share in either of those experiences?

But if God is manifold, then it will be very easy for me to accept that people are different too, that they have different experiences, and that I can share in those different experiences. This is borne out by the historical record. When the Romans encountered the Persian Ahura Mazda, the Jewish Adonai Tzevaot, and the Egyptian Amun, they did not denounce them as evil or imaginary beings. Instead they equated them with their own supreme God and worshipped them as Jupiter Orimasdes, Jupiter Sabazius, Jupiter Ammon. Later in history, we find that Jews, Christians, and Zoroastrians came to India, escaping from their monotheistic persecutors. The first two groups were so comfortable there that they believed that they had always lived in India since the founding of their religion.[7] It is very easy for any different religion, even a monotheistic one, to be embraced and welcomed and made to feel at home by a polytheistic society.

What makes countries like America or France both tolerant and bearable is the fact that in addition to being 'Christian countries', they are also heavily influenced by the tolerant, pagan, polytheistic traditions of Greece and Rome. For the first century of its existence, the coins of the American republic had two mottoes only, 'Liberty' and 'E Pluribus Unum'. There was no mention of God or religion.[8] But in the year 1864, the government surrendered to a bullying, religious fanatic and added the words 'In God We Trust'.[9] How anyone can have true liberty, and at the same time be deprived of the right to decide whether there is one God or not, and whether that God should be trusted or not, is a mystery that surpasses human understanding. How a country could be a union of many different parts, and yet every part should be obliged to believe the same thing, is beyond human comprehension. Nevertheless, American coins and bank notes still bear these contradictory mottoes, celebrating the natural, republican relationship between freedom and diversity, but also shamefully surrendering to the claims of monotheistic orthodoxy. The Civil War was drawing to a close when these fatal words were added to the coins of America, but ever since then a different type of civil war has raged in America: a battle between Greco-Roman liberty and Fundamentalist Christian theocracy, between the free republic of the Founding Fathers and the hideous tyranny of the Pilgrim Fathers.

The French Republic had a similar religious motto on the edge of its coins, 'God protect France'. At the end of the nineteenth century, a group of monarchists, nationalists, and conservative Catholics decided to challenge the Republic by attacking Captain Dreyfus, whose only crime was that he had refused to betray his country to the Germans. The temporary victory of the monarchists and fanatics forced the Republic to retaliate, and in 1906 the monotheistic motto was removed from the edge of its coins, and replaced with 'Liberty, Equality, Fraternity'. In both America and

France, religious freedom is in alliance with ancient paganism against the globalizing demands of monotheism.

There is, therefore, a natural affinity between the open tolerant world of Greco-Roman paganism and the compassionate world of the *dharma* traditions. I would like to look closely at two Greek thinkers who were heavily influenced by Hinduism, and to examine the impact this relationship had on their lives and thought. The first is the Greek scientist and religious guru, Pythagoras. The second lived almost a thousand years later. He was a Greek-speaking subject of the Roman empire who came from West Asia (Cappadocia in modern Turkey), Apollonius of Tyana.

Pythagoras

Pythagoras lived in the 6th century BC, and he is probably most famous nowadays for the theorem that bears his name, though the Babylonians had figured out this problem a thousand years earlier. In ancient Greece, however, he was even more famous as an innovative religious thinker. In his biography of Pythagoras, the pagan philosopher Porphyry (3rd century AD) sums up his religious teaching as follows:

It was very well known by everyone that Pythagoras said:

- first, that the soul is immortal;
- next, that it changes into other types of living things;
- in addition, that what has already happened will happen again some time at regular intervals, so nothing is absolutely new;
- and that we should consider everything with a soul as being related.

It seems that Pythagoras was the first person to introduce these doctrines into Greece.[10]

In effect, Pythagoras had introduced Vedantic Hinduism into Greece. If we recall that sacrificing an animal and sharing its meat among the community was the most important way of communicating with the gods in ancient Greece, we will realize how radically different and strange the religion of Pythagoras must have seemed to everyone around him. His belief in reincarnation and in the fellowship of all living things, everything with a soul (*empsukhos*), meant that his followers "not only had to abstain from living things (*empsukha*), but also could never associate with butchers and hunters."[11] Most Greeks thought that the dead survived as ghosts in the underworld, but some groups such as the Orphics believed that if you performed the correct rituals and purified your soul, you would reach a special heaven with the gods. Pythagoras was always close to the Orphics,[12] since they both believed that the soul was immortal, but he introduced the idea of transmigration to the Orphics.[13] Again, as in Vedantic Hinduism, he placed less focus on ritual, and provided a more ethical and intellectual path to heaven. In effect, he was reforming the Orphic cult, and making it more respectable socially and intellectually.[14]

Like special Indian saints, Pythagoras had the ability to recognize his previous incarnations. During his first incarnation, when he was the human son of the Greek God Hermes, his divine father had granted him this ability to remember all his lives.[15] During a later incarnation, Pythagoras demonstrated this ability in a spectacular way by walking into a temple of Apollo, and correctly identified the weapons that had been seized from him centuries earlier when he had lived as the Trojan warrior Euphorbos.[16] He could even recognize the previous incarnations of other people.[17] Through these demonstrations and his own personal charisma, he won many people over to his teachings throughout Italy.[18] A century later, the ruling family of Akragas (modern Agrigento) in Sicily believed in transmigration.[19]

In their general attacks on Greek religion, Xenophanes, who was a younger contemporary of Pythagoras, and Heraclitus, who was born later, mocked not only the traditional gods of Homer, but also the new religion of Pythagoras.[20] The mockery of these writers shows that his new beliefs were already widespread enough to merit an attack. By the fifth century, he was famous throughout the Greek world. The poet Ion referred to Pythagoras as an expert on what happens to the soul after death,[21] and the historian Herodotus called him "by no means the weakest thinker among the Greeks." Herodotus regarded him as the man who taught the Thracians about the immortality of the soul.[22] By the fourth century, the Pythagorean doctrine of transmigration was so well known that a comic poet could refer to him as "thrice-blessed Pythagoras,"[23] and everyone in the audience knew that he was referring to the many incarnations of Pythagoras.[24] This was also the century in which Plato accepted his teachings and guaranteed that Pythagoreanism would play a major role in Western philosophy.[25]

There was a second important aspect to the teaching of Pythagoras that made his religion very different from what had gone before. The believers formed a special sect that was personally devoted to Pythagoras and separated itself from other people. Pythagoras was a very charismatic person, and he inspired complete devotion or violent hatred.[26] Of course, he had to be that type of person in order to spread his new teachings around southern Italy, in order to charm the government of Croton and turn it in to a Pythagorean state, in order to win over Greeks and Italians elsewhere[27] and bring them to a "new level of consciousness."[28]

His followers believed that he could tell the future and perform miracles,[29] and his authority was unquestioned. One of their sayings was, "Do not distrust any miraculous thing about the gods or about the divine teachings."[30] No matter what Pythagoras taught you, you had to trust him completely and believe everything he told you. They coined the phrase "he himself said it" (αυτόζ εφα *ipse dixit*), because "he himself," Pythagoras, was the ultimate authority that ended any dispute.[31] This intense loyalty to a holy man with special powers shows that he was, in effect, their guru.[32] His followers proclaimed that he was above other humans and living things, that he was some kind of spirit.[33] They told the story that a messenger was sent by the God Apollo from the far north, and this messenger proclaimed that Pythagoras was an incarnation of Apollo Hyperboreas himself.[34] Pythagoras was not just a guru, therefore, but a *sadguru*, one who is identical with the God who has sent him among men.

Anyone who wanted to join the inner circle of devotees who spoke with Pythagoras himself had to undergo a period of testing for five years, part of which involved keeping a vow of silence.[35] Once a person was accepted, there were no limits to the loyalty of his new Pythagorean friends. Once again they had a special saying that encapsulated this bond: "What friends own is shared by all."[36] On the other hand, if someone had failed his probation, he was considered dead by the commnuity.[37] The Pythagorean community has all the characteristics of a *satsanga*.

But if Pythagoras was a Greek *guru* and trusted like a God by his *sanga*, if he brought Indian ideas to Greece, his followers did not have to abandon their own religion completely. One difficult point was that animals had to be sacrificed to please the Greek gods, but transmigration made this impossible. Pythagoras found a way out of this dilemma by allowing some of his followers (those outside the élite innermost circle of believers) to eat meat, but only meat offered to the gods at a sacrifice, because he declared that such sacrificial victims were (by a lucky coincidence) those animals into which a human soul would never transmigrate.[38] Without this loop-hole, the Pythagoreans could never have governed or even lived in a city, because sacrifices were essential for citylife in Greece.

The *sanga* was also typically Greek. Since the Greeks could not conceive of a social group that was not also a political one, Pythagoras could only establish his community by turning it into a political force, by taking control of a city-state, Croton in southern Italy.[39] This meant that the Pythagoreans were both a religious group within the state and the government of that state. This political involvement ultimately led to their downfall in Croton. Keith judges this involvement rather harshly: "The fate of the movement was adverse, as it deserved to be."[40] We might regret the élitist stance of the Pythagoreans, but every ancient religion had to be social and political. The connection between Pythagoreanism and an élitist political system never went away, and it became a central feature of Plato's thought.

The case of Pythagoras and Hinduism tells us something very important about inter-religious dialogue. If two religious systems are very open, if they can enter into a free discussion with each other, they can have a very rich and productive relationship. Hinduism could offer something to the Greeks, because it did not insist on converting them, it did not insist that they should abandon their own world view. And the Greeks could accept Hindu ideas, because their religion was not exclusive, it did not reject new and different ideas. The case of Pythagoras also shows us that in such a dialogue, the speaker and the listener are equally important. It is not a one-way monologue directed at a passive convert. It is a whole range of suggestions being offered to someone who can make a wide range of choices. The listener is equally powerful, the listener has the power to decide what he or she wants to hear. So we end up with a *guru* who is a professor of mathematics, a vegetarian who allows some of his followers to eat meat on special feast days, a sacred *sanga* that is also a secular government, a metaphysical insight that is also a political program. The result is something completely new, a child that shares the features of both its parents. Rather than a clone produced by one alone.

There are, however, two puzzles about Pythagoras that I must mention. The first is that nobody knows how he learned about these Hindu ideas. The messenger who proclaimed that Pythagoras was an incarnation of the God Apollo came from Thrace (modern Bulgaria), so some scholars think that these ideas came to Pythagoras through Central Asia. Others have pointed out that the Persian Empire included both Greeks and Indians, so these ideas must have come to Greece through West Asia. The second puzzle is even more mysterious. Nobody in Greece realized at the time that these ideas were Indian. Herodotus, the father of Greek history, wrote that the idea of transmigration came from Egypt,[41] but it was typical for Greeks at this time to believe that everything came from Egypt.[42] Herodotus also claims that the Greek gods themselves are Egyptian.[43] The Greeks respected Egypt as a very ancient civilization, and Plato later says that the Egyptians regarded the Greeks as mere children compared to themselves.[44] So it is not surprising that the Greeks would guess that the Hindu system of Pythagoras came from Egypt, since Pythagoras had not told them the real answer. Perhaps it was taught to Pythagoras as a secret doctrine (it was after all Upanishadic), and he was not told or was not allowed to reveal its source. Pythagoreanism is, therefore, a strange case of inter-religious dialogue, because one of the interlocutors remains anyonymous, though its identity is perfectly obvious.

Apollonius of Tyana

My second case of inter-religious dialogue between Greco-Roman paganism and Hinduism is much more clear and obvious. It involves a Greek follower of Pythagoras who came from what is now Turkey. He lived in the first century AD, and his name was Apollonius of Tyana.[45] His father sent him to the neighboring Roman province of Cilicia to study philosophy, and Apollonius became a Pythagorean "by some secret wisdom."[46] His philosophy teacher was interested only in food and sex, he had no belief or interest in the teachings of Pythagoras, he simply repeated them like a parrot. But in spite of his dreadful teacher, the Pythagorean system appealed to Apollonius and he decided he was going to follow that path by himself. He became a vegetarian, he refused to wear any animal products, he grew his hair long, he lived in the local temple of the God Asklepios.[47] After his father died, he left the family property to his brother, and took a vow of chastity.[48] He was thus free from all social ties, and he spent his time as a *sadhu*, wandering around from temple to temple and talking with the priests there.[49]

It is at this point in his life that he decides to visit "the nation of India and the wise men living there who are called *Brakhmanes*."[50] When he reaches India, he is told that "the truly wise men live half way between the Beas (*Huphasis*) and the Ganga (*Gangēs*),"[51] and even though he does not name the place, he is talking about Kurukshetra. Since these men are *sadhus*, they have long hair and they are able to levitate.[52] There he learns, what he obviously must have suspected all along, that India is the source of the teaching of Pythagoras, and that it was also brought to Egypt by the Ethiopians, who had originally lived in India.[53] This strange story about the Ethiopians coming from India was obviously invented to explain how Pythagoras could have learned about Indian philosophy in Egypt. Apollonius makes the connection explicit when he later has to defend his entire life in Rome. He justifies his refusal to kill any animal or to eat any meat as follows: "The Indian *Brakhmanes* themselves did not approve of this, and they taught the Naked Men of Egypt not to approve of it. Pythagoras got his teaching from there, because he was the first Greek to associate with the Egyptians."[54]

By the time Apollonius comes back to Greece, he regards himself as an Indian thinker. He later visits Egypt and protests against their sacrifice of a bull. The Egyptians ask what person would have the authority to denounce their practices, and he replies: "any wise person who has arrived from India!"[55] Using the typically Indian practice of ritual substitution, he sacrifices a bull made of incense instead of a living animal.[56] The reason he happens to be in Egypt is that he is on his way to the Naked Men or *sadhus* of Ethiopia, who taught the doctrine of transmigration. They are slightly annoyed when he keeps talking about India, but he explains to them how their own philosophy and Pythagoreanism derive from India.[57]

Being a holy man, Apollonius like Pythagoras has the ability to recognize previous incarnations. He can tell that a tame lion he saw in Egypt is actually a reincarnation of the Pharaoh Ahmose,[58] or that a young boy in Tarsus (Cilicia) is a reincarnation of the Trojan hero, Telephos.[59] In spite of his explicitly Indian religious views and his supernatural powers, he does not in any way reject the everyday practices of his own people. He defends the religious customs of Greece at length in his discussions with the Naked Men of Ethiopia,[60] and he even refuses to attack people who eat meat.[61] He continues to visit the sanctuaries of Greece and to live in them.[62]

When he is asked about his philosophy in Rome, he summarizes it as follows: "*theiasmos* and how to pray and sacrifice to the gods."[63] *Theiasmos* is usually translated as 'religion' or 'theology', but it means more than that. It means to be inspired or possessed by a God, and therefore implies a much closer union with a God than is normal in Greco-Roman religion. This is why people proclaimed in public that he was a God,[64] and why the Spartans were prepared to honor him as a divine epiphany (*theophania*), but Apollonius modestly discouraged them.[65] A century after his death, the emperor Caracalla visited Tyana, the town where Apollonius was born, and had a shrine built in honour of the pagan saint.[66] A decade later, the emperor Alexander Severus had a statue of Apollonius in his personal shrine at the palace.[67] So even though he was openly and explicity preaching Hinduism, Apollonius never abandoned his own gods and was ultimately included among them.

In the fourth century, when Christians and pagans fought for the soul of the Roman Empire, Apollonius became a very important figure for both sides. In some ways, he was too similar to Jesus—both of them urged people to live better lives, both of them taught about the next life, both of them performed miracles. The argument between Christians and pagans about Apollonius turned quite nasty. It is a great example of how an inter-religious dialogue should not be conducted. Christian writers naturally denounced Apollonius as a magician and a trickster; they could not allow any rival to the one, true God. The Christian writer Arnobius gives a list of pagan holy men, including Apollonius and Zoroaster (an interesting choice!), and he asks whether any of them could match the achievements of ordinary Christians.[68] Eusebius denounces Apollonius as an ass in a lion's skin, a sophist who is trying to make money out of people, and a wizard.[69] Eusebius conceded that Apollonius may have performed miracles, but if so, it was only with the help of demons.[70] This reaction is only to be expected, but what is very unusual is that the pagans respond to the Christians in the very same way. Hierocles attacks the Christians for being so gullible, and he claims that the stories about Jesus have been exaggerated by Peter and Paul, who were "liars, uneducated, and wizards."[71] From a pagan, polytheistic perspective, this attack makes no sense. There is no reason why another foreign God should not join the others; there is no reason why a pagan should refuse to welcome the contribution that Jesus might make to his view of the world. As a pagan, Hierocles could not, of course, accept Jesus as the only God and the only Savior, but he should be quite happy to embrace him as yet another God and yet another Savior.

It is impossible, however, for an open-minded polytheist to have a real dialogue with a determined monotheist. The monotheist is forbidden by his or her religion to make any concession whatsoever, the monotheist is obliged to conduct a monologue. This tactic changes the matter under debate because the only question that can now be discussed is whether or not you accept Jesus as the one and only true God and Savior. Instead of a real dialogue, we have a monologue directed by an aggressive salesman against his victim. It changes the entire nature of the debate, because it forces the other party to adopt the same tactic and initiate a monologue on the theme of 'No!' Perhaps the most damaging feature of the bullying imperative to convert is that it forces its victims either to surrender their identity completely and agree to conversion, or if they wish to resist, it forces them to surrender an essential part of their identity, their belief in the diversity of the divine, and become a mirror-image of their persecutors. The dialogue degenerates into a shouting match, with two monologues facing each other but not really interacting. This zero-sum game can only be decided by force, and that in fact is how it ended.[72]

So what can we learn from these stories? First, if we are to communicate as human beings, if we are to respect each other, if we are to show compassion for each other, conversion has to be taken off the agenda. If I am speaking to you with the goal of converting you, you are listening to a telemarketer, you are trying to have a conversation with a machine, and that cannot work. Neither Pythagoras nor Apollonius converts to Hinduism; they adopt it, and when you adopt a new child, you do not have to get rid of your own previous children. The cruel and horrible thing about converting religions like Christianity and Islam is not that they want everyone to believe in Christ and Allah; that is perfectly all right, that is wonderful. The cruel and horrible thing is not that they want you to adopt their God, but that they want you to kick your own gods out of your life. Second, in a real conversation based on compassion and mutual respect, the listeners, are as important as the speaker. The listeners can reject everything I say, and that means I have not been paying a great deal of attention to them, I have not respected them. I have been conducting a monologue and they have fallen asleep. On the other hand, the listeners can accept everything and decide to convert to my point of view, and that means that they have not respected themselves. It has not been a real conversation, it has once again been a monologue. I have been talking all the time, and they have been nodding their heads in silent agreement. These are not real dialogues, these are not proper responses. The only legitimate response is that they will adopt some of what I say and they will bring it up as their own child. This means that both of us have contributed something to the conversation. The outcome, the 'child', will resemble both of us. So the Hinduism of Pythagoras and Apollonius is Greek Hinduism, Pythagorean Hinduism. When Apollonius is in India, he goes to Indian *mandirs* and worships Indian gods; when he is at home, he goes to Greek temples and worships Greek gods. His *guru* Pythagoras is not an *avatara* of Vishnu or Shiva, he is an *avatara* of the Greek God Apollo. When each side treats the other with compassion and respect, when each side listens to the other and does not try to kill what is different and unique about that other person, everyone leads a richer and happier life. Pythagoras and Apollonius did not lose anything or surrender anything when they adopted Hinduism; on the contrary, they greatly enriched their own lives and the entire world of Greco-Roman paganism. They paved the way for the synthesis of Neo-Platonism and Neo-Pythagoreanism which was one of the great religions of the world, even if it has rarely been acknowledged as such.

Monotheism and Dialogue

If a converting monologue is wrong, if it is wrong to ask someone to surrender their identity, we have to ask some awkward questions about monotheism. Is an interchange of ideas based on mutual respect only possible among polytheistic religions? Have monotheists locked themselves out of genuine religious dialogue? If a monologue is all they can offer, won't that kill the conversation? Worse still, won't it generate an equal but opposite monologue from the other side? Are monotheists doomed to shouting and permanent deafness?

There is, however, one very important exception to this depressing tendency in monotheism, there is one group of monotheists who do not behave in this dreadful way, and that is the people who invented West Asian monotheism in the first place, the Jews. They did indeed try to make converts during the period of the Second Temple (516 BC to AD 70), and there were even forced conversions in Israel itself,[73] but after the destruction of the temple, there was a great change. After the first century AD, the Rabbis actually discouraged people from converting, warning them that it was extremely difficult for a newcomer to adhere to the demanding rules of Judaism.[74] Any newcomers who converted to Judaism would have to restrict themselves to the worship of one God, they would have to obey a complex series of laws, where as non-Jews were free to think and act as they pleased. This does not mean that the Rabbis sympathized with these other religious beliefs, but they did sympathize with the believers themselves and accepted that maybe these people might be better off adhering to their non-Jewish beliefs. Such people are not Jewish, their beliefs are not Jewish, but they suit each other perfectly, they are perfectly happy together.[75] It is obviously a wonderful match, so why would anyone want to interfere, why would anyone want to ruin it?

The Jews invented West Asian monotheism, they taught it to the Christians and the Muslims, but unfortunately their open-minded and sympathetic attitude, which goes far beyond tolerance, is not to be found in their Christian and Islamic imitators. Christianity was legalized throughout the Roman Empire in 313, and throughout the second half of the fourth century, Christian emperors passed laws that gradually forbade the citizens of the empire to practice their old pagan beliefs. From now on there was only one path to God. By 393, the Olympic Games had been abolished, and in 529 the Emperor Justinian closed down the philosophy schools. In an act of extraordinary ingratitude, the Christian emperors even passed laws restricting the rights of Jews, biting the hand that had fed them.

An old pagan Senator, Quintus Aurelius Symmachus (who was Consul in 391) protested against the unreasonable persecution of paganism, and he made a very simple, very humane statement which is a profound argument in favor of religious diversity: "It is not possible to reach so great a Mystery by one road alone."[76] He had discovered the essence of these new Christian laws: monotheism does indeed declare that there is one road alone. It may allow its rivals to walk across the fields instead, in the rural areas which give us the word 'pagan',[77] but its natural tendency is to prevent this, to force everyone to walk on the one and only road. This is how the monotheists behaved to their pagan enemies, but their behavior to each other was even worse. For over a thousand years, Christians and Muslims have launched crusades and *jihads* against each other, they have conducted an endless propaganda war of hatred and vilification against each other. Even within their own camps they have fought vicious religious wars, Catholic against Protestant, and Sunni against Shia, because once you decide that there is only one perfect answer to the Great Mystery, you can always find some little flaw in anyone else's answer, no matter how close their answer is to your own.

If any compassion is to survive on this earth, the monotheistic religions must seriously evaluate their attitude to themselves and to others. Conversion cannot be a duty. If someone wishes to join a monotheistic religion, they are taking an irretrievable step, because monotheism forces them to reject everything they have previously believed in. There is one road alone, and any other path you have followed is wrong, it does not exist. A compassionate person would not ask them to take so cruel a step. And even if they wanted to do so of their own free will, even if they had not been subjected to any bullying or cajolement or intimidation, a compassionate person would follow the example of Judaism and urge them to reconsider.

Tolerance is not enough. We cannot reject other people's beliefs as absurd or marginal, and congratulate ourselves for allowing them the legal right to be so very wrong. There is no compassion or empathy in that. We must again follow the example of Judaism and ask ourselves whether this belief might not be right, at least for them. But compassion would go even further and require us to ask whether their belief might not also be another correct answer, not just for them but for all of us. It might be another road to the Great Mystery.

If we turn to the polytheistic religions, the religions that can visualize the Supreme Being in more than one way, we will discover the proper way to treat other religions, and that way is with compassion and respect. The pagan emperor Alexander Severus (who reigned from 222 to 235) had a private little shrine in his palace: this shrine had statues of the emperor's ancestors, and a very interesting group of sacred people. The four holy men honored by the pagan emperor were Abraham the founder of Judaism, Jesus the founder of Christianity, Orpheus the mythical founder of Orphism, and the Greek holy man we have been talking about, Apollonius of Tyana. Severus Alexander had a place in his heart for Judaism, Christianity, and three very different branches of paganism—ancestor worship, Orphism, and Pythagoreanism. He personally worshipped all of these images when he got up every morning.

We find a similar openness and respect in the Birla Mandir of Delhi. The temple has images of Vishnu and Lakshmi in the Hindu style; an image of the Buddha in the Buddhist style; and a non-iconic plaque honoring the Sikh Guru, Gobind Singh, because Sikhs do not allow images in their Gurudwaras. In this architectural conversation, the Hindu speaker pays attention to the Sikh listener and the Buddhist listener. Perhaps this respect and compassion for others is expressed most simply and most effectively in the simple Indian rhyme: *Īśvara Allah tere nām, mandir masjid tere dām* (Lord and Allah are your names, temple and mosque are your homes).

The destruction wreaked by Christians and Muslims on the minds and on the feelings, on the lives and on the cultures of other people violates the spirit of the Genocide Convention and it is a crime against all of humanity, because it involves the destruction of a part of our shared human heritage.[78] It is worth quoting the words of this convention.

In the present convention, genocide means any of the following acts committed with intent to destroy, in whole or in part, a national, ethnical, racial or religious group, as such:

(a) killing members of the group;
(b) causing serious bodily or *mental harm* to members of the group;
(c) deliberately inflicting on the group conditions of life *calculated to bring about its physical destruction* in whole or in part.[79]

So we cannot kill or ill-treat people because they are pagans or infidels. We cannot manipulate other people's minds and cause them mental harm so that they will abandon their religion. We cannot calculate ways of obliterating a religion from the face of the earth. We must therefore accept the polytheistic view that there is more than one path to God, there is more than one road to the Great Mystery, because if we continue to pursue the monotheistic path of mutual destruction, we will inevitably come to a point when there will be nobody left on this earth to worship God in the 'right' way or the 'wrong' way.

NOTES

1. Polybius, *Histories*, 21: 28, p. 9.
2. Aristotle, *Problemata,* 886a, p. 25.
3. Philo, *De Migratione Abrahami,* p. 178.
4. Aristotle, *Physiognomica, p.* 808a.
5. Euripides, *Hippolytus*, pp. 1078-09.
6. The belief that everyone should be the same is the 'exclusive' view, the belief that they are really the same without knowing it is the 'inclusive' or 'pluralist' view analysed by Rita Gross. See Gross,

Religious Diversity, pp. 60-64 (exclusivism), 66-69 (inclusivism), 69-75 (pluralism).

7. The Syrian Christians believe they came over with Saint Thomas in the 1st century AD, the Binai Israel believe that the prophet Elijah had visited India.
8. In a free republic, a person's religion or lack thereof is utterly irrelevant (United States Constitution, Article Six and First Amendment). A 'Christian republic' or an 'Islamic republic' is therefore an absurd contradiction in terms.
9. The fanatic's name was Mark Richards Watkinson, and for some peculiar reason he is frequently referred to as the 'reverend' Watson, the Watson "who must be revered." I fail to see why anyone should have to revere or respect this appalling bully.
10. Porphyry, *Vita Pythagorae*, p.19.
11. Ibid., p. 7.
12. Both Herodotus and Ion of Chios assume that Pythagoras was the creator of the Orphic system of belief, Burkert, *Lore and Science*, pp. 127, 129; Riedweg: *Pythagoras*, pp. 53, 55.
13. Burkert, *Lore and Science*, p. 133.
14. Keith, *Pythagoras and Transmigration*, p. 584; Burkert, *Lore and Science*, p. 132; Philip, *Pythagoras and Early Pythagoreans*, p. 155; Riedweg, *Pythagoras*, pp. 63, 75.
15. Diogenes Laertius, *Vitae Philosophorum* 8:4. See Burkert, *Lore and Science*, p. 138; Riedweg, *Pythagoras*, p. 5.
16. Diogenes Laertius, *Vitae Philosophorum* 8:5. See Burkert, *Lore and Science*, pp. 140-41; Riedweg, *Pythagoras*, p. 5.
17. He tells Myllias of Croton that he had been King Midas in a previous life (Iamblichus, *De Vita Pythagorica*, 28, p. 143). See Philip, *Pythagoras and Early Pythagoreans*, p. 152; Burkert, *Lore and Science*, p. 142; Riedweg: *Pythagoras*, p. 4.
18. Porphyry, *Vita Pythagorae* 19. See Riedweg, *Pythagoras*, pp. 12, 61-62.
19. Pindar, *Olympian*, p. 2. See Philip, *Pythagoras and Early Pythagoreans*, p. 155. Philip suggests that people in Sicily and southern Italy had already believed in transmigration before Pythagoras came along.
20. Xenophanes, fr 7 Diels-Kranz; Heraclitus, fr 40 and 129 Diels-Kranz.
21. Ion of Chios, fr 31 West.

22. According to Herodotus 4:95, the Thracians believed that the dead join the God Salmoxis, but Salmoxis had been a human being who learned about the immortality of the soul from Pythagoras. See Philip, *Pythagoras and Early Pythagoreans*, p. 153; Burkert, *Lore and Science*, p. 157; Riedweg, *Pythagoras*, pp. 56-57.
23. Antiphanes, fr. 168 Kock.
24. Burkert, *Lore and Science*, p. 139. Pythagoras had, in fact, died more than three times, but in calling him 'thrice blessed' (*tris makarites*, which refers to the blessed dead alone), the comic poet is punning on the common phrase 'thrice blessed' (*tris makar*, which can be used of anyone, dead or alive).
25. Plato's version of Pythagorean philosophy was so important that it makes it difficult for modern scholars to trace the original, pre-Platonic version of that system. See Burkert, *Lore and Science*, p. 13; Riedweg, *Pythagoras*, pp. 20-25. Pythagoras was regarded as the first Platonic philosopher, Kahn, *Pythagoras and the Pythagoreans*, p. 65.
26. Riedweg, *Pythagoras*, p. 60.
27. Ibid., pp. 12, 61.
28. Burkert, *Lore and Science*, p. 136.
29. Riedweg, *Pythagoras*, pp. 2-4; Burkert: *Lore and Science*, p. 142.
30. Riedweg: *Pythagoras*, p. 72.
31. Ibid., p. 100.
32. Among other things, Pythagoras "is represented as...a guru with supernatural powers," Riedweg, *Pythagoras*, p. 1.
33. Philip, *Pythagoras and Early Pythagoreans*, pp. 156-57; Riedweg, *Pythagoras*, p. 35, 72.
34. Philip, *Pythagoras and Early Pythagoreans*, pp. 156-57; Burkert, *Lore and Science*, p. 143; Riedweg, *Pythagoras*, p. 2.
35. Riedweg, *Pythagoras*, p. 101.
36. Timaeus fr. 13. See Riedweg, *Pythagoras*, pp. 39, 102.
37. Riedweg, *Pythagoras*, p. 103.
38. "The soul of a human being does not enter those animals alone which it is customary to sacrifice. Therefore, people who are allowed to eat them must only eat sacrificial victims and no other animal." Iamblichus, *De vita Pythagorica*, 18, p. 85. See Riedweg, *Pythagoras*, p. 69.
39. "What is really interesting about the Pythagorean society is that, unlike the Buddhist, it endeavoured to be, and for a time succeeded

in setting itself up as, a state organization superseding the ordinary state machinery." Keith, "Pythagoras and Transmigration," pp. 599-600.

40. Keith, "Pythagoras and Transmigration," p. 600.
41. Herotodus, 2: 123.
42. Burkert, *Lore and Science*, p. 128; Riedweg, *Pythagoras*, p. 7.
43. Herodotus, 2: 50, p. 2.
44. Plato, *Timaeus,* p. 22b.
45. His home town, Tyana, was in Cappadocia, which was originally a Princely State within the Roman empire, but became a Roman province in AD 17, around the time when Apollonius was born.
46. Philostratus, *Life of Apollonius*, 1: 7, p. 2.
47. Philostratus, *Life of Apollonius* 1: 7, pp. 2-3. He even refuses to wear wool, Philostratus, *Life of Apollonius* 1: 32, p. 2.
48. Philostratus, *Life of Apollonius* 1: 13, p. 3.
49. Philostratus, *Life of Apollonius* 1: 16, p. 3.
50. Philostratus, *Life of Apollonius* 1: 18, p. 1.
51. Philostratus, *Life of Apollonius* 2: 33, p. 1.
52. Philostratus, *Life of Apollonius* 3: 15.
53. Philostratus, *Life of Apollonius* 3: 19, pp. 1, 20.
54. Philostratus, *Life of Apollonius* 8: 14.
55. Philostratus, *Life of Apollonius* 5: 25, p. 1.
56. Philostratus, *Life of Apollonius* 5: 25, pp. 1-2. Compare the way in which Empedocles, another Greek who believed in transmigration, offered a pastry bull instead of a real one (Philostratus, *Life of Apollonius* 1: 1, p. 3).
57. Philostratus, *Life of Apollonius* 6: 11, pp. 13-14.
58. Philostratus, *Life of Apollonius* 5: 42.
59. Philostratus, *Life of Apollonius* 6: 43, p. 2.
60. Philostratus, *Life of Apollonius* 6: 19-20.
61. Philostratus, *Life of Apollonius* 8: 15.
62. Philostratus, *Life of Apollonius* 4: 40, p. 4.
63. Philostratus, *Life of Apollonius* 4: 40, p. 1.
64. Philostratus, *Life of Apollonius* 8: 19.
65. Philostratus, *Life of Apollonius* 4: 31, p. 1.
66. Philostratus, *Life of Apollonius* 8: 31, p. 3; Cassius Dio, *Roman History* 78: 18, p. 4.
67. *Historia Augusta. Life of Alexander Severus* 29, 2.
68. Arnobius, *Against the Nations.* 1:52.

69. Eusebius, *Against Hierocles*, p. 5.
70. Eusebius, *Against Hierocles*, p. 31.
71. Sossianus Hierocles, *The Truth-Lover* (quoted at Eusebius, *Against Hierocles*, p. 2).
72. The pagan Emperor Julian adopted the intolerant language of the Christians, but he never persecuted Christians. See Armstrong, "The Way and the Ways," p. 7. The dispute between the two world views ended with "the final establishment of Christian intolerance under Theodosius" (Armstrong, "The Way and the Ways," p. 1).
73. Rosenbloom, *Conversion to Judaism*, pp. 94-96.
74. *Yevamot* translated in Cohen, *Beginnings of Jewishness*, p. 199.
75. A later Rabbinic text (the *Gerim*) says that if someone decides not to covert after all, "he is dimissed and wanders off" (Cohen: *Beginnings of Jewishness*, p. 199). Cohen points out that this is implicit in the original *Yevamot*, and summarizes the principle behind both texts: "a convert should not be hindered if after the examination he decides to withdraw" (Cohen, *Beginnings of Jewishness*, p. 212).
76. Symmachus, *Relatio*, 3: 10.
77. A *paganus* is someone from the *pagus*, the countryside, the rural district.
78. "...having a universal, common religion would not significantly improve anything. In fact, it would rob us of a lot [of] interesting religious and spiritual alternatives..." (Gross, *Religious Diversity*, p. 83).
79. *The Convention on the Prevention and Punishment of the Crime of Genocide*, Article 2. The italics in the text are mine, because I wish to emphasize the phrases that illustrate the criminal nature of the imperative to convert others.

REFERENCES

Armstrong, A.H. "The Way and the Ways: Religious Tolerance and Intolerance in the Fourth Century A.D." *Vigiliae Christianae*, 38 (1984), pp. 1-17.

Burkert, Walter. *Lore and Science in Ancient Pythagoreanism.* Translated by Edwin L. Minar, Jr., Cambridge, MA: Harvard University Press, 1972.

Cohen, Shaye J.D. *The Beginnings of Jewishness: Boundaries, Varieties, Uncertainties*, Berkeley: University of California Press, 1999.

Gross, Rita. *Religious Diversity—What's the Problem,* Eugene: Cascade Books, 2014.

Kahn, Charles H. *Pythagoras and the Pythagoreans,* Indianapolis, IN: Hackett Publishing, 2001.

Keith, A. Berriedale. "Pythagoras and the Doctrine of Transmigration", *Journal of the Royal Asiatic Society,* 1909, 569-606.

Philip, James A. *Pythagoras and Early Pythagoreanism,* Toronto: University of Toronto Press, 1966.

Riedweg, Christoph. *Pythagoras: His Life, Teaching, and Influence.* Translated by Steven Rendall, Ithaca, NY: Cornell University Press, 2005.

Rosenbloom, Joseph R. *Conversion to Judaism: From the Biblical Period to the Present*, Cincinnati: Hebrew Union College Press, 1978.

□

PART II

Compassion in Our Relationships with the Natural World and with those We Serve

4
Compassion in the Four Dharmic Traditions: Relationship with the Natural World and Our Environment

—*Bal Ram Singh*

Introduction

Dharmic traditions and nature are almost synonymous in their philosophies and practices, both outwardly and inwardly. *Dharma* by definition is the nature and, by derivation, is the source of all that exists. Thus, nature and environment are corollary to *dharma*, and people following dharmic traditions compassionately embrace the nature and environment.

Vaisesika philosophy principles are quite compatible with modern chemistry and vice versa (Singh, 2003). *Vaisesika-sutras* begin with the definition or purpose of the *dharma*—*Yato'bhyudayanihsreyasasiddhihsadharmah*, meaning *dharma* is the one which lifts up everything to the greatest realization (salvation or *Moksha*). In other words, anything that is destined to life (existence) and death has to follow the *dharma*. *Padaartha* is created by the *dharma*, and subsequently *Padaartha* expands itself into different entities and categories encompassing the universe we know as made of the substance or matter. Thus, *dharma* in fact is cause of the universe and pervades it throughout.

Compassion is natural in dharmic traditions, first due to its philosophical root with its Sanskrit and Hindi translation as *sahanubhuti* to mean experience together. From humans and off of nature being extension of the same supreme force comes the idea of humans and all of nature sharing the same experience. Compassion is highly regarded in Buddhism as that is an integral part of enlightenment. Because of compassion towards other animals, Jainism has prescribed only vegetarian diets for human consumption, perhaps the only tradition in the world to make such a prescription to its followers. In Sikhism, *daya* (pity or compassion) is considered one of the five essential virtues, along with *sat* (truth), *santosh* (contentment), *namrata* (humility) and *pyar* (love). In Hinduism, God is referred to as *karunanidhan* (lord of compassion) or *dayanidhan* (lord of mercy) putting such a strong emphasis on compassion. All four dharmic traditions emphasize non-violence, which is another sign of compassion towards others.

Compassion in one form or another is part of every religious tradition, dharmic or non-dharmic. However, in the case of dharmic traditions, compassion is an essential part of understanding self and achieving self-enlightenment. Compassion, being integral part of practicing the principles of *dharma*, leads these traditions to connect well with the entire cosmos. Thus, nature and environment are intrinsically part of these traditions. Armed with this foundation one can look at the relationship of dharmic traditions with nature in the modern context and examine the approach rationally.

Unifying Hypothesis for the Nature Living and Non-living Matter

The ayurvedic system, which is primarily derived from *Nyaya* (concerned with establishing facts) and *Vaisesika* (concerned with formation of substance from elements) philosophies, with incorporation of *Sankhya* (concerned with interconnectedness of the universe) philosophy in a unifying hypothesis, links both living and non-living matter; the ayurvedic system considers humans and plants in the hierarchy of the cosmic evolution to consist of the same basic matter (*panchabhootas* or five elements—earth, water, air, fire, and ether) (Chopra and Doiphode, 2002). Consciousness (*satva*), motion or action (*rajas*), and the inertia that resists them (*tamas*) are the three omnipresent non-material qualities (*gunas*) which govern the structure and function of all material forms of the basic matter (Chopra and Doiphode, 2002). The basic matter produces three life forces or energy known as *doshas* that pervade all existing matter. These three *doshas—vata, pitta,* and *kapha*—are the primary physiological forces which govern the biomotor, metabolic, and preservative (homeostasis) activities, respectively. This concept provides a practical observable basis of unity amongst the humans, animals, inanimate matter, and the environment.

In modern times, there is so much concern about the effect of human activities on the environment (pollution, climatic changes) and nature (extinction of plants and animals). At the fundamental scientific level, these issues can be examined in terms of evolution, a concept that presupposes interaction of organisms, plants, animals and humans to adapt to the nature under changed environment as part of evolution. Humans generally invoke the survival of the fittest paradigm to rationalize their exploitation of nature which results in changed environment. Therefore, it may be a worthwhile exercise to apply the *dharma* paradigm to the evolution process to develop a better understanding of human relationship with nature and the environment.

Origin of species (or diversity) and evolution may thus provide a good example to explore how the *dharma* paradigm can be used to rationalize and even reveal new concepts in this very contentious discipline of scientific inquiry.

One of the major features of the Darwinian theory of evolution involves the presence of diversity within and between genera of organisms from bacteria to mammals. While the basic mechanism of evolution of different species (or diversity) is explained by assuming random genetic mutations, some of which allow better adaptation to the nature, and thus natural selection resulting into continuous stream of new species, it is not known how the random mutation is initiated and what is the role of the nature in creating those mutations and selecting the species. Different *karma* aspects emphasized in various dharmic traditions can be contrasted with modern scientific and philosophical concepts to elaborate them to the modern world, and explain some of the unresolved questions of interaction between the nature and organisms.

Karma as the Basis of Diversity

The concept of *karma* being responsible for the variation in human behavior and for the state of society as explained in Buddhist philosophy can be contrasted with the concept of evolution to clear concepts, and address missing points of even scientific theories. In Buddhist philosophy, it is the difference in *karma* which determines the birth in a given state of beings, high and low, base and exalted, happy and miserable, beings as beautiful and ugly, high-born or low-born, well-built or deformed, or the worldly conditions of beings such as gain and loss, disgrace, blame and praise, and happiness and misery.

Clearly, these concepts refer not just to the physical existence, survival, and evolution. They refer to physical, mental, and intellectual aspects of a being. While there is a general concept that mental and intellectual features only belong to humans or some other higher animals, modern scientific evidence and ancient dharmic traditions place intelligence in the lowest of the low organisms (and in dharmic traditions even in non-living objects) as well, albeit not to the same degree as humans.

Current Theory of Evolution and its Limitations

The biological evolution, however, largely refers to the physical features of organisms, from complexities of organs and tissues to the variability in cells and size of nuclear materials. This approach counts on fossilized records on one hand and the brain size and genetic mapping on the other. While the scientific approach is considered largely objective, it has been marred with a certain degree of manipulation as it relates to the discussion of evolution. Whereas Darwin published his book *Origin of Species* to explain the diversity of biological organisms, and potential evolution of one organism from the other through the process of adaptation and natural selection, evolution itself has been viewed as a trait for superiority. There have been attempts by scientists to find a way to place human beings on top of the evolutionary ladder by deriving an "encephalization" factor that neatly dictates superiority of man by the ratio of the brain size to the body as compared to those of other animals.

Similarly, an unwritten hypothesis and expectation in the human genome project was that humans will have the largest number of genes and perhaps the largest genome—both of which have turned out to be not true. Humans have about 30,000 genes whereas plants and mice have over 60,000 genes. In fact, onions, amphibians, and Whisk fern have six times, 30 times, and 3,000 times, respectively, larger DNA in their genomes than humans.

The larger issue is whether in being so biased in our approach at the fundamental level, we are compromising the science. Taking the example of evolution and its basic assumptions, one can see how a perspective can change the scientific explanation of an observation. The following are the core assumptions of evolution.

1. The diversity of species we see in the world basically evolved from unicellular organisms through the process of natural selection.
2. Natural selection occurs when a given species adapts to the change in nature through its variation in the biological system.
3. The basis of the variation in the biological system is random mutation in the genetic material of the organism.
4. For an organism to accumulate a large number of random mutations, it must undergo many generations over a long period of time.

Humans being in existence for about only one million years, and with their reproduction cycle of about 20 years, would have gone through only about 500 iterations. On the other hand, anaerobic bacteria with a record of existence for about two billion years would have gone through 2.16 trillion iterations, considering even eight hours for their life cycle. The anaerobic bacteria thus have 4.32 billion times advantage over humans to go through the adaptation and natural selection process compared to humans. It is thus important to consider the bacteria being superior evolutionarily. This is especially relevant since the bacteria have survived in nature throughout the time other organisms and species have appeared. Similar arguments can be made for plants and animals.

Although there are no written rules or expectations for humans to be most evolved in terms of superiority, it has been generally accepted that human species is the most evolved and most superior among the current species of organisms. This has sometimes led to bending or accommodating the rules to suit the human superiority.

As mentioned earlier, when the human genome project was undertaken this idea of superiority led to the thought that the human genome would be the largest, containing the largest number of genes to justify their status of most complex set of organs, physiology, cognition, etc. However, as it turned out not to be the case, scientists are still struggling with this question, and are looking for ways to justify the concept of human superiority.

In the case of bacteria, with only about five million base pairs of DNA and about 5,000 genes, about 80 percent of the genetic material is utilized for genes. This compares with 1.4 percent utilization of the genetic material (approximately 3 billion bp) for genes (30,000). Thus, on the basis of efficiency in using its genetic material, bacteria seem to be more evolved.

Bacteria, plants, and animals other than humans can readily live in the nature, thus demonstrating their adaptation and natural selection trait, whereas humans generally live an artificial life, which not only shows their inability to cope with the natural living, but it has also been suggested that, as there is no adequate interaction with nature their further evolution is in jeopardy.

Darwin on Diversity

In his famous book, *Origin of Species*, Charles Darwin cited a study (Sinclair, 1826) which demonstrated that when several types of grasses (Clover, Trefoil, Lucern, Saintfoin, etc.) were planted together there was a higher yield for each compared to when each grass was planted separately (Fig. 1). In *Origin of Species,* Charles Darwin writes, "It has been experimentally proved that if a plot of ground be sown with one species of grass, and a similar plot be sown with several distinct genera of grasses, a greater number of plants and a greater weight of dry herbage can thus be raised." By this he demonstrated the principle of divergence in the natural selection and evolution process. This is the key force driving diversity even from an evolutionary point of view.

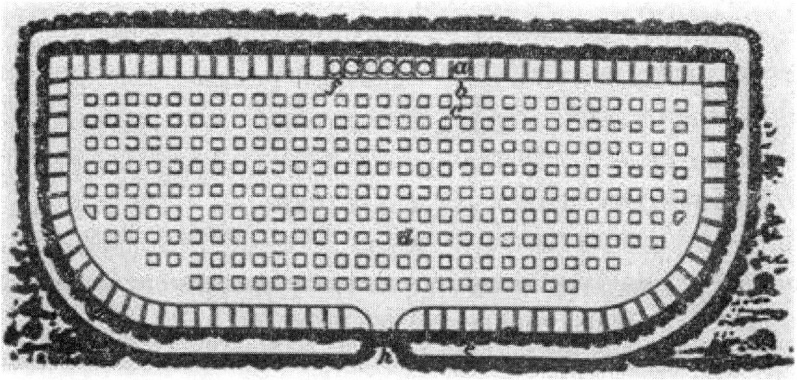

Fig. 1. Schematics of 242 experimental plots – 4 × 4 ft; 85 beds Clover, Trefoil, Lucern, Saintfoin, etc. that were used to show that different species of grass grown together produce larger yields than when grown separately. [Schematics taken from Hector and Hooper, 2002]

What is missing in this observation is the origin of the force that drives this diversity. Both the yield- and entropy- (thermodynamic measure of randomness) based arguments pertain to the consequences, not the cause. *Karma* and the origin of *karma* (the author of the *Rājavārttika* in Jaina tradition points out that which is performed out of the result of the vibrations of the self is called *karma,* which is similarly described in *Nasadiya suktam* as Big Bang Singularity, the state before which everything was pure existence and pure consciousness, *ānīd avātam* without vibration, and thus the world begins with vibration) point towards the origin of the force that drives the diversity.

Evolutionary Superiority of Bacteria and Plants

Humans have inhabited this planet for merely a million years. By virtue of being on Earth for a longer time period—plants and other organisms have inhabited the planet for over a billion years more—one would imagine that organisms such as bacteria would have undergone an even higher level of evolution through the iteration of adaptation and natural selection, particularly because their reproductive cycle runs at a shorter time scale.

Such a realization is likely to be more in tune with dharmic traditions, which value and respect earlier creations to the extent that some of them even worship them. This may reflect the longer memory and observations by continual civilizations based on existence of *dharma* traditions, and their integral approach to the universe and understanding of the existence of various species and organisms—more a reflection of *karma* than a particular hierarchy. There are many stories in epics and *puranas* which suggest at times animals and plants having a higher level of consciousness than humans. This is also reflected in reverence displayed towards nature (plants and animals) in dharmic traditions.

Dharmic Traditions, Joint Family System and Environmental Preservation

Accepting dharmic values allows one to be free of bias, and thus create a more just system which can build a progressive and developed society. One of the systems that has remained a pillar of Indian society is its joint family system. A joint family system is not sustainable unless dharmic values are employed where selflessness becomes the operating principle. Scientific research has shown that the joint family system is critical for environmental protection.

According to a report (Lazarof, 2003), researchers have found that across the world, in both developed and developing countries, households are getting smaller, and there are many more of them. Multigenerational living arrangements are giving way to couples or individuals moving out on their own. In addition, rising divorce rates mean families that used to live in one dwelling now occupy two, and aging populations mean more parents living in households separate from their grown children. The result is often urban sprawl and less efficient housing for the same number of people. For example, a refrigerator uses about the same amount of energy whether it belongs to a family of four or a family of two. Each household takes up space, requires resources to construct, and fuel to heat and cool it. Increased energy consumption also increases the emission of greenhouse gases, which is believed to contribute to global warming. The study was carried out by scientists from Michigan State University (MSU) and Stanford University. Professor Jiaguo 'Jack' Liu of MSU said, "Freedom and privacy come at a huge environmental cost."

The research findings suggest that in 76 countries containing biodiversity hotspots, between 1985 and 2000 the number of households grew by 3.1 percent a year, whereas the population increased only 1.8 percent. Meanwhile, the number of people living in a single dwelling dropped from 4.7 to 4.0. It was estimated by scientists that had average household size remained the same in hotspot countries during the 15 year period, there would have been 155 million fewer households overall, meaning less pressure on biodiversity. Hotspot countries studied included Australia, India, Kenya, Brazil, China, Italy and the United States.

"Ignoring population growth, reduction in household size alone is projected to add 233 million households to hotspot countries between 2000 and 2015," said Stanford ecologist Gretchen Daily. In the 65 non-hotspot countries, similar trends were found, although the magnitudes of change were less. In 1985, the average household size was 4.7 in hotspot countries and 3.7 in non-hotspot countries. The average household size in hotspot countries is expected to be 3.4 persons, and in non-hotspot countries it is expected to be 3.6 persons.

Professor Liu has contended (Liu et al., 2003) that the increase in household numbers even in non-hotspot countries directly influences important biodiversity on a national and local scale. Indirectly, global environment will be affected in such patterns as more energy consumption and release of more greenhouse gases.

Even in regions where population size decreased such as in New Zealand, the number of households increased because of a reduction in household size.

Scientists believe that a reduction in average household size takes a 'double toll' on the environment, which includes more land use and more materials consumed for construction, and a lower efficiency of resource use per person. In hotspot countries, where this trend is most prevalent, the Liu and co-workers (Liu et al., 2003) believe that there may be severe limits on efforts to conserve species, thus "degrading the ecosystem services that biodiversity delivers to humanity."

Concluding Remarks

Going back several millennia, the dharmic traditions contain robust philosophical, scientific, cultural, and ritualistic practices of respecting nature and protecting the environment for sustainable progress of humans materially, intellectually, and spiritually. These practices need to be modernized and presented to the world as complementary and alternative approaches to the current scientific and technological efforts being employed for sustainability.

REFERENCES

Chopra, A. and Doiphode, V.V. (2002), Ayurvedic medicine. Core concept, therapeutic principles, and current relevance. *Med. Clin. North Am.*, 86, 75-89.

Hector, A. and Hooper, R. (2002), Darwin and the first ecological experiment, *Science*, 295, 639-40.

Lazaroff, C. (2003), Smaller Households Lead to Vanishing Biodiversity, Environmental News Service.

Liu, J., Daily, G.C., Ehrlich, P.R. and Luck, G.W. (2003). Effects of household dynamics on resource consumption and biodiversity. *Nature*, 421, 530-33.

Sinclair (1826), London's Gardener Mag. 1, 14.

Singh, B.R. (2003), Use of Chemistry to Understand Vedic Knowledge in *Contemporary Views on Indian Civilization* (B.D. Sharma, Editor), World Association of Vedic Studies, 388-99.

□

5

Compassion and Selfless Service

—Radheyshyam Dwivedi

Introduction

Compassion is the emotional response to perceived suffering and involves a genuine desire to help. It is not the same as empathy, which is an emotional experience of another person's feelings, or altruism, which is an action that benefits someone else. These terms are related to compassion but they are not identical.[1] Compassion does have elements of both, but it is also accompanied by a real desire to help relieve the suffering.

Why would someone stop on a busy highway to help a stranded stranger whose vehicle has become disabled when many others ignore it; some others volunteer their services in homeless shelters and hospitals, do dishes or sweep floors; or give ride to the needy to a doctor's office or for shopping, or help them with essential services? Why does anyone engage in such acts of kindness, and in extreme cases, even jump down onto the tracks of an oncoming subway train to save a total stranger's life as Wesley Autrey, a 50 year old man, did in New York in 2007, or rush into a burning home to save a little sister, as ten-year-old Antoine Burks did?[2] All this is because of their innate compassion.

Compassion is widespread in the biological world, even among wild animals. Both animals and humans have what Dacher Keltner, Professor of Psychology at UC Berkeley, calls a 'compassion instinct'.

It is a natural and automatic response that has ensured our survival. Even rats are driven to empathize with another suffering rat and to go out of their way to help. Studies with chimpanzees and infants too young to have learned the rules of politeness also support such claims.[3] Thanks to YouTube, many well-documented videos are freely available that dramatically demonstrate compassion in wild beasts. In one amazing video, a leopard kills a mother monkey and drags her up on the tree with an infant baby clinging to the mother's underside. Scared to death, the infant monkey instinctively runs away from the killer leopard and tries to hide in the branches but the leopard feels so compassionate to the baby that she grabs hold of the helpless fearful infant, caresses it and comforts it in her kind loving embrace and protects it from the other predators. The baby monkey, gradually feeling secure in the protective care of the surrogate mother leopard, follows her unafraid everywhere.[4]

Evolution of Compassion

Widespread as it is throughout the biological world, compassion is not an uncontroversial topic. There is no consensus as to how it evolved. According to Goetz et al.,[5] there are at least three main lines of arguments that converge on the hypothesis that compassion evolved as a distinct effective experience with its primary function to facilitate cooperation and protection of the weak and those who suffer. Among the theorists of morality, compassion is considered by some to be an unreliable guide to judgments of right and wrong, whereas others view it as a source of principled moral judgement.[6-7] Those considering compassion mainly as altruistic in nature think that it is a proximal determinant of pro-social behavior.[8-10] Within evolutionists, opinions differ whether compassion and sympathy are the products of evolution, as Darwin assumed,[11] or it cannot be so because it is generally too costly to the individual.

Psychology and Physiology of Compassion and Related Behaviors

Philosophers and scientists have long argued whether or not

compassion as altruism exists. Jill Suttie of Greater Good Science Center, UC Berkeley, says: "Those on one side say that people act selflessly to benefit others out of a natural, inherent quality of goodness; those on the other side say that behind every act of altruism there is an ulterior motive such as wanting to appear 'good' in the eyes of the community, which is ultimately selfish."[12]

David Sloan Wilson, President of Evolution Institute and SUNY Distinguished Professor of Biology and Anthropology at University of Binghamton, in his book *Does Altruism Exist*,[13] argues that what really drives altruism in society is not the intention of the person, good or bad, but the altruistic act itself and its effect on the community—in other words, its evolutionary function.

Practicing kindness has benefited people immensely. In the last few decades, mindful meditation techniques from Buddhist and other traditions have gained momentum as practical methods for acquiring peacefulness, tranquility of mind, productivity in work, and overall good mental health. "The field of mindfulness research is exploding," says Kira M. Newman.[14]

In a recent study, researchers at Purdue Univ. and UC Berkeley recruited volunteers separately for a discussion course and a meditation course. Both courses were beneficial. After initially taking the discussion course, the discussion group felt more positive and less negative toward themselves than the group that hadn't started the experiment yet. The participants who did just the meditation course also showed improvements in their positive and negative attitudes toward themselves—but they also felt more positivity toward others. The book-learning didn't seem to add as much as the practice. After taking both courses, the discussion group reported no benefits that the other group didn't enjoy from meditation alone.

Vicky Zakrzewski, education director of GGSC at UC Berkeley, in a recent post titled "Social-Emotional Learning: Why Now?," writes:[15]

> Social-emotional learning (SEL) is becoming very popular not only in the United States, but also in the UK, China and Singapore. Many reasons exist why a school might adopt SEL,

> all of which have been validated by research: to increase academic success and, somewhat ironically, to lower the stress-levels of students as they strive towards that success; to prevent negative behaviors such as drug use, violence, and bullying; to equip students with the 'soft skills' they will need in today's work environment; and to promote positive relationships and attitudes.

In his book *Born to Be Good,*[16] UC Berkeley professor and GGSC director Dacher Keltner counters the centuries-old argument that we are hard-wired for selfishness, making us naturally competitive as we strive to satisfy our self-serving desires. Keltner makes the case, based on research in psychology, sociology, and neuroscience that we are also wired for good. "The origins of human goodness," writes Keltner, "are rooted in our emotion, and these social instincts may be stronger than those of any other instinct or motive."

Kindness and helping others are inborn qualities, says Zakrzewski.[15]

Some of the most compelling proof that we are wired for altruism, kindness, and compassion comes from numerous studies that demonstrate children as young as 14 months have innate altruistic tendencies, well before socialization can have a major influence on their development. For example, psychologists Felix Warneken from Harvard and Michael Tomasello from the Max Planck Institute in Germany found that an 18-month old child, without prompting, readily help another person. In one experiment, a toddler opened a cupboard for Warneken who, while carrying a stack of books, indicated non-verbally that he wanted to place the books in the cupboard but could not do so because his hands were full. In another study, the toddlers disengaged from playing with a toy to help the adult in the room, suggesting that they were motivated to help, even though it required effort on his or her part.

Additionally, it was also found that toddlers' happiness levels increased significantly when they gave away one of their own treats rather than a treat that belonged to another person. In other words, these children may have been motivated to help, not because someone told them to, but because it felt good.

All of these studies support Keltner's view that we are moved to do good and that our altruistic, compassionate tendencies may be motivated, in part, by positive emotions elicited through our interactions with others.

Neurologic Basis of Compassion

In modern times, when the world is experiencing cut-throat competition and selfishness rules the day, how does compassion make any difference? The answer lies in which aspect—selfish or altruistic—gets cultivated through our environment, our interactions with people such as teachers, parents, friends, colleagues, customers, and our personal choices.[15]

Emotion researchers have found that negative emotions close us off, making us less resilient and unable to relate with and connect to others; whereas positive emotions such as gratitude, tranquility, love, and joy come with a myriad of benefits, including an expansion of our hearts and minds that helps us to see our common humanity.

If we can become aware of our emotions and learn to work with them in a healthy way—to see them as information rather than as overpowering responses that control our actions—then we can choose to respond to situations in a manner that brings out the good in us and in others. Instead of acting out of fear, hate, and anger, we can take a deep breath and try to empathize with what the other person is feeling or experiencing and then make the choice to respond with care.

Scientists have found that when we feel compassion, regions of the brain linked to empathy, care giving, and feelings of pleasure light up,[17] thus further encouraging us to help others. The boost of positive emotions that comes from acting compassionately motivates us to continue doing so in the future. We also know from research that compassion is contagious: when people see us caring, they want to follow in.

Emiliana R. Simon-Thomas[18] in her recent article "Is There a Biological Fingerprint for Compassion?" says that compassion can be measured:

> Two scientific teams, one led by Zoe Taylor at Purdue and the other by Jenny Stellar at UC Berkeley, have found that the answer may lie in the Vagus nerve. That's the cranial nerve in the body with the widest reach, influencing speech, head positioning, digestion, and—importantly for these two studies—the parasympathetic branch of the autonomic nervous system's influence on the heart. The parasympathetic branch (PNS), as the 'rest and digest' branch of the autonomic nervous system (ANS), controls bodily functions that we're not aware of when we're relaxed and feeling content. The PNS is also called the 'feed and breed' branch—and recently, social psychologist Barbara Fredrickson added the label 'tend and befriend' to the PNS, suggesting that it also supports functions that enable social engagement and nurturing behaviors.

The new research[18] suggests that the Vagus may be the key to the emergence of compassionate behavior during development as well as day-to-day experiences of compassion in studies with children 3-4 to 7 years. The data showed that warm, sensitive parenting for three years old predicts greater focused concentration in the children one year later, which in turn predicts greater sympathy at ages six and seven. Vagal tone in the kids at three years also predicts sympathy three and four years later. As was the case for parenting style, the Vagal tone effect was largely related to the children's concentration skills as four years old.

The data further suggest that warm, sensitive, authoritative parenting may support skills such as managing emotions and focusing attention, and that children with higher Vagal tone are more likely to have these skills, which in turn paves the way for sympathy for other peoples' suffering.

Jenny Stellar's UC Berkeley team took a different approach: they measured Vagal tone while adults were in the midst of feeling compassion. In particular, they wanted to know whether Vagal tone increases—in other words, if the Vagus exerts more influence on the nervous system during an actual experience of compassion.

The results show that the Vagus nerve appears to be intimately tied to experiencing compassion towards other people's suffering. More specifically, these studies show that what happens in your Vagus affects whether or not you can handle the feelings provoked by another person's suffering and whether or not you'll feel concerned and motivated to help.[18]

"The research of recent years has shown that compassionate people have better mental health. They are much less likely to be depressed, anxious and stressed and are much more likely to be happy, resilient and optimistic about their future" says Kristin Neff of the University of Texas at Austin.[19] "Feeling good triggers the release of oxytocin, a hormone whose increased levels are associated with increased feelings of calm, generosity, safety, trust and connectedness. It facilitates the ability to feel warmth and compassion for ourselves and others. Feelings of anger, fear, self-criticism, etc. have an opposite effect on our body. When we are confronted with threatening situations, the fight or flight response is triggered. The amygdala, a part in the brain, sends signals that increase blood pressure, adrenaline and the hormone cortisol supplying energy and strength needed to face or avoid the threat. Research has shown that feelings of self-compassion decrease the cortisol levels."

Marsh et al.[20] using structural and functional-magnetic resonance imaging (FMRI) of the brains of extraordinary altruists (such as altruistic kidney donors) have shown that the neural anatomy and functioning of the altruist's brain is very different from psychopaths, who are usually callous and antisocial.

The subject has been reviewed in detail by Goetz et al. and in an excellent YouTube lecture presentation by Goldin Phillippe of Stanford.[21]

Genetics of Compassion

Scientists have found the genetic basis for traits such as compassion, altruism, empathy, and in general, feeling good about such benevolent behaviors.

Reuter et al.[22] have investigated the role of the COMT Val158Met polymorphism, gene, which has been implicated in the metabolism of Dopamine, and which is responsible for eliciting the effect of (feel good) hormones oxytocin and vasopressin. In their words:

> Altruism was assessed by the amount of money donated to a poor child in a developing country, after having earned money by participating in two experiments. Carriers of at least one Val allele donated about twice as much money as compared with those participants without a Val allele. Results indicate that the Val allele representing strong catabolism of dopamine is related to altruism.
>
> The evolutionarily highly conserved neuropeptide oxytocin is a key mediator of social and emotional behavior in mammals, including humans. A common variant (rs53576) in the oxytocin receptor gene (OXTR) has been implicated in social-behavioral phenotypes such as maternal sensitivity and empathy. Activation and interregional coupling of the amygdala during the processing of emotionally salient social cues was significantly affected by genotype. In addition, evidence for structural alterations in key oxytocinergic regions emerged, particularly in the hypothalamus.[23]

Gong et al.[24] have shown that the Dopamine beta-hydroxylase gene modulates an individual's empathic ability. Dopamine beta-hydroxylase (DBH), an enzyme that converts dopamine to norepinephrine, has broad influences on social functions. Their results showed that individuals with the CC genotype, which is associated with higher DBH activity, manifested greater empathic ability than those with CT/TT genotypes establishing a genetic basis of empathy and in predicting individual differences in social and affective processing.

Compassion is an adaptively evolved trait that has played a critical role in the survival of human species through the evolutionary process because it has enormous benefits for both physical and the mental well-being, which are essential prerequisites for healthy living. The 'survival of the fittest' has also been the story of 'the survival of the kindest.' Not only the physically strong, but also the compassionate must have ensured the survival of the 'not-so-strong' in the community. It follows then, that in human survival, it is not just gross physical strength that has ensured the survival of human species over historical proportions, but also the compassionate mind that has played a crucial role in adapting to the changing environment.

Studies have shown that compassion can be cultivated. Meditation practices of Buddhist tradition—Mindfulness meditation[21, 25-26] and 'loving kindness' meditation—[27] help cultivate compassion in a very short time. It was found that a seven-minute intervention was enough to increase feelings of closeness and connection to the target of meditation on both explicit and the implicit measures that participants could not voluntarily control; this suggests that their sense of connection had changed on a deep-seated level. The Center for Compassion and Altruism Research and Education (CCARE) at Stanford School of Medicine (www.ccare.stanford.edu), has been doing pioneering research in the field of compassion and kindness. Its founder and director, James Doty, says: "When health care is delivered with kindness and compassion, it has a significantly greater effect than when it is given in a dispassionate fashion that assumes that human connection has no benefit." Emma Seppala, associate director, and her team have made significant contribution in the field of compassion research. She gives 18 scientific reasons loving-kindness meditation[28] to cultivating compassion for good health.

It is beyond the scope of this article to review in detail the research in this area, which is expanding by leaps and bounds. The main purpose of this article is to highlight the scientific basis of compassion, which has been the subject of intense research in the last few decades at the National Institutes of Health and many major universities.

Compassion in Indic Religions

In the context of Indic religions, compassionate acts of kindness are considered as the observance of the *Dharma*. I am reminded of a story of the 'Sadhu and the Scorpion'.[29] A Sadhu, while taking bath in a river, saw a scorpion that had fallen into the water struggling for life. Because scorpions don't swim, this one was sure to die if not rescued. The sadhu, out of love and compassion, could not bear the plight of the unfortunate creature. He lifted it out of water to take it to the shore but the scorpion, now secure in the palm of his savior, stung him. Excruciating pain shot up the arm of the kind sadhu, causing him to fling his arm up in the air and drop the scorpion back in the water. But the sadhu would not give up until the scorpion was saved. He tried again and again, only to be stung repeatedly, every time experiencing the debilitating pain. Finally, he succeeded in landing the scorpion safely on the ground.

One of his disciples was watching this drama. Perplexed, he asked why his guru ji was persistent in saving the scorpion that stung him every time he tried to save him from drowning. The sadhu replied: "The *Dharma* or nature of scorpion is to sting and the nature or *Dharma* of a sadhu is to rescue a being from distress—and in this case sure death by drowning. If the scorpion cannot give up its *Dharma* why should I give up mine? The *Dharma* of fire is to burn, of water is to be cool, of wind is to blow. So, the *Dharma* of man is to be humane. I was only following my *Dharma*."

On January 27, 1868, Sri Ramakrishna was going on a pilgrimage to the sacred places of northern India with a party of 125 arranged by Mathur Nath Biswas, the rich landlord and owner of the Dakshineshwar Kali Temple where Sri Ramakrishna was employed as a priest. On the way, in Vaidyanath, in Bihar state, when Shri Ramakrishna saw the inhabitants of a village reduced by poverty and starvation to mere skeletons, he requested his rich patron to feed the villagers and give each a piece of cloth. Mathur demurred at the expense. Sri Ramakrishna then declared that he is not going to Varanasi but he would rather live with the poor and share their miseries. He actually left Mathur and sat down on road with the villagers whereupon Mathur had to yield.[30] Ramakrishna was so compassionate that he could truly empathize with the suffering destitutes.

In another fairly recent story, one of the disciples of the Dalai Lama was severely tortured for years by his captors in a Chinese jail and finally let go. He had no bad feelings for his torturers. He had no malice for them; he had forgiven them. He was all smiles when he finally came to meet his Master, the Dalai Lama in India. Asked how he was able to be so calm and collective under the brutal punishment, he replied, "I only thought of you, O Master, and your teachings, I didn't feel any pain; it is all because of your grace." Humility is one of the hallmarks of compassion, and of strength. "When you have the strength to strike a strong blow to the opponent and you choose non-violence instead; that is *Ahimsa*. Not that you are weak and helpless and use this as an excuse," says Swami Vivekananda.

While it is easy to become angry, arrogant, and violent or break down under the pressure of persecution, it is also possible to do just the opposite—to feel love and compassion for those who sting like a scorpion—do us harm deliberately—and this under all odds. This ideal strength of character comes after great *sadhana*—religious practice—of *Ahimsa* (non-violence) and love. It is like treading the razor's edge: it is not for the weak.

Buddha is considered as 'compassion incarnate'. Born in India as a prince and surrounded by luxuries, he left home at the age of 29 after witnessing widespread suffering in the world. He gave up everything in search of truth and to find a cure for suffering. He lived the very austere life of a monk and preached unconditional love and compassion until his last breath. Under his influence not only India but most of the East Asia became Buddhist. If he became the moral guiding force and inspiration to millions in his own life time, it was not accidental. He worked extremely hard, persevered, and failed many times but did not give up until he succeeded. His life is a shining example that human life is not for luxuries but for serving one and all with loving kindness. Birth as a human being is considered a special privilege in all Indic traditions and especially in Hinduism.

Glory of Human Birth

Human birth, according to Adi Shankaracharya,[31] is a rare blessing that comes only to those who have earned it by great *punyas*—self-earned credits—of hundred crores (one billion) of births in other species, because it is through this (human) body alone that the spiritual quest is possible. Man can speak, communicate, control nature, and become civilized and cultured. He can know the world, but more than this he can also know himself. This knowledge is important not only for his ultimate spiritual destiny but also for the all-round welfare of humankind. It is this science of self-knowledge that Vedanta delineates and which Shankara so brilliantly expounds in his book, *Viveka Chudamani*. Self-knowledge is exclusively a human phenomenon. Therefore, Shankara says, among all living beings, birth in a human body is indeed a rare privilege "*nar janma durlabham*".[31]

Human birth is indeed a rare privilege since it is only through the human body that an intense desire for liberation—*mukti*—and the company of the great souls—*maha purusha samshrayah*—is possible. The company of the great souls is a rare blessing because all the truly great men/women are endowed with a highly compassionate nature. Their consciousness is so expanded that they can feel the pain of all creatures, including plants and animals. An anecdote from the life of Ramakrishna Paramhansa will make the point. One day while sitting by the shore of the river Ganga Sri Ramakrishna saw two persons quarreling in a distant boat. In a violent fit of anger, one man slapped the other on the back. Sri Ramakrishna was so moved by the sight that not only he felt the pain of the man who was so mercilessly struck but the painful red finger marks appeared on his back.

The company of holy men is a rare blessing. It can awaken the dormant inherent instincts for compassion even in a savage and transform his life. Angulimar was a notorious highway robber who delighted in killing passersby and, true to his name, always wore a garland of cut fingers of his victims. Terror ran supreme in the region where he lived. Afraid for their lives, people stopped going there. The news reached Buddha one day and out of compassion for the terrorized masses, he decided to do something about it. So, he went where Angulimar lived to talk to him to stop the killing of innocent people. Angulimar learned that Buddha was coming his way. He came out laughing and making fun of the holy man and warned him not to come close, but Buddha fearlessly kept on going. This was unprecedented for Angulimar who had never seen such boldness. He ran towards the Buddha with a dagger in one of his raised hands, determined to kill him. But no sooner had he come close to Buddha than his whole demeanor changed. He felt so hopelessly weak that he could not even think of harming Buddha let alone strike a blow. He was overwhelmed by the guilt of his savagery that he became deeply remorseful. He fell down at the feet of the holy man and begged for his forgiveness. His life was changed forever by the mere sight of compassionate Buddha. He was transformed instantly into a loving and kind person.

Swami Vivekananda in his book *Raja Yoga*[32] talks about the glory of human birth as follows:

> This human body is the greatest body in the universe, and the human being the greatest being. Man is higher than all animals, than all angels; none is greater than man. Even the *Devas* (gods) will have to come down again and again and attain to salvation through a human body. Man alone attains to perfection, not even the *Devas*. This human birth is the greatest birth we can have. The animal is dull, and made mostly out of *Tamas*. Animals cannot have any higher thoughts, nor can the angels or *Devas*, attain to direct freedom without human birth.

Our bodies are made up of three subtle natural elements, the *gunas*: *Tamas* (dullness/ignorance) and *Satva* (purity/serenity), as two extremes, with *Rajas* (restlessness/activity) in between. Self-effort—*Rajas*—as the driving force properly motivated makes all the difference between an ignorant/dull and illumined/enlightened.

Swami Vivekananda narrates a story from *Chandogya Upanishad* (Chapter 8, sections 7-9), to point out the nature of the *Tamasic* and the *Satvic* personalities:

A god (Indra) and a demon (Virochana) went to learn about the Self from a great sage (Prajapati). They studied with him for a long time. At last the sage told them "You yourselves are the being you are seeking." Both of them thought that their bodies were the Self. They went back to their people quite satisfied and said, "We have learnt everything there was to be learnt; eat, drink, and be merry; we are the Self; there is nothing beyond us." The nature of the demon was ignorant, clouded, so he never enquired any further, but was perfectly contented with the idea that he was God, that by "Self" was meant the body. The god had a purer nature. He at first committed the mistake of thinking "I, this body, am *Brahman*; so keep it strong and healthy, and well dressed, and give it all sorts of enjoyments." But, in a few days, he found out that that cannot be the meaning of the sage, their master; there must be something higher. So, he went back and said "Sir, did you teach me that the body was the Self? If so, I see all bodies die; the Self cannot die." The sage said, "Find it out; thou art that." Then the god thought that the vital forces which work the body were what the sage meant. But after some time, he found that if he ate, the vital forces remained strong, but, if he starved, they become weak. The god then went back to the sage and said, "Sir, do you mean that the vital forces are the Self?" The sage said, "Find out for yourself; thou art that." The god returned home once more thinking that it was the mind, perhaps, that was the Self. But in a short while he saw that the thoughts were so various, now good, again bad; the mind was too changeable to be the Self. He went back to the sage and said, "Sir, I do not think that mind is the Self; did you mean that?" 'No' replied the sage, "Thou art That, find out for yourself." The god went home, and at last found that he was the Self, beyond all thought, One without birth or death, whom the sword cannot pierce, or the fire burn, whom the air cannot dry or the water wet. The beginning-less and endless, the immovable, the intangible, the omniscient, the omnipotent Being; that It was neither the body nor the mind, but beyond them all. So he was satisfied (that he has found the truth), but the poor demon did not get the truth, owing to his fondness for the body.

This vast humanity is intricately connected in more ways than we would like to think. Moreover, it is not a homogeneous mass. All kinds of variations exist. The 'haves' and 'have-nots' of great variety are globally widespread and all are the children of the Mother Earth. The natural resources were here since eternity and will be here long after the last of the humans departs. Good for all is a shared concern for the well-being of all, and compassion invariably helps bring about the much-needed change in our outlook when we start thinking about others and take action. That is the first step, for as long as we are addicted to the complacency of our own comforts, not much will change. Everything in this phenomenal world is changing, including our minds. It is inevitable but it can also be directed for the good of all by practicing compassion. Morality tempered with ethical code of conduct helps.

Yama and *Niyama*

Yama and *Niyama* are considered the 'outer' and the 'inner' observances, respectively, as a guide for living soulfully. Patanjali teaches that there are five *yamas* and five *niyamas*. Compassion by itself as a noble virtue draws its sustenance from love and kindness. The practice of *Yama* and *Niyama* as moral disciplines helps refine the personality of an individual; they are an integral part of Patanjali Yoga.[33]

Yama

Ahimsa: Non-violence, avoiding injury to anyone by thoughts, speech or action.
Satya: Truthfulness or honesty.
Asteya: Non-stealing, abstention from theft.
Brahmacharya: Purity of mind.
Aparigraha: Non-possessiveness.

Niyama

Saucha or *shaucha:* Purity or cleanliness. This is both internal and external. It's how we treat our bodies and our energies (internal) and how we treat our environment (external).

Santosha: Contentment. The practice of contentment leads to inner peace.

Tapas: Self-discipline, it is viewed as a way to cleanse the mind and body of the daily residue that may color one's perceptions.

Svadhyay: Regular study of scriptures and chanting the holy name of God.

Ishvara Pranidhana: Surrendering the fruits of work to *Ishvara* (God).

Practicing Compassion: *Seva*, the Selfless Service

Seva is a Sanskrit word, meaning service. Ideally, it is offered with humility and without any thought of receiving a reward or even gratitude in return. Rather, one should be grateful that there is a deserving someone to do the favor of accepting it.

Seva is extolled as one of the noblest of all virtues. It is recommended as a 'holistic' practice that helps purify the mind and advance the spiritual growth of any person, even the most selfish. It is an attitude that can be cultivated. The overriding concern here is the mindset: not for 'me' but for 'you'—the deserving 'other', even the totally unknown.

Service as Yoga

Service offered as duty, where the doer knows that he/she is not the real doer but only an instrument, is the essence of *Karma Yoga*. The same service to others becomes the worship of the *ishtadeva* in *Bhakti Yoga*—the recipient is his ideal deity of worship appearing in yet another form, and in *Jnana Yoga* with the realization that there is no *other* but the same divinity pulsating in all.[32] The ultimate beneficiary is the person who develops such service attitude; she/he progressively becomes a better person. Practiced to the perfection, yoga offers anyone the opportunity to rise above the conflicts of thought, word, and deed (*manasa*, *vacha*, and *karmana*), where there is absolute congruity in thought, speech, and action. Such a person lives a simple, unpretentious life, totally dedicated to serving others. His life inspires a transformation in thousands from within, making them progressively better persons, constantly less selfish and ultimately totally unselfish. Truly selfless service holds this promise.

Seva as Dharmic Duty

Indian (*Paurānic*) literature is replete with stories of great souls like Maharaja Shibi, who did not hesitate to give up his own life to save that of a lowly bird that came flying into his lap, looking for shelter in his personal care.[34] Another was Maharaja Rantideva who, starving and thirsty for over forty days, happily offered the last few drops of remaining water, which he had saved for himself and his family, to a total stranger, who appeared from nowhere, and who was from the ranks of the lowliest of the low in the social order, so that the suffering of the miserable man be minimized.[35] Yet another tale of performance of one's Dharmic duty, well known to most Indians, is the story of the maid servant Panna Dhai of Rajasthan,[36] who gladly sacrificed the life of her own son to save the life of the crown prince Uday Singh. And there are many others. In each case, all that was done by the noble individual, was done in the spirit of '*seva*', following the dictates of the conscience as the '*dharma*' under the circumstances. No sacrifice was too great or too small in the call of duty when it came to selfless service.

Seva as Dedicated Service to Masses

Buddha, Mahavir, Adi Shankaracharya, Shri Chaitanya, the Sikh Gurus—starting with Guru Nanak down to the last one—and their disciples, Ramakrishna Paramahansa, Ramana Maharshi, Swami Dayananda Saraswati of Arya Samaj, and others like them, lived a life with the attitude of *Seva* and inspired millions to serve society with that spirit. Swami Vivekananda boldly declared, "They alone live who live for others, the rest are more dead than alive."

By 'live' he meant living in *seva*—selfless service to the most wretched of all, the millions of poor and destitutes. Selfless service to humanity, for him, was like serving God '*Narseva, Narayanaseva*'. The poor, the wretched and the most miserable were like the 'living gods' to him. "Why go looking for Him in the temples?" he asked, "Open your eyes and see His living presence in the poorest of the poor and serve Him." This was his ideal; he lived it and preached it, and inspired millions to do the same.

Raja Ram Mohan Roy, Ishwarchand Vidyasagar, Mahatma Gandhi, Mahamana Malaviya, Acharya Vinoba Bhave—just to name a few—dedicated their lives in the selfless service of the masses of India in the field of social reform, education, and political awakening, and inspired thousands to follow in their footsteps. To them, the country was not just a piece of land but the divine mother incarnate—"Bharat Mata"—to millions of inhabitants with all their problems, to worship; that is, to look after and care for. Selfless service to all, regardless of their caste, creed, religion, pelf, and power, was the real service to the country and humanity at large. And such examples are not only in India, but they are all over the world.

Mary Esther Middleton, a yoga teacher,[37] has put it very aptly:

> Seva is a win-win, the total source of victory. The moment you serve with heart and head, and without grinding any ax, you win the person forever. You deliver another person facing difficulty to their own strength. You save the person in the face of calamity. You protect him in the face of non-reality and bring home the reality. In any form, shape, or projection, if you can elevate a person's consciousness, his spirit, his self, his environments, his life—it is Seva.

The attitude of anyone offering service is not how good she/he feels, but how the other, the recipient, feels as a result of the service. Serving others with this spirit is not an exercise in ego-boosting or a "holier than thou" mindset, or feeling pity for someone; it transcends all these. Compassion, gratitude, humility and love are the hallmarks of this attitude.

When we help others without any thought of personal gain, we can actually gain a lot. In that sense, *seva* is not just for the 'religious'. There are atheists and agnostics who do not believe in, or they are skeptical about, any divinity or God looking after the affairs of mankind or the universe. A large majority of such people are also very kind-hearted and pragmatic humanitarians. They feel deeply about the sufferings of fellow human beings. They go about their business, live and let others live, do not pose any threat to humanity, and have, in fact, made enormous positive contributions to advancing the welfare of their fellow human beings. Ironically, it is the so-called 'religious' groups who have wreaked havoc in historical proportions through millennia and still continue with that agenda in the name of religion.

Is Selfless Service Really Possible?

Skeptics of selfless service ask: "Is it really possible for any ordinary person to serve others in a truly selfless fashion—without expecting anything in return, not even feeling good for his/her altruistic behavior—or is this something reserved only for saints?"[38]

This question, well intentioned as it may be in professional terms, misses the core concept of selfless service. The motivation for service in general, and selfless service in particular, is not for getting anything in return for 'me'. It is for the 'other'. The only purpose of selfless service is to benefit the recipient in any and every way possible, physically and mentally.

Questioning selfless service, without any reference to the cultural context, also ignores the underlying innate cultural diversity of people. While this lack of concern for the sufferings of others may be a typical characterization for a large majority of those living comfortably, brought up under the materialistic culture, it is not so common a trait of many millions in other regions and cultures. This especially is the case for those belonging to many ancient cultures globally, and especially the Indic cultures—Hindu, Buddhist, Jain, Sikh, and their numerous denominations. The ordinary person here is very different—is typically not looking for any reward in return for his/her altruistic service. '*Neki kar aur kuen me dal*' (do the kind work and throw it in a well)—meaning serve the needy respectfully and then forget it—is a common colloquial axiom in India. When the work is done as duty with mind unattached to the result, it transcends even the 'feeling good' option. This, in fact, is the essence of *Karma Yoga*. Actions (*karmas*) are determined by the doer's *dharma*, which has no English equivalent. It stands for his/her *swabhava*, or intrinsic nature on the one hand, and his/her duty, ethics, morality, etc., on the other hand under the circumstances although she/he may or may not be religious or saintly in a typical sense.

This, however, should not give a false impression that selfless service is reserved for a specific ethnic group, or for people of any particular culture, religion, or geographic location. It's universal; there are examples all over the world where such 'ordinary' people, including those from the Western culture, have spontaneously come up to help others, totally unknown to them. They have a compassionate mind that feels the suffering of the other. Most of them are ordinary civilians who may stop to help a stranger stranded on a busy highway with a disabled vehicle, or volunteer their services in homeless kitchens serving food or sweeping floors or washing dishes, or provide of their selfless service to patients in a hospital or in disaster relief work. They are indifferent to any reward in return, don't expect even a 'thank you' expect to feel better afterward. Unknown to themselves, they are the great humanitarians. They are not incarnations of love and compassion but they do not miss any opportunity when presented where their actions can help minimize or eliminate the suffering of a fellow human being or even an animal. They rise to the occasion and answer the call of duty in emergency or non-emergency situations. They do not have any trace of expectation of a reward in return for their altruistic action. They make the lives of others better by serving them, simply by being there at a time and place by some divine plan indifferent to a reward in return, let alone the glory, publicity, or any name and fame.

Selfless Service as Moral Duty

Selfless service is the ideal of true service. The doer is not looking for anything in return as a reward, but considers the service to the needy as a moral duty. In the context of Hinduism, it is believed that human birth is a rare blessing that comes after many births of different species. It is the cumulative effect of many *punyas* (meritorious deeds) of the past lives. With such a rare gift, the purpose of life cannot be just for 'me' or 'mine'. It has to be much more than that. For Hindus, and those who believe in *karma*, it may be to exhaust the karmic load and get out of the endless cycles of birth and rebirth, and be free, the ultimate goal being the realization of the true nature of the Self as *sat-chit-ananda*. Purity of mind is the essential requirement for such an exalted achievement.

Seva—just the service to others, even if not entirely selfless—helps to free the mind from the clutches of *Kama* (lust), *Krodha* (anger), and *Lobha* (greed), which are at the root of all the evils that motivate selfish pursuits (*Srimad Bhagavadgita*, ch. 16, verse 21). Hindus also believe that we are born with some inherent debts, one of which is the *Bhutarina* (indebtedness to the living, including animals and plants). It follows then that we have an obligation to share what we have and serve others and make this world a better and safe place for all to live and enjoy. This also means doing all that we can to help eliminate pain and suffering of others, regardless of race, religion, ethnicity, geographic, and political affiliation, and to safeguard the protection of the environment.

Vasudhaiva Kutumbakam—the whole world is a family—is not just a slogan. It came as an expression of deep experience and feeling of belonging and concern for humanity spread across the globe. The full verse, which puts this expression in proper perspective, goes like this:

> *Ayamnijahparoveti, gananalaghuchetasam,*
> *udarcharitanamtu, vasudhaivakutumbakam.*

Paraphrased, it means: "This is mine, that is others is the thinking of the petty-minded; for the large-hearted, the whole earth—the entire world—is one family."

We all share the bounties of Mother Nature. We also share common aspirations of life, liberty, and pursuit of happiness, regardless where we are or who we think we are. What makes one individual different from the other is the refinement of the attitude which brings about a positive change in him/her, elevating him/her to a higher *udar charitanam* or humane level. Some have this naturally in their genes or because of *samskaras* (deep impressions) from their past lives. For many others, it is an acquired habit that they cultivate, over time, to become more loving, compassionate, sensitive, and responsive to the needs of the fellow beings. Gradually, this brings about an inner transformation. A feeling of fellowship dawns, shared care and collective good for all, including the well-being of the planet earth and a peaceful living experience for all, becomes a dominant part of their day-to-day life.

Selfless service is an ideal of *Seva*, and while serving others in selfless manner may be difficult, it is not impossible, and it is not only for the selected few. It can be learned by any one at any age, and any selfless service to the deserving/needy in any shape or form, by itself, is an ennobling experience. It is an invitation to sublimate the all-too-common egoistic selfish human nature. In Swami Vivekananda's words, it is for

> "*Atmanomokshartham, jagathitayacha*"—one's own salvation and for the good of the world at large.

It is an opportunity knocking at the door for self-upliftment.

Giftivism: Generosity—Giving Selflessly—is Good

Pavi Mehta of the Service Space organization[39] has a new word for selfless service—Giftivism. The Service Space is something of a paradigm shift in the field of innovative selfless service. Its model is not based on conventional fund-raising, as is so common in most others. Donating or collecting funds is not so unusual; it is the personal involvement part of the service that makes the difference. In one of the invited featured talks of Centifolia in 2013 in France,[40] Mehta tells the story of a depressed photographer who jumped off the Golden Gate Bridge in California in a suicide attempt and a man who was robbed by a knife-wielding teenager. She also tells of her own grandfather, an ophthalmologist, who started a free eye hospital with only 11 beds, which in time became Aravind Eye Hospitals in India, treating millions of poor patients free. The Aravind Hospital initiative of preventing blindness in populations that cannot afford the treatment turned out to be such an innovative successful business model that Harvard Business School featured the story in its publications. All the stories that Pavi tells in her video presentation are unique. All started with no money or money as focus but with the foundation of unconditional generosity.

All the talk about selfless service has no meaning unless someone takes it upon himself/herself to change him/her self and change the others. Mahatma Gandhi as a freedom fighter, and Dr. Karve, as champion of women's education in India, Dr. Albert Schweitzer (originally from Germany), who chose to work selflessly in remote jungles of Africa, and Nelson Mandela of South Africa, are just a very few names that everyone knows, but the list of the selfless service activists is long.

Seva is Wholesome Humanitarian Activity

Service to others is an opportunity to get out of our comfort zone and do our part. There are many worthy institutions of all sizes, and from local to truly global in scope, looking for volunteer workers for serving the community or for supporting their charitable activities. The range is enormous from education to health, from serving disadvantaged anywhere to disaster relief and much more—the opportunities are endless. All the information is at the tips of the fingers on the Internet for anyone who is interested.

In conclusion, even if one does not believe in altruistic activity and is looking for "what is in it for me," or at least wants to feel good with the investment of time, talents and resource, the return in terms of overall personal happiness is enormous. It may possibly even make someone a more compassionate, loving, and caring person, which also means a stress-free and egoless person.

Compassion and selfless service are not just fancy talk any more. The scientific evidence, supported by hundreds of research papers from topmost researchers, from behavioral and social sciences to human physiology and from genetics to neuroscience, has been building up in the last few decades[41-46] to show that we are 'hardwired' for compassion and altruism. Kindness and service to others have been part of our nature for millions of years and it can be cultivated. It has survived because it is so natural and healthy for the personal and collective welfare of all.

As the Dalai Lama says, "Be kind whenever possible. It is always possible."

NOTES

1. Seppala, Emma M. 2013. The compassionate mind. *Observer* (APS). 26 (5)
2. Jill Suttie, 2013. Where do heroes come from? GGSC Newsletter, August 28, 2013.
3. F. Warneken, M. Tomasello, 2006. Altruistic helping in human infants and young chimpanzees. *Science*. 311: 1301-03.
4. Leopard kills a monkey, YouTube, 2015.
5. Jennifer L. Goetz, K. Dacher, and E. Simon-Thomas, 2010. Compassion: An evolutionary analysis and empirical review. *Psychol. Bull.* 136(3): 351-74.
6. J. Haidt, 2003. The moral emotions. In: Davidson, RJ.; Scherer, KR.; Goldsmith, HH., editors. *Handbook of Affective Sciences*. New York: Oxford University Press; pp. 852-70.
7. M.C. Nussbaum, 1996. Compassion. *Social Philosophy and Policy*. 13: 27-58.
8. C.D. Batson and L.L. Shaw, 1991. Evidence for altruism: Toward a pluralism of prosocial motives. *Psychological Inquiry*. 2: 107-22.
9. N. Eisenberg and P.A. Miller, 1987. The relation of empathy to prosocial and related behaviors. *Psychological Bulletin*. 101: 91 19.
10. M.L. Hoffman, 1981. Is altruism part of human nature? *Journal of Personality and Social Psychology*. 40: 121-37.
11. C. Darwin, 1871. The descent of man, and selection in relation to sex. London: Penguin Books; 1871/2004.
12. J. Suttie, 2015. Why does altruism exist? 2015. GGSC Newsletter, April 15, 2015.
13. David S. Wilson, 2015. *Does Altruism Exist*? New Haven: Yale University Press, 2015.

14. Kira M. Newman, 2015. You need more than a book to learn loving kindness. GGSC Newsletter, March 23, 2015.
15. Vicky Zakrzewski, 2015. Social emotional learning: Why now?. GGSC Newsletter, Jan. 7, 2015.
16. Dacher Keltner, 2009. *Born to be Good: The Science of Meaningful Life*. New York: W.W. Norton and Co. Inc.
17. Ji-W, Kim 2009. *Neurophysiopsychologia*. 47(10): 2073-81.
18. Emiliana Simon-Thomas, 2015. Measuring compassion in the body. www.greatergood.berkeley.edu/article/item/measuring compassion in the body. Google search.
19. Kristin Neff, 2015. The physiology of self-compassion. http://self-compassion.org/the-physiology-of-self-compassion/
20. Abigail A. Marsh et al., 2014. Neural and cognitive characteristics of extraordinary altruists. *PNAS*. 111(42): 15036-41.
21. G. Phillippe, 2008. Cognitive neuroscience of mindful meditation. http://YouTube.be/sf 6QOG1iHBl
22. Martin Reuter et al., 2010. Investigating the genetic basis of altruism: The role of COMT Val 158 Met polymorphism. *Soc. Cogn. Affect. Neurosci.* 2010: 1093.
23. H. Tost et al., 2010. A common allele in oxytocin receptor gene (OXTR) impacts prosocial temperament and human hypothalamic-limbic structure and function. *PNAS*. 107(31): 13936-41.
24. Pingyuan Gong et al., 2014. Dopamine beta hydroxylase gene modulates individual empathic ability. *Soc. Cogn. Affect. Neuroscience.* 9(9): 1341-45.
25. Vipassana meditation. www.dhamma.org/en/vipassana.shtml
26. Mindfulness meditation. Wikipedia, the free encyclopedia. http://youtu.be/3nwwKbM_vJC
27. Loving-kindness meditation. http://YouTube.be/sz7cp V7ERsM
28. E.M. Seppala, 2014. 18-Science based reasons to try loving-kindness meditation. Huffington Post. Healthy Living. www.huffingtonpost.com/...seppala.../18-science based reasons-t-b-582395
29. Saint and scorpion, 2011. *The Times of India*. www.timesof india.indiatimes.com/life-cycle/the saint and the scorpion
30. Swami Nikhilananda, 1942. The Gospel of Sri Ramakrishna, eighth printing 1992. pp. 35-36. New York: Ramakrishna-Vivekananada Center.

31. Swami Ranganathananda, 2008. *The Message of Viveka Chudamani: The Significance of Birth in a Human Body*. 1-24: 312-43.
32. *The Complete Works of Swami Vivekananda,* Vol. 1. Karma Yoga, pp. 25-118, Raja Yoga, pp. 140-141, 1986 edition; Vol. 2. Jnana Yoga, pp. 57-288, 1983 edition; Vol. 3. Bhakti Yoga, pp. 29-100, 1984 edition; Advaita Ashrama, Dehi Entally Road, Calcutta. (These are also available as separate books by the same title at any Ramakrishna Vedanta Center.)
33. Swami Bhaskarananda, 2001. Meditation, Mind and Patanjali's Yoga. *Yama and Niyama*, pp. 39-67. Viveka Press, Seattle.
34. www.moralstories.wordpress.com/shibi, Google search.
35. Swami Tapasyananda, 1980. *Srimad Bhagavatam* (Skandha 9, ch. 21), Vol. 2: 475-76.
36. www.royalheritagehaveli/wordpress.com/Panna Dhai, Google search.
37. Middleton, Mary Esther. www.yogasense.net. Google search.
38. John A. Johnson, 2013. Selfless Service, Part 1: Is selfless Service possible? (Cui Bono, Psychology Today.com/blog/cui-bono/201305/selfless-service-I-is selfless-service-possible)
39. www.servicespace.org, posts inspiring stories on daily basis.
40. Pavi Mehta 2013. YouTube, Centifolia 2013 Fr. Google search.
41. Emma M. Seppala, 2013. Compassion: Our First Instinct. Psychology Today-Google search.
42. Dacher Keltner and Jeremy S. Smith, (Eds.). 2010. The Compassionate Instinct: The Science of Human Greatness. New York: W.W.Norton and Co.
43. Graham J Thompson, Peter L. and Bernard J. Crespi, 2013. Genes underlying altruism. *Biol Lett*, 9: 20130395. (http://dx.doi.org/10.1098/rsbl.2013.0395)
44. Jennifer L Goetz, D, Keltner and E. Simon-Thomas, 2010. Compassion: An Evolutionary Analysis and Empirical Review. *Psychology. Bull.* 136(3): 351-74.
45. Greater Good Science Center (GGSC) publications, 2015. The Science of Meaningful Life. GGSC reports on groundbreaking research into the roots of compassion and happiness (www.greatergood.berkeley.edu).
46. Richard J. Davidson and A. Lutz, 2008. Buddha's Brain: Neuroplasticity and Meditation. *IEEE Signal Process Mag.* 25(1): 174-76.

□

6

Nature Connection in the *Yogavāshiṣh-ha*

—Christopher Key Chapple

Part One: Elements

The *Yogavāshiṣh-ha* served both as a resource and an inspiration for Kashmir Saivism. Composed in the early years of the second millennium of the common era, this text concatenates and amalgamates the spiritual insight of India, drawing lightly yet profoundly from Vaisnavism, Jainism, Buddhism, Yoga, and even Islam. One feature of the text that must be noted is its ornate use of language and abundant honoring of the natural world. The *Yogavāshiṣh-ha* includes descriptions of India's vast and varied landscape, from the desert of King Lavaṇa's banishment to the listing of India's great mountain ranges. For most of the text, the natural world serves as a backdrop for the many stories gathered into this collection. Nature also serves as a metaphor for difficulty, with people enduring privation for the purpose of spiritual purification. However, toward the latter part of the final section of the book, nature becomes the context in which Vasiṣ-ha describes his own experience of freedom, an experience that qualified him to become Rāma's teacher.

Nature has been articulated in Indian philosophy through the five great elements (*mahābhūta*): earth, water, fire, air, and space. These are carefully listed in the *Sāṃkhya Kārikā* and in various philosophical literature of the Hindus and Buddhists. They receive prominent mention in the Abhidharma literature of early Buddhism as well as in the later literature of Hindu and Buddhist Tantra. Ritual in Indian traditions involves the sanctified presence of these elements in the earthen form of the altar shaped with terra cotta bricks, cleansed with water, filled with fire, into which offerings of food and incense and ghee are burned, released into the air, reaching into space. Buddhist stupas portray the elements in order of ascension, with the square base representing the earth, the bowl-like second tier evoking the holding of water, the spiral third tier rising above the water-like flames, air cascading above through a cloud-like architectural flourish, topped with sun and moon representing movement through space.

Furthermore, each of these five elements correlates to sensory processes and bodily functions: earth with smell and evacuation, water with taste and reproduction, fire with sight and power, air with touch and heart and legs, space with ears and sound. Visual symbols combine with mantras to create a functional cosmology, a human-felt connection. To know the elements, senses, and body constitute an important foundation for knowledge in Indian thought and literature. This chapter will explore the role of the elements in Vasiṣ-ha's spiritual journey, a journey that leads through the world into reverie, and from reverie back into the world.

Nature and the Elements in Indian Thought

The earliest of India's texts, the *Ṛg Veda*, composed over 3500 years ago, celebrates Agni as the God of heat and light, Indra as the deity of the thunderstorm who releases the waters of each year's monsoons, and Soma, the creator of a special herbal elixir. The Vedas also extol Dyaus, the Lord of the heavens (referred to by the Greeks later as Zeus), and Pṛthivī, the Goddess of the earth.

The *Atharva Veda*, written a few hundred years later, acknowledges that all works and endeavors rely upon the earth, and that medicines arise from the earth. It praises mother earth in various ways, stating that "on her body food is grown everywhere and on her the farmer toils...the earth is home to cows, horses and birds...sacred are your hills, snowy mountains and deep forests.... You are the world for us and we are your children."[1] Without the beneficence of the earth, all would perish.

The Upaniṣads, which were composed starting 2,800 years ago, praise the body and senses. In particular, the Upaniṣads honor the power of the breath. They redefine the self as beyond name and form, and introduce methods of Yoga and meditation. These ideas find distillation in the texts of Yoga and Sāṃkhya around two thousand years ago, which discuss the operations and functions of the elements, the body, and the emotions in regard to transcendental consciousness.

The *Mārkaṇḍeya Purāṇa* (ca. 400 C.E.) makes correlations between the senses, the elements, and the *cakras*, outlining an ascendant interiority similar to that found in Emerson. Beginning with the earth and increasing in subtlety through water, fire, air, and space, this text suggests that one enter into full understanding of one's thoughts and one's soul, correlating a *cakra* to each of these seven steps. The Yogi of the *Mārkaṇḍeya Purāṇa* begins with the *mūla cakra* at the base of the spine and disappears at the seventh stage into supreme bliss.[2] The text states:

> The yogi should contemplate the seven objects,
> starting with the earth.
> He should contemplate the subtle earth;
> when he deems the earth to be
> his soul, he leaves behind its bonds.
> Then he transcends the subtle taste in water,
> the form in fire and the touch in wind.
> As he moves into the subtle form of the mind,
> he leaves behind engagement with the sky and sound.
> He enters with his mind into the mind of all created beings in a subtle condition.
> From there he develops religious devotion.
> Having traversed all seven
> (earth/smell; water/taste; fire/form; wind/touch,
> space/sound, mind/thought, intellect/devotion),
> he moves to supreme bliss,

leaving behind all attachment.
(*Mārkaṇḍeya Purāṇa*, XL:15-23)[3]

Vasiṣ-ha's Liberation: The World Within the Rock

In a narrative entitled by Swami Venkatesananda "The World Within the Rock", the sage Vasiṣ-ha, preceptor of the young Rama, enters into a darkened cave where he sees Lord Śiva in meditation. A shadow calls his attention to the presence of the Goddess. As he gazes upon her body, she dances, creating the world, carrying mountains and forests on her shoulders and arms. When she ceases to dance, the world stops and begins to dissolve. The presence of this magical Goddess intrigues Vasiṣ-ha. She instructs Vasiṣ-ha about how she creates the material universe from her body. She inspires him to take up a sequence of concentration exercises (*dhāraṇā*) through which he sees how his own body is connected with the fundamental elements that comprise the world.[4] Vasiṣ-ha celebrates all that emanates from and remains connected with his body. He enters into an experience of the anthropocosmic, a term used by Eliade from the 1940s through the 1970s "to account for the correspondences between microcosm and macrocosm that appear throughout the history of religions" and more recently used by Tu Wei Ming "to describe the dynamic interconnectedness of Heaven, Earth, and humanity."[5]

There is a close relationship between the philosophy of Sāṃkhya and the process through which Vasiṣ-ha reaches liberation. According to the *Sāṃkhya Kārikā* and the *Yoga Sūtra*, Nature (*Prakṛti*), personified in this tale by the Goddess, serves two functions, providing experience and liberation.[6] In the story of Vasiṣ-ha's realization of liberation through his direct encounter with Nature, we find that a Goddess starts him on his quest. He employs the named Yoga technique of *dhāraṇā* to enter deep states of interiority. His narrative takes the form of a personal confession. He seems delighted, surprised, and even overwhelmed as he discovers that the powers of the elements themselves reside in his own body.

The narrative begins when Kālī shuts down the world through her dance of cosmic dissolution. It then shifts to a reconstruction of the world within the body of Vasiṣ-ha himself, celebrated element by element. It concludes (or rather transitions to yet another story) by placing Vasiṣ-ha in dialogue with an ascended sage, who gives advice on how to maintain purified consciousness while moving about in the world. The sage tells him:

The infinite consciousness (*cid-ākāśa*) is I,
it is the three worlds,
it is the *puruṣa* (cosmic being)
and it is you.[7]

This philosophy affirms the validity of the constructed realm and hence forms a foundation for Vasiṣ-ha to exhort Rāma to resume his duties.

In order to capture a sense of the rich imagery employed by the author in praise of Nature, new translations of portions of successive chapters describing Vasiṣ-ha's encounter will follow.[8] In this narrative, Vasiṣ-ha undergoes a shift in awareness. He assumes the position of a sovereign king, overseeing the landscape of his domain from a birds-eye view. What begins as rhapsody about the beauties of nature becomes a celebration of the material powers contained within his own body. Vasiṣ-ha, as we will see, becomes anthropocosmic.

The Earth

In volume VII, chapter 89, Vasiṣ-ha describes looking down upon the earth. From this vantage point, he sees soil, plants, mountains, rivers and relates them to his own body:

58. Through performing concentration on the earth,
I dissolved into the form of the earth.
While still retaining this expanded consciousness,
I became like a universal ruler (surveying his domain).
59. And indeed, through my concentration on the earth,
I went to the mines at the root of the earth.
I came to understand my body as the trees,

the grasses, the mountains, the continents, and more.
60. As I took possession of the throne of the earth,
forests sprouted from my body.
I became adorned with cities
as if laced with strings of pearls.
61. ....
My arms embraced the mountain ranges
and my continents were encircled with oceans like bracelets.
62. I felt my body covered with grasses like hair,
as well as tree-tangled mountains,
held up by the heads of ten elephants
and the hundreds of heads of the primal serpent Śeṣa.
64. The beautiful ridges of the Himalayas and the Vindhyas,
the clouds high on Mount Meru,
the abundance of the rivers such as the Ganges:
all this evokes a delicate string of pearls.
65. Caves and thickets and marshes
appear to encircle the ocean.
The white salts of the desert
shimmer like a beautiful garment.
67. Repeatedly, the ground is plowed and turned:
cooled by the winds of the winter,
warmed by the heat of summer
and moistened by the waters of the rainy season.
68. My chest became the expansive plains.
My eyes became pools of lotuses.
My crown was the light and dark clouds.
My body (*mandiram*) contained the ten regions.
72. Filled with floods, deserts, farms, kingdoms, as well as people,
on named continents of stone with rivers, forests,
and oceans to the end of the horizon,
the Earth is an assemblage of vessels and designs
connected with various adorning marks,
as if flecked with groups of lotuses in a raging river,
or like a pond laced with vines.

Vasiṣ-ha describes the planet with great precision and emotion. He sees mountains, forests, deserts, caves, plains, and oceans. He describes the seasons and, like the anthropocosmic sections of the *Bṛhadāraṇyaka Upaniṣad*, makes correlations between his body and the body of the world. He feels vegetation sprout from his body. His arms embrace the mountains. His chest becomes the broad plains, his eyes become lotus pools, and clouds gather around his head. He becomes entranced and absorbed into the beauty of the earth.

The Waters

In the next chapter, Vasiṣ-ha explores various forms of water. He again performs *dhāraṇā*, defined by Patañjali as "the binding of the mind to a place" (*deśa-bandhaś-cittasya dhāraṇā*, *Yoga Sūtra*, III:1). This practice, when extended, moves one into a state of meditation (*dhyāna*) and ultimately into *samādhi*. Patañjali describes *samādhi* as a state of emptying (*śūnya*) that allows the higher self to shine forth.[9] Vasiṣ-ha attained a state of transparency first to earth and then to water, blending and merging with the experience of each:

90.9. Just as I experienced the earth-plane
by earth contemplation (*pṛthivī dhāraṇā*),
then, just as I saw those many worlds
held in the form of the earth,
so also I became water, which was seen
by me in the same way (as from above).
10. By concentration on water, I became water,
as if this unconscious (substance)
took on consciousness
inside the abodes of the oceans with its quiet gurgling.
11. [The water] slowly rose up into the veins
and trunks of creeping vines, grasses, trees,
tendrils, and groves, as if a caterpillar
were mounting your limbs.
12. That [water] lifts everything like the [rising of sap in]
the trunk of a tree, cutting patterns like bracelets,

roiling the water worms gently
with undulating movements in its hollows.
13. Having rested, [the water] formed beautiful lines,
its full shape taking the form of the leaves and fruits
of vines, hardwood trees, and palm trees.
14. [Water] enters into the hearts [of plants]
as if through their mouths.
It lets the roots in the bodies [of plants]
hold firm during the adversity of the [monsoon] season,
[growing back] when cut, shaken, eaten, or harvested.
15. [Water] takes the form of drops of dew
asleep in the beds of leaves,
constant at all times,
tirelessly gleaming in all directions.
16. Along its endless journey,
[water] takes a home in various lakes and rivers,
occasionally resting gracefully by a bridge,
like an old friend.
19. Having arisen from the woods in the form of mist
into the ocean of the sky,
this indwelling gem stuck
as tear drop jewels in the blue stars.
20. [Water] took rest in the thrones of the clouds,
accompanying Lady Lightning
whose blue sapphire light
illuminated Vasudeva on his Snake Throne.
21. Atoms of water gush forth in tiny drops.
Each holds its essential nature,
like Brahman is found in all souls.
22. Having reached a connection with the highest experience
through the taste buds, my soul was delivered
from the body to the singularity of knowledge.
23. That sweetness is not achieved by me,
nor by my body, nor by anything else.
It is revealed inside, to consciousness.
At that point, ignorance disappears.

24. The bee tastes and takes nectar from various flowers
in all directions across all seasons.
It takes this enjoyable elixir and
passes it along to the next bee.
25. In the connecting joints of the fourteen classes of beings,
water dwells as if it were conscious,
though by its inert nature it has no consciousness.
26. In the form of a rising mist,
[water] ascends on the chariot of the winds,
bestowing joyous fragrance in the channels
of the pure sky.
27. Rāma, by dwelling in that [water concentration]
from the smallest particle
to the ultimate experience of it,
the whole world comes into existence.
28. Through this unconscious thing appearing as if conscious,
through the sameness of myself with this water,
all inner meaning of what is known
and unknowable was revealed to me.

Vasiṣ-ha experiences water in its various forms. Just as he discussed the fragrance of the earth, he mentions the sense of taste in regard to water. In Sāṃkhya, foundational awareness of the earth arises from the power of smelling, and the capacity of tasting is known through and linked with water. He describes dew, drops of rain, the gathering of moisture in clouds, mist, rivers, and waterfalls. Vasiṣ-ha talks of how sap rises in plant life. He also discusses how the beauty of water brought him again to a deep appreciation and awareness, stilling his thoughts and revealing vast empty space.

Fire

Fire (*agni, tejas*) finds an important role in the earliest literature of India. The very first hymn of the *Ṛg Veda* offers praise to the God Agni (cognate with the Latin word ignite) and more Vedic hymns address Agni than any other deity. Vasiṣ-ha finds fire in a myriad of forms, from the sun and moon and stars to the simple oil lamp. Through light one experiences deep delight and a feeling of safety and security. The correlated sense, seeing, can only function through the presence of light. For Vasiṣ-ha, light becomes truly revelatory:

91.1. Then I disappeared into fire
through the brilliant concentration on fire.
I became linked with its various parts such as
the moon, lightning, stars, flames, and so forth.
2. From its essential nature as eternally luminous,
it spreads light like a beloved prince.
It makes all things visible. It makes all things right.
Thieves fail to conceal themselves in its glow.
3. Through its gentle, friendly lamps
it provides thousands of delights.
It allows all purposes to be seen
in every house, like a good prince.
4. It brings good cheer to all the world
through the sparkling rays of the moon and sun.
Through its singular delights it casts light
into the distance, lifting up and pervading
the circumference of the sky.
5. Light destroys the combined qualities
of blindness and affliction.
It possesses the quality of
revealing all truth and awakening.
6. The people proclaim with gusto:
"[Fire] is the axe [that cuts] the tree of darkness.
It provides the foothold for making things exceedingly pure.
It is golden, the ruby among gems."
7. It [energizes] reds, blacks, and whites;
it abides eternally through its gleaming limbs,
like a father gives shape to the bodies
of all his sons.
8. Fire, through its blessings, chooses
to spare the house of children from destruction.

It also protects [the people] from piercing winds
throughout the land.
10. I saw [fire] in the abodes of the gods,
where illumined souls are eternally in great splendor,
as well as the light on the ruined huts of the people
and in the recesses covered in great darkness.
11. [I saw] that stainless radiant virgin sky
become smeared with the color of saffron [at sunset],
making way for the illumination of the moon and stars,
as well as the winds that bring night dew.
12. Her grace causes the fields of corn each day
to ripen and grow up out of the darkness.
Her radiance [draws water up] into the clouds
that fill the vast crystal dome [of the sky]
and bring cleansing rains.
13. By her, meaning is bestowed.
Through her, comes illumination.
Like a younger sister, she reveals the highest truth:
there is consciousness only.
14. Her lustre on the lotus pool reflects
the actions of living beings on the earth and below,
just as from consciousness emerges
the wonderment of thought, perception, and form.
15. A necklace of innumerable jeweled stars
is called together from the mist.
Light increases with the days and seasons throughout the year
and froths in fires under the ocean.
16. The moon and sun move briskly
inside the great darkness of the night sky,
just as the one who stands deep in the great universe
is the one eternally moving and imperishable.
17. Fire is the brilliance in gold,
the strength in men,
the crystal gleam in all jewels,
and the flash in lightning storms.

18. It is the splendor in the phases of the face of the moon.
It is the mark of beauty in long eyelashes.
Its undying love flows abundantly.
It glitters in the laughter of friends.
19. Fire is in the love that arises and shines forth
and can be found in the innate allure of the movement
of a face, an arm, an eye,
an eyebrow, a hand, or a lock of hair.
20. Fire shows that these three worlds are as flimsy as straw.
It burns in the slap of one's worst enemies.
It starts the thunderclap
and dwells in the heart of the strong lion.
21. Among excellent, active warriors,
fierce fire can be found in the sound
of their clashing swords, breaking through armor,
and in their harsh, noisy battle cries.
22. ....
Fire is the force that moves all beings.
It causes plants to sprout upward.
23. Bright-eyed one, I experienced those things
in these coverings of space that make up the world
as if they were shimmering in the desert.
24. I saw the phoenix sun as its streams of light
scattered over all ten points of the horizon.
I saw its limbs flash on chosen mountains,
making them appear as if they were villages
on the face of the earth.
25. The wheel of the sun is filled with treasure
like the desire within a flower's blossom.
Light sits within the universe
like phosphorescence in the darkened sea.
Its continuous line of days unfolds just as fruits ripen on the tree.
26. The face of the moon in the sky
forms a pool of elixir.
Each evening it smiles cheerfully

on the people of the night.
27. (The moon's) power reflects
all lovely good fortune in the world.
His wife, Rohini, (shines) in the might
as the most beloved white lotus flower.
28. To me appeared a gentle trail of stars,
arrayed like nectar flowing through the heavens,
like a web of shining flowers on a vine,
twisted and heaped together.
(The Milky Way!)
[**Note:** commentary suggests *maranda* (nectar) in place of *maśaka* (mosquito).]
29. I saw jewel-like waves in the hands of the oscillating ocean,
as if merchants' hands were tossing them
on their scales to weigh them.
30. I see whirlpools of fish in the water of the ocean,
multitudes of sunbeams on that water,
and in the delicate clouds,
(portents of) lightning igniting a forest fire.
31. I saw the beautiful burning of the sacrificial fire,
its tenacious flames devouring the wood,
spreading throughout all that can be burned,
roaring, strong, and crackling.

Vasiṣ-ha explores various metaphors of fire and light including its ability to dispel ignorance, its ability to provide comfort "like a good prince," its ability to protect and illumine. Like a Buddhist, he proclaims that fires remind us that all things are fleeting. Like a Vedāntin, he hints that just as fire can be found in all manner of things, so also resides the soul.

Air and Wind and Space

When Vasiṣ-ha practiced concentration on the wind (*vāyu dhāraṇā*), he proclaimed:

VII.92.1. Next I came to concentrate
on the operations of the wind,

spreading my thoughts resolutely
to examine the world and satisfy my curiosity.
2. I rose up into the wind [that surrounds] the earth,
playing with the people, the trees,
and the beautiful blooming flowers,
protecting the water lilies.
4. I became the teacher of the dancing leaves
of grasses, trees, and tender vines.
I was adorned with the fragrance of flowers
and the splendor of medicinal plants and fruits.
6. In heaven, I carry the earth's honey and pollen.
I lift up the scent of jasmine that adorns the trees in paradise.
In hell, my gathered fires illuminate the thick fog.
7. In the ocean my undulating movements
can be seen in the pounding of the surf.
In the sky, I move the clouds to hide
and then reveal the mirror of the moon.
8. I support that beneficial vehicle,
the powerful army of stars,
moving perfectly through the three worlds
on their powerful, speedy chariot.
9. Closely resembling how thought
quickly appears and disappears,
the air touches the body though it has no body,
inducing bliss through its movement (*spanda*)
like the fragrance of sandalwood.
10. [The wind drives] the hard showers of rain and snow.
It brings infirmity to the old.
It makes the young drunken with joy.
For the gentle ones, it brings silence and innocence.
11. Its course lifts up sweetness,
and brings the nectar of happiness to the heavens.
The beloved [winds] of March take away
the fatigue that comes with long love making.
13. Though its caresses, it bends the abundant flowers

and the vines waiting like wives in springtime.
It incessantly shakes and moves the palm fronds.
It dislodges bees from the plants.
15. The wind, like a horse, moves through the sky,
established in and combined with the clouds.

In these verses, Vasiṣ-a feels the touch of wind upon his skin and feels the power that comes as the wind reaches far and wide, even "teaching the grasses how to dance." The power of breath, associated elsewhere in text with yogic *prāṇāyāma*, enables one to fly freely, as far as the expanse of space.

Space

In the elemental narratives and meditation manuals, space often received scant mention, no doubt due to its subtlety. However, in his rendering of the description of space, Swami Venkatesananda uses the category of space to visit the entire human body. Vasiṣ-ha claims:

The netherworlds were my feet,
the earth my abdomen,
and the heavens my head...
I was spread in all directions
everywhere at all times
and I did everything.
I was the self of all.
I was all.
Yet I was pure space.
I experienced being something and being nothing.
I experienced universes within every atom
and universes within the atoms of those universes.
I myself became all these universes.[10]

In this proclamation, Vasiṣ-ha's body expands to encompass the universe. He has attained the pureness of space and hence liberation.

Conclusion

In this narrative, nature speaks to and moves Vasiṣ-ha to a place of deep connection. The bliss engendered by Vasiṣ-ha's process of immersion in the elements and their correlative senses, one by one, culminates in a universal vision not unlike that experienced by Arjuna in the eleventh chapter of the *Bhagavad Gītā*. In the *Gītā*, Kṛṣṇa draws all the Mahābhārata warriors into their destruction, like moths to a flame. Vasiṣ-ha's epiphany begins as Kālī performs her dance of destruction. This entices him into rarefied states of contemplation that culminate in universal consciousness, an immersion into the *cid-ākāśa*.

Vasiṣ-ha's liberation takes place through the very tools of experience. Vasiṣ-ha does not retreat from the earth or its smells; he does not disdain water or its tastes; he does not reject light and the forms it reveals; he does not recoil from the various forms of wind. He celebrates each with elation. Each condition becomes a moment for the expansion of consciousness, an important moment in the process of purification. The journey of Vasiṣ-ha affirms, piece by piece, the vital importance of the creative powers of the Goddess, the powers of nature herself. By contemplating the elements, Vasiṣ-ha comes to highest consciousness. By experiencing nature, he experiences liberation.

The human body, according to Sāṃkhya, is composed of five sense organs (nose, mouth, eyes, skin, ears) and five action organs (anus, genitalia, hands, legs, and voice) that allow one to perceive and operate in the realm of the five elements (earth, water, fire, air, space). Without the senses and the body there could be no engagement of the world. Without engagement, there can be no experience, and without experience, there can be no liberation. Without the story told by the mind and enacted by the body through the senses, there could be no reflection, no suffering, no spiritual journey. Rāma, at the very beginning of the *Yogavāshiṣh-ha*, balks at being asked to venture forth from safety to defend the homeland of sages. Vasiṣ-ha's advice points out to Rāma that one cannot avoid the unavoidable, but one can engage the world from a place of wisdom. Vasiṣ-ha, having encountered the Goddess, having seen the process of world creation emanate from his own body, having followed a great sage from space back into the world of subject and object, encourages Rāma to take up his duty. Knowing the world gives one power over the world; without the loss of innocence, there can be no knowledge, no liberation.

Vasiṣ-ha writes poetically about the beauties of nature. From nature he learns firsthand of immediacy and evanescence. He also learns intimacy through his successive encounters with the elements and the senses. One truth remains constant through the lessons taught in the *Yogavāshiṣh-ha*: once we learn of the ways of nature, we are confined only by our freedom to pay honor to her, to configure and reconfigure our lives as cultivators and agents of renewal. Like Vasiṣ-ha and Rāma, we must return.

Part Two: Sorrow, Birth and Rebirth

The *Upaśama Prakaraṇa*, the fifth book of the *Yogavāshiṣh-ha*, consists of instructions and examples given to Rāma by Vasiṣ-ha on how to pacify his mind, establish himself in a state of yogic equipoise, moving toward living liberation (*jīvanmukti*). It provides stories that illustrate how one can effectively dissolve attachment to the world through reasoned reflection and meditation.

As a mind-only text in the tradition of Yogācāra Buddhism, the *Yogavāshiṣh-ha* posits a pan-psychic world. The world utterly depends upon our construal of it as shaped by past influences (*vāsanā*). The movement from consciousness to the realm of the five senses and the five elements depends upon the structures of the mind. Psychic constructs shape and inform our interaction within the external world. The core message of the *Yogavāshiṣh-ha* entails clearly seeing this relationship. Recognizing the constructive power of the mind, one is urged to apply yogic techniques to reverse the outward flow of the mind, which habitually relies upon past conditioning and karmic accretions. This stabilization leads to the negation of compulsive entanglement with the external realm and establishes one in a state of equilibrium informed by an insight into the fleeting nature of reality. This insight into the experience of pure consciousness enlivens and empowers all things but allows one to remain unperturbed by them.

At the conclusion of the *Upaśama Prakaraṇa*, Vasiṣ-ha speaks of three 'virtues': knowledge of essential truths (*tattva-jñāna*), restraint of the mind (*mano-nāśa*), and abandonment of desires (*vāsanā-kṣaya*) (*YV*, V:92:14). Swami Venkatesananda translates these as "realization of truth, cessation of the mind, and the ending of conditioning" (*CYV*, 254). This triad reflects Vasiṣ-ha's insistence on the psychic nature of the troublesome aspects of the human condition. Humans suffer due to desire. Desire arises within the mind and habituates individuals toward particular actions. By understanding the connection between one's psychic state and one's relationship with the world, one gains insight into mental control and eventually is able to bring about transformation of the mind. Once committed to the practices of Yoga, one can reverse the influences of past desires, purify one's mind, and bring a lighter, enlightened approach to the world.

Puṇya and Pāvana

In one story from the *Upaśama Prakaraṇa*, two brothers face the death of their parents. A playful cascade of poetic narrative describes the process of reincarnation. It suggests that because all humans have once been animals, insects, and even trees, that we can feel empathy for each of these life forms. Through reflecting on these other existences, we can lessen our attachment to this particular precious human birth.

Puṇya, the older brother, has attained the state of liberation (*jīvanmukta*). Their father, a holy man named Dīrghatapā, dies. His wife and the mother of the boys, using yogic techniques, follows him in death. Pāvana, the younger brother, is inconsolable in his grief. Puṇya instructs him regarding the fleeting nature of the body and eventually frees his brother from his affliction, bringing him to liberation through tales of birth and rebirth. His teachings admonish Pāvana to remember his past births as a myriad of beings. By reflecting on the joys and pains of various past births, Puṇya prompts his brother to gain a new perspective on his current circumstance. Ultimately, this insight liberates Pāvana. The dialogue includes the following:

> You are a spiritual substance (*liṅga śarīra*)
> and have undergone many births.
> You have had many friends and properties in your past lives.
> Why not think of them also?
> You had many friends in the flowery plains
> where you had your pasture in your former form as a stag.
> Why not think of those deer,
> who were once your dear companions?
> Why do you not lament for your lost companions of swans,
> in the pleasant pools of lotuses, where you dove
> and swam in the form of a gander?
> Why not lament for your fellow trees in the woodlands,
> where you once stood as a stately tree among them?
> You had comrades of lions on the rugged crags of mountains.
> Why not lament for them also?
> You had many friends among the fishes
> in clean lakes adorned with lotuses.
> Why not lament your separation from them?
> You have been a monkey in the green woods of Dasārṇa.
> You have been a prince in the land of frost.
> You have been a raven in the woods of Puṇḍra.
> You have been an elephant in the land of Haihayas,
> a donkey in Trigarta, a dog in the country of Sālva,
> a bird in the wood of sāl trees.
> You have been a papal tree on the Vindhya Mountains,
> a wood insect in a large oak,
> a rooster on the Mandara Mountain,
> and then you were born as a Brahmin in one of its caverns.
> You were a Brahmin in Kosala, a partridge in Bengal,
> a horse in the land of snows,
> and a beast at the sacred grounds of Puskara.
> You have been an insect in the trunk of a palm tree,
> a gnat in a big tree, and a crane in the Puskara...
> Now you are my younger brother.

You had been an ant for six months,
laying within the thin bark of a bhugpetera tree
in a glen of the Himalayan foothills.
You are now born as my younger brother.
You were a millipede in a dung-hill at a distant village,
where you dwelt for a year and a half.
Now you are my younger brother.
You were once the baby of a hill tribe woman
and dwelt at her breast like a honey-sucking bee...
You are now my younger brother.
In this manner, you were born in many other shapes
and had to wander all about this continent for years.
You are now my younger brother.

(*YV*, V:20:8-22, adapted from Mitra)

Under the tutelage of his older brother, Pāvana achieves liberation through reflecting on the many past lives that he has experienced. By seeing his connections with past embodiments, Pāvana gains the dispassion needed to heal his grief and engage the world through a state of equanimity. According to Vasiṣ-ha, the two brothers lived for many years in the forest, perfect in their spiritual knowledge (*jñānavijñānaparagau*). Through moving himself away from self-concern, Pāvana becomes free to act again within the world without depression or fear, important lessons for the young Rāma.

Toward the end of the *Upaśama Prakaraṇa*, Vasiṣ-ha explains to Rāma that, on the one hand, his true self has no association with anything at all. On the other hand, it can be proclaimed:

I am the space. I am the sun.
I am the directions, above and below.
I am the gods. I am the demons. I am all beings.
I am darkness. I am the earth, the oceans,
the dust, the wind the fire, and all this world.
I am omnipresent. How can there be anything other than me?

(*YV*, V:73; *Vasiṣ-ha's Yoga,* p. 295)

This theology combines a rejection and embrace of the world. Everything is suffused with soul. The very desires and manifestations and objects that cause attachment and pain cannot be separated from the consciousness that pervades them. Hence, the world itself, with the myriad experiences it provides, becomes an occasion for spiritual insight.

At the end of the *Upaśama Prakaraṇa*, Vasiṣ-ha tells the story of Vītahavya as an example of a Yogin who conquered all desires and attained a state of liberation:

Repeating aloud the sacred syllable Om,
the sage obtained internal peace,
having gotten rid of thoughts
and become free of desires...
He drew his mind inward,
away from internal and external organs,
as also from gross and fine feeling
and the sensibilities of his heart and body.
He dismissed all things of the three worlds
and converted all his desires to indifference...
His mind was like the clear firmament...
and his heart was bright,
without the light of the sun, moon, or stars.
His intellect was unclouded
by the fumes, dust, and clouds of ignorance.
His soul was as clear as the autumnal sky.
Then, raising his voice from the ventricle
to the top-most part of his cranium,
his mind transcended the region of the sensations...
He then beheld a flood of light in himself.
Having attained to that state of ineffable light,
he found his mental urges burnt down quickly...
This sage stopped the course of his thought,
as a current of wind stops its motion...
He was joyous in his joylessness
(*nirānando'pi sānanda*),

existing in nonexistence
(*saccāsaccapi*).
He became that transparent substance,
which is pure and purifying,
which is all pervasive, yet without body.
(*YV*, V:87:1-17, Mitra)

The text goes on to state that he became the emptiness of the Mādhyamika Buddhists, the Brahman lauded by Vedāntins, the knowledge of the *Jñāna-Yogis*, the *Puruṣa* of the Sāṃkhya philosophers, the *Īśvara* of the Yogins, and the Śiva of the Śaivites.

It could be argued that having attained this state of rarefied spirituality there would be no incentive to stir from that bliss to exhibit any concern about the affairs of the world. However, Vasiṣ-ha states that Vītahavya entered into a state with form (*svarūpa*) through which he manifested friendliness and other such qualities (*maitrādayo guṇaḥ*). The term *svarūpa* refers in the *Yoga Sūtra* to the state that the mind attains after having achieved the cessation (*nirodha*) of thought and desire (*Yoga Sūtra*, I:3, 43; II:23, 54; III:3, 44, 47; IV:12, 34). Friendliness (*maitri*) is the first of the Brahma Vihāras, the four 'immeasurables' of Buddhism that indicate the enlightened view and the modalities through which the awakened Yogin operates within the world: friendliness toward those who experience pleasure, compassion for those who suffer, happiness toward the virtuous, and equanimity toward the vicious (*Yoga Sūtra*, I:33). Though the sage is "freed form the pains of repeated births," he nonetheless "has best wishes for all living beings" (*YV*, V:90:18). His "joy shines forth like the light of the moon" (*YV*, V:90:20). In terms of the *Yoga Sūtra*, he would enter into the state of *dharma megha samādhi*, wherein, according to Patañjali, there would be no impure actions (*Yoga Sūtra*, IV: 29-30).

The compassionate aspect of Vītahavya's accomplishment can be seen in the gratefulness expressed by him toward his former state of adversity. He proclaims that his entry into the path (*mārga*) was prompted due to his suffering (*duḥkha*) and he thanks and blesses his former difficulty. He even asks forgiveness of his desires and avarice now that he has attained a state of non-attachments (*vairāgyam*) (*YV*, V:86:39).

Conclusion

The *Yogavāshiṣh-ha* displays Vasiṣ-ha's vast knowledge of Indian thought and mythology, from the Upaniṣads to the Purāṇas. Vasiṣ-ha espouses a view that sees God in all things and all things as not different from God. He teaches Rāma that an enlightened awareness will allow him to move through the world without being affected by its allure or its disappointments. The following verse encapsulates this message, translated first by Vihari Lal Mitra, and then by Swami Venkatesananda:

> Though the spiritual man is engaged in worldly affairs
> and is subject to *rāga* and *dveṣa*,
> yet he is unstained by them in his heart,
> as the lotus bud is unsullied by water.
>
> (*YV*, 64:8, Mitra)

> Even if you engage yourself in the activities relating to your daily life
> and even if likes and dislikes arise in you,
> your inner being will never become impure.
>
> (*Vasiṣ-ha's Yoga*, p. 286)

The psychology of the *Yogavāshiṣh-ha* assesses the human condition in terms of karmic conditioning. If one is subject to karmic residues and attachments, then one will inevitably experience discomfort and suffering (*duḥkha*). If one takes the time to examine the root causes of desire and applies the effort (*pauruṣa/yatna*) to purify oneself through reflection, breathing, and meditation, then one can overcome attachment and attain the state of living liberation while in the body (*sadeha jīvanmukta*). Vasiṣ-ha argues for the re-engagement of the world after having undergone the purification process.

Due to its emphasis on the importance of action, *Yogavāshiṣh-ha* holds a deep ethical message with profound implications for environmental thought and action. The ultimate good entails the cessation of desire and the temporary withdrawal from an unthinking, unreflective involvement in worldly affairs. For Vasiṣ-ha, it also requires taking up the tasks of the world following this transformative experience.

Indian traditions have often been criticized, particularly by Christian missionaries, for their over-emphasis on other-worldliness. David Haberman, citing the *Maharaj Libel Case* in Bombay Court, 1862, has noted that the opinion of Oriental scholar and Christian missionary John Wilson was used to define "legitimate forms of Hinduism as...ancient, ascetic, individualistic, transcendent, world-denying...[with] the singular goal of *mokṣa.*"[11] The *Yogavāshiṣh-ha* conforms to this notion that the world must be transcended. However, in contrast to the characterization that religion in India requires rejection of the world, it also emphasizes that one must return and embrace the world. The ultimate good entails cessation and action.

The ethic of the *Yogavāshiṣh-ha* requires a refined, purified psychological state, carefully cultivated through effort (*yatna*) and creativity (*pauruṣa*). This process eschews reliance on past cultural norms, though one might and probably will embody those same cultural norms after returning from the transformative experience. By clearing one's psyche and body of the cobwebs of the past, one attains a clarity that brings one a place of immediate sensory perception. Without expectation of the future or reliance on the past, the liberated person is able to act freely and set an example for others.

Many ethical systems, in India and elsewhere, present a fixed code of expected behaviors or commandments. Yoga and Jainism set forth five rules to be followed: abstention from violence, lying, stealing, sexual misadventures, and hording. Buddhism abides by the same set, but substitutes abstention from intoxicants for not hording. The *Yogavāshiṣh-ha* propounds a method for purifying action that focuses on one's attitude rather than fixed behaviors.

By first erasing one's attachment to the world through meditation and reflective realization, one is then able to re-enter and reconstruct the world from a fresh perspective.

Environmental ethics requires knowledge of and engagement with the world of nature. The field biologist carefully observes and gains intimacy with her or his chosen object of study, whether a particular plant such as pickleweed within a salt marsh or a miniature red fox on California's Channel Islands. The scientific process of observation may be seen as kin to the *pañca mahābhūta dhāraṇā*, the sustained observance of the five great elements, with similar results. Just as Vasistha saw the myriad connections between earth, water, fire, and air and was drawn into a state of elation, so also the research scientist comes to recognize a plethora of connections, seeing that plant life, insect life, reptiles, mammals and more live in a web of mutual dependence. From this realization arises an ethic of care, a sense that one must act responsibly for the whole rather than seeing all nature as merely instrumental for human comfort. Becoming larger than ourselves, making the move from anthropocentrism to anthropocosm, from self-centered concern to an embrace of the largest of the large, the universe itself: such is the calling of meditation, a meditation that connects the individual through elevated consciousness with the cosmos.

NOTES

1. *Pṛthivi Sukta,* verses 4, 5,11, 16. O.P. Dwivedi, translator.
2. *Mārkaṇḍeya Purāṇa*. T. Eden Pargiter, translator (Reprint Delhi: Indological Book House, 1969), p. 200.
3. F. Eden Pargiter, *The Mārkaṇḍeya Purāṇa,* translated with Notes (Calcutta: The Asiatic Society of Bengal, 1904), p. 200.
4. This is the title of the story given in the translation by Swami Venkatsananda. This segment is referred to with various chapter titles in Ravi Prakash Arya's editing of Vihari Lal Mitra's 1890s translation, starting with "Description of the Last Night of Death or General Doom" [VII:81] and ending with "Description of the Current Air, as the Universal Spirit" [VII:92].
5. Sam Mickey, "Contributions to Anthropocosmic Environmental Ethics", *Worldviews: Global Religions, Culture, and Ecology,* XI:2, 2007.

6. *Sāṃkhya Kārikā*, verses 21, 56-62; *Yoga Sūtra*, II:20-22.
7. *Vasiṣ-ha's Yoga*, 588, VII:96.
8. The translations that follow are by Christopher Key Chapple, with assistance from various students including Jodi Shaw, Wynanda Jacobi, Viresh Hughes, Benjamin Zenk, Daniel Levine, and Randall Kraus.
9. *Yoga Sūtra*, III:1-3.
10. *Vasiṣ-ha's Yoga*, 582-583, VII:92.
11. David L. Haberman, *River of Love in an Age of Pollution: The Yamuna River in Northern India* (Berkeley: University of California Press, 2006), p. 28.

□

7

"Animals are Persons Too": Ancient Indian Narratives and the Contemporary Question of Animal Compassion

—Veena R. Howard

> The greatness of a nation and its moral progress can be measured by the way its animals are treated.
>
> *—M.K. Gandhi*

> ...[T]hose who advocate the moral right of non-human things, and seek a philosophical basis for such rights, do so by identifying what human beings, as archetypal persons, hold in common with other objects of concern. In the case of non-human animals, the important questions are whether they are sentient, can suffer pain, have the capacity for emotional experience.
>
> *—Kay Milton*[1]

On April 23, 2014, the *New York Times* published an article and posted a YouTube video entitled "Animals are Persons Too," which focuses on lawyer Steven Wise's unprecedented lawsuit for animal protection in New York's appellate court. Authors Chris Hegedus and D.A. Pennebaker stated that Wise, who was influenced by philosopher Peter Singer's book *Animal Liberation*

(1975), "showed the world how...an animal can transition from a thing without rights to a person with legal protections." The authors went on to say that, "in many ways, the lawsuits have already been won: They have brought animal personhood to the forefront of the conversation surrounding our society's relationship with animals."[2]

Each year many conferences, colloquia, and collegial blogs focus on the 'animal question' in fields such as ethics, bioethics, ecology, literature, and philosophy. Wise's lawsuit takes the debate of animal rights to a new stage, not just talking about animal rights but instead seeking to secure those rights legally. During the last several decades, philosophers have considered the moral questions regarding the rights and equality of non-human animals and human responsibility toward them. More recently, in the ever-expanding field of animal studies, scholars and ethologists have engaged with questions that traditionally concerned only human animals. For example, "Do animals have agency?", "Can animals experience emotions?" and even more intriguing, "Can animals be moral agents?" Animal behaviorists seek answers through empirical evidence and philosophers through logical inference.

Peter Singer, the leading animal ethicist, argues the case of animal equality by drawing attention to the reality of 'speciesism', which is defined as "prejudice or discrimination based on species, especially against animals."[3] This nomenclature is often used by advocates of non-human animal rights who argue that speciesism is a prejudice similar to racism and sexism.[4] Singer points to Hindu and Buddhist thought for compassionate treatment of animals: "Concern for animal suffering can be found in Hindu thought, and the Buddhist idea of compassion is a universal one, extending to animals as well as humans, but our Western traditions are very different. Our intellectual roots lie in Ancient Greece and in the Judeo-Christian tradition. Neither is kind to those not of our species."[5] Because animals are unable to communicate their suffering, it is important that humans show concern for their pain and well-being. Singer argues that, "We should not discount their [animals'] interests in not suffering because they cannot talk or because they are incapable of reasoning; and we should not discount their interests in enjoying life...."[6] I suggest that Hindu and Buddhist narratives provide voices to animals in order to provide humans a glimpse into the animal mind and invoke compassion toward them.

Concerned with the world's ecological predicament and humanity's ethical responsibilities, leaders and scholars of religions have joined the environmental conversation, wrestling with religion's role in confronting the exploitation of the environment, which includes non-human animals. This is not surprising: since the nascence of structured religion, the subject of animal treatment—ranging from rules for animal sacrifice and dietary laws, to systems against animal exploitation—has been addressed in the ethical discourse of religious literature. Kimberley Patton remarks, "Religious traditions contain extremely long and rich and ancient commentaries on the topic of animals. They are very interested in animals as existential beings."[7] Patton goes on to observe that engagement with the question of animals in ancient religious commentaries can guide our present-day discourse on animal welfare. However, this paper expands on this perspective by uncovering how religious narratives of various traditions in India (in the context of this paper, Hinduism) are not only "interested in animals as existential beings," as Patton puts it, but also, through various narrative tropes, challenge the human/animal binary—a binary that has been at the heart of animal exploitation for centuries.

I specifically call attention to the animal narratives found in Hindu-sacred literature such as the *Rāmāyaṇa* and the *Mahābhārata*, in which the portrayal of animals and the relationship between nature and humans take a form that invokes ethical questions regarding the treatment of animals. The many narratives of the *Mahābhārata* argue not merely for the sameness of all beings, nor for 'speciesism', but instead set up a more complex framework that allows the reader to experience a world in which animals, humans, and gods co-exist and often share their existence on equal footing, even to the point of interchanging their bodies through disguises. Readers of the *Mahābhārata* cannot help but be struck by the ubiquitous stories of animal transformations.

The narratives that explore these shared concerns can be an important supplement to present-day discussions of animal rights. The strategies used in these narratives disorient readers/listeners by transporting them into a world in which the chasm between non-human and human animals begins to disappear; thus these are strategies that have the potential to create an ethical framework for coexisting with animals beyond the hubris of speciesism. To this end, I analyze narratives from the *Mahābhārata,* including both humans disguising as animals and animals as agents advocating their own protection. These animals are presented as the advocates for the protection of nature and present an ideal of compassion that arises from Indian philosophical and ethical foundations. The stories invoke the precepts of *dharma* (one's sacred duty or nature) and the law of *karma* (consequence of one's actions) from the animals' vantage point to communicate the ethics of responsibility towards all living beings.

Among the most didactic of these tales are the stories of Pāṇḍu's curse by a wounded deer who in fact was an ascetic (Book 1) and King Śibi's test by Hawk and the Dove, who were Indra and Agni in disguise (Book 3). These narratives are exemplary and demonstrate the *Mahābhārata's* approach to human's engagement with animals. Specifically, they bring into focus the emotional lives of animals, the intrinsic value of animals, and the way the text seeks to evoke compassion toward animals in the hearts of readers/listeners. This model can serve as a tool for constructing a psychological mindset of compassion toward animals for the modern world, as has been explored in modern theories of eco-psychology, a discipline that seeks to explore the human's bonds with nature.

In Book 1 of the *Mahābhārata,* a Brāhmin disguised as a deer curses the hunting King Pāṇḍu for interrupting his *kāma* (love-making).[8] Upon being interrupted, the deer cries out:

> King....But out of kindness you should have waited until I was done mating! For what man of sense would kill a buck that is

> mating in the woods, at a time beneficent to all creatures and wanted by all creatures? Needlessly to frustrate a cherished goal of man [*purusśārtha*] was not worthy of you.... This cruel act is decried by all the worlds: it is ungodly, utterly against the Law. You know the niceties of the pleasure of women. I mated with a doe because I shy away from humans, and as a deer I live with deer in the depths of the forest.... You killed me in the body of a deer when I was overcome by love. (1.109.20)

The deer curses Pāṇḍu: "When you are lying with a woman you love, blinded by your passion, you too in that very same state will depart for the world of the dead" (1.109.27)—a serious karmic consequence. Indeed Pāṇḍu suffers the consequence of his action, and the epic of *Mahābhārata* takes a tragic turn because of King Pāṇḍu's demise.

As this example shows, the *Mahābhārata* employs narrative strategies that give voice to animals and shift physicality between beings, thus setting up a complex matrix that blurs the boundaries among humans, animals, and gods. More importantly, these narratives prompt a series of questions and concerns by demonstrating interspecies communication and shared existential concerns, and not simply through codified rules to be prescriptively followed. In other words, rather than prescribing rules about animal treatment, these stories show animals' concerns by providing them voices.

Animals' rights to basic needs are similarly raised in the parable of the Hawk and the Dove in Book 3, a story that can also be found in the Buddhist narratives. In this tale, the God Indra disguises himself as Hawk and the fire God Agni as Dove in order to test the righteous King Śibi, as the gods wanted to know if the king was equal to them. Hawk begins chasing Dove and Dove, trembling with fear, settles on the king's thighs for protection. Hawk invokes the moral law (*Dharma*) and demands that the king release Dove because it is Hawk's food. Hawk argues that his right to food is equivalent to a human's, saying:

> Great Lord, it is through food that all creatures find their being, by food that they thrive, by food that they live.... If I am deprived of my portion...my spirits will desert my body and go the way of no return. When I predecease them, Law-spirited Kind, son and wife will perish: so by protecting this dove you will kill many lives (3.131.25).[9]

Hawk intelligibly argues for his right to eat Dove, and demonstrates a responsibility to family that is generally considered the purview of humans alone but that has been observed by some animal behaviorists among non-human animals. But the king defends his protection of the bird on the basis of the law requiring protection of one seeking refuge. King Śibi looks for an alternate way to placate Hawk, arguing, "then how do you think it right to abandon a refugee?... I shall have a steer, a board, a deer, or even a buffalo cooked for you, or whatever you want" (3.131.15), Hawk insists on his right to the dove: "Let that dove loose for me. Hawk eats doves; that is the everlasting rule" (3.131.18). Hawk thus presents the king with the dual *dharma* problem: on the one hand, protection of Hawk's right of access to his natural food and, on the other, the protection of the one who has taken refuge.

Understanding the complexity of *dharma*, the king seeks to appease Hawk: "You that are adored by the hosts of the birds, reign over the rich kingdom of the Śibis. Or I shall give you whatever you want, Hawk, but not this bird that has sought shelter in me! Tell me what should I do?" (3.131.20). Hawk agrees to relinquish his claim to the dove on one condition: "If you love the dove, over lord of kings, cut off a piece of flesh and weigh it against the dove. When your flesh balances the dove's, king, you will give it to me, and I shall be satisfied" (3.131 28).

The king happily agrees: "Your request I deem a favor," and cuts a piece of his flesh to be weighed against the dove. But he finds that the dove is heavier than the piece of flesh. The king cuts more of his flesh but is not able to balance the scale. The Dove is still heavier. Finally, exhausted by cutting pieces of his flesh, the king mounds his entire cut-up body onto the scale as an offering for the protection of the Dove (3.131.20-25). Hawk, pleased with King Śibi's commitment, shows his true form of God Indra and discloses his intention of testing the king. "I am Indra, Law-knowing King, and this Dove is the sacrifice carrying fire. We came here to you in your offering grove to test you in the Law (*Dharma*). This shall be your shining glory, to master the worlds, lord of the people, that you cut the flesh from your limbs!" (3.131.30). This story can be interpreted as the display of "macho Kshatriya virtue and a badge of ascetic conquest of the body," as Wendy Doniger proposes.[10] However, I see a story not about the 'machismo' of King Śibi, but rather a metaphor designed to convey ethical meanings regarding the intrinsic value of animals and questioning speciesism.

The tale judges the issue of ethics on the basis of the value of all life. It presents the subtlety of *dharma* ethics and challenges humans with the responsibility of having equal ethical obligations toward other living beings. The story presents a shocking proposition: there is no equivalence to the body of the dove other than the whole body of the king. If we are to see the symbolic meaning of scales as justice, then it poses a serious moral question: Is a dove's life equal to a king's? Through its use of gods in animal disguises, the text creates an understanding of the following ethical issues: an awareness of animals' equal rights to the basic needs of food, shelter, and individual biology; the human responsibility to protect animals, even ones that do not hold non-violence as virtue and are simply bound by their instincts; and an unexpectedly equal value placed on the life of a dove and the life of the righteous king—a model contrary to speciesism, which modern animal activists and scholars have just begun to challenge. By virtue of his commitment to justice and protection of a helpless being, King Śibi passes the test and proves that he is equal to the gods, as to be god-like is to embrace the equality of all beings.

This tale presents a moral challenge by equating a human life to a dove's life. In doing so, it invites the reader to consider the difficult moral decisions by challenging the hubris of humans. Indeed, these narratives illustrate animals having emotional lives that modern scholars studying animal behaviors have begun to explore. For example, Jeffrey Masson, who analyzes the emotional lives of animals, draws upon folk tales to show that "animals have the potential to connect emotionally with humans."[11] However, humans may need to imagine 'personhood' in order to connect with non-human animals. Henry Salt, an early advocate of animal rights, emphasizes the need for 'sensibility and sympathy'. He argues, "The cruel man is cruel because he cannot put himself in the place of those who suffer, cannot feel with them and imagine the misfortunes from which he is himself exempt. The cure for cruelty is therefore to induce men to cultivate a sympathetic imagination."[12] The narratives of the *Mahābhārata* do precisely this—use various devices to connect humans with animals in order to create sensibility and sympathy toward animals. However, by appearing in a major religious text and piece of epic literature, they are not merely fables; rather, they claim the 'intrinsic value' of animals by asserting their distinctive agency.[13]

These stories present counter-voices pleading for equality and justice in response to those crowing for the domination of animals by humans. Mark Rowland underscores that "[t]here is a game that is played when animals are discussed in a philosophical or scientific context. The game is: don't give them anything more than you absolutely have to. Cognitive abilities—assume only the bare minimum required to explain their behavior.... Above all else: don't get attached to them."[14] Yet the *Mahābhārata* narratives overturn this construction. Was this unique approach to animals motivated by a desire to alter the natural dominating human behavior toward animals? Might this model serve as a tool for constructing a psychological mindset of compassion toward animals for the modern world?

Notably, the stories recounted above do not claim a universal ethic of non-violence but rather raise moral questions of justice and equality with respect to animal ethics. These tales do not present lessons that are easily learned, but they do offer a glimpse of the highest form of ethics based on compassion and embodied by particularly righteous beings such as King Śibi.[15] In the *Mahābhārata*, the stories of animals as ethical agents and their representative voices present complex *Dharma* lessons that can aid in developing a fresh and environmentally sound mindset. The *Mahābhārata* insists readers realize the human responsibility toward non-human animals and to all living beings.

The sacred Hindu epic of the *Mahābhārata* presents a framework with which eco-critics, eco-psychologists, and eco-philosophers may investigate questions regarding the relationship between the humans and the natural world. Jeffery Masson asserts: "When animals are no longer colonized and appropriated by us, we can reach out to our evolutionary cousins. Perhaps then the ancient hope for a deeper emotional connection across the species barrier, for closeness and participation in a realm of feelings now beyond our imagination, will be realized."[16] What Masson hopes for, the *Mahābhārata* models through its paradoxical and surprising stories of animals appealing to human emotions and sensibilities.

NOTES

1. Kay Milton, *Loving Nature: Towards an Ecology of Emotion* (New York: Routledge, 2002), 28.
2. Chris Hegedus and D.A. Pennebaker, "Animals Are Persons Too" (*The New York Times*: N.p., 23, April 2014). The lawsuit was filed on behalf of species of great apes, elephants, and cetaceans (dolphins and whales) on the basis of their cognitive abilities.
3. Peter Singer (2009) uses this term "to make a parallel with other 'isms' that we are familiar with, particularly racism and sexism" (572). Singer uses the term to draw attention to the sometimes arbitrary distinctions we draw between the animal and human worlds, distinctions which he considers analogous to racial and sexual distinctions.
4. 'Speciesism': "prejudice or discrimination based on species; *especially*: discrimination against animals," Merriam-Webster.
5. Peter Singer (1985), 1.
6. Ibid. (2009), 575.
7. Quoted in Lisa Kemmerer, *Animals and World Religions* (Oxford: Oxford University Press, 2012), 4.
8. Ibid. (Vol. 1, 1973).
9. Ibid. (Vol. 1, 1975).

10. Wendy Doniger, *The Hindus: An Alternative History* (New York: The Penguin Press, 2009), 273.
11. Jeffrey Masson, *When Elephants Weep: The Emotional Lives of Animals* (New York: Bantam Doubleday Dell Publishing Group, Inc., 1996), 233.
12. Henry Salt, *Humanitarianism: Its General Principles and Progress*, 18.
13. Psychoanalyst Sudhir Kakar observes the significance of the medium of story for the purpose of conveying essential messages: "The spell of the story has always exercised a special potency in the oral-based Indian tradition and Indians have characteristically sought expression of central and collective meanings through narrative design." Sudhir Kakar, *Intimate Relations* (Chicago: University of Chicago Press, 1990), 1.
14. Mark Rowlands, *Can Animals be Moral?* (New York: Oxford University Press, 2012), x.
15. Mahatma Gandhi, who was deeply influenced by stories such as these, presents an example of the embodiment of this mindset in the modern world. He notes the view of those who commit themselves to not harming animals: "Man's supremacy over animals meant not that the former should prey upon the latter, but that the higher should protect the lower, and that there should be natural aid between the two as between man and man" (Welch, 246). In 1920, Gandhi also wrote in *Navjivan* on the Hindu attitude which might be a result of such stories, stating: "A good many snakes sting and kill animals and human beings, but the Hindus not only abstain from killing them, they actually consider it a sin to kill them." (http://www.internationalpeaceandconflict.org/profiles/blogs/mahatma-gandhi-and-goddess-kali#.VeKCr7xViko, accessed, August 29, 2015.)
16. Masson, 236.

REFERENCES

Doniger, Wendy. *The Hindus: An Alternative History*. New York: The Penguin Press, 2009.

Hegedus, Chris and D.A. Pennebaker. "Animals Are Persons Too." *The New York Times*: N.p., 23 April 2014. Web. 29 Aug 2015. <http://www.nytimes.com/video/opinion/100000002839672/animals-are-persons-too.html>.

Kemmerer, Lisa. *Animals and World Religions*. Oxford: Oxford University Press, 2012.

Masson, Jeffrey. *When Elephants Weep: The Emotional Lives of Animals*. New York: Bantam Doubleday Dell Publishing Group, Inc, 1996.

Milton, Kay. *Loving Nature: Towards an Ecology of Emotion*. New York: Routledge, 2002.

Rowlands, Mark. *Can Animals Be Moral?*. New York: Oxford University Press, 2012.

Salt, Henry. *Humanitarianism: Its General Principles and Progress.* 1891. *Humanitarismo*: N.p., 16 Feb 2011. Web. 16 Feb 2015. <https://humanitarismo.wordpress.com/2011/02/16/humanitarianism-its-general-principles-and-progress-h-s-salt-londres-1891>.

Singer, Peter. "Speciesism and Moral Status." *Metaphilosophy*, 40.34 (2009): 567-81. Web. 10 Aug 2015. <http://www.oswego.edu/~delancey/Singer.pdf>.

—.Ethics and the New Animal Liberation Movement (ed.) *In Defense of Animals*. New York: Basil Blackwell (1985), 1-10. Accessed August 2015. <http://www.animal-rights-library.com/texts-m/singer01.htm>.

'Speciesism'. *Merriam-Webster.com*. Merriam-Webster, n.d. Web. 29 Aug 2015. <http://www.merriam-webster.com/dictionary/speciesism>.

Kakar, Sudhir. *Intimate Relations: Exploring Indian Sexuality*. Chicago: University of Chicago Press, 1990.

van Buitenen, J.A.B. (Trans.). *The Mahābhārata* (Vol. 1). Chicago: University of Chicago Press, 1973.

—.*The Mahābhārata* (Vol. 2). Chicago: University of Chicago Press, 1975.

Welch, Jerry. *The Encyclopedia of Your Observations*. Bloomington, IN: Trafford Publishing, 2015.

□

PART III

Compassion from the Perspective of Dharma Traditions

8

Creating Enlightened Society: Compassion in the Shambhala Tradition

—Judith Simmer-Brown

It is wonderful for Naropa faculty members like myself to join with the experts of the Uberoi Foundation to celebrate the fortieth anniversary of Naropa University around the theme of compassion. Naropa's Founder, Chögyam Trungpa Rinpoche, wished to create a university that would be of benefit to its faculty, staff and students certainly, but especially to the world. He wished to draw out the natural compassion of Naropa's students and empower them to "see the world as it is and change it for the better," as the Mission Statement expresses. You might say we are in the compassion business. Our graduate and undergraduate programs teach mindfulness-awareness meditation and compassion practices, and prepare students for compassionate vocations in a variety of fields. Our alumni serve as therapists and activists, teachers and chaplains, mediators and social workers in a variety of settings. Our artists, translators, and poets enrich culture with their compassionate expressions of the beauty of human life.

Buddhism has always been associated with compassion. The Buddha said that he instructed his monastics to go forth and teach "for the good of the many, for the happiness of the many, out of compassion for the world, for the welfare, the good and the happiness of gods and humans."[2] Compassion teachings pervade all Buddhist lineages, and they are among the most compelling practices currently being pursued by Western practitioners. From *mettā* or loving kindness practices to the *brahmāvihāras, tonglen* and contemporary self-compassion practices, Buddhism has introduced profound and pragmatic ways for practitioners to actually become more caring and responsive to themselves and others. As the Dalai Lama famously said, "We can reject everything else: religion, ideology, all received wisdom. But we cannot escape the necessity of love and compassion.... This, then, is my true religion, my simple faith."[3]

While there are many sources on compassion in Buddhism, and some excellent papers in this important conference, very little has been written about the founding tradition of Naropa University, and the very special teachings of Naropa's founder. The tradition of Shambhala "is rooted in the contemplative teachings of Buddhism, yet is a fresh expression of the spiritual journey of our time. It teaches how to live in a secular world with courage and compassion" according to the Shambhala International website.[4] This paper will address Shambhala's unique and visionary teachings on compassion and creating enlightened society.

Shambhala History and Lineage

> While it is easy enough to dismiss the kingdom of Shambhala as pure fiction, it is also possible to see in this legend the expression of a deeply rooted and very real human desire for a good and fulfilling life.
>
> —*Chogyam Trungpa*[5]

Tibetan Buddhism has always promoted powerful methods of personal transformation focused on transmuting the habitual energy of aggression, attachment and bewilderment into compassion and wisdom. These methods begin with individual commitment to unmask the egocentric preoccupation that has, from beginningless time, caused such harm to others as well as oneself. With the realization that all beings, like ourselves, have the simple yearning to be happy and to avoid suffering, it is difficult to ignore the cries of the world. In the tradition of the *bodhisattva*, the compassionate meditations have served as the core of personal and societal transformation. In Tibet, these meditations serve as reminders that we can individually place the needs of others before our own needs, sparking the 'turning of the tide' of egocentric concerns. These are at the core of Tibet's treasury of compassion practices.

However, in contemporary society many agree that the factors that contribute to a degradation of dignity of human life are systemic, environmental and complex, rendering merely individual efforts insufficient to the task. For this reason, the Tibetan Buddhist teacher Ven. Chögyam Trungpa, Rinpoche (1939-87) brought the transmissions of another important but less known Tibetan tradition to his communities in the United States, Canada, and Europe. This is the tradition of Shambhala that is named for the legendary enlightened kingdom, beloved in Tibet right into contemporary times. Through centuries of interaction with Buddhism, Shambhala became an esoteric transmission regarding the cultivation of 'enlightened society', universal in scope, compassionate in intention, and peaceful in methods. Shambhala teachings blend influences from three primary sources: the Kālacakra-tantra tradition from 11th century India, Tibetan lore from the Gesar epic, and the Dzogchen tradition of the Nyingma.[6]

The Kālacakra-tantra teachings were given by the Buddha in the last year of his life to the king of Shambhala at Dhānyaka-aka, in southern India in the place known as Amrāvati. Shambhala, literally "the place where tranquility is certain," was a kingdom hidden north of the Himālayas in Inner Asia, "north of the River Sīta."[7] King Sucandra (Dawa Sangpo in Tibetan) requested teachings from the Buddha that would allow him to reverse the traditional trajectory of renunciation, leaving home and responsibilities in order to pursue the path of *dharma* as a mendicant monk. He asked instead for teachings that would empower him to rule his kingdom in an enlightened manner, bringing wisdom and compassion together with strong leadership in order to directly benefit his subjects and his entire kingdom. He envisioned a completely enlightened society in which the citizens value the simplicity and beauty of human culture and harmonious community. The Buddha taught the king what has been considered the most subtle, sophisticated, and advanced *dharma* teachings in the world based on the Vajrayāna tradition of tantra.[8]

A second stream of influence with the Shambhala teachings comes from the indigenous Tibetan tradition of Gesar, the legendary warrior king who battled enemy forces in order to create a peaceful and harmonious society. The legend of Gesar is the last undiscovered epic in world literature, the first volume of which has recently been translated.[9] Gesar operated under the spiritual mandate of Padmasambhava to lead his kingdom against corrupting and divisive forces in order to create an enlightened society. Beloved by the Tibetan people, Gesar is considered a magical being whose inconceivable skill established the foundations of Tibet's sacred culture. While his battles are described conventionally, the subtext of the epic points to shamanic mastery of natural and human elements that make his leadership powerful. For example, Gesar's enemies are former tantric yogis whose arrogant misuse of the practice turned them against the *dharma* itself. Defeating them brings integrity and authenticity back to Tibet's sacred practices while restoring the yogis to their *dharma* commitments.

In modern times, the Gesar epic has been deeply influenced by Chinese culture from the Yuan emperors, bringing elements of Confucian political philosophy into Tibetan culture.[10] When Chögyam Trungpa taught about enlightened society, he drew from post-antiquity Sino-Tibetan notions of the philosopher-king who blended Tibetan indigenous and Indian Buddhist elements together with Chinese medicine and astrology.[11] From his perspective, these teachings have tremendous relevance in the contemporary West where respectful, visionary leadership is so rare and the need is so dire.

Thirdly, the Shambhala teachings are also closely associated with the Mahā-ati or Dzogchen lineages of Tibet. Dzogchen, or the 'great perfection', is considered the highest, most ancient and direct teachings of Buddhism, closely related to the pre-Buddhist, indigenous traditions of Tibet. The Great Perfection is not an outward goal to which we strive, but the fundamental perfection that is already present in the mind-stream of beings, the completeness and goodness in the very nature of life. It cannot be perfected, because it is already inherently present, like the vast purity of the sky in which clouds may suddenly appear. The clouds cannot impede the sky or change its vastness, clarity, or accommodation. The focus of Dzogchen meditation practice is simply to realize that inherent purity and perfection of the basic nature. The great 20th century Dzogchen master, H.H. Dilgo Khyentse Rinpoche wrote: "The practice is simply to realise the radiance, the natural expression of wisdom, which is beyond all intellectual concepts."[12]

The tantric teachings of Dzogchen come from two Buddhist sources: the long transmission (*ka-ma*) of teachings traced back to the great masters of India, found in some of the essential tantras of the Nyingma lineage; and the short transmissions of treasure teachings (*terma*) hidden by the great adept Padmasambhava and his consort, Yeshe Tsogyal, to be revealed at auspicious moments throughout history.[13] *Terma* teachings are especially potent for practitioners in the Nyingma lineages, for the blessings are fresh and undiluted and the message addresses particular circumstances and contexts in a particularly relevant way. In the Dzogchen lineage, certain realized teachers who have special qualities can discover the hidden treasure teachings through visionary means. They are called *tertöns*, or treasure discoverers; often it is their spiritual heirs who propagate the *terma* teachings, and these heirs are called *terdak*, or treasure propagators.

Chogyam Trungpa, Rinpoche, received Shambhala transmissions in both the long transmission, from his root guru Jamgon Kongtrul of Shechen; and as a *tertön*, through mind discovery in a series of visionary transmissions both in Tibet and the United States.[14] These teachings apply the ancient Kālacakra vision of enlightened society to the contemporary complexities of militarism, consumerism, and environmental degradation, as well as to the malaise and hopelessness that accompany them. He passed these teachings on to his *dharma* heir, Sakyong Mipham Rinpoche, his eldest son who is the propagator (*terdak*) of his father's treasure teachings. Together they have founded the Shambhala lineage.

The three main streams of influence on the Shambhala teachings weave together naturally in the culture of Kham and Golok regions in East Tibet. It was customary for monastic and lay culture in this region to weave together the Kālacakra, the post-antiquity Gesar epic, and Dzogchen practice and indigenous cultural elements into a single fabric of sacredness.[15] These streams became a living tradition under the influence of the great Jamgon Ju Mipham, the nineteenth century Rime (non-sectarian) master known for prodigious scholarship, instigation of Nyingma philosophical renaissance, and special connection with the Kālacakra-tantra and the Gesar epic. When he died in 1912, Mipham famously told his students he would not be conventionally incarnated, but would be reborn in Shambhala.[16] The current Shambhala lineage-holder, Sakyong Mipham Rinpoche, is his present emanation.

Trungpa Rinpoche had a particular passion and urgency about the transmission of the Shambhala vision and practices he had received. These were teachings of utmost relevance for this time, for they provided a spiritual path with a social vision that shored up visionary solutions for the depression and hopelessness of our time. Having fled a medieval and isolated Tibetan society overrun by militant Communist China, he was deeply affected by the forces of materialism that drive contemporary international values, and he devoted his final decade of teaching to ways to ameliorate the violence and greed he observed. Central to his Shambhala teachings were those of the importance of 'enlightened warriorship' based on gentleness and courage.

Warriorship in the Shambhala Lineage

A true warrior is never at war with the world.

—*Chogyam Trungpa, Rinpoche*

The Shambhala teachings are based on the warrior traditions of Asia, including cultures of India, China, Japan, and Tibet. While they reject the outward violence and unscrupulousness of the combat fighter, the Shambhala teachings embrace the discipline of the warriors' training and the bravery and confidence necessary to sustain the strength of constantly facing challenges. Trungpa Rinpoche wrote:

> Warriorship here does not refer to making war on others. Aggression is the source of our problems, not the solution. Here the word 'warrior' is taken from the Tibetan *pawo*, which literally means "one who is brave." Warriorship in this context is the tradition of human bravery, or the tradition of fearlessness.[17]

In this, the Shambhala teachings embrace the Tibetan folk hero Gesar, who exhibited bravery without aggression.

We live in an era where such bravery is necessary, for we are faced with daunting problems that can easily give rise to aggression or to hopelessness and depression. The forces of militarism, globalization, and environmental degradation have weakened the fabric of our human communities and have undermined the life-force (*sok*) of individuals, rendering them helpless against these forces. The path of the warrior requires that we not give up on humanity or the earth community. Instead, we raise our gaze to look carefully and reflectively at our communal human life and identify how we can be of help. The answer to the world's problems will come from within our everyday experience, not from ideologies, political philosophies, or economic theories.

It is always assumed in the Shambhala teachings that compassion is the motivation of the warrior, though the way compassion is spoken of differs somewhat from the Buddhist teachings alone. In this essay, we will explore the core teachings of the Shambhala teachings in order to trace the contours of its presentation.

It is important to understand something of cosmology and the Shambhala lineage for context. According to the Kālacakra-tantra, the future of humanity will be increasingly threatened by barbarians (*lalo* in Tibetan), harbingers of the decline in the quality of life and the increase in warfare, greed, and environmental destruction.[18] In the meantime, the teachings of Buddhism are guarded and protected by a lineage of seven enlightened kings (*dharmarājas*) and twenty-five bodhisattva kings (*kalki*, or *rigden*) who protect the Buddhist teachings and guard the dignity of humanity under duress.[19] Each of these kings was predicted to live one hundred years. Eventually, when the forces of the degenerate age advance and the world descends into intractable violence and greed, the twenty-fifth Kalki (Rigden) king will appear with his enlightened army to bring about a new Golden Age, restoring the peace, harmony, and humanity of the world.[20] Various predictions from the Kālacakra system suggest this will occur in the 25th century, though others suggest that the degenerate forces are accelerating this time sequence.

In the contemporary Shambhala teachings, the forces of degeneration are already apparent, rendering gentle warriorship a timely response. With the help of the Kālacakra-tantra and Shambhala teachings, trained warriors are not daunted by the degenerate age. Instead, they find power and clarity in the midst of chaos and see the basic goodness and humanity in every situation. They are resilient in the midst of challenge, contented in the maelstrom of greed, and peaceful in the face of aggression. Their tantric training shows them how to turn the distractions of the life of a householder into a good human society. Their enlightened army wields weapons of kindness, strength, and wisdom to invigorate the life-force of their communities and the world.

Basic Goodness

> The world is in constant turmoil because beings have not discovered their basic goodness.
>
> —*Sakyong Mipham Rinpoche*[21]

The secret teaching of Shambhala sounds simple, and it is. It is the teaching of basic goodness, *domine sangpo*.[22] Human beings are good. We are complete, unmistaken, and there is nothing we lack. No matter what happens to us, no matter what we do, our underlying motivations are based on human feeling, the human heart. Everything that arises—doubt, fear, irritation, boredom—is an expression of that goodness. This is called "the great cosmic secret" transmitted by King Sucandra to the subjects of Shambhala.

> The essence of all beings from beginningless time, this universal truth has always existed. It transcends the notions of good and bad; therefore it is primordial. It is beyond time and space; therefore it is inconceivable. It surpasses thought and non-thought; therefore it is remarkable.... This rare human gift is at our fingertips day or night, whether we are walking, sleeping, or talking. It constantly pulsates within our being, ever transmitting wakefulness that has never known doubt or fear.[23]

The teaching of basic goodness is not a tenet or article of faith; it is presented as a quality that must be experienced. The Kālacakra says, "The nature of the primordial cannot be expressed in words, but with the eyes of the master's teaching it will be seen."[24] We can speak of basic goodness as much as we like, but without a direct experience of it, there is little understanding.

The most direct way to experience basic goodness is through the sitting practice of meditation. We are taught by a lineage teacher to synchronize body and mind so that we can experience nowness, the present moment. This simple practice is an expression of accepting ourselves, our experience, and the world without judgment or bias. Then we can experience the goodness of our humanity.

According to the Shambhala teachings, the most daunting aspect of the degenerate age is the endemic sense of worthlessness and hopelessness that most people feel, no matter what cultural environment they may inhabit. We have given up on human nature and human society. While we may find exceptions in a few remarkable people, we feel that most humans, especially ourselves, are disappointing and inadequate. We are convinced that society especially is flawed. The 20th century confirmed our worst opinions about how humans behave in groups, and the 21st century is making strides to intensify that view.

These self-defeating views contribute to the dilemma of modern life. Our inner defeat leads to external disaster, and vice versa. The Shambhala warrior sees that the true antidote to the degenerate age is found in deep investigation of human nature through meditation. Then we see that the true nature of basic goodness is never distorted by circumstances, and that impurities are merely temporary ripples.

The Genuine Heart of Sadness

Sadness is precisely the heart of warriorship.

—*Chogyam Trungpa*[25]

When we sit in nowness, we discover a kind of nakedness in our experience where we just are. We are not doing, we are being. This does not mean we have no thoughts or emotions. It means that whatever is occurring in our minds happens against a backdrop of utter simplicity, openness, and immediacy. There is no exaggeration, and no minimizing. Everything is very straightforward.

This experience, however, is not merely a blank or vast empty sky. We discover this simplicity by tasting our own human heart, which is an experience of what is called the "genuine heart of sadness." We find ourselves with ourselves, with all the storylines and habits, all the misgivings and hopes, and we are just there. Fundamentally, there is nothing happening. Within the space of that moment, we feel a quality of tenderness, vulnerability, and unconditional sadness. It is a poignant moment in which we are most in touch with our genuine humanity.

The genuine heart of sadness comes from feeling your nonexistent heart is full. You would like to spill your heart's

> blood, give your heart to others. For the warrior, this experience of sad and tender heart is what gives birth to fearlessness.[26]

The sadness described here is distinctly different from depression; it is not sadness about anything in particular, and is a constant companion as a kind of subtle mood. It is a kind of tenderness that makes us more open to others, rather than wishing to withdraw into ourselves. The tenderness is about feeling our own experience, and being touched by the beauty of human life. It is always there, not dependent upon circumstances, and it is never tragic. "Whatever you do to try to forget that sadness—sadness will always be there. The more you try to enjoy yourself and the more you do enjoy, nonetheless there is still the constant sadness of being alone."[27]

The experience of the genuine heart of sadness has tremendous poignancy and joy as well. It is associated with aesthetic appreciation, being touched by the beauty and preciousness of human life. The samurai traditions of Japan place tremendous emphasis upon this kind of subtle and pervasive sad enjoyment. While appreciating the vividness of sense perceptions—of the placement of a stone in the garden, of the taste of bitter tea on the tongue—sadness about the transitory and vibrant beauty of the moment fills our empty hearts.[28] In this experience, we discover our humanity in a personal and intimate way.

The warrior practices joining sadness and delight together as a way to taste sadness rather than indulging in it. That is authentic tenderness, the experience of human goodness. As Trungpa Rinpoche wrote,

> You should feel that way with everything you do. Whether you have a good time or a bad time, you should feel sad and delighted at once.... Joining sadness and joy is the only mechanism that brings the vision of the Great Eastern Sun.[29]

The Great Eastern Sun is the full bloom of Shambhala vision of basic goodness and its manifestation as enlightened society.

Sadness and *Bodhicitta*: The Seed of Compassion

> The warrior's duty is to generate warmth and compassion for others.
>
> —*Chogyam Trungpa, Rinpoche*

The experience of the genuine heart of sadness is an aspect of what both the Buddhist and Shambhala teachings speak of as *bodhicitta,* the awakened heart or the supreme thought. *Bodhicitta* is the topic of many Indian Mahāyāna texts, from the Prajñāpāramitā-sūtras and Samòdhinirmocana-sūtra to the sìāstras of Sìāntideva and Kamalasìīla. No Buddhist teaching is complete without an extensive exposition of *bodhicitta,* for the tender motivation to benefit beings, generally associated with relative *bodhicitta,* is always coupled with the recognition of the ultimate insubstantiality and interdependence of all phenomena, associated with absolute *bodhicitta.*

Bodhicitta teachings became foundational in Tibetan Buddhism from the time of Ātiśa in the 11th century, and sources on *bodhicitta* abound in the Tibetan tradition. Sìāntideva is considered the most venerable source of exposition of *bodhicitta,* and his 8th-century composition, the Bodhicāryāvatāra, the entrance to the way of the *bodhisattva,* is the most popular Indian text in Tibet. As Sìāntideva famously said of compassion,

> All the joy the world contains
> Has come through wishing happiness for others.
> All the misery the world contains
> Has come through wanting pleasure for oneself.[30]

This quote has become a slogan used by many Tibetan teachers, often glossed as "If you want to be miserable, think of yourself. If you want to be happy, think of others." Throughout Sìāntideva's presentation, *bodhicitta* is described as the motivation to benefit others embedded in the recognition that other beings do not inherently exist and that their relative happiness cannot be separated from our own. His luminous verses guide the practitioner to transform personal preoccupations and fixations into compassionate care for others.

In the Sakyong lineage of Shambhala, Sìāntideva is also beloved, serving as the foundation for most of the teachings on compassion.[31] *Bodhicitta* is nicknamed 'the supreme thought', *lhaksam* in Tibetan, which means that compassion and care for others are the pinnacle of human life, the "most supreme thought that the mind could possibly have."[32] *Lhaksam* is spontaneous and natural, arising from the best of human nature, basic goodness. It is also considered the seed of enlightenment, for the essence of Buddhahood is wishing perfect happiness for all.

Such an attitude takes bravery, and so those who commit to *bodhicitta* are considered to be *bodhisattva*-warriors, those for whom their love is greater than their fear. When confronting the challenges of life—from life-threatening illness to warfare to disasters—they are the ones who choose not to retreat into mere personal survival, but who recognize that suffering affects everyone. They are the ones who are willing to work for the greater good of human society, seeing the fundamental potential of human life. They know that individual, personal happiness is not possible and that our human life must involve placing the happiness of others as primary. When *bodhisattva*-warriors have a terminal illness, they do not just retreat into their rooms, but start a support group for others with the same illness. When disaster strikes, they do not merely bail their own basements but organize teams bailing the flooding in the streets and preventing future floods.

This care for others is deeply motivated by the sadness the *bodhisattva*-warrior feels when encountering suffering, especially unnecessary suffering. This is not a tragic sadness, but recognition of how suffering works in human life.

> In a moment of horror, one realizes that there is no source of this pain. The suffering is completely unnecessary. It would be another matter if there were, in fact, a self that was causing it. However, the only source—if it can be considered to be a source—is the mind's confusion.[33]

Bodhisattva-warriors feel the poignancy of the human condition, sadness for the unnecessary suffering mixed with joy of connection and care for others, and this becomes a motivating force in working for the benefit of others. "When the supreme thought occurs in the mind, one becomes fearless and brave," especially in working for the benefit of others.[34]

The reason the *bodhisattva* is a warrior is that feeling the pain of others does not end the journey. "Instead of overwhelming and defeating us, the plight of human existence has the power to spark our deep-seated human valor and nobility."[35] The challenge of helping the world becomes a life-giving purpose that uplifts and cheers the warrior, even while sadness touches her heart. The fundamental inspiration comes from the personal experience of basic goodness, and the confidence that comes from affirming this goodness throughout life.

The Supreme Thought and Enlightened Society

> Our hearts long to beat together. Naturally, there is warmth, kindness, and love.
>
> —*Sakyong Mipham*[36]

There is a slightly different emphasis in how teachings on *bodhicitta* are used in Shambhala, and the key is a larger, more societally-oriented motivation. Generally speaking, the compassion teachings in Buddhism emphasize individually working to benefit other beings, specifically, one at a time. The Shambhala teachings speak of social benefit—creating a society that highlights human goodness and ripens the capacity to manifest that goodness in community. The purpose of warriorship is to create an enlightened society.

The emphasis on societal happiness influences the Shambhala reading of Mahāyāna Buddhist history. It is well known that the Gupta period in India (320-700 C.E.) during which Mahāyāna flourished was a classical age of Indian art, commerce, and culture.[37] As Sakyong Mipham observes,

> ...the dynamic power of raising the supreme thought of *bodhicitta* to benefit others created a flourishing culture that celebrated human goodness and extolled the beauty of the world. This transformed Buddhism from an individual pursuit to a cultural pursuit. The arts and philosophy blossomed. We Shambhalians should draw great inspiration from the tradition of the Mahayana. It is part of our heritage.[38]

From a Shambhala point of view, when we embrace of *bodhicitta* and the path of warriorship we enjoy the same possibility of celebrating community and culture, developing the arts and philosophy, and nurturing a new golden age of humanity.

The reason for the emphasis on society is found in basic goodness teachings themselves. If all beings are basically good, a fundamental tenet of Shambhala, this means that human society is also good. In Tibetan, this is expressed as *mi sipasangpo*: sangpo refers to the non-dual sense of goodness or completeness (as opposed to *yakpo*, which means good versus bad)—intrinsically good. Mi is 'human'. Sipa usually refers to the confused aspect of human life, saṃsāra, suffering. In this context, sipa refers to connectivity and community of all beings, full of the "desire to communicate, touch, and love one another."[39] It refers to the universe of relationships, and even to politics, usually considered to be irredeemable but in this case 'possible' to awaken into deep goodness. Those polluted elements of human life are, in their intrinsic nature, awakened, harmonious, pure and full of possibility.[40] Society is basically good, already, in its very nature.

This means that the Shambhala teachings are not utopian. They are not referring to a future society in another place, another time, with another model. Enlightened society is the human society in which we already live; it is the society where everyone lives. We only need to awaken to the fundamental goodness and wakefulness embedded in the fabric of humanity. Everyone wishes to raise their children in an environment of peace and harmony, in which the customs and traditions of the family and community are passed along to the next generation. Every culture has its celebrations and ceremonies, its rites of passage, and its meaningful work. Every community takes pride in its food and crafts, its manufactured goods and trade, its hobbies and occupations. Even communities held hostage by warfare or sectarian strife, pitched into flight as refugees, or secularized by rapid industrialization and urbanization have longing for these cultural practices, and these are all evidence of the inherent enlightenment of society, according to Shambhala.

The Warrior's Training in Compassion

> The essence of warriorship, or the essence of human bravery, is refusing to give up on anyone or anything.
>
> —*Chogyam Trungpa, Rinpoche*[41]

Like Buddhism, the warrior's compassion practices involve supreme thought (*bodhicitta*) and loving kindness practices, as well as *sādhana* practices that take the basic goodness of humans and of society as their object. The warrior commits to the sacred outlook (*daknang*) of seeing basic goodness in oneself, in others, and in society through formal vows and *sādhana* practice.[42] These are practiced, however, with special attention to the core Shambhala transmission regarding the life-force of humanity.

Among the causes of the current degenerate age is the weakened life-force (*sok*) that is core to the quality of life of individuals and communities.[43] In Tibetan medicine, yoga and cosmology, the life-force is a psychophysical element in our ability to connect with inherent enlightenment or basic goodness and have harmony with others. If our life-force is low, our meditation practices—no matter how profound—will be of limited success. In the Shambhala teachings, the life-force is enhanced by the experience of *lungta*, literally 'wind-horse', bringing the vitality of the warrior's horse into energetic connotation. *Lungta* is closely related to the practices of *ch'i* in China and *prāṇa* in India, arousing psychophysical energy coursing through the body.[44] *Lungta* is an actual warrior mind-body practice enhanced by a combination of lineage blessings, community life, and healthful lifestyle. Teachings on *lungta* are associated with both the Buddhist and indigenous shamanic traditions of Tibet, and are linked with the *dralas*, or divine beings who protect the lives of individuals and communities.

While the name *drala* literally means "gods against enemies," in the Shambhala teachings *dralas* protect against anything that jeopardizes the life-force of humans.[45] *Dralas* are closely related to the Rigdens, the *bodhisattva* kings of the Kālacakra-tantra. The way humans can reawaken their life-force draws on the blessings of dralas found in a visionary realm, in the natural world, and on the human body and the mind itself. *Dralas* can also be human saints, *bodhisattvas*, who work tirelessly for the benefit of others. Through the blessings of the *dralas*, human *lungta* can strengthen and radiate, attracting and nurturing the continued influence of the *dralas*.

Fundamentally, *drala* is not a deity, however. *Drala* is the power of things as they are in the world and especially in our own beings—our own wisdom, our ability to connect directly with how things are in our experience. You might say that *drala is* our life-force, and it is found in gentleness and kindness rather than aggression.

> But true magic is the magic of reality, as it is: the earth of earth, the water of water—communicating with the elements so that, in some sense, they become one with you. When you develop bravery, you make a connection with the elemental quality of existence.[46]

Altogether, *drala* is the magical, synchronistic aspect of the world when seen without the limiting influence of merely self-centered perspectives. Magnetizing *drala* and raising *lungta* are the fundamental practices of warriorship.

When a warrior trains, Buddhist practices of sìamatha-vipasìyanā meditation are foundational for connecting them with basic goodness. In addition to these practices, however, those that rouse *lungta* and attract the *dralas* are especially important, for they strengthen the confidence (*ziji*) of the warrior. In the degenerate age when humans become quickly discouraged or burned out, this confidence brings a resilient compassion that can fulfill the vow to create enlightened society. These practices include meditations, ceremonies, warrior practices, and community celebrations.

When invoking *drala* and arousing *lungta*, gradually the world becomes alive, vibrant and sacred. "When you invoke *drala*, you begin to experience basic goodness reflected everywhere—in yourself, in others, and in the entire world."[47] This experience fills the warrior's mind with possibilities, and problems do not seem intractable anymore. The fundamental goodness and healthiness inherent in circumstances seem more apparent, and an ancient optimism and vitality bloom both in the warrior's mind and within circumstances themselves. This experience brings greater likelihood of finding allies and collaborators, and discovering organic solutions for society's deepest difficulties.

Creating Enlightened Society

> The warrior's approach is that, rather than trying to overcome the elements of existence, one should respect their power and their order as a guide to human conduct.
>
> —*Chögyam Trungpa, Rinpoche*[48]

The ultimate commitment of warriorship is to create enlightened society. At first, this commitment might seem almost messianic, invoking the aspiration of a crusader. But that approach is actually ego-centered and aggressive, manifesting more conventional than mystic. The crusader's approach to social change is the most common, and has not been successful. Instead, the warrior begins a journey of personal transformation first, and then continues this journey with further magical and actual engagement with the natural elements of existence. This approach discovers that "creating enlightened society" is seeing the inherent, unacknowledged sacredness of society and the world and becoming harmoniously attuned with it.[49]

This journey begins with investigating the fundamental nature of humanity, identifying whether basic goodness is true and clear.

How we feel about ourselves has a tremendous impact on everything we are and do.

> When we feel goodness, a shift occurs: We get curious, which sparks care. We begin to see goodness happening in so many ways—rational and irrational, visible and invisible, and through signs, words, and examples. From that arise virtues like patience, exertion, and generosity.[50]

When warriors develop confidence in basic goodness, they become stakeholders in the society in which they live, and their activities are committed to bringing out the goodness of those societies. Becoming stakeholders depends upon appreciation, not merely critique. Still, bringing out basic goodness in society is not a quick-fix. It requires tuning into our communities and identifying ways to help its members to awaken to basic goodness. The gateway to basic goodness is through feeling, through affirming that our sense perceptions and emotional undertones are accurate, authentic, and worthy of respect. It is impossible to tune into feeling when we are speedy, and so finding time to connect to others through feeling is foundational for creating enlightened society. Sharing joy, sorrow, tenderness, and excitement builds relationship with others; learning to truly listen to others is the key. Doing so with kindness and gentleness ensures that we can honor our connection with others in a way that builds genuine community.

Communities connect with each other through the ceremony of daily life—formally through celebration of holidays, religious and secular, and informally through the rhythms of the life-stages, calendar and seasons. Civic life routinely acknowledges community in a variety of ways, through governance, commerce, education, and change. Whether through the farmers' market, the opening of a new library, sporting teams' events, graduations, or funerals, communities have a way of acknowledging who they are and what they want to be. By bringing forward the intention to foster human goodness, warriors can contribute to ceremonies creating community contexts of meaning. They can infuse these ceremonies with kindness and appreciation in order to strengthen the fabric of connection.

For that matter, when the warrior begins to experience the sacredness of life, then all life is a ceremony. Every interaction is special. Each meal has specialness in its preparation, its enjoyment, and in its clean-up. Going to work is joining the ceremony of the workplace, and returning home reactivates the ceremony of household and family. Everyday life is an opportunity to appreciate the inherent goodness of human life and human discourse, no matter how many people it may involve. The warrior can be present for life, and when doing this, a huge reservoir of *lungta* that animates life is waiting.

When life is viewed in this way, the warrior has an opportunity to choose how to participate in the global ceremony of human life. How does this influence our buying patterns, our relationship with our natural resources, our responses to threats and attacks? The warrior can choose a life ceremony that considers long-term effects on the planet and its inhabitants. Sakyong Mipham writes:

> What happens next on earth is totally up to us. If we are willing to work for a wholesome future, then humanity's future truly does lie in our hands, for it will come about only through manual labor powered by our illumination. This creates a twinkle in the eye, brings a smile to the lips, and broadens our sense of conviction. In this light, humanity's future can occur because we are willing to hold it in our own hands.[51]

Because current circumstances represent the ceremony of sleep and denial, the biggest responsibility of the warrior is to join with others to change society's ceremony to one that honors, respects, and loves all of humanity. The future ceremony of society will be determined by what values we put in place.

Conclusion: Gentle Urgency

> The world does need your help so badly, very badly. So, on behalf of this world (smiling), I would like to request you to come and do something about it.
>
> —*Chogyam Trungpa*[52]

From certain perspectives, this kind of training of a warrior might be viewed as having little effect on the cataclysmic challenges of contemporary life. A critic would suggest that developing *lungta* and compassion is an anemic contribution to creating enlightened society, contributing little concrete solution to the current crisis. But Shambhala is part of a worldwide 'engaged Buddhism' movement that suggests a new approach, one that does not fall into adversarial methods or quick fixes. It is more a paradigm shift about what it looks like to systemically change the basis of conflict. Spiritually-based social engagement like this suggests that the problems of our time belong to us as well, and that there can be no change without personal transformation. We cannot simply create an alternative system that works; instead, we endeavor to use our understanding of the disease or symptom as a way to grow personally and societally to more caring, penetrating compassion.[53]

One of the hallmarks of engaged Buddhism is giving up an adversarial approach. The basis of the analysis is different: there are no clear enemies. Thich Nhat Hanh writes, "Where is our enemy? I ask myself this all the time."[54] For the Shambhala warrior, the enemy is not external. Instead, warriors battle their own fear and disheartenment. With confidence in basic goodness, the fundamental impulse to demonize others is put to rest, providing a completely different ground for activism.

Decades ago, in a penetrating essay shortly before being nominated for the Nobel Peace Prize, the Dalai Lama asked the human question, what are the real solutions for widespread warfare and violence in the world? If they could be ended through waging war, then we should turn every resource of our world toward warfare and not rest until violence is defeated once and for all. But, as the Dalai Lama observed, we have tried that over and over again, and this has not been the solution to violence. He writes, "The time has come to try a different approach. Of course, it is very difficult to achieve a worldwide movement of peace of mind, but it is the only alternative. If there were an easier and more practical method, that would be better, but there is none."[55]

The Shambhala tradition has provided the basis for a powerful transformation of the motivation that seeks the welfare of the world, and asks its citizens to step in and find a tangible, enduring way to help. Some Shambhala warriors have become activists; many have become leaders and visionaries in their fields. Most have become inspired by the dignity and beauty of everyday human life, and have found a way to contribute to the long-term goal of enlightened society. Through the transmissions of the Shambhala lineage, warriors have resilience and stamina and an ancient optimism about human potential. Within daily practice, they enjoy themselves by celebrating human capacity through appreciation of beauty through the arts, of human connection through community, and of wisdom through cultivation of curiosity and investigation of the world. This means meeting friends new and old over coffee, having dinner parties and family celebrations, organizing community events, and going back to school for more education. Done with the proper attitude, these activities inspire confidence in the basic goodness of humanity. They also have the potential for contributing to the long-term goal of creating enlightened society.

NOTES

1. A previous version of this paper was published in the online journal, *The Arrow: The Journal of Wakeful Society, Culture and Politics*, Fall 2014. http://www.arrow-journal.org/creating-enlightened-society
2. *Vinaya*, IV.20.
3. Dalai Lama, *The Ethics for a New Millennium* (New York: Penguin Books, 2001), Chapter Sixteen.
4. 'Shambhala Vision," http://www.shambhala.org/about_shambhala.php (accessed on July 16, 2014).
5. Chögyam Trungpa, *Shambhala: The Sacred Path of the Warrior* (Boston: Shambhala Publications, 1984), 27.
6. Other influences not treated in detail here are Confucian and Hindu Purāṇa sources, and indigenous apocalyptic lore.
7. The Sīta River is sometimes identified with the Tarim River in Eastern Turkestan. Shambhala is considered north of Tibet, Khotan, and China—which places it north of the Tian Shan. John Newman, "Itineraries to Sìambhala," *Tibetan Literature: Studies in Genre*, Jose

Ignatio Cabezon and Roger R. Jackson, ed. (Ithaca: Snow Lion, 1996), 487.

8. For further information on the Kālacakra origins of the Shambhala teachings, see: Khedrup Norsang Gyatso, *Ornament of Stainless Light: An Exposition of the Kālacakra-tantra* (Boston: Wisdom Publications, 2004), 1-20.
9. Robin Kornman, Sangye Khandro, and Lama Chönam, *The Epic of Ling: Gesar's Magical Birth, Early Years, and Coronation as King* (Boston: Shambhala Publications, 2012).
10. Robin Kornman, "The Influence of the Epic of King Gesar of Ling on Chögyam Trungpa," *Recalling Chögyam Trungpa*, edited by Fabrice Midal (Boston: Shambhala Publications, 2005), 350.
11. R.A. Stein refrained from using the term Bön, calling the indigenous sources of the Gesar tradition 'nameless'. Stein, 191-229.
12. From a teaching on the Longchen Nyingtik Guru Yoga, given by Kyabje Dilgo Khyentse Rinpoche in Dordogne, France in August 1984, at the request of Sogyal Rinpoche and the Rigpa Sangha. http://www.rigpawiki.org/index.php?title=Dzogchen
13. Geoffrey Samuel, *Civilized Shamans: Buddhism in Tibetan Societies* (Washington: Smithsonian Institution Press, 1993), 228-30.
14. Carolyn Gimian, "Introduction to Volume Eight," *The Collected Works of Chogyam Trungpa*, Vol. VIII (Boston: Shambhala Publications, 2004), xii-xiv.
15. Kornman, 369-70.
16. Khenchen Jigme Phüntsok, *Lama Mipham's Miracles: The Sound of the Victorious Battle Drum which Accompanies the Supplication to Omniscient Mipham Gyatso*, translated by Ann Helm (Halifax: Nalanda Translation Committee, 1999).
17. Trungpa, *Sacred Path*, 28.
18. The Shambhala teachings share South Asia's view of time, with ever-declining conditions of auspiciousness, culminating in the Kāli-yuga. The notion of the degenerate age is the backdrop of the Kālacakra-tantra, providing an opportunity to awaken through the special skillful means of tantra.
19. Dalai Lama, *The Kālacakra Tantra, Rite of Initiation for the Stage of Generation: A Commentary on the Text of Kay-drup-ge-lek-bel-sang-bo*, edited by Jeffrey Hopkins (London: Wisdom Publications, 1985), 65.
20. Gyatso, *Ornament*, 40-49.

21. Mipham J. Mukpo, *Shambhala Sadhana* (Halifax: Kalapa Court, 2012), 7.
22. The Kālacakra-tantra speaks of basic goodness as the primordial mind, *nyuk-ma sem*.
23. *Shambhala Sadhana*, 2.
24. Gyatso, 55.
25. Chogyam Trungpa, *Great Eastern Sun* (Boston: Shambhala Publications, 1999), 185.
26. Trungpa, *Sacred Path*, 46.
27. Trungpa, *Great Eastern Sun*, 149.
28. In Japanese traditions, this is spoken of as *wabi-sabi*, two of the aesthetic moods that characterize appreciation. For more information, see D.T. Suzuki, *Zen and Japanese Culture* (Princeton: Bollingen, 1957), Chapter Two, and Andrew Juniper, *Wabi-Sabi, The Japanese Art of Impermanence* (New York: Tuttle, 2003).
29. Trungpa, *Great Eastern Sun*, 111.
30. VIII.129, Padmakara Translation Group, *The Way of the Bodhisattva* (Boston: Shambhala Publications, 1997), 128.
31. The great Dzogchen master Paltrul Rinpoche (1808-87) revived Tibetís interest in Sìāntideva as he emphasized the importance of the Bodhicaryāvatāra as the foundation of Dzogchen practice. His students included Ju Mipham Gyatso, whose work spawned the popularity of Shambhala as a tradition.
32. Dradul, *Supreme Thought*, 22.
33. Ibid., 26.
34. Ibid., 49.
35. Ibid., 10.
36. Dradul, *Supreme Thought*.
37. Stanley Wolpert, *A New History of India*, Seventh Edition (New York: Oxford University Press, 2004), 88-104.
38. Dradul, *Supreme Thought*. In Tibetan, mi'isrid pa zangpo, transcribed sometimes as 'sepa' and others as 'sipa'. See Holly Gayley, "Society as Possibility: On the Semantic Range of the Tibetan Word *Sipa*," *The Arrow: A Journal of Wakeful Society, Culture and Politics*, http:/ /www.arrow-journal.org/society-as-possibility (accessed on July 21, 2014).
39. Dradul, *Supreme Thought*, 5.
40. Gayley, "Society as Possibility: On the Semantic Range of the Tibetan Word *Sipa*," *The Arrow: A Journal of Wakeful Society, Culture, and Politics*, http://www.arrow-journal.org/society-as-possibility (accessed on July 31, 2014).

41. Trungpa, *Sacred Path*, 33.
42. These vows, roughly analogous to refuge and *bodhisattva* vows, are the Shambhala Vow and the Enlightened Society Vow, followed by practice of the *Shambhala Sādhana: Discovering the Sun of Basic Goodness*, composed by Jampal Trinley Dradul (Halifax: The Kalapa Court, 2012).
43. R.A. Stein, *Tibetan Civilization*, translated by J.E. Stapleton Driver (Stanford: Stanford University, 1972), 202-12; Robin Kornman, "The Thirteen Dralas of Tibet" (Halifax: Nalanda Translation Committee), 3. http://nalandatranslation.org/media/Thirteen-Dralas-of-Tibet-by-Robin-Kornman.pdf (accessed on July 17, 2014).
44. Stein, *Tibetan Civilization*, 223-24.
45. Kornman, 'Thirteen Dralas', 3.
46. Trungpa, *Sacred Path*, 109.
47. Ibid., 126.
48. Ibid., 129.
49. Sakyong Mipham wrote that perhaps the reason his father spoke of 'creating' had to do with the mood of the times in which he taught, a mood that emphasized dismantling, destroying. Perhaps the word 'create' brought encouragement to "bolster humanity's confidence in its ability to create a better world." Sakyong Mipham, *The Shambhala Principle: Discovering Humanity's Hidden Treasure* (Boston: Shambhala Publications, 2012), 36.
50. Sakyong, *Shambhala Principle*, 31.
51. Sakyong, *Shambhala Principle*, Chapter 8.
52. Chogyam Trungpa. *Stafa*. "Crazy Wisdom—The World Needs Your Help." MP3, 0.40 http://m.stafaband.info/download/mp3/X3HIFIZIzLk.html (accessed on July 16, 2014).
53. Robert Aitken, *The Mind of Clover* (Toronto: HarperCollins, 1984), 3-15; Kenneth Kraft, "Prospects of a Socially Engaged Buddhism," *Inner Peace, World Peace: Essays on Buddhism and Nonviolence*, edited by Kenneth Kraft (Albany: State University of New York Press), 11-30.
54. Thich Nhat Hanh, "Please Call Me by My True Names," in Fred Eppsteiner, *The Path of Compassion* (Berkeley: Parallax Press, 1988), 33.
55. Tenzin Gyatso (HH XIVth Dalai Lama), "Hope for the Future," in Fred Eppsteiner, *The Path of Compassion* (Berkeley: Parallax Press, 1988), 7.

REFERENCES

Aitken, Robert. *The Mind of Clover*. Toronto: Harper Collins, 1984, 3-15.

Arnold, Edward A. *As Long As Space Endures: Essays on the Kālacakra Tantra in Honor of H.H. the Dalai Lama*. Ithaca: Snow Lion, 2009.

Bernbaum, Edwin. *The Way to Shambhala: A Search for the Mythical Kingdom Beyond the Himalayas*. Garden City, N.Y.: Anchor/ Doubleday Books, 1980.

Dalai Lama. "Hope for the Future," in Fred Eppsteiner, *The Path of Compassion*. Berkeley: Parallax Press, 1988.

—.*The Ethics for a New Millenium*. New York: Penguin Books, 2001.

—.*The Kālacakra Tantra, Rite of Initiation for the Stage of Generation: A Commentary on the Text of Kay-drup-ge-lek-bel-sang-bo*, edited by Jeffrey Hopkins. London: Wisdom Publications, 1985.

Dhargyey, Geshe Lharampa Ngawang. *A Commentary on the Kālacakra Tantra*. Dharamsala: Library of Tibetan Works and Archives, 1994.

Dradul, Jampal Trinley. *Shambhala Sadhana: Discovering the Sun of Basic Goodness*. Halifax: Kalapa Court, 2012.

—.*The Supreme Thought*. Halifax and Cologne: Dragon Books, 2013.

Gayley, Holly. "Society as Possibility: On the Semantic Range of the Tibetan Word *Sipa*," *The Arrow: A Journal of Wakeful Society, Culture and Politics*. http://www.arrow-journal.org/society-as-possibility (accessed on July 21, 2014).

Gimian, Carolyn. "Introduction to Volume Eight," *The Collected Works of Chogyam Trungpa*, Vol. VIII. Boston: Shambhala Publications, 2004.

Gyatso, Khedrup Norsang. *Ornament of Stainless Light: An Exposition of the Kālacakra-tantra*. Boston: Wisdom Publications, 2004.

Juniper, Andrew. *Wabi-Sabi, The Japanese Art of Impermanence*. New York: Tuttle, 2003.

Kraft, Kenneth. "Prospects of a Socially Engaged Buddhism," *Inner Peace, World Peace: Essays on Buddhism and Nonviolence*, edited by Kenneth Kraft. Albany: State University of New York Press, 11-30.

Kornman, Robin, Sangye Khandro, and Lama Chönam, tr. *The Epic of Ling: Gesar's Magical Birth, Early Years, and Coronation as King*. Boston: Shambhala Publications, 2012.

Kornman, Robin. "The Influence of the Epic of King Gesar of Ling on Chögyam Trungpa," *Recalling Chögyam Trungpa*, edited by Fabrice Midal. Boston: Shambhala Publications, 2005.

Kornman, Robin. "The Thirteen Dralas of Tibet" (Halifax: Nalanda Translation Committee), 3. http://nalandatranslation.org/media/Thirteen-Dralas-of-Tibet-by-Robin-Kornman.pdf (accessed on July 17, 2014).

Mipham, Sakyong. *The Shambhala Principle: Discovering Humanity's Hidden Treasure*. Boston: Shambhala Publications, 2012.

Nhat Hanh, Thich. "Please Call Me by My True Names," in Fred Eppsteiner, *The Path of Compassion*. Berkeley: Parallax Press, 1988.

Newman, John. "Itineraries to Sìambhala," *Tibetan Literature: Studies in Genre*, Jose Ignatio Cabezon and Roger R. Jackson, ed. Ithaca: Snow Lion, 1996.

Padmakara Translation Group. *The Way of the Bodhisattva*. Boston: Shambhala Publications, 1997.

Phüntsok, Khenchen Jigme. *Lama Mipham's Miracles: The Sound of the Victorious Battle Drum Which Accompanies the Supplication to Omniscient Mipham Gyatso*, translated by Ann Helm. Halifax: Nalanda Translation Committee, 1999.

Samuel, Geoffrey. *Civilized Shamans: Buddhism in Tibetan Societies*. Washington: Smithsonian Institution Press, 1993.

Stearns, Cyrus. *The Buddha from Dölpo: A Study of the Life and Thought of the Tibetan Master Dölpopa Sherab Gyaltsen*, 2nd Edition. Ithaca: Snow Lion, 2010.

Stein, R.A. *Tibetan Civilization*, translated by J.E. Stapleton Driver. Stanford: Stanford University, 1972.

Suzuki, D.T. *Zen and Japanese Culture*. Princeton: Bollingen, 1957.

Trungpa, Chogyam. *Great Eastern Sun*. Boston: Shambhala Publications, 1999.

Trungpa, Chögyam. *Shambhala: The Sacred Path of the Warrior*. Boston: Shambhala Publications, 1984.

—.*Stafa*. "Crazy Wisdom—The World Needs Your Help." MP3, 0.40. http://m.stafaband.info/download/mp3/X3HIFIZIzLk.html (accessed on July 16, 2014).

Wallace, Vesna. *The Kālacakratantra: The Chapter on the Individual Together with the Vimalaprabhā*. New York: American Institute of Buddhist Studies, Columbia University, 2004.

Wolpert, Stanley. *A New History of India*, Seventh Edition. New York: Oxford University Press, 2004.

□

9

Compassion and Religious Diversity—Some Buddhist Perspectives

—*Rita M. Gross*

I chose to write on compassion and religious diversity for this symposium because I have recently published a book, *Religious Diversity—What's the Problem?: Buddhist Advice for Flourishing with Religious Diversity*. The link between these two topics— religious diversity and compassion—is obvious, though some might not recognize that link immediately. Some people seem to think that the compassionate thing to do about religious diversity is to try to convince others to join their own religion because it has served them well. They would argue that differences make people uncomfortable and that agreement and sameness are more conducive to peace. They think the problems brought up by religious differences would disappear if only everyone had the good sense to join them in the one true faith. They might also argue that among the world's religions, only one can be true and merit adherence, that belonging to the 'wrong' religion is actually dangerous to adherents of that religion.

Religious Diversity—The Actual Problem

By contrast, my thesis is that, while religious diversity does cause discomfort, that discomfort is due, not to the presence of different religions co-existing within the same geographic area or on our one small planet, but to our own discomfort with diversity and our preferences for uniformity and conformity. Those are the problems we must cope with and defuse, rather than seeking for religious uniformity, sameness, or agreement. What needs to change is not the existence of religious others but our own discomfort with difference. We have to learn the spiritual and psychological skills to be willing to let others be different.

Why is it so difficult to let others be different? The default mode of human consciousness is oppositional duality. Without deep training, we will usually respond to most experiences of difference with oppositional dualism, with up/down, right/wrong evaluations in which those most like us always come out 'on top', and 'right'. Such oppositional dualism has to be replaced by some version of non-duality, by the willingness to give up 'either/or' logic and become more comfortable with 'both/and' logic, which is well known and accepted in many Indian systems of thought. Such oppositional dualism is what we need to work to transform and eliminate. That is essentially an internal, 'subjective' issue. Discomfort with diversity is about 'us' not about 'them'. We are the problem, not them.

I find it interesting that the major theologies of religion on the table from Western theologians of religion evaluate and judge 'them' on how closely 'they' conform to 'us'. Mainly, they ask the question "Are you enough like us to be okay?" The major answers are 'Definitely not' (the exclusivist position), "In some ways, but we are still the best" (the inclusivist position), and "At the most basic level, we are all the same" (the pluralist position). Problems with the exclusivist and inclusivist positions are quite obvious but problems with the pluralist position are more subtle and less obvious, especially to more liberal religious thinkers. However, many more conservative religious people rightly claim that for them to fit within the pluralist position, many of their most distinctive beliefs and practices would have to be eliminated, which is unacceptable to them. Any real solution must be able to let religions remain distinctive from one another while also giving up the exclusive or inclusive positions—positions which in one way or another claim that if the world were working correctly, everyone else would join us, or at least join our religion.

Flourishing with Religious Diversity

But, as I argued extensively in my book, people do not need to fundamentally change their religious beliefs in order to flourish with religious diversity. They only need to give up their attachment to beliefs, the fixation and rigidity with which specific words and concepts are clung to. In other words, religious beliefs themselves do not necessarily need to be changed or given up, but the manner in which they are held does need to change. Such a change involves looking inward, evaluating one's own ethics, one's own conduct vis-à-vis others. Can claims that we alone possess religious truth, accompanied by heavy duty missionary projects and internal religious education that teaches scorn for other religions, possibly be ethically upright? Such thinking, both in terms of how we negotiate identity and how we evaluate otherness, does need to change. We return again to the fundamental problem with religious diversity, which lies within our own psyches, not externally in the existence of religious others. We need to look inward to determine why we are so uncomfortable with religious diversity and take such pleasure in the unreasonable and unethical belief that we alone have a monopoly on religious truth. Such a belief is so self-cherishing, and, at least according to Buddhism, such self-cherishing is at the root of all suffering.

Buddhist Best Practices for Becoming Comfortable with Religious Diversity

Regarding discomfort with diversity, I claim that Buddhism offers many suggestions that are extremely helpful in coming to terms with religious diversity, but which are not part of current conversations about religious diversity or the prevailing theologies of religion. The claim that undue attachment to one's own religious convictions and other ideologies is dangerous, both to one's own spiritual maturity and freedom as well as to religious others, is especially well known and central to Buddhism. It is also one of the most useful contributions Buddhists could make to discussions of becoming comfortable with religious diversity. To be free of unhealthy, fixated attachment to one's own views and opinions requires a flexible, relaxed mind, a mind that is well trained and pliable, a mind that has the stability not to be shocked by surprises. This comfortable, cheerful, relaxed, and contented state of mind is greatly prized by Buddhists, whose age-old disciplines of mind training are extremely adept in fostering such a state of mind. Given the extreme ideological and verbal aggression that plagues all public discourse in the United States, widespread adoption of such disciplines would be more than helpful and appropriate.

Developing more flexible and less rigid states of mind would help reduce the hard oppositional dualism that eagerly proclaims and acts on the claim that "we are right and they are wrong, period." Nevertheless, a softer dualism, the dualism of believing in the real and separate existence of self and other still remains. This too is part of the default mode of human consciousness. It takes considerable contemplative and meditative work for the realization that self and other are actually interdependent and inseparable to begin to dawn on one. Nevertheless, with deeper reflection, those conclusions become inevitable. The Buddhist parable of the ten blind people and the elephant clearly demonstrates how partial and incomplete subjective conclusions about the 'other', what is 'external' to oneself, can be, especially if one makes uneducated snap judgments about others. One's own subjectivity literally creates 'the other' in one's mind; one does not have direct, unmediated, accurate access to that other. That subjectively created 'other' then impacts one's own identity, one's own view of who one is. Beginning to recognize how much our version of 'the other' can be subjectively created has obvious implications for our views on religious diversity and greatly aides the dawning realization that our discomfort with diversity is actually a much bigger problem than the mere presence of religious diversity. Most or all of that discomfort is our own creation and has nothing to do with anything religious others represent. We just don't like the challenge of dealing with the fact that there are many ways such as theistic, non-theistic, or atheistic, to construct the world we all share and no way to objectively delineate whether any of these metaphysical or theological views is 'correct', whatever that might mean. But the implications of this subjective creation of the other for theologies of religion have not been taken into account by the prevailing theologies of religion in the English-speaking world.

The inseparability and co-arising of self and other have other implications for our views of religious diversity when we examine more carefully yet the subjective pole of that interdependent matrix. Without reflection, people have a knee-jerk impression that there is an independently existing, permanent, singular self to be found somewhere beneath the flux of our experience. There is no need to go into the complexities of Buddhist views of egolessness in this context. We need only focus on one word used to describe the self most people believe in—'singular'. Most people talk about their identity as if it were a monolith, whereas a bit of reflection reveals that everyone has multiple identities, that we are all hybrids with hyphenated identities. This means that one's religious identity is not one's only identity, even if one is more focused on one's religion than are most people. It is not the monolith many people assume their religious identities to be when they discuss religious others and religious diversity. Other identities can easily trump religious identity, which is shown very clearly when co-religionists on opposite sides in a war pray to the same God for victory over their political 'enemies', who are of the same religion but of a different national persuasion. On the other hand, people with vastly different religious identities often recognize that they deeply share common cultural, racial, or gender identities and that those common concerns are at least as important as their religious differences. Realizing that we all actually have multiple identities could go far to defuse the rigidity and self-righteousness with which religious others are sometimes approached. And again, this perspective on religious identity as one component of a hyphenated, ever-changing identity is absent from current theologies of religion and discussions of religious diversity.

Basic Points about Buddhism and Compassion

These four points from the standard Buddhist repertoire for negotiating the complexity of our worlds and our lives—recognizing the need for detachment from views and ideologies; the need for tools to develop a flexible, pliable state of mind; the interdependence of self and other; and our hyphenated identities—contribute greatly to an improved discussion of religious diversity. They also all have obvious and direct implications for a discussion of compassion and religious diversity. Nevertheless, before we move directly into a discussion of compassion and religious diversity, a few words about Buddhist perspectives on compassion itself are required. I think it is crucial to understand that, from the perspective of Vajrayana Buddhism, if compassion is to be effective and genuine, it does not and cannot stand alone. It must be paired with its partner, wisdom. The two are inseparable and one without the other does not yield positive results. Though their relationship is ultimately non-linear, if one were to put their relationship into linear perspective, one would have to say that wisdom takes the lead and compassion is the inevitable, natural result of true wisdom, of being in tune with things as they are in interdependence and emptiness. This means that true compassion is not a deliberate choice or strategy, nor is it the result of feelings or emotion. It is simply the spontaneous upwelling of appropriate actions taken in the light of interdependence and emptiness. A truly wise person is compassionate without a lot of theorizing about compassion. Buddhists are very suspicious of deliberate or strategized compassion because such compassion often has much more to do with making the subject feel better than with truly helping others. We are often encouraged to look into our motivations for activities we might undertake—to ask, for whom are we really doing what we are doing? Are we doing something because we take ego-satisfaction in our 'compassion', or is it genuinely useful and appropriate for those to whom our activities are directed? 'Idiot compassion' is something we are always warned against. Whenever I hear someone proclaim that they are compassionate, I cringe because their ego-involvement is so obvious. People who are heavily invested in being viewed as compassionate should arouse suspicion.

To begin our discussion of compassion and religious diversity from a Buddhist point of view, we need first to recognize that it is extremely unrealistic to imagine that a single religious ideology or set of practices could be satisfying and transformative for all the different cultures and people living on our planet. Wisdom should tell us that and Buddhist have a category for dealing with the need for differing religious methods to meet the differing spiritual needs of people—skillful means. The traditional Buddhist ways of discussing skillful means are not completely adequate for the modern situation of global religious diversity, but Buddhist ideas about skillful methods can easily be developed and augmented to help people become more accepting of the inevitability of religious diversity.

The question so often asked by so many religious people—"is my religion the true religion?"—is irrelevant. It isn't even worth discussing or debating. There are no grounds or criteria by which one could definitively determine that one of the world's religions is superior to the others, truer and better. Even if there were some grounds on which one could determine that one of the world's religions is 'truer' or 'better', it would not matter because it will never be the case that everyone would join the same religion.

People generally prefer their own religion, just as they prefer their own culture or their own cuisine. But to leap to the conclusion that everyone else should also prefer that religion or culture or cuisine simply because the subject prefers it is illogical in the extreme and quite unwarranted. People simply prefer their own distinctive ways, no matter what evidence outsiders may bring to bear about the superiority of other ways. It is as unrealistic to expect that everyone would adopt the same religion as that people everywhere would adopt the same language, even though a common language would actually be useful, whereas a universally accepted religion would only mean the disappearance of many interesting religious and spiritual options, with no corresponding benefits.

Even if, somehow, against all logic, expectations, and precedents, people did universally adopt the same religion, that mega-religion would soon fragment into sects. The history of religions clearly demonstrates that people simply cannot agree over the long term on even the basics within any given religion. Each of the world's major religions has splintered into many sects or denominations, which often conflict with each other as seriously, even more seriously, than the different religions conflict with one another. It should be completely obvious to any observer that, regarding religions, disagreement and diversity always displace agreement and uniformity. That is simply an observable, incontrovertible fact. Whatever one may think of that reality, however one may evaluate it, it is simply a fact. Disapproving of facts is rather beside the point and does not help one respond well to those facts or engage in helpful conduct concerning such facts. The first priority is to accept facts and learn how to deal with them with humor and compassion. Religions sometimes have had a difficult time accepting facts such as that the earth is round, not flat. But at a certain point, fighting such facts becomes counter-productive. As others, including the great philosopher of religion, John Hick, have argued, it is time for a Copernican revolution among religious thinkers regarding religious diversity. A claim that we could demonstrate the real superiority of one among the world's religions is as untenable as an attempt to demonstrate that the earth is flat, despite photographs from space of the round earth floating in space. To return to the main claim, made above, religious diversity itself is not the problem; it is simply a fact. Our discomfort with diversity is the problem and that is what we must learn to cope with.

Learning about Religious Others as the Way to Flourish with Religious Diversity

Given the extent of inter- and intra-religious hostility and ridicule, and the extent of the discomfort from which it stems, the chief question becomes what is the most urgent and compassionate counter-measure to that hostility, ridicule and discomfort? I would claim that regarding religious diversity, both within any given religion and external to it, the most compassionate step we can take is to learn about religious others from their own texts and in their own terms. Internal religious education, the training given to newer members of a religious community by their elders, routinely includes justifications for one's own religion that compare it very favorably to other denominations within the same religion or to completely different religions. But that training rarely, if ever, includes empathetic discussions of those religious alternatives or materials taken from their own texts and scriptures. The question "What do they actually believe or practice?" with information taken from the literature of religious others, is rarely asked. Instead, ages-old insider defenses are repeated, as if those accounts of "this-is-what they-believe-and-this-is-what's-wrong-with-them" actually sufficed as accurate accounts of religious others. Anyone who has undergone any traditional religious indoctrination can give countless examples of such propaganda pretending to be religious education, if they would be honest enough to reflect critically on what they were taught. For examples, as a young Christian, I was taught that Judaism is a heartless religion of laws that people cannot possibly keep and that Christianity provides relief from that burden. That assessment pales beside the litany of incorrect beliefs held by Catholics that were repeatedly taught to me. No one ever attempted to explain why Jews or Catholics find their own religions satisfying and remain within them, leaving us to surmise that stupidity or stubbornness accounts for their religious intransigence. Sadly, the same dynamic prevails regarding intra-Buddhist sectarianism. Within the past month, I have heard an esteemed Tibetan teacher spew misinformation about Theravada Buddhists and pre-Mahayana Buddhisms while glorifying Mahayana/Vajrayana Buddhisms as not only different but superior. Buddhism, especially in its Mahayana/Vajrayana forms espouses non-duality. Nevertheless, many fall into an up/down, right/wrong dualism when differences among Buddhists are being discussed and these evaluations often involve serious misunderstandings of the actual teachings and practices of other Buddhists. Why can differences not be allowed to simply be different? Why must they also be 'wrong?' Why the discomfort and defensiveness? Of course, in some contexts, Theravada Buddhists return the favor, claiming that Mahayanists are actually 'non-Buddhists'.

Instead of such confrontational dualism, I call for empathy between religions. Empathy involves use of one's imagination to enter into the subjectivity of others to the extent possible with education and good will. And if the education and good-will are present, empathy can significantly defuse the misunderstandings and discomfort that accompany religious difference. However, empathy and education are absolutely necessary. I would claim that somewhere between 75 and 90 percent of religious sectarianism and inter-religious hostility could be overcome if people would only take the time and effort to really understand 'the others'. But I ask them to "take the time and effort to really understand 'the others'" and it does take time and effort to do so. Taking that time and effort, including studying the texts and interpretations internal to religious others, usually results in realizing that their beliefs and practices are not so scary or stupid, even if they are different. Just as 'we' have good reasons for our own beliefs and practices, so do 'they'. Thus, our immersion into the empathetic study of religious others would cure the tendency of religious people to make claims for the exclusive relevance and worth of their own system of beliefs and practice, though not necessarily for universal ethical norms. (More on this point later.)

Refusal or reluctance to engage in such empathetic study of religious others on the part of religious institutions and leaders makes me very frustrated. At my most frustrated, it leads me to suggest that leaders of religious institutions are fundamentally not interested in truth. They are more interested in defending their own brand name and increasing its market share, something that strikes me as fundamentally unworthy of any human enterprise, let alone religions. If they were more interested in truth and less concerned to promote the name brand, they would be more open-minded about religious others, more willing to learn accurate information about them and to drop ages-old stereotypes about religious others found in their own texts and scriptures. The modern situation in which all the world's major religions now live in close proximity to one another requires a new attitude towards religious others. When the major religions were more isolated from one another, accurate knowledge about religious others may have seemed like a luxury, but it no longer is, as any daily newscast reveals.

Fortunately, modernity has also resulted in new ways of thinking about religion and studying religions, namely the academic study of religion and the presence of scholar-practitioners who participate in both the academy and the various religions. This modern development means that religions can be studied not only confessionally by insiders who mainly defend their own tradition and know little about other religions, even other denominations within their own tradition, but also more critically and comparatively by scholars who have primary allegiance to accuracy and non-sectarianism, no matter where that may lead them regarding their home traditions. When these two enterprises bifurcate into two enterprises, very unfortunate results are frequent. Religious insiders are often extremely uninformed about many aspects of other religions, and, in many cases, about the complexity and ambiguity of their own tradition. They often insist on sanitized and censored versions of their own traditions as the only part of them that should be presented to the general public, for example in university classes on their tradition. Partly because of the many ways in which religions have often limited critical, free inquiry and sought conformity to an orthodoxy, many scholars of religions, especially in earlier times, became very unsympathetic to religious institutions. Their teaching and scholarship became anti-religious and they refused to participate in the more experiential dimensions of religions, the dimensions that actually give those traditions meaning to their own adherents. As a result, insiders have often responded vehemently that such scholars misrepresent their tradition, don't understand it, and shouldn't be teaching it.

It should not require too much sophistication to realize that both positions are extremes, between which a middle way should be sought. That middle way is represented by scholar-practitioners who know their home tradition well, and participate in it, but who also know how to study religions in a more critical and comparative way, who know other traditions besides their own well, and are more interested in truth than in either promoting or debunking the name brand. As is often the case with those who will not take an extreme or a dualistic position, critics on both sides are quick to castigate those who seek a middle between extremes. The purely academic scholars often insist that we scholar-practitioners cannot be 'objective', though claims that there could be a neutral no-place from which scholars could observe human phenomena has been thoroughly debunked by post-modernism. On the other hand, insiders who lack academic training and know only their own tradition can also be untrustworthy in representing that tradition to the wider world. They will often adamantly claim that they should be the sole spokespersons for their tradition because they speak out of an insider's orthodox, traditional position—the tradition as it really is, not as misrepresented by scholars and modernists, they would claim. However, while such spokespersons can speak well for a slice of the tradition—the orthodox, often anti-modern perspective—they can speak only for that slice of the tradition. In doing so, they often whitewash or overlook less savory aspects of the tradition such as its treatment of women or of heterodox elements within the tradition, and they downplay its socially oppressive elements. They also often do not present accurate versions of that tradition's history, telling only the stories the tradition has told itself for centuries and refusing to take aspects seriously of that tradition's history that come to light in broader, more comparative and less sectarian inquiries into the history of the tradition. In addition, when, as has happened in some recent cases, such traditionalists also try to censor or suppress the results of more modern and academic scholarship, the situation becomes very problematic. As a Buddhist scholar-practitioner, I know well whereof I speak. Buddhist insiders who do not know the whole Buddhist tradition but only their version of it and who have no acquaintance with modern academic methods of studying religion are much more troublesome than the non-Buddhist, secular, even anti-religious scholars, who at least try to be more comprehensive in their methods and results. Especially when we are dealing with issues of religious diversity and all the havoc resulting from insiders' claims about the unique relevance of their own traditions, historical consciousness and the comparative methods brought into the discussion by modern academic methods of studying religion are indispensible.

A key thesis of this chapter is that the most compassionate thing we can do regarding religious diversity is to learn about religious others by studying their own texts and teachings, by empathetically entering into their worlds. Of course, it must be stated that such empathy must be reciprocal. It would be a dead-end, even self-destructive, to practice such empathy with those whose only goal is conversion to their way of being. That mutual pursuit of empathy being agreed upon, what methods then offer the most promise? Many people immediately jump to the alternative of dialogue, but for many reasons which I detailed in my book, I would argue that the first task should be empathetic study of the world's various religious options such as is offered by a well-constructed course on world religions or a competent survey text on that topic. I make this argument because it seems to me that many people's default modes of thinking regarding religious diversity are still either a dualism concerned with right and wrong, truth and falsity, or a very mushy claim that all religions teach the same thing, which is simply not accurate and robs religions of their own distinctiveness. People who hold either position are not well prepared to dialogue with religious others. Those who hold the first position are not really prepared to put their religion and the religions of others on a level playing field, viewing the religions as equals and their own task as learning accurate information and empathetic insight regarding religious others. Those who hold the later position are ill-prepared to appreciate how different religions are from one another, thus missing the whole point of learning how to flourish with religious diversity.

With the foundation of mutual empathetic understanding well in place, dialogue can then become a useful, though not a necessary next step for all participants. Many contemporary religious leaders, from the leaders, including the Dalai Lama, have written and spoken about how much they have learned from encountering their counterparts in other religions and coming to understand and appreciate them in ways that are difficult to learn from textbooks alone. Nevertheless, for the average member of any religion I continue to regard the accurate knowledge about and empathetic insight into various religious traditions that can be gained through a competent introduction to the world's religions as the indispensable foundation for anything else. Furthermore, whether empathetic learning or dialogue is one's major tool for working with religious diversity, we must all agree that mutual understanding, not agreement or conversion, is our goal.

Much more critical than widespread or universal participation in inter-religious dialogue is better education about religious others in seminaries and other institutions that train ordinary pastors, priests, rabbis, and other religious leaders. Lamenting the negative attitudes towards other religions, I often encountered my university students, I reflected that there are only two places from which my students learned that negativity—their parents and their pastors. And their parents in turn had learned their negativity from the previous generation of pastors and others. Thus, seminaries and other such institutions are the weak link regarding better inter-religious understanding that must become a lynchpin in a future in which religious institutions and leaders flourish with religious diversity rather than regarding it as a problem. The kind of religious indoctrination I received as a child and the scorn for other religions that was recommended to me simply have no place in the world of inevitable religious diversity in which we must live.

However, among the various options for interaction among religious leaders, I am very skeptical of one that has been favored in some Indian contexts, including Buddhist contexts. That is the practice of debate, which I do not regard as a helpful option. I make this claim because debate is confrontational and combative. Debate is generally an enterprise in which there are winners and losers, sometimes with high stakes, including forced religious conversion, for the debate's losers. Such behavior seems more appropriate to sports than to religious sensibilities. Furthermore, debates are 'won' by those who have better debating skills, which does not necessarily mean that they hold the more cogent position. In the future, a better debater from the 'other side' might well win the debate. What does that then mean about the cogency of either position? Debate clearly does not seek or promote reconciliation and mutual respect, both of which are solely needed in a world in which religions are mainly hostile toward each other.

Is Anything about Religion Worth Debating?

However, if we are going to debate about religious differences, it is important to know what is worth debating and what is not. The same comment should be made about simply discussing religious differences. These questions are tied in with the oft-repeated request for 'respect', rather than 'mere tolerance' for any and all religious points of view. What deserves respect, and what does not? I will argue that a great deal of time and energy is wasted discussing the truth or falsity of religious and metaphysical ideas and not enough time discussing their practical utility, that is to say, the ways in which religious ideas lead to the alleviation of suffering or increase suffering, a question that has much more to do with ethics than with metaphysics. In this discussion, I draw upon the historical Buddha's de-emphasis on metaphysical questions and his insistence that suffering and its alleviation were uppermost among his concerns.

It may seem to outsiders that Buddhists have nevertheless focused a great deal on seemingly metaphysical concepts such as egolessness and emptiness. Many people also mistakenly assume that Buddhism is an atheistic religion and regard Buddhist non-theism as a theological claim opposed to theism. However, Buddhist would claim that such concepts are not metaphysical claims at all, but that they grow out of deep reflection, without metaphysical presuppositions, on our experience as it is. It is claimed, most definitely, that they are not the results of revelation or transcendent intervention into the matrix of interdependence, and it is also claimed that, in the long run, they are not absolute truth because words and concepts cannot capture absolute truth. The best that they can do is to be good pointers beyond themselves to things-as-they-are. As for Buddhist non-theism, Buddhists have never declared that deities don't exist, at least relatively, but only that they cannot confer liberation because they cannot cut a person's attachment and fixation; only the person in question can do that.

Because the Buddhist assessment is that metaphysical and theological concepts are somewhat beside the point, I always wonder why anyone would care so much about someone else's metaphysical or theological beliefs or try to change them. Why should it matter to me whether someone else believes that Jesus is their only savior, that the Qur'an is the deity's final revelation to humanity, or meditates correctly on emptiness, so long as they do not try to force their beliefs onto me, disrupt my life because of their beliefs, or even try to convince me that their beliefs are 'superior' to mine? I have always likened such debates or discussions to arguing about whether romantic or baroque classical music is 'better', whether classical music or jazz is better, or whether one style or art or architecture is better. These are personal preferences, as is the preference for theism versus non-theism or a preference for Vajrayana Buddhism over a simpler form of Buddhism. It may be fun and entertaining to argue about such preference, but is much more at stake?

Whenever I make such an argument, which I have made many times in many contexts, someone then always asks me if my position is one of thorough-going relativism, if 'anything goes' and will I endorse any religious position whatsoever? Am I completely 'laissez faire' regarding religious beliefs and symbols? My answer is always that some things matter a great deal. The ethical outcomes of religious beliefs matter a great deal. Thus, if any religion or religious position can be directly linked with negative ethical outcomes, that religious position cannot be respected or garner my approval, nor, I hope, anyone else's respect and approval. The problem with any possible judgments about whole religions, or even denominations within a religion, is that, as John Hick pointed out long ago, if one of the various religions is qualitatively and quantitatively better than the other options, then adherents of that religion should demonstrate consistent ethical superiority over adherents of other religions. What other test could possibly be relevant? But it is impossible to demonstrate actual, on-the-ground ethical superiority for any of the world's religions. Temporary lapses on the part of a segment within any religion such as the Christian religious wars of the sixteenth century, current Muslim violence on the part of some Muslims, or Buddhist repression of Muslim minorities in Burma prove nothing about the religions as a whole, except that no matter what one's theology may be, ethical lapses are easy to make and are very common.

What about specific religious ideas? Many feminists, myself included on some occasions, have argued that the exclusively male god-language of monotheistic religions contributes to male dominance in those religions, and I have no doubt that it is one factor contributing to male dominance in those religions. But Mahayana and Vajrayana Buddhisms have plenty of highly revered female personifications of virtue in their symbolic repertoire but are nevertheless as male dominated as are monotheistic religions. It seems that links between specific religious concepts or symbols and ethical behavior are difficult to pin down. Such conclusions strengthen claims that there are no grounds for declaring any set of religious symbols of beliefs superior to others. Therefore, all deserve respect, not merely tolerance.

Nevertheless, there are limits to this respect and tolerance. Religious leaders often claim religious grounds for what can only be considered their ethical lapses, especially their propensity to condone and support social oppression in societies in which their religions arc dominant. I can respect, and even find interesting, virtually any religious symbol system or set of religious beliefs. That does not translate into respect for practices such as not educating girls, marrying them off at the age of twelve or fourteen and expecting them to spend their lives taking care of men and children. It does not translate into respecting social systems such as racism or caste institutions, in which some people are automatically condemned at birth to having few opportunities and to lifelong social inferiority. And religious leaders often condone and support such oppressive practices, even though no specific warrant for those practices can be found in their religions and some reformers claim that such practices are actually contrary to the religion.

Some might claim cultural relativism, saying that if I am so relativistic regarding religious beliefs and symbols, should I not equally recognize that people simply have different ideas about how the sexes and other social groups should interact in different societies? And to some extent, yes. Some societies practice arranged marriages and others practice marriage by individual choice. Some practice polygamy, some practice serial monogamy, and others practice lifelong monogamy. None of these choices is perfect and all can result in individual discomfort. In fact, these days a good bit of anti-colonial rhetoric seeks to claim that democracy, women's equality, and human rights are only Western impositions on the rest of the world and on societies that have their own ways of doing things. Such claims, in fact, amount to extreme cultural relativity, to claims that practices that are harmful to some individuals should not be interferred with because any social system is as good as any other. If we cannot judge between religious symbol systems and theologies, how can we judge between different norms regarding gender, race, sexual orientation, caste, etc.?

The difference is that social practices such as male dominance, castism, racism, heterosexism, etc. always result in benefits to the dominant group and disadvantages to the suppressed or scorned groups. In other words, different theologies or religious symbol systems are, in and of themselves, harmless. We simply cannot demonstrate that any specific theology or religious symbol system results in harm, either to its own members or to others. But it is very easy to demonstrate that some ethical norms such as male dominance, do result in harm to some, even though they may benefit others. As I've often commented, how convenient for men to have the other half of the human race dedicated to taking care of them and their offspring while they are free to pursue interesting and rewarding intellectual, artistic, and spiritual practices! Just think of all the prefaces to books by male authors in which they thank their wives for watching the kids while they worked on their book, and, in addition, typed the manuscript as well! Where do we women find that kind of support for our vision and our competence?

But can it not be argued that overall social good is served by having some members of a society be inherently disadvantaged by their very birth, compared with other members of society? To answer this question, I would call up the deepest Buddhist argument about why I should be kind to others. We know, in an incontrovertible way, that we do not want to suffer and that we seek happiness. It is obvious that all creatures are the same. Inherently, masochistic species or individuals are difficult to find. Then we are asked to practice reversibility, the silver rule of not doing to others what we don't want them to do to us. This argument is used to demonstrate why we should be willing to blow mosquitoes off ourselves when they land and bite, rather than just squashing them. How much more so with other human beings. What man would really want to be treated the way women are treated in male-dominant societies? That's why in some religions, they daily thank God for not making them a woman! What upper caste person would really be willing to trade places with a dalit? What white person could bear the scorn and oppression experienced by people of color in the United States and other parts of the world?

It should give spiritually inclined people pause to realize that, whatever their theology or religious symbol system may be, it has condoned social oppression in the past, and in most cases still does so today. So when I am asked to respect, and not merely tolerate, other religions, what am I being asked to do? Their symbols and theologies may be beautiful and easy to respect. What about their ethics? Unfortunately, no religion is immune to disrespect because of ethical lapses on the part of its members and because of widely condoned social practices that hurt some members of that religion. To give blanket respect in spite of those ethical lapses would not be consistent with the practice or compassion.

□

10

Compassion in Hinduism through the Preservation of Human Rights

—*Samir Kalra*

Introduction

Psychological researchers define compassion as "the feeling that arises when you are confronted with another's suffering and feel motivated to relieve that suffering."[1] Under this definition of compassion, one acts on feelings of empathy and a desire to help others.[2]

Beyond this emotional and psychological interpretation of compassion, the concept is spiritually intrinsic to the Dharmic religions of Hinduism, Buddhism, Jainism, and Sikhism, and is frequently manifested through *seva*, or selfless action. This paper will delve into the connection between the Hindu ideas of compassion and *seva* as manifested through the promotion and preservation of human rights.

The concept of compassion in Hinduism, in its broadest sense, can be viewed as an extension of *ahimsa* and applies to all living beings, not just humans. *Ahimsa* is "the Hindu belief that symbolizes love, genuine care, and compassion towards all living beings. The principle of *ahimsa* extends far beyond avoiding causing physical harm; it also includes avoiding causing harm through speech and thought. *Ahimsa* is non-injury in mind, speech, and action towards any creature."[3] Compassion is similarly "based on notions of *atman*, and the ability to feel for others as we feel for ourselves."[4]

Several Hindu scriptures expound on the importance of compassion. Verse 6.28-32 of the *Bhagavad Gita*, for instance, provides that,

> The infinite joy of touching the Godhead is easily attained by those who are free from the burden of evil and established within themselves. They see the Self in every creature and all creation in the Self. With consciousness unified through meditation, they see everything with an equal eye.
>
> I am ever present into those who have realized Me in every creature. Seeing all life as My manifestation, they are never separated from Me. They worship Me in the hearts of all, and all their actions proceed from Me. Wherever they may live, they abide in Me.
>
> When a person responds to the joys and sorrows of others as if they were his own, he has attained the highest state of spiritual union. (*Bhagavad Gita,* 6.28-32)

Similarly, verse 12.13 of the *Gita* states "That one I love who is incapable of ill-will, who is friendly and compassionate" (*Bhagavad Gita*, 12.13), while the Yajur Veda 36.18 posits, "Strong One, make me strong. May all beings look on me with the eye of friend! May I look on all beings with the eye of friend! May we look on one another with the eye of friend!" (*Yajur Veda,* 36.18)

This emphasis on compassion within Hindu scriptures is closely intertwined with and essential to the act of *seva*. Indeed, the Hindu conception of *seva,* or selfless service to others without thought of personal reward or the existence of one's own identity,[5] is predicated on a sense of compassion for another's condition.[6] It requires one to act for the larger group without consideration of one's own benefit, whether spiritual or worldly. In other words, *seva* must be carried out in a manner that is free from ego and "...should flow out of deep compassion for the pain, hunger, feelings of rejection, loss, or any other problem from which either an individual or a group is suffering."[7]

Conceptualizing Compassion through Human Rights Law

An individual who acts in *seva* toward his or her fellow human beings is acting out of a sense of compassion for the collective good, which lies at the core of human rights. This conceptualization of compassion is embodied in modern human rights law.

Human rights, as defined under international law,

> ...are rights inherent to all human beings, whatever our nationality, place of residence, sex, national or ethnic origin, colour, religion, language, or any other status. We are all equally entitled to our human rights without discrimination. These rights are all interrelated, interdependent and indivisible. Universal human rights are often expressed and guaranteed by law, in the forms of treaties, customary international law, general principles and other sources of international law. International human rights law lays down obligations of governments to act in certain ways or to refrain from certain acts, in order to promote and protect human rights and fundamental freedoms of individuals or groups.[8]

International jurisprudence contains multiple sources of law that govern the behavior of nation states and their relationships with individuals. These include international conventions and treaties, customary international law, general principles of law recognized by civilized nations, and the judicial decisions of individual nations as a subsidiary source of law.[9]

Although not legally binding, the United Nations Declaration of Human Rights provides a basic expression of human rights norms that have been incorporated into international conventions and treaties, and reflects a global paradigm applicable to all countries. According to the Declaration, human rights are "inalienable rights of all members of the human family," and should be applied equally to all persons.[10]

In particular, Article 2 states that all people are entitled to human rights and freedoms "without distinction of any kind such as race, colour, sex, language, religion, political or other opinion, national or social origin, property, birth or other status," while

Article 7 provides for equal protection before the law, and Article 18 protects the individual's freedom of thought, conscience, and religion.[11] Furthermore, under Article 8: "Everyone has the right to an effective remedy by the competent national tribunals for acts violating the fundamental rights granted him by the constitution or by law."[12]

The International Covenant on Civil and Political Rights (ICCPR), the International Convention on the Elimination of All Forms of Racial Discrimination (ICERD), and the International Covenant on Economic, Social and Cultural Rights (ICESCR) comprise the major human rights treaties that prohibit discrimination based on religion, race, nationality, sex, colour, language, or political affiliation.[13]

Under Article 2 of the ICCPR, all states party to the convention must respect the rights of any individuals residing in their territory without distinction based on race, religion, sex, or any other category, while Article 26 guarantees equal protection under the law without discrimination.[14] Additionally, Section 3(a) of Article 2 requires a state party to provide a remedy in the event an individual's rights or freedoms have been violated under the ICCPR.[15]

In addition to treaties and conventions, custom is firmly recognized as a source of law in the Statute of the International Court of Justice, and reflects "generally accepted state practice."[16] As a result, regardless of whether a country is a signatory to a particular convention or treaty, it remains bound by generally accepted norms and principles of law. The principles enunciated in a specific convention are indicative of a broader legal standard that is recognized under customary international law. Customary international law has been codified in the Vienna Convention on the Law of Treaties, and has equivalent authority over the actions of states as compared to conventions and treaties.[17]

Similarly, under Article 53 of the Vienna Convention, the concept of *jus cogens* applies to the actions of nation states. *Jus cogens* is defined as "a norm accepted and recognized by the international community of States as a whole, as a norm from which no derogation is permitted and which can be modified only by a subsequent norm of general international law having the same character."[18] Furthermore, according to the Restatement (Third) of the Foreign Relations Law, a norm of international law is established "where there is acceptance and recognition by a 'large majority' of states, even if over dissent by a very small number of states."[19]

The right to property, equal protection under the law, and freedom of religion are some of these basic norms and principles that are widely recognized and accepted as state practice by most civilized nations around the world. Moreover, almost all countries have constitutional protections for minorities and prohibit discrimination based on religion or race.

The shifting paradigm of conflict, the increasing prevalence of asymmetric warfare, and the rise of quasi-governments exerting control over vast expanses of land have similarly led international law to impose obligations on non-state actors to protect human rights.

Spiritual and Scriptural Foundations for Human Rights in Hinduism

The codification of human rights in the modern era through human rights conventions and treaties, and customary international law, however, does not imply that these are new ideas. To the contrary, many ancient civilizations and religious traditions have well-developed notions of human rights and fundamental freedoms.

Hinduism, in particular, has deep spiritual and scriptural foundations for human rights, with a particular emphasis on the concepts of equality and religious freedom.

The Hindu view of equality is based on accepting the divinity and diversity of all beings, which encompasses not only humans, but the complete spectrum of living organisms.[20] Since God permeates and exists in all beings,[21] the universe is considered one family, or *vasudhaivakutumbakam*.[22] The Hindu concern for universal well-being is commonly expressed through the following invocation:

Om sarvebhavantusukhinah.Sarvesantuniraamayaah. Sarvebhadraanipashyantu.Maakaschiddukhbhaagbhavet.

May all beings be happy. May all beings be healthy.
May all beings experience prosperity. May none in the world suffer.[23]

In the context of human rights, the fact that all individuals have the same soul dictates that all humans should be treated equally.[24] This interpretation of equality transcends distinctions of gender, race, religion, and nationality, and is reflected in the Universal Declaration of Human Rights and many of the human rights treaties referenced above.

The theoretical underpinnings of religious freedom are similarly embedded in Hinduism. Indeed, respect for religious freedom as defined in both the Universal Declaration of Human Rights and the ICCPR can be found in one simple verse in the Rig Veda: *Ekam sat viprahabahudhavadantior* (The truth is one, the wise call it by many names).[25] In addition, Chapter 4 of the *Bhagavad Gita* provides "Whoever approaches Me in whatever manner, I accept him. All paths men are struggling through lead unto Me."[26]

The centrality of both equality and religious freedom to Hinduism expressed through the underlying unity of all beings and the acceptance of a multiplicity of paths to the divine, form a spiritual foundation for modern human rights frameworks.

From this belief in the inherent divinity of all beings naturally flows compassion for the state and condition of others, and a desire to act in service of the common good. Hinduism, however, goes further than merely respecting the divinity of all beings, and places a duty on humans, as the most spiritually evolved, to protect and preserve the underlying equality and unity of all beings.[27] The manner in which human rights are framed in Hindu thought differs from modern Western conceptions, though, in that duties toward the collective good are accorded greater esteem than focusing on one's own individual rights.[28]

Compassion Manifested through the Preservation of Human Rights

The practical application of compassion to the preservation and promotion of human rights can be achieved in a multitude of ways, and by states and non-state actors alike.

A state's adherence to human rights norms and its implementation of laws that protect the most vulnerable segments of society, for instance, is driven at least in part by compassion for the needs of the people it governs. The behavior of a state and its leaders, however, is not entirely dictated by compassion or a desire to serve its citizens selflessly. Instead, a state often complies with treaty obligations and human rights norms out of self-interest and political expediency.

Arguably, when a state provides humanitarian aid or attempts to protect the human rights of civilians caught in the middle of civil conflicts or large-scale wars outside its own borders, it is motivated to a higher degree out of compassion for their suffering. While strategic geopolitical factors certainly must also be taken into account, these acts can be said to comport more closely with *seva* and concern for the plight of such civilians.

Similarly, a third party state's acceptance and/or resettlement of refugees is significantly motivated by compassion towards the humanitarian suffering of displaced and persecuted populations. Despite the existence of the 1951 Refugee Convention, its 1967 Protocol, and customary international law,[29] a state is far less obligated to act towards refugees than on behalf of its own citizens.

In fact, the definition of a 'refugee' under Article 1(A)(2) of the 1951 Refugee Convention requires a third party state or international institutions to act out of compassion for their predicament. Specifically, a refugee is defined as someone who:

> ...owing to well-founded fear of being persecuted for reasons of race, religion, nationality, membership of a particular social group or political opinion, is outside the country of his nationality and is unable or, owing to such fear, is unwilling to avail himself of the protection of that country; or who, not having a nationality and being outside the country of his former

> habitual residence as a result of such events, is unable or, owing to such fear, is unwilling to return to it.[30]

The U.S. resettlement of nearly 80,000 Bhutanese refugees from United Nations High Commissioner for Refugees (UNHCR) administered camps in Nepal can be considered an example of compassionate action, devoid of geopolitical factors or treaty obligations. During the early 1990s in Bhutan, more than 100,000 mostly Hindu Bhutanese of Nepali descent were stripped of their citizenship and forced to leave the country under the 'One Nation, One People' policy aimed at homogenizing a multi-ethnic and multi-religious society.[31] Repressive tactics and violence, including harassment, arrests, and the burning of ethnic Nepali homes, ultimately led these Nepali Hindus to seek refuge in UNHCR camps in Nepal.[32]

Bhutan's obstinate failure to repatriate the refugees and Nepal's unwillingness to locally integrate them, led the U.S. and other Western nations to agree to resettle these Bhutanese refugees who had been languishing in the camps for nearly 20 years.[33] Subsequently, the U.S. federal and local governments provided a range of services to help the refugees adjust to life in their new surroundings, including assistance with housing, food, clothing, medical care, and employment services.[34] These actions epitomize the connection between compassion and *seva* through the provision of direct assistance and preservation of basic human rights.

Even when a country does not grant official refugee status to a group of persecuted individuals or formally resettle them, it can still follow the principle of non-refoulement. Non-refoulement, under Article 33 of the 1951 Refugee Convention[35] states that no country, "shall expel or return ('refouler') a refugee in any manner whatsoever to the frontiers of territories where his life or freedom would be threatened on account of his race, religion, nationality, membership of a particular social group or political opinion."[36] Although non-refoulement is technically binding on nations under customary international law,[37] though not enforceable, most states presumably follow this principle out of a sense of compassion. India has followed this principle with Pakistani Hindu refugees, thousands of which have fled religious persecution in recent years. Although these refugees have not been accorded refugee status, they have not been sent back out of concern for their well-being and fundamental human rights.[38]

Compassion can also be demonstrated following a conflict or the mass violation of human rights through the use of transitional justice mechanisms. According to experts on transitional justice in post-conflict societies, these "mechanisms may take a number of forms. Most prominently these include the international criminal court, international tribunals, special courts, truth commissions, local courts and traditional methods of justice."[39] Such mechanisms can assist in achieving accountability, justice, sustainable peace, and stability for a nation that is attempting to move forward and heal the wounds of the past.[40]

A state's desire to seek closure on a conflict period, when not imposed by the international community, is debatably one of the highest forms of compassionate behavior. Acknowledging past wrongs and taking concrete steps to redress them, as required by transitional justice mechanisms, can often pose the greatest obstacle to a state's ability to protect and preserve human rights.

It took Bangladesh, for instance, nearly 40 years after the horrific events of the 1971 War of Independence from Pakistan, to establish the International Crimes Tribunal (ICT) in 2010 to investigate war crimes committed during the conflict. The ICT was authorized through an amendment to the International Crimes (Tribunals) Act, originally enacted in 1973 by Bangladesh to "provide for the detention, prosecution and punishment of persons responsible for genocide, crimes against humanity, war crimes, and crimes committed in the territory of Bangladesh, in violation of customary international law, particularly between the period of 25th March to 16th December 1971."

Despite the existence of the 1973 Act, those responsible for committing crimes against humanity were not held accountable until the tribunals began in 2010. In the interim, 195 members of the Pakistani military initially charged with war crimes were granted immunity by a 1974 agreement signed by Bangladesh, Pakistan, and India. Similarly, a large number of local Bangladeshi collaborators from Islamist militias were granted amnesties following the conclusion of the war.[41] True transitional justice, albeit flawed, did not begin in earnest until the establishment of the ICT in 2010, as successive Bangladeshi governments failed to both provide justice to the victims and hold the perpetrators responsible for their actions.

While state actors can certainly act out of compassion, as noted above, independent human rights advocates and non-governmental organizations (NGOs) are more clearly motivated to engage in *seva*. In particular, the activities of advocates and NGOs are almost entirely based on compassion for the suffering of others, although a degree of self-interest cannot also be overlooked. Specifically, these entities pursue multiple avenues of *seva*, including, but not limited to: (1) investigating alleged human rights violations by state and non-state actors; (2) providing direct humanitarian aid or legal assistance to victims; (3) training or educating human rights defenders or state institutions on human rights; (4) raising awareness of human rights violations amongst the general public; and (5) conducting direct advocacy to state governments and international bodies.

Conclusion

The concepts of compassion and *seva*, or selfless service, are closely interwoven in Hindu scriptures and philosophical texts. *Seva* can be viewed as the practical manifestation of compassion, as true ego-less *seva* cannot be carried out without a sense of empathy for the suffering of others. This compassion for the collective good is based on the acknowledgment of the unity of all beings and their inherent divinity, and leads one to engage in *seva*.

In the context of human rights, notwithstanding other factors, the behavior of states in upholding and protecting the human rights of their own citizens, as well as those of external or displaced populations, can be viewed as a form of compassionate action. Similarly, human rights advocacy and activism by non-state actors and NGOs can be said to be motivated to a large extent by compassion. Thus, human rights in the modern era is a vehicle to carry out acts of compassion for the benefit of universal brotherhood.

NOTES

1. The Greater Good: The Science of a Meaningful Life, http://greatergood.berkeley.edu/topic/compassion/definition
2. *Id.*
3. Hindu Beliefs: Service – Seva, BAPS Swaminarayan Sanstha, http://www.baps.org/Spiritual-Living/Hindu-Beliefs/Service—Seva.aspx
4. The Heart of Hinduism, International Society of Krishna Consciousness, http://hinduism.iskcon.org/concepts/202.htm
5. Hindu Beliefs: Service – Seva, BAPS Swaminarayan Sanstha, http://www.baps.org/Spiritual-Living/Hindu-Beliefs/Service—Seva.aspx
6. John A. Johnson, "Cui Bono: Human Behavior Unpacked," *Psychology Today*, http://www.psychologytoday.com/blog/cui-bono/201306/selfless-service-part-ii-different-types-seva
7. Phyllis Krystal, "Taming Our Monkey Mind" (p. 39), http://www.psychologytoday.com/blog/cui-bono/201306/selfless-service-part-ii-different-types-seva
8. Office of the High Commissioner for Human Rights, http://www.ohchr.org/EN/Issues/Pages/WhatareHumanRights.aspx
9. Summary of Customary International Law and Jus Cogens as Pertains to Juvenile Offenders, 2003/2004, The International Justice Project, http://www.internationaljusticeproject.org/juvJusCogens.cfm
10. Legal Information Institute, Cornell University Law School, http://www.law.cornell.edu/wex/international_law
11. The Universal Declaration of Human Rights, The United Nations, http://www.un.org/en/documents/udhr/#atop
12. *Id.*
13. International Law, Office of the High Commissioner on Human Rights, http://www2.ohchr.org/english/law/index.htm.
14. International Covenant on Civil and Political Rights, Office of the High Commissioner on Human Rights, http://www2.ohchr.org/english/law/ccpr.htm

15. *Id.*
16. Summary of Customary International Law and Jus Cogens as Pertains to Juvenile Offenders, 2003/2004, The International Justice Project, http://www.internationaljusticeproject.org/juvJusCogens.cfm
17. Legal Information Institute, Cornell University Law School, http://www.law.cornell.edu/wex/international_law
18. Summary of Customary International Law and Jus Cogens as Pertains to Juvenile Offenders, 2003/2004, The International Justice Project, http://www.internationaljusticeproject.org/juvJusCogens.cfm
19. *Id.*
20. Dipti Patel, "The Religious Foundations of Human Rights: A Perspective from the Judeo-Christian Tradition and Hinduism," The University of Nottingham Human Rights Law Centre, http://www.nottingham.ac.uk/hrlc/publications humanrightslawcomm entary.aspx
21. *Id.*
22. Hinduism Basics, Hindu American Foundation, http://hafsite.org/resources1?q=resources/hinduism_101/hinduism_basics
23. *Id.*
24. Dipti Patel, "The Religious Foundations of Human Rights: A Perspective from the Judeo-Christian Tradition and Hinduism," The University of Nottingham Human Rights Law Centre, http://www.nottingham.ac.uk/hrlc/publications humanrightslaw commentary.aspx
25. Hinduism Basics, Hindu American Foundation, http://hafsite.org/resources1?q=resources/hinduism_101/hinduism_basics.
26. *Id.*
27. Hinduism Basics, Hindu American Foundation, http://hafsite.org/resources1?q=resources/hinduism_101/hinduism_basics
28. Dipti Patel, "The Religious Foundations of Human Rights: A Perspective from the Judeo-Christian Tradition and Hinduism," The University of Nottingham Human Rights Law Centre, http://www.nottingham.ac.uk/hrlc/publications humanrightslaw commentary.aspx
29. International Refugee Law, Rule of Law in Armed Conflicts Project, The Graduate Institute Geneva, http://www.geneva-academy.ch/RULAC/international_refugee_law.php

30. *Id.*
31. "Hindus in South Asia and the Diaspora: A Survey of Human Rights, 2013," Hindu American Foundation, http://hafsite.org/resources/human_rights_report
32. *Id.*
33. *Id.*
34. *Id.*
35. International Refugee Law, Rule of Law in Armed Conflicts Project, The Graduate Institute Geneva, http://www.geneva-academy.ch/RULAC/international_refugee_law.php
36. 2013 UNHCR Regional Operations Profile, UNHCR, http://www.unhcr.org/pages/49e4876d6.html#; UNHCR Note on the Principle of Refoulement (November 1997), UNHCR, http://www.unhcr.org/cgi-bin/texis/vtx/refworld/rwmain?docid=438c6d972
37. International Refugee Law, Rule of Law in Armed Conflicts Project, The Graduate Institute Geneva, http://www.geneva-academy.ch/RULAC/international_refugee_law.php
38. "Victims of History: The Untold Story of Pakistani Hindu Refugees in India," Hindu American Foundation, http://hafsite.org/resources/human_rights_report
39. Eirin Mobekk, Chapter 9 Transitional Justice in Post-Conflict Societies – Approaches to Reconciliation, www.bmlv.gv.at/pdf_pool/publikationen/10_wg12_psm_100.pdf
40. *Id.*
41. Sudha Ramachandran, "Flawed Justice in Bangladesh" (October 31, 2013), *The Diplomat*, http://thediplomat.com/2013/10/flawed-justice-in-bangladesh/2/

□

11

Morality and Compassion in Hinduism

—*Subhash Kak*

Introduction

Moral and compassionate behavior, as part of conduct, is derived from ideas regarding the nature of reality and man's place in it. Hinduism sees itself as a path of self-knowledge in which the individual's *dharma* depends on station in life and understanding. General principles are enunciated that help determine what is ethical and compassionate in the complexities and ambiguities of life-situations.

Dharma is one of the most complex and all-encompassing terms in Hinduism: it can mean religion, law, duty, proper conduct, morality, and righteousness. It fundamentally underlies conceptions of morality and ethics in Hinduism. The very name by which Hinduism knows itself, *Sanātana Dharma* or Vedic *Dharma* (*sanātana* = eternal, *veda* = knowledge) in Sanskrit, indicates focus on knowledge and right conduct. The various sects of Hinduism take the Vedas, which are collections of hymns, to be their canonical texts. But the Vedas are difficult to understand, and for practical reasons, most Hindus rely on later texts such as the Upaniṣads, Bhagavad Gītā, Āgamas, Śāstras, Sūtras, Purāṇas, the epics, and the teachings of spiritual teachers for guidance (Klostermaier, 2010). These teachings include philosophical ideas but above all they emphasize good conduct. Vyāsa, the author of the

Mahabharata, explains that for such conduct it is essential not to envy anyone in thought, action, or word and treat everyone with love, charity, and compassion.

Although the Vedic tradition speaks of a unity from which all diversity springs, it also acknowledges that polarities must underlie embodied reality, and there exists duality in lived life (Heesterman, 1985). At each felt moment we are stretched between body and spirit, possession and renunciation, and apartness and belonging. According to the Vedas, evil is a manifestation of ignorance that emerges from lack of knowledge of one's true self. For the wise person, who has sensed and felt commonality with all beings, compassion is the natural state.

Ethical conduct has a utilitarian angle, for it promotes harmonious existence that makes it possible for more people to know themselves. Since it affirms a spiritual side to human existence, ethical life not only includes consideration of other humans but also other sentient beings. The deeper basis of this is the Vedic idea of a recursive nature of reality that argues for our own nature to have as much variety as there exists in different kinds of beings. What is true for the individual has parallels for the group and society. Just as *dharma* guides the individual, it must also guide each group and society at large. The Vedas have many passages enjoining ethical behavior.

The *Bhagavad Gītā* has served as the book of guidance for countless people. It sets the conflict of life as an ethical problem. It is about the crisis facing Arjuna, hero of the Pāṇḍavas, facing his relatives, the Kauravas, on the battlefield of Kurukshetra. Overcome by despair at the thought of killing his kinsmen in the battle, Arjuna lays down his arms. But his charioteer Krishna, who is incarnation of Viṣṇu, teaches that Arjuna should do his duty and do battle. Krishna says that inactivity cannot be the answer. One should act without attachment to the result and without personal interest. By doing his duty a person will find salvation no matter what his station. The human soul is not different from the universal soul and, thus, is immortal. When duties are performed without attachment to success or failure, one is not stained by action. Krishna teaches Arjuna the essence of *karma yoga* (yoga of works), *jñāna yoga* (yoga of knowledge), and *bhakti yoga* (yoga of devotion). He also teaches that the human being has free will that permits him to make intelligent choices, which bear on his *karma*. By taking the battlefield of Kurukshetra as symbolic of life's struggles, the lessons of this text are applied to everyday situations (Pande, 2001).

Elaboration of the social code is found in other episodes of the Mahābhārata and in Rāmāyaṇa. The four great aims of human life are *dharma* or righteousness, *artha* or wealth, *kāma* or enjoyment and *moksha* or spiritual liberation. Life runs through four stages: studentship, householdership, forest-dwelling, and renunciation. The four large social classes (*varṇa*) are: the teacher or brahmin, the warrior or kṣatriya, the trader or vaiśya and the worker śūdra, viewed as being born from the head, the arms, the thighs, and the feet of *puruṣa*, the primal Man (*puruṣa*). In reality, the aims of life run somewhat concurrently; each individual is not only a life long student, a member of a family while also detached from it and trying to form a new foundation by renouncing what he has, but due to having the same *puruṣa* within, he has attributes of each of the four classes.

The evolution of the ideas of Hinduism is tied up with the history of India whose archaeological record has been traced, in an unbroken tradition, to about 8000 BC. Prior to this we have records of rock paintings that are believed to be considerably older. The astronomical references in the Vedic books recall events of the third or the fourth millennium BC and earlier (Feuerstein et al., 2001). The Brāhmaṇas describe the Vedic ritual, and the Upaniṣads address philosophical issues. Ethical questions are directly addressed in the Sūtra literature, the Rāmāyaṇa and the Mahābhārata, the Purāṇas and the commentaries on these texts that have been written from time to time. In modern times, the Bhagavad Gītā and the Rāmāyaṇa have influenced millions, including Indian leaders like Bal Gangadhar Tilak, Sri Aurobindo, and Mahatma Gandhi (Klostermaier, 1994).

Academic narratives of Hinduism emphasize issues related to social hierarchy, customs, and sectarian divisions around the worship of Viṣṇu, Śiva, and the Goddess. In reality, the social classes are not rigid, and most Hindus worship several deities, although they might personally be more devoted to one of them. They also recognize that devotion to a personal deity is just the first step in a journey that takes one to experience the formless and the transcendent.

The centrality of ethical life is stressed in the earliest texts. One of the heroes of ancient India is King Hariścandra who is lauded in the Ṛgveda for his ideal conduct, for never having told a lie and for keeping every promise. The gods wish to test him, so they ask the great sage Viśvāmitra to approach Hariścandra and inform him of a promise made in dream to donate his kingdom! The virtuous Hariścandra gives his entire kingdom to the sage and additionally he is forced to sell his wife and son in servitude and to seek employment as a worker at the cremation ground. Further misfortunes befall the family but Hariścandra's conduct is always perfect regardless of the cost to him and his family. Impressed by this conduct, the gods eventually restore his kingdom together with his wife and son to him. Gandhi claims that Hariścandra's story influenced him greatly.

Another famous heroic tale is that of King Sibi who is famed for his justice. A dove comes flying in to him in his court for refuge and the king promises protection. Soon the dove's pursuer, an eagle, arrives and asks the king to release the dove—his food—to him. The king accepts the eagle's argument about natural law but since he has promised to protect the dove, he offers the eagle his own flesh equal in weight to that of the dove. He lets his leg to be cut off but the scales show that the dove is heavier. As he now offers his whole body, the dove and the eagle transform into Agni and Indra and restore his leg, explaining that they had staged the drama to test his justice.

Daṇḍa (punishment) was needed as a tool of *dharma* for self-protection and protection of the weak. In the absence of *daṇḍa*, humans will follow the principle of 'might is right' that is equivalent to the morality of the fishes (*matsya-nyāya*), where the big eats the small.

The ideal conduct of Rāma and Sīta has served as model for the lives of people for centuries. Some of the first lines that my father taught me from Tulasi Dās's Rāmāyaṇa are: *Prāṇa jāyen par vacana na jāyī/ Raghukula rīta yahī calī āyī* (I may lose my life but shall never go back on my word; this is the tradition of the Raghus, the lineage of Rāma.) My father had embraced this principle for his own life. There are other mythological and real-life exemplars whose stories form essential part of the instruction of the child. These include Śravaṇakumāra, known for his filial devotion, who carries his blind parents in baskets slung over his shoulders on pilgrimage.

Virtue and Social Welfare

Manu Samhitā lists ten virtues necessary for a human being to live a dharmic life: *dhṛti* (courage), *kṣamā* (forgiveness), *dama* (temperance), *asteya* (non-covetousness), *śauca* (inner purity), *indriyāṇi-graha* (control of senses), *dhī* (reflective prudence), *vidyā* (wisdom), *satyam* (truthfulness), *and akrodha* (freedom from anger). In later verses, this list was shortened to: *ahimsā* (non-violence), *dama* (self-restraint), *asteya* (non-covetousness), *śauca* (inner purity), *and satyam* (truthfulness).

Patañjali's *Yoga Sūtra* speaks of the need for moral and ethical preparation before any spiritual progress can be made. This preparation includes moral restraint (*yama*), comprising non-harming, truthfulness, non-stealing, chastity, and non-covetousness; and discipline (*niyama*), consisting of purity, contentment, asceticism, self-study, and devotion to the Lord. The remaining limbs are to prepare oneself for a mystical union with the Self: posture, breath control, sense withdrawal, concentration, meditation, and absorption. This elaboration makes it clear that ethical behavior is essential to prepare oneself to receive knowledge and to live life meaningfully.

Like the *Yoga Sūtra*, the law book of Gautama lists the following practices for a virtuous person: "compassion for all beings, patience, contentedness, purity, earnest endeavor, good thoughts, freedom from greed, and freedom from envy."

Among the social virtues are included hospitality, courtesy, and duties to parents, grandparents, spouse, children, and grandchildren. If all were virtuous, there would be no social discord. In Chāndogya Upaniṣad, King Aśvapati Kaikeya describes such a place: "In my kingdom there is no thief, no miser, no drunkard, no man without an altar in his home, no ignorant person, no adulterer, much less an adulteress."

Ethical action calculated to promote social welfare is enjoined upon all, although it is recognized that conflict between groups with different *dharma* is inevitable. Without ethical restraint follows chaos that is detrimental to the development of virtue and self-knowledge. When a student had completed education in the guru's ashram, he was enjoined to speak the truth, follow *dharma*, and not be lazy in self-study, and honor parents and the teacher. Ethical behavior in Hinduism is not only treat all other humans with kindness and compassion but do the same to animals.

Each person has within him three different kinds of tendencies: godly (*daivika*), human, and demonic (*āsuric*). If the godly is the identification with the spirit and with freedom, the demonic is the identification with the body and with possession, and the human lies in between the two. In the Bṛhadāranyaka Upaniṣad 5.1, there is the charming story of the instruction by Prajāpati to the gods, men, and demons. He asks each if they know the meaning of the syllable 'da'. The gods say it means *dama* for self-control, the men say it means *datta* for charity, and the *asuras* (demons) say it means *dayadhvam* for compassion. So when the thunder says '*da, da, da*', it is exhortation for self-control, charity, and compassion.

Varṇa and Jāti

Hinduism has often been criticized for the textual support for hierarchical classes, popularly called the 'caste system'. This system is much misunderstood and the textual descriptions are a result of the Indian predilection to report reality as exists rather than an imagined community. The Ṛgveda hymn 10.90 speaks of a society comprising four classes and the social system as an organism with limbs doing several specialized functions. The Bhagavad Gītā describes the qualities of a Brahmin: control of the mind and the senses, austerity, cleanliness, forbearance, uprightness, scholarship, insight, and faith. He possesses a minimum of worldly assets, accepts voluntary poverty, and is satisfied with simple living and high thinking. Both a priest and a teacher, he is the leader of society and an adviser to king and commoner. A custodian of the culture, he occupies his high position in society by virtue of his spirituality, and not by the power of arms or wealth.

The qualities of a kṣatriya are heroism, high spirit, firmness, resourcefulness, bravery in battle, generosity, and sovereignty. Agriculture, cattle rearing, and trade are the duties of a vaiśya. The main duty of a śūdra is action entailing labor. The respect earned in society was partly determined by the degree of voluntary renunciation and self-control, and also by the degree of intellectual and spiritual attainment. A brahmin must live according to the highest standards of virtue. A kṣatriya enjoys power and pleasure, but he must be ready at any time to lay down his life for the protection of society. A vaiśya must be practical in his pursuit of wealth and he must do it not only for his own enjoyment but also for the welfare of society. A śūdra must excel at his occupation. The Viṣṇu Purāṇa adds: "Besides these their respective obligations, there are duties equally incumbent upon all the four castes. These are, the acquisition of property, for the support of their families; cohabitation with their wives, for the sake of progeny; tenderness towards all creatures, patience, humility, truth, purity, contentment, decency of decoration, gentleness of speech, friendliness; and freedom from envy and repining, from avarice, and from detraction. These also are the duties of every condition of life."

The higher one's position in the class system, the greater the obligation to members of the lower classes, and the more stern is the injunction of renunciation of personal comforts. Although people in different classes at various points in their own life may live according to different norms, it was understood that the wise individual lives for the greatest good for the society. Mohandas

Gandhi stressed vegetarianism and non-violence. He argued that this leads to courage. These views influenced much modern thinking on ethics today, especially in the peace and ecology movements.

There is much misunderstanding of the Indian social organization and some ill-informed people tend to equate caste with Hinduism and it is assumed that strict caste rules trumped virtuous behavior. It is no doubt true that in historical times the social organization in many parts of the country had deteriorated greatly. But many scholars see that as a consequence of the impoverishment of India during the English rule. Economists estimate that India's share of the world economy declined from about 27 percent in 1700 to less than 3 percent in 1950 (Madison, 2006; Kumar and Desai, 1985).

India's technology was very competitive until the beginning of the 19th century and in fact the British imposed heavy tariffs to keep Indian textiles out of Britain. The British became masters of India at a very opportune time. First, they cut off India's export markets. Soon the innovations of the dawning industrial revolution gave their products a cost advantage that became permanent in the absence of new investments to upgrade Indian factories.

As India became de-industrialized, it turned into a huge monopoly market for British products. British Raj made token investments in science and technology. In 1920, India's scientific services had a total of 213 scientists of whom 195 were British! With accelerating poverty and hunger, social classes turned against each other.

Evidence demonstrates that there was no caste system based on birth in the Vedic times. The Purāṇas say that during the golden age (Satya Yuga) everyone was a brahmin. That these categories illustrate psychological states is illustrated by Brahma Purāṇa (Chapter 7) where two people are described who were first vaiśya and then became brahmin. The mention of the four varṇas in the Ṛgveda has been taken to indicate that a caste system existed in the Vedic times. But it is repeatedly mentioned elsewhere that each human is in the image of the *puruṣa* which would indicate that each human internalizes aspects of all the *varṇas*. The Vedic gods are themselves classed as belonging to different *varṇa* as in different situations. Thus, the application to a person of the label of a specific *varṇa* indicates a judgment on that person's temperament and conduct.

The texts proclaim that one's nature alone, and not birth, determines to which *varṇa* one belongs. In the famous dialogue between Yudhiṣ-hira and Yakṣa in the Mahābhārata, Yudhiṣ-hira is asked whether a person is a brahmin based on "birth, learning, or conduct" and his answer is that only 'conduct' makes a person a brahmin and not birth. Brahmin is not a racial category emerging from a mythic fair race; some of the darkest Indians are brahmins.

In the ancient Aryan society, the *varṇas* were functional groupings and not closed endogamous birth-descent groups. It has been suggested that the *jāti* system in its modern form developed very late, perhaps not before 1000 A.D. The Chinese scholar Hsuan Tsang in the seventh century was not aware of it. The emergence of the modern jāti system can be traced as a response to historical events. It was indeed the next fundamental change in the Indian polity that occurred with the invasions of the Turks.

There is no synonym for caste in any Indian language. The Indian words that caste supposedly translates to are *jāti*, which means a large kin-community or descent-group, and *varṇa*, which implies a classification based on function. The dynamics between the *jātis* was influenced a great deal by historical and political factors. During periods of economic growth, the *jātis* were relatively open-ended; during periods of hardships the *jātis* tended to draw in for the sake of survival. The word 'caste' comes from the Portuguese *casta*, a word that was meant to describe the *jāti* system, but slowly it has come to have a much broader connotation.

Megasthenes, the Greek ambassador to India about 2,300 years ago, noted the existence of seven classes, namely that of philosophers, peasants, herdsmen, craftsmen and traders, soldiers, government officials and councilors. These classes were apparently *jātis*. It has been argued that these classes were treasury or tax categories. Nowhere does Megasthenes speak of four *varṇas*.

In its long history, India has had diverse social and religious currents. It is only in the exception that the reality has conformed to the theory of the conservative *dharmaśāstras*. The Vaiṣṇavas emphatically define *varṇa* based on one's actions. This is repeated by the Bhagavad Gītā and the Bhāgavata Purāṇa. Brahma Purāṇa (Chapter 223) says, "People are classed differently according to their nature. Conduct is the cause for brahminhood, not birth, sacramental rites, revelation, lineage. When established in a brahmin's conduct, even a śūdra becomes a brahmin." The Śaivites, likewise, do not subscribe to a caste system. Those who follow the conservative law books have always been a miniscule minority of the population.

Although *jātis* may pay lip service to the priest as an intermediary to the gods when he performs the rituals, each community considers itself to be the highest in status (Kak, 1993). The priest need not be a brahmin. Most *jātis* do not know where they belong in the theory of four *varṇas* classification. Although current self-identities of the communities are generally a snapshot freezing the equations and attitudes of the late nineteenth century, when the British sought caste classification, changing economic and political equations are now having an effect on class equations.

In the equations between the communities, hierarchy is not clear. If the brahmins were to be accepted as the highest community then other communities would have no hesitation in marrying their daughters off to them. But in reality they do not. The Rajputs consider the brahmins to be other-worldly or just too poor; the traders consider the brahmins to be impractical; and so on. In classical Sanskrit plays, the fool is always a brahmin. In other words, each different community has internalized a different outlook on life but these outlooks cannot be placed in any hierarchical ordering. The internalized images of the other must, by its very nature, be a gross simplification and it will never conform exactly to reality.

Some scholars argue that at the village level the cultivator is analogous to the king and he treats priests, washerman, and drummer alike. It appears that the best way to see the role of castes is in terms of relationships with the dominant economic and political community (Hocart, 1970). Note further that only small minorities of Brahmins were ever priests (Madan, 1989); also there have always been non-Brahmin priests.

Caste is a sociological phenomenon that transcends religion since Indian Muslims and Christians also have castes. The 18th-century German society was divided into princes, nobles, burghers, peasants and serfs between whom no marriage other than morganatic was possible. Korea and Japan also had the practice of untouchability. The Buddhist dogma about non-killing appears to have led to the ostracization of those people whose trades involved hunting, slaughtering of animals or other trades that were considered polluting.

Circles of Morality and Freedom

Socially, one lives in two somewhat overlapping circles: one determined by morality and law; and the other determined by one's notions of self. One may choose to live according to the expectations of one's familial and social group, do one's duties, and be a good citizen without worrying about larger questions of meaning. Or one may ask who one is beyond one's name and history and wonder why one likes certain things and doesn't like other things.

The first circle is the domain of Viṣṇu, and the second is that of Śiva. Viṣṇu is the deity of morality, friendship, and devotion, whereas Śiva is the deity of consciousness, of the being within whom is hidden one's deepest self. Indeed one can say that when viewed as the ethical principle, Brahman is Viṣṇu; as the inner Self, it is Śiva; and seen as the energy of Nature, it is the Goddess. Although at one level Viṣṇu and Śiva are the Preserver and the Destroyer, at another level, due to recursion, Viṣṇu and Śiva, as well as the Goddess, are each the Creator, the Preserver, and the Destroyer. Furthermore, each God has a Goddess as the consort, emphasizing the complementarity of the two. Śiva and Goddess are also viewed as a single deity, as half of each, called Ardhanārīśvara, and Viṣṇu and Śiva as a single deity called Harihara.

Outwardly, the path of Viṣṇu is relatively straight because it requires following the laid out rules and exercising self-control. On the other hand, the path of Śiva calls for self-questioning that may involve abandoning what one started out with. People pick one or the other path based on their innate temperament. The path of inward search soon raises troubling questions related to several selves within. At a more philosophical level, in the transitions between several selves, the individual dies many deaths and is reborn. This is the dance of Śiva that destroys and creates at each moment and at many levels. Without Viṣṇu there is chaos, without Śiva there can be no creativity.

The two circles also characterize human conduct. If we lived our lives mechanically, just doing what we area expected to do, we would be unable to rise to unexpected and new challenges. A morality based on virtue and altruism rather than any specific prescriptive rules is likely to bring happiness to most people.

Our understanding of what is right conduct should be informed by the connections between our outer and the inner worlds. At one level, the outer is merely the contents of the inner. In other words, the exploration of the outer is only the exploration of the inner. The fact that we can even make sense of the outer world is due to the connections (*bandhu*) between the outer and the inner. Ancient mythologies acknowledge these connections: the gods and the demons reside in the sky and also in the firmament of our inner space.

The yoga books speak of three skies which are the physical sky (*bhautika ākāśa* or *bhūtākāśa*), the sky of the mind (*citta ākāśa*), and the sky of consciousness (*cid ākāśa*). Of these, the sky of consciousness is the most subtle and powerful and it is this that engenders the connections with the other two skies. The sky of the mind is not fully illumined and it is this darkness that causes the individual to think that the physical sky is the primary reality. If the light of consciousness is allowed to shine in its full glory in the sky of the mind, then the individual becomes enlightened. Yogic practices make the individual aware of the three skies and the relationship between their contents. More importantly, they help the individual to erase invalid links that they have imposed on the three which resulted in their confusion about the nature of reality.

Hinduism takes phenomenal reality to be a projection of God (Brahman), who is both transcendent and immanent. In its transcendent form, Brahman is beyond any attributes; in its immanent form it may be visualized in many different ways, leading to a multiplicity of representations. The evolution of the universe is by laws, yet sentient beings have freedom. The law of *karma* constrains ordinary action, but a realized person is free.

The Vedic texts claim that language cannot describe reality completely, although its mystery can be experienced fully. Knowledge is classified in two ways: the lower or dual; and the higher or unified. The lower knowledge, that describes the objective world, is obtained using logic and it is accessible by language. The higher knowledge concerns the experiencing self and it is beyond ordinary language. The seemingly irreconcilable worlds of the material and the conscious are aspects of the same transcendental reality. Hinduism is supportive of all scientific exploration, believing that at its end one become aware of its limitations and the need to reach the mystery of the experiencing self. From a personal perspective, Hinduism is concerned with strategies that make self-transformation possible.

Hinduism approaches the world in an ecological sense. Not only humans, but also animals are supposed to be sentient and, therefore, deserving of compassion. The Hindu approach to reality is through *jñāna* (intuitive understanding) that includes subjective and objective knowledge, value and fact, and consciousness and reality. *Jñāna* presupposes *jijñāsā*, a reaching out to understand, that leads to a spark of illumination. Ethical behavior is an indispensable condition for knowledge, which thus is not value free.

Vedic Cosmology

Briefly, the Vedic texts present a tripartite and recursive view of the world. The universe is viewed as three regions of earth, space, and sky that in the human being are mirrored in the physical body, the breath (*prāṇa*), and mind. The processes in these regions are assumed to be connected in consequence of the binding (*bandhu*) between various inner and outer phenomena. At one level, it means awareness that certain biological cycles such as menstruation, have the same period as the moon. At another level, equations such as the 360 bones of the infant (which fuse into the 206 bones of the adult) correspond to the number of days in the civil year.

The connection between the outer and the inner cosmos is seen most strikingly in the use of the number 108 in Indian religious and artistic expression. Elementary geometrical reasoning establishes that this number is the approximate distance from the earth to the sun and the moon in sun and moon diameters, respectively. The diameter of the sun is also approximately 108 times the diameter of the earth, but that fact is not likely to have been known to the Vedic sages. The number of dance poses given in the *Nātya Sāstra* is 108, as is the number of beads in a rosary. The *distance* between the body and the inner sun is also taken to be 108, to span which one symbolically one uses 108 names of the deity in worship. The number of weak points in the body in Āyurveda is 107, because in a chain 108 units long, the number of weak points would be one less. The centrality of this number in Indian life shows the importance of the idea of recursion across time and scale.

The Vedas are primarily concerned about universal laws related to the inner self (*adhyātma vidyā*) that are true for all times. The Hindu experience is thus not contingent on a particular account of history, or an event that cannot be replicated. Complementing the Veda, which is the *heard* revelation (*śruti*), is the remembered tradition (*smṛti*). As custom, *smṛti* is considered appropriate for time and location and thus subject to change. This is the reason behind the adaptability of Hinduism to contemporary change.

In Hinduism, the dividing line between objective sciences and *adhyātma vidyā* (spiritual knowledge) is the logical or linguistic paradox. Logical argument and rational proof using *Nyāya* is the way to obtain correct knowledge. But where paradox (*parokṣa*) begins, one must let go of linguistic associations to experience paradox-free deeper knowledge.

Nyāya's beginnings go back to the Vedic period, but its first systematic elucidation is Akṣapāda Gotama's *Nyāya Sūtra*, dated to the third century BC. Its text begins with the nature of doubt and the means of proof, and it considers the nature of self, body, senses and their objects, cognition and mind.

The *Nyāya* system supposes that we are so constituted as to seek truth. Our minds are not empty slates; the very constitution of the mind provides some knowledge of the nature of the world. The four *pramānas* through which correct knowledge is acquired are: *pratyakṣa,* or direct perception; *anumāna,* or inference; *upamāna,* or analogy; and *śabda,* or verbal testimony. Four factors are involved in direct perception: the senses, their objects, the contact of the senses and the objects, and the cognition produced by this contact. The mind mediates between the self and the senses. When the mind is in contact with one sensory organ, it cannot be so with another. It is therefore said to be atomic in dimension. It is because of the nature of the mind that our experiences are essentially linear, although quick succession of impressions may give the appearance of simultaneity.

Medical Ethics

The idea of the Hindu medical ethics may be gleaned from initiation ceremony of the physician (*vaidya*). Called the *upanayana*, the ceremony involved the teacher leading the student three times around the sacred fire. This ceremony made the student thrice-born (*trija*), distinguished from the twice-born (*dvija*) non-physicians.

At the closing of the initiation, the guru gave a solemn address to the students in which the guru directed the students to a life of chastity, honesty, and vegetarianism. The student was to strive with all his being for the health of the sick. He was not to betray patients for his own advantage. He was to dress modestly and avoid strong drink. He was to be collected and self-controlled, measured in speech at all times. He was to constantly improve his knowledge and technical skill. In the home of the patient, he was to be courteous and modest, directing all attention to the patient's welfare. He was not to divulge any knowledge about the patient and his family. If the patient was incurable, he was to keep this to himself if it was likely to harm the patient or others.

The normal length of the student's training appears to have been seven years. Before graduation, the student was to pass a test. But the physician was to continue to learn through texts, direct observation, and through inference. In addition, the *vaidyas* attended meetings where knowledge was exchanged. The doctors were also enjoined to gain knowledge of unusual remedies from herdsmen and forest-dwellers. The *vaidya* was assisted by nurses. The great doctor Suśruta describes the ideal nurse as devoted, friendly, watchful, not inclined to disgust, and knowledgeable.

There is reference to free hospitals in ancient India. There were also hospitals for animals and shelters for old animals.

Regarding the unborn, the Garbha Upaniṣad claims that the subtle body enters the embryo in the seventh month. Although the Hindu law books condemn abortion, the modern Hindu is wont to defer to the scientist in determining the time that the fetus becomes viable. Since the individual is not just the physical body but also the subtle body, cloning the physical body is not problematic. For similar reason, Hindus are not opposed to stem cell research (Crawford, 1994).

Concluding Remarks

Moral and compassionate conduct is a theme that runs through most Hindu teachings. The exhortation below in the Viṣṇu Purana (Chapter 8) sums up Hindu attitudes about correct behavior:

> Viṣṇu is most pleased with him who does good to others; who never utters abuse, calumny, or untruth; who never covets another's wife or wealth, and who bears ill-will towards none; who neither beats nor slays any living being; who is ever diligent in the service of the gods, of the Brahmans, and of his teacher; who is always desirous of the welfare of all creatures,

> of his children, and of his own soul; in whose pure heart no pleasure is derived from the imperfections of love and hatred.

Hinduism recognizes that at one level all creatures are placed in a hierarchical system, where the big fish eats the small. While this physical aspect of life represents the animal self, the role of Hinduism is to raise the individual beyond the animal self to a state where one sees the interconnectedness of reality and develops compassion for all beings. Non-violence is lauded as the highest principle, with the acknowledgement that the real world has violence in it that reflects the degree of the development of society.

The Hindu belief is that science and technology must be harnessed in a manner that furthers man's inherent quest for self-knowledge. Since an individual is defined not in isolation, but through his interactions with other persons, this quest of knowledge cannot ignore the larger good of the society, and it requires ethical preparation on the part of the individual. In the Upaniṣads, this is addressed as the coming together of both *vidyā* (spiritual knowledge) and *avidyā* (material knowledge) (Kak, 2008). The Hindu ideal is to embrace life and its challenges without losing sight of the larger world and remaining compassionate in dealings with others.

REFERENCES

Crawford, S.C. (1994). *Dilemmas of Life and Death: Hindu Ethics in North American Context*. Albany: State University of New York Press.

Feuerstein, G., Kak, S. and Frawley, D. (2001). *In Search of the Cradle of Civilization*. Quest Books.

Heesterman, J.C. (1985). *The Inner Conflict of Tradition*. Chicago University Press.

Hocart, A.M. (1970). *Kings and Councillors.* Chicago University Press.

Kak, S. (1993). *Understanding Caste in India*. Mankind Quarterly, Vol. 34, pp. 117-23.

Kak, S. (2007). *The Prajña Sūtras*. DK Printworld.

Kak, S. (2012). *Mind and Self.* Stillwater: OSU, 2012.

Klostermaier, K.K. (1994). *A Survey of Hinduism*. Albany: State University of New York Press.

Klostermaier, K.K. (2010). Vidyaranya Swami's 'panca viveka' and Thomas Aquinas' 'quique viae' in the light of today's science. *Journal of Hindu-Christian Studies*, Vol. 23, Article 9.

Kumar, D. and Desai, M. (ed.) (1985). *The Cambridge Economic History of India*, Volume 2, c.1751-c.1970.

Madan, T.N. (1989), *Family and Kinship*. Oxford University Press.

Madison, A. (2006). *The World Economy*, Vols. 1-2. OECD Publishing.

Pande, G.C. (ed.) (2001). *Life, Thought and Culture in India*. New Delhi: Centre for Studies in Civilizations.

□

12

Compassion in Sikhism: A Scriptural, Traditional and Historical Perspective

—Dilpreet Singh Jammu

Introduction

Founded by Guru Nanak Dev Ji in the late 14th century, Sikhi, or Sikhism, is the youngest of the Dharmic traditions at barely 500 years of age. It has been described by some as a true universal religion; its message is for all of humanity, not just for Sikhs. Sikhi is not well known in the Western world as very few early scholars focused on Sikh Dharma (Max Arthur Macauliffe, J.D. Cunningham) and it has only recently attracted the attention of modern Western experts. Compassion is a central and critical tenant within Sikhism, and also within the teachings of its holy scriptures, the Sri Guru Granth Sahib Ji. This paper analyses the text of the Sri Guru Granth Sahib Ji and examines the concept of compassion within the Sikh faith. It also discusses compassion within the key values of the faith and then provides historical examples.

Definition of Compassion

Before discussing compassion, one may find it helpful to begin with a definition. Oxford dictionary defines compassion (noun) as "Sympathetic pity and concern for the sufferings or misfortunes of others." Merriam-Webster provides a more full and comprehensive definition of compassion as "sympathetic consciousness of others' distress together with a desire to alleviate it." It is the proactive desire to eliminate another humans' suffering that distinguishes true compassion from basic pity. A quick examination of any thesaurus shows that similar words may include 'grace', 'mercy', 'kind', 'kindness' and 'compassionate'.

The Sikh holy scripture, the Sri Guru Granth Sahib Ji (SGGS), is written in the Gurmukhi script. This script was codified by the second Sikh Guru, Guru Angad Dev Ji. The closest Gurmukhi word that translates to the English equivalent of compassion is ਦਇਆ. This word is often written in English transliteration as '*Daya*' but is correctly pronounced as 'the-i-ah'. ਦਇਆ is one of many Gurmukhi words which English speakers may translate to include the word 'mercy'.

Word Analysis of Compassion in Sri Guru Granth Sahib Ji

Because the incidence and context of a word within a document is an indicator of its relative importance, this paper provides a numeric analysis of the word incidence of 'compassion' as broadly defined within the Sri Guru Granth Sahib Ji. The author began with the original text of the Guru, and then considered a number of English translations; Bhai Gopal Singh Translation, Manmohan Singh Translation, Gurbachan Singh Talib Translation, Pritam Singh Chahil Translation and the Dr. Sant Singh Khalsa Translation, before settling on the Khalsa Translation, which is also referred to as the "Khalsa Consensus Translation." This is a more modern translation with minimal archaic words that would be difficult and cumbersome for the modern English reader. The Sri Guru Granth Sahib Ji is a unique document in that it is not divided by chapters but by musical *raags* (measures). It consists of 1,430 pages of poetry and 5,864 verses, and each verse has an identifiable musical measure, and thus can be sung by the congregation.

As shown in Fig. 1, the Khalsa Consensus Translation was downloaded onto a Windows-based computer and then searched using basic software and web-based tools. Word incidence was determined, and then the lines and verses were collated for additional analysis. Figure 2 shows the incidence of keywords within the Sri Guru Granth Sahib Ji.

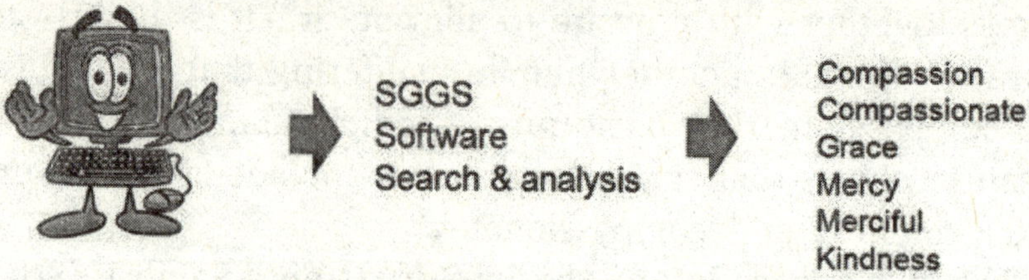

Fig. 1. Overview of Methodology.

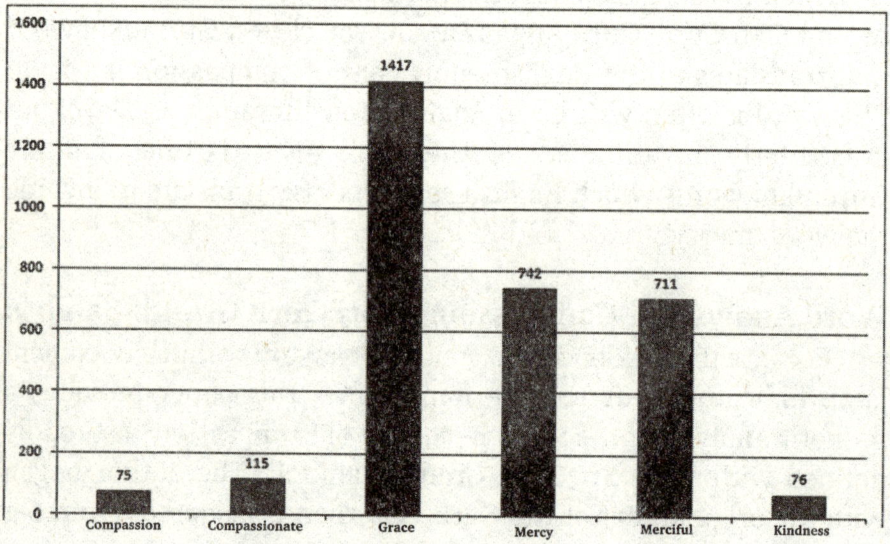

Fig. 2. Incidence of Keywords.

There are over 3,136 references to words that broadly include 'compassion'. The English translation of 'Grace' appears 1,417 times, with 'Mercy' and 'Merciful' appearing 742 and 711 times, respectively. These three words have the highest incidence. The words 'Compassionate' and 'Compassion' are found in translation 115 and 75 times, respectively. Though this appears to be a simple analysis, when one considers that there are 5,864 verses, the sheer number of references (3,136) covers a substantial portion of the SGGS. It also speaks to the importance of compassion within the Sikh scriptures and for practitioners of the Sikh faith.

Since the number of references, with a broad search criteria, would require an analysis of the entire Sri Guru Granth Sahib Ji, this paper focused on those words which were translated directly to 'Compassion' and 'Compassionate'. This reduced the number of references to a manageable 190 verses. It should be noted (as an example) that 'Grace' and 'Mercy' may have multiple contexts within the SGGS and thus, may complicate the discussion. By focusing only on two key English translated concepts, it becomes possible to do a preliminary and manageable analysis of the Sri Guru Granth Sahib. 'Grace' and 'Mercy' may be considered for a future study.

Context of Compassion in the Verses of the Sri Guru Granth Sahib Ji

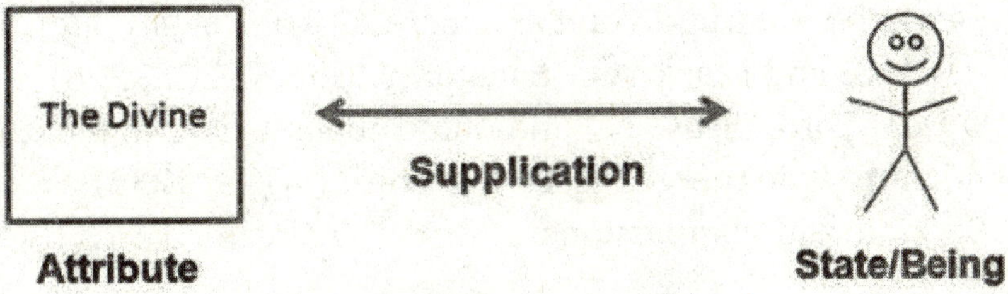

Fig. 3. Overview of Relationship.

Once the 190 references were examined for context, they fit one of three major categories as shown in Fig. 3:

(i) The reference was a description of the Divine or exemplified an attribute or quality of the Divine.

(ii) The reference was a supplication to the Divine.

(iii) The reference describes the State of Human existence or the State of Being.

We will look at each of these in turn along with examples from the Sri Guru Granth Sahib Ji.

(i) A Description of the Divine or an Attribute

Examples of this included the following English lines from the Sri Guru Granth Sahib Ji. The page numbers have been provided in brackets.

> He is the Lord of the Universe, the Compassionate Lord, the Supreme Lord God, the Formless Lord. (SGGS, 614)
>
> I seek Your Sanctuary, and bow to You, O Compassionate Lord. (SGGS, 1119)

> Suffering in pain, I have come to Your Door, O Compassionate Lord. (SGGS, 793)

The description of the Divine as being 'compassionate' is a theme that runs throughout the Sri Guru Granth Sahib Ji.

(ii) *A Supplication to the Divine*

The second major group was a supplication to the Divine. In this case, the supplicant asks the Divine to transfer the attribute of compassion to the Human existence, thereby elevating the Human existence. Examples include:

> Please be kind and compassionate, O Lord of my life; I am helpless, and I seek Your Sanctuary, God. (SGGS, 208)
>
> O Dear Lord, please be kind and compassionate to me, that I might remain merged in You, O Lord. (SGGS, 1232)
>
> Be kind and compassionate to me, O Creator Lord. (SGGS, 897)

(iii) *The State of Human Existence or Being*

The final category speaks to the state of the human being or also to the state of being human. These verses or lines describe the import of a human that has either achieved the state of compassion or is devoid of this higher state. Compassion is considered to be a Divine quality and thus anything that increases the ability to experience compassion for all of creation moves us closer to the Creator. The following lines provide insight to the state of being:

> You have no compassion; the Lord's Light does not shine in you. (SGGS, 903)
>
> Purity, contentment, compassion, faith and truthfulness—I have ushered these into the home of myself. (SGGS, 379)
>
> He alone obtains meditation, austerities, self-discipline, compassion and Dharmic faith, whom the Lord so blesses. (SGGS, 966)

The number of incidences for each verse is provided in Fig. 4:

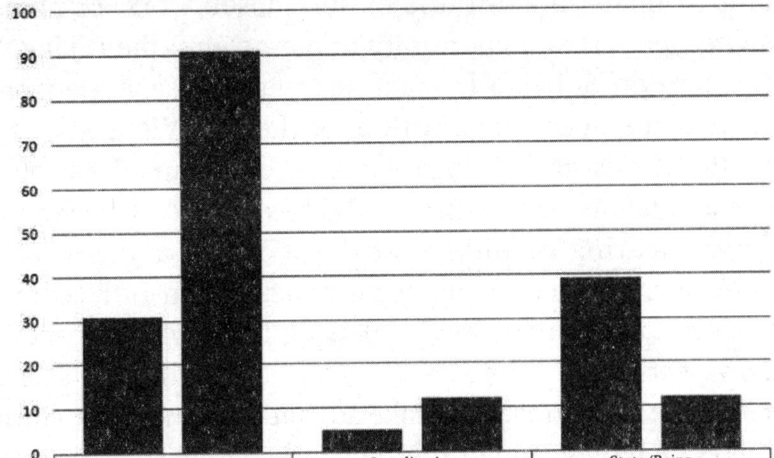

	Attribute	Supplication	State/Being
■Compassion	31	5	39
■Compassionate	91	12	12

Fig. 4: Numeric Word Count as a Function of Category.

As this analysis shows, the word 'Compassionate' is used, to a greater degree, to refer to the Divine attribute (91 references) with fewer references to State/Being (12 references). The word 'Compassion' is used comparably, both as a Divine attribute (31 references) and in the context of being in this more positive human state (39 references).

Three Values of Sikhism and Traditions/History

The three key values of Sikhi are:

(i) **Naam Japna**—Remember and meditate upon God.
(ii) **Kirat Karna**—Living and working honestly.
(iii) **Vand Chhakna**—Sharing with others.

Every Sikh is reminded that these three values are intertwined and work in harmony to guide one's daily actions. Compassion and remembering or meditating upon Divine attributes, as well as supplication to the Divine were covered in the context of the Sri Guru Granth Sahib (see above).

What about *Kirat Karna*? One's career and livelihood are a major part of the day. To have compassion, and to be compassionate in and through our chosen work, combined with *Naam Japna*, is an opportunity to merge with the Divine. Work is an extension of being human, and yet, still separate from us, as our vocation does not go with us at the end. What will go with us are the deeds and actions we take onto ourselves; our fellow humans and our environment. A Sikh is reminded to avoid stealing, lying, cheating or killing while at work, and not to pursue professions which promote negative actions. In 14th century India, it was not unusual for inn keepers and highway robbers to attack unsuspecting travelers. Nor was it unusual for unscrupulous businesses to mistreat or to take advantage of workers. Guru Nanak admonished these and furthermore asked us to consider our actions on all beings and forms within creation.

Vand Chhakna has been described as sharing with others. The *Langar* (free community kitchen) is the key manifestation of this value. The *Langar* existed from the time of Guru Nanak, but was codified and institutionalized by Guru Amar Das Ji, the third Guru of the Sikhs. Every Gurduara serves free food to all, regardless of caste, creed, vocation, social status, religion or wealth. The *Langar* not only feeds the poor, but it takes it one step further, in that one cannot just throw alms at those who are less fortunate, and then walk away feelıng good about oneself. The *Langar* requires that all of us sit with those whom our minds may consider lower or higher. It ensures that we have an opportunity to engage with those who are less fortunate, and to have a sense of their lives.

Today, and at the time of the living Gurus, it was not uncommon to reside within one's own caste or social status. The *Langar* afforded not only an opportunity to feed the poor, but also to interact with them by serving them and to better understand others and thus develop greater compassion. For over 500 years the *Langar* has been a part of Sikh living. All Gurduaras have a *Langar* at the end of a service and many large Gurduaras have langar available 24/7 for anyone who walks through the doors. The *Langar* physically expresses the oneness of humanity. *Langar Seva* (service) is considered by modern Sikhs as a way to give back to the community.

At the time of Guru Tegh Bahadar Ji, the Mogul emperor Aurangzeb had begun the forced conversion of the Kashmiri Pandits (Hindu Priests). His strategy was to convert the priests, with the expectation that the followers would convert more willingly to Islam. The Khasmiri Pandits approached the 9th Guru and requested his help. Guru Tegh Bahadar Ji advised the Pandits to deliver a message to the emperor, that if Aurangzeb could convert him, then all would willingly submit to conversion. The Guru then travelled to Delhi, was arrested and, as expected then, was mistreated and tortured. He refused to accept Islam and was publically executed. The key message for Sikhs is that it is not enough to defend our own right to worship. We must defend the rights of all religions to worship and be willing to sacrifice ourselves for 'the others'. True compassion requires Sikhs to respect other religious traditions.

The third example of compassion in tradition and history is in the actions of Bhai Kanhaiya Ji (1648-1718). During the time of the 9th Living Guru, Bhai Kanhaiya Ji was seen giving water to all wounded soldiers on the battlefield. The Sikh soldiers complained to the Guru that Bhai Kanhaiya Ji was aiding and providing comfort to the enemy. This was taxing already dwindling resources and was making it difficult for the Sikh soldiers. Upon speaking with Bhai Kanhaiya, the Guru reminded his followers that compassion is to be extended to all and all wounds on the battlefield are to be treated. Any fallen soldier is to be provided with water and with care. In the Sikh tradition, it is incumbent upon us to treat all of humanity as one, regardless of how we may see them.

Conclusion

Compassion is central to the human experience and critical within Sikh *Dharma*. The Sri Guru Granth Sahib Ji (English Translation) has over 3,000 references to Compassion, and to its synonyms.

Compassion is a Divine attribute. As humans, we can achieve this state of being, through prayer and meditation. Supplication is a path to recognizing the Divine within us, here and now, not just for the afterlife, but for living in this life.

Compassion is not a theoretical construct, but also a part of daily being. Compassion is to be extended to the poor, to our colleagues at work, to all those who worship and to those on the battlefield. Regardless of our religion, caste, creed, social status or wealth, compassion is the precursor to The Divine.

REFERENCES

Khalsa, Sant Singh. Sri Guru Granth Sahib (English Translation). USA: Sikhnet, 2013.

Macauliffe, Max Arthur. The Sikh Religion, Its Gurus, Sacred Writings and Authors, Oxford University Press, 1909.

Singh, Gopal. Sri Guru Granth Sahib (English Translation). New Delhi: World Sikh University Press, 1978.

Sri Guru Granth Sahib (English Translation). Sikhitothemax and various online websites.

□

13

Compassion and Service in Buddhism

—Frank Tedesco

> Cherishing and caring for others is the source of all happiness. Cherishing ourselves over others is the source of all suffering and negative conditions.
>
> *—Śāntideva*

Compassion as an impetus for selfless service to others in the Dharmic tradition of Buddhism is a compelling topic for our troubled times. Sudden and unexpected tragedies due to human folly, accidents and environmental fluctuations are occurring simultaneously in all regions of the globe. Relatively isolated populations on distant continents are now aware of each other and interconnected as individuals and groups. Thanks to satellite television and Internet streaming video, viewers on every continent can see, hear and feel the distress of distant people within their own country and around the world instantaneously as if they were close neighbors. They can also re-experience traumatic events over and over again around the clock due to news rebroadcasts and media manipulation by governments and corporations.

The world has recently witnessed the grief of victims of the mysterious disappearance of Malaysian Airline over the Indian Ocean, the shooting down of a civilian aircraft over war-torn Ukraine, the spread of Ebola in western Africa and demonstrations and militarized police response after the police shooting of an unarmed teenager in Ferguson, Missouri.[1] These events have been featured in the media against the grim, benumbing background of the everyday horrors in Gaza, Iraq, Syria and Afghanistan. Outside of war zones, neither the very poor nor the very privileged regions of the planet are exempt from the ravages of global warming. We will share the effects of global climate change directly whether we live on the Pacific Rim, Africa, North America, South America, Central Asia, Europe, or elsewhere.[2]

Information technologies have shattered traditional, hierarchical relationships between the powerful and the weak, the younger generations and the old. The ownership and control of knowledge and technological expertise are shared by more people than ever before because of global educational exchange opportunities and the Internet universities. So, too, vast numbers of people are migrating or being dislocated to neighboring nations and distant regions because of regional conflicts, famines, floods, earthquakes, mudslides, sea-level raise, droughts or varieties of human environmental degradation. At the same time, partly due to advances in food production and medicine, the world population is increasing faster than ever, major debilitating diseases are being eradicated or controlled, and longevity has increased dramatically.[3] Some scientists in the wealthier countries envisage an almost unlimited extension of human life.[4] Yet parallel to these futurist hopes, obesity and diabetes, have become widespread and have become serious health issues among the more 'developed' or 'advanced' classes East and West.[5]

As isolated people become increasingly exposed to the pain and suffering of others near and far and they seek answers to explain misfortune, many are seeking understanding, consolation and guidance in the ancient Indian *Dharma* teachings of Buddhism. Unlike popular theistic faiths, Buddhism does not require belief in God or gods, hereditary priests, divinely-inspired scripture or particular allegiance to a troubled, geographic motherland. Its earliest teachings as in the *Dharmapada*[6] point to the seeker's own mind as the cause of happiness or unhappiness in this life. For many, the Buddhadharma has emerged as a way to analyze, evaluate and more deeply understand the causes of their personal experience of suffering (*dūkha*), the First Noble Truth. It is not just a play of philosophical ideas for bemusement in chat rooms: as comprehensive guidance for ethical living, Buddhist teachings and reflections provide an analysis of existential causes and conditions and an empirical, 'psychosocial technology' (ethical lifestyle guidelines and practices)—the Eightfold Path to Enlightenment—to help individuals better understand themselves as intentional agents of their '*karma*' introspectively. Practitioners claim that the process itself is transformative of their 'inner world'. Personal insights encourage consequent, wholesome actions (*kusala karma*) that lead to the elimination (*nirodha*) of the origin of suffering ('thirst' or 'craving' (tasha), the Second Noble Truth. As the painful trauma of multiple disruptions of 'satisfaction' lessen and disappear, contentment and happiness arise accompanied by compassion or more empathy for those around us who are trapped by "greed, hatred and foolishness."

According to the senior nun Venerable Adrienne Howley who was both ordained by the Dalai Lama and has the highest ordination vows in the Vietnamese tradition,

> Following the Buddha's way and studying the *Dharma*...is meant to develop sympathetic understanding, gentleness and the ability to see the reasons for another's behavior. If you did no more than act with real compassion in every situation, you would almost be a Buddha. The sincere practice of *universal compassion* leads to enlightenment. A mind set on this path seeks to see clearly what needs to be done—or not done—and the best and most compassionate way to go about it. Seeing *clearly* is the way.
>
> Universal compassion means *awareness* at all times that all sentient beings—all things that live—experience suffering. Awareness of *universal suffering* is the first step toward *universal compassion*.

Thinking is a very rare activity. Thinking is what the Buddha tried to teach, thinking about existence—not in the manner of worrying and speculating but of being *fully aware of the way things have become in any given moment.*[7]

The notion of universal compassion applies to all Buddhists—the four-fold *sangha* of monks and nuns and laymen and lay women—and followers of other traditions and philosophies or no philosophical orientation at all. Everyone can share in the benefits of developing *karuṇā*, 'compassion' ('empathy'). It is the wish that others be free from suffering (*dūkha*).[8]

In the Pāli or Nikāya Buddhism as practiced by contemporary Theravāda Buddhists, compassion (*karuṇā*) is traditionally listed as the second of the four brahmavihāra or divine abidings after loving-kindness (Pāli: mettā, Sanskrit: Maita), and preceding empathetic joy (*muditā*) and equanimity (*upekḥā*). In a widely observed early Buddhist guided meditation practice, compassionate intentions are systematically applied to oneself, then to widening circles person-to-person, from those closest to the indifferent, then to those hostile to you ('enemies') and lastly to everyone in the surrounding vicinity, the region, the country, the continent, the globe and lastly all directions in the cosmos.

Karunā was not only considered a focus of meditation but also a call for action. According to Buddhaghosa, whose commentaries are the central authority for the interpretation of the Pāli scriptures in Theravā da Buddhism, analysis of the word '*karuṇā*' shows that in Pāli Buddhism:

> the concept of compassion calls for aggressive action for the relief of the suffering of others. When others suffer it makes the heart of good people tremble (*kampa*), thus it is *karuṇā*; it demolishes others' suffering, attacks and banishes it, thus it is *karuṇā*; or it is dispersed over the suffering, is spread out through pervasion, thus it is *karuṇā*.[9]

Compassion is widely extended across all planes of existence in the Buddhist cosmos in the exalted Mahāyāna ideal of the *bodhisattva* who generates *bodhicitta*, the vow or commitment to achieve buddhahood for the purpose of liberating all beings from suffering (*mahākarunā*—'great compassion'). We are all familiar with the famous moral exemplar of His Holiness Tenzin Gyatso, the current exiled 14th Dalai Lama of Tibet, who is considered an emanation of the *Avalokiteāvara bodhisattva*, the "Lord who Looks Down in Empathy," who responds to the desperate cries of worldly beings and assuages their suffering as a savior with wisdom and compassion both spiritually and in practical service. His Holiness considers compassion the 'supreme emotion':

> ...our innate capacity for empathy is the source of the most precious of all human qualities, which we in Tibetan call *nying je*. Now while generally translated simply as 'compassion', the term *nying je* has a wealth of meaning that is difficult to convey succinctly, though the ideas it contains are universally understood. It connotes love, affection, kindness, gentleness, generosity of spirit, and warm-heartedness. It is also used as a term of both sympathy and endearment. On the other hand, it does not imply 'pity' as the word compassion may. There is no sense of condescension. On the contrary, *nying je* denotes a feeling of connection with others, reflecting its origin in empathy,...a combination of empathy and reason...when we act out of concern for others, our behavior towards them is automatically positive...we have no room for suspicion when our hearts are filled with love.[10]

In this chapter, I attempt a brief overview of what we may call 'compassionate service' (sometimes '*bodhisattva* action') in contemporary Buddhism as practiced 'on the ground' in the 'real' world as it appears today. Other scholars at our meeting will address the scriptural and theoretical understanding of compassion in Buddhism at greater depth from its birth in pre-literate India to its dissemination beyond the Indian sub-continent over more than two millennia. This paper will also overlap with topics of other Uberoi Experts' Meeting panelists. Some notable Buddhist leaders and organizations motivated by compassion for others choose to concern themselves primarily with broad socio-political issues of violence, conflicts, war and worrisome environmental challenges affecting our complex, interdependent planet. This modern Buddhist movement is collectively called 'socially engaged Buddhism' in the West (See Christopher S. Queen, "Introduction: A New Buddhism" in *Engaged Buddhism in the Online Academic Room*, 2005).

Socially-engaged Buddhism: At Home and Afar

The term 'socially-engaged Buddhism' is attributed to the renowned Vietnamese peace activist and Zen monk Thich Nhat Hanh who as a practicing monk during wartime in Vietnam was impelled to serve his bloodied and suffering country men and women in the battlefield firsthand rather than simply praying for them in a temple. As charismatic speakers and gifted and prolific writers, the Dalai Lama Thich Nhat Hanh, Sulak Sivaraksa, A.T. Ariyaratne and other talented leaders have brought socially engaged Buddhism as 'love in action' wider public recognition as an activist faith throughout the world. Buddhist sensitivity to others' suffering (compassion), however, is not just for people experiencing violence, human rights violations and sexual degradation in distant places, it begins with oneself at home with those near to you. According to Kenneth Kraft,[11] "For Thich Nhat Hanh, engaged Buddhism encompasses meditation, mindfulness in daily life, involvement in one's family, and political responsiveness." Echoing Buddhist critics of the phrase 'socially engaged', the Zen monk "at times even dismisses the term he coined as a misnomer: 'Engaged Buddhism is just Buddhism. If you practice Buddhism in your family, in society, it is engaged Buddhism.'"[12] Of relevance to our theme of compassion and service in Buddhism, I must add another quote from the revered Vietnamese sage:

> We talk about social service, service to humanity, service for others who are far away, helping to bring peace to the world—but we often forget that it is the very people around us that we must live for first of all. If you cannot serve your wife or husband or child or parent—how are you going to serve society?[13]

Another senior monk from Vietnam, Australia-based Venerable Thich Quang Ba emphasized the inherently 'engaged' nature of Buddhism from its inception in India. He noted that:

> (1) The place of 'interdependence' (*pamicca samuppāda*—the "conditionality of all physical and psychical phenomena") in Buddhist philosophy predisposes Buddhism to social engagement; (2) In the Buddha's lifetime, very few *bhikkhus* asked for or were granted permission to live solitary lives of practice. His followers were deeply engaged in work at the village level; (3) We are constantly being engaged by life. It is extremely difficult to be disengaged from life. It is how we engage life as Buddhists that matters; (4) The (historic) Golden Ages of Buddhism in India, China and Vietnam provide significant examples of socially-engaged Buddhism. The term may provide an emphasis in practice which is appealing to Westerners but it is not a new form of Buddhism.[14]

The historical Buddha's forty-five year teaching career in India was a mission of direct compassionate service to the people of his time, extending to animals as well (all sentient beings). Buddha taught 'compassionately-engaged *Dharma*' for all. Legend goes that he was driven by a profound compassion he felt for their suffering as beings subject to the inescapable existential reality of impermanence (*anicca*), specifically the experience of painful gestation and birth into the world from the womb, the discomforts and anxieties of the stages of maturation leading to inevitable illnesses, disabilities, decrepitude and inexorable death. He taught that individuals must rely on their own ethical actions and insights into their own patterns of thinking in order to achieve liberation from the karmic bonds of their circumstances without relying on gods, incontestable divine scriptures, public opinion, traditional blood sacrifices or a hereditary priestly caste.

From what can be surmised from the voluminous legends, stories and teachings that have been passed down to us, the Buddha was a brilliant and well-seasoned yogi who was also compassionately attuned to society around him. Though born in a ruling family of wealth and provided the education of a future king, he left his worldly good fortune behind for the life of an ascetic. He became a leader of a voluntary association (*sangha*) of homeless mendicants who were dependent on a hospitable local populace for sustenance in exchange for teachings. His single-minded purpose was guiding all individuals within the tribes and castes of the warring society of his time (~2300-2600 BCE) toward personal, inner spiritual cultivation and outer, socially-responsible, ethical behavior. In short, his primary guiding platform was adumbrations of the Middle Way of the Four Noble Truths and the Eight-fold Path for forty-five years. This deeper insight into 'the existential present'—the results of previous actions (*karma vipka*)—and his positive teachings of ethical, 'mindful' living for householders and the ordained *sangha* focused on inner freedom and harmonious social interactions.

According to Professor Achariya Vijaya Samarawickrama, the former Director of Nalanda Institute in Selangor, Malaysia:

> When we reflect on the lives of the Buddha both in his long career as a Bodhisatta as well as the Enlightened One, the unique characteristic that stands out is his selfless service to all beings. In the very first story which marks his career as a Buddha-to-be until his last life as King Vessantara (before he was born as Prince Siddhartha), he gave away all his possessions for the benefit of others. Even as a Buddha his primary concern was to bring to humanity the ultimate bliss of Nibbāna.
>
> The Buddha gained nothing personally by serving others, but he did it out of his deep compassion and his determination to end the suffering of all beings. Therefore we can say that if we want to follow in the footsteps of the Buddha, then we must selflessly serve all those who share this planet with us out of love and compassion. In this service we leave out no one: the long, the short, and the middling, the seen and the unseen, the strong and the weak. There is none whom we cannot serve.[15] (my own)

Achariya Samarawickrama's call for a Buddhism of selfless service is directly contrary to untutored, common opinion that Buddhism is a kind of passive, navel-gazing faith for self-absorbed narcissists or those who have been wounded in love. Quite the opposite he avers, "if one wants to be a Buddhist then one must begin by serving others to reduce and finally eliminate the illusion that one has a permanent self, which is why we call it selfless service." Although a teacher of Theravada Buddhism for primarily English-speaking Sri Lankan and overseas Chinese in Malaysia, he exalts the Mahayana ideal of the *bodhisattva* using the Pāli term *bodhisatta* rather than Sanskrit terminology, "A Buddhist is one who, while actively working to purify his or her own mind, also ceaselessly works for the welfare of others, to reduce suffering at all costs. This noble aspiration is embodied in the Bodhisatta ideal in which the disciple vows to serve others while at the same time working towards self-perfection. One cannot call oneself a Buddhist without actively working to relieve the suffering of others."[16]

The vow to "serve others while at the same time working toward self-liberation" is reminiscent of a phrase I heard frequently in South Korea during my years living there and studying Buddhism academically and practicing with the gray-robed ordained sangha: *sang gu bori, ha hwa jungsaeng,* "Seek to awaken (attain Buddhahood), save all sentient beings": 上求菩提下化衆生 (literally, "seek enlightenment above, transform sentient beings below").[17] Like the Taoist yin yang symbol of interlocking but inseparable black and white halves forming a full circle, inner spiritual cultivation and outer service for others form an integral and balanced whole. Within communities of meditators there must exist individuals that serve them and take care of daily business. Those who serve others selflessly must continually fortify themselves with personal spiritual practice and periods of repose to be effective. The circle is not static but in motion, more of a turning *Dharma* wheel or spinning top, sometimes tottering more in one direction than the other, rectifying itself and eventually finding proper balance after rotating from one extreme to the other like a compass settling on the true north direction.

One of the guideposts of the socially-engaged Buddhist charity Buddhist Global Relief (BGR) founded by the senior American monk Venerable Bhikkhu Bodhi is inward 'self-cultivation'. The BGR statement of its Core Values is very clear about its balanced inner and outer perspective:

> Self-cultivation: We recognize that our outward-directed relief work must be accompanied by an inward effort to purify the mind of greed, hatred, and delusion—the root causes of personal and collective suffering. We try to integrate our relief work with our self-cultivation, so that the outer work becomes a means of self-purification and inward self-cultivation strengthens us to accomplish our mission more effectively.[18]

In his inspiring essay to goad Western Buddhists to become more active to decrease suffering around the world, "Socially Engaged Buddhism Today: A Challenge to Buddhists" (2007), Bhikkhu Bodhi addressed the 'inner-outer focus' polarity in much of the Buddhist world.

> It is true that Buddhist meditation practice requires seclusion and inwardly focused depth. But wouldn't the embodiment of *dharma* in the world be more complete by also reaching out and addressing the grinding miseries that are ailing humanity? I know we engage in lofty meditations on kindness and compassion and espouse beautiful ideals of love and peace. But note that we pursue them largely as inward, subjective experiences geared toward personal transformation. Too seldom does this type of compassion roll up its sleeves and step into the field.
>
> Too rarely does it translate into pragmatic programs of effective action realistically designed to diminish the actual sufferings of those battered by natural calamities or societal deprivation. Buddhist teachers often say that the most effective way we can help protect the world is by purifying our own minds, or that before we engage in compassionate action we must attain realization of selflessness or emptiness. There may be some truth in such statements, but I think it is a partial truth. In

> these critical times, we also have an obligation to aid those immersed in the world who live on the brink of destitution and despair. The Buddha's mission, the reason for his arising in the world, was to free beings from suffering by uprooting the evil roots of greed, hatred, and delusion. These sinister roots don't exist only in our own minds. Today they have acquired a collective dimension and have spread out over whole countries and continents. To help free beings from suffering today therefore requires that we counter the systemic embodiments of greed, hatred, and delusion.[19]

Bhikkhu Bodhi concludes his rallying cry to modern Western Buddhist converts with:

> In each historical period, the *dharma* finds new means to unfold its potentials in ways precisely linked to that era's distinctive historical conditions. I believe that our own era provides the appropriate historical stage for the transcendent truth of the *dharma* to bend back upon the world and engage human suffering at multiple levels—even the lowest, harshest, and most degrading levels—not in mere contemplation but in effective, relief-granting action illuminated by its own world-transcending goal.
>
> The special challenge facing Buddhism in our age is to stand up as an advocate for justice in the world, a voice of conscience for those victims of social, economic, and political injustice who cannot stand up and speak for themselves. This, in my view, is a deeply moral challenge marking a watershed in the modern expression of Buddhism. I believe it also points in a direction that Buddhism should take if it is to share in the Buddha's ongoing mission to humanity.[20]

In quick response to Venerable Bodhi's call in *Buddhadharma* magazine's 2007 editorial essay quoted above, several of his students decided to form a Buddhist relief organization dedicated to alleviating the suffering of the poor and disadvantaged in the developing world afflicted by hunger and poor agricultural productivity. Cooperating with other Buddhist groups in the greater New York area before long, Buddhist Global Relief emerged as an 'inter-denominational' organization comprising people of different Buddhist groups who share the vision of a Buddhism actively committed to the task of alleviating social and economic suffering. The BGR stated service mission is clear: to sponsor projects that promote hunger relief for poor communities around the world by:

1. providing direct food aid to people afflicted by hunger and malnutrition
2. helping develop better long-term methods of sustainable food production and management appropriate to the cultures and traditions of the beneficiaries
3. promoting the education of girls and women, so essential in the struggle against poverty and malnutrition
4. giving women an opportunity to start right livelihood projects to support their families.[21]

In the Anguttara Nikaya 5:37, "In giving food, one gives five things to the recipients: one gives life, beauty, happiness, strength, and mental clarity. In giving these five things, one in turn partakes of life, beauty, happiness, strength, and mental clarity, whether in this world or in the heavenly realm."

From Santa Clara County in California, New York City, Detroit, Vietnam, Sri Lanka, Rwanda and Malawi, India, Haiti, Ethiopia, Ivory Coast, China, Cambodia and Bangladesh, Buddhist Global Relief supports direct food aid and educational right livelihood projects, as a 100% volunteer-only organization with about 90% direct program costs in service to international projects and less than 4% for administrative overhead! Few charities can boast such figures![22]

It is no surprise that the energy that drives the volunteer effort of Buddhist Global Relief is the emotion of compassion, for it is compassion "that makes the hearts of the good tremble with the suffering of others." This thoughtful sentiment is what enables humans to escape the 'cocoon of self-centeredness' and awaken a universal consciousness. Like Avalokiteś vara, compassion opens us to the anguished cries of misery rising up from countless living beings that live in despair. Compassion moves us to dispel their suffering and secure their well-being and happiness. As for the value of service, to follow the call of compassion is to enter into service to others, and to find in service a source of strength, power, and joy that far surpasses the superficial satisfaction gained from self-centered projects aimed at domination and exploitation"[23]

The many service projects of Buddhist Global Relief require substantial funding. Many charities in the United States hire costly public relations and fund-raising agencies to acquire donations for their work. BGR keeps its fund-raising campaign costs very low because its members are generous. They also voluntarily organize fund raising events and activities to inform the general public about BGR's good works and solicit donations. BGR's Walks to Feed the Hungry have been very successful in boasting the morale of participants and in raising dāna-spiritual gifts (funds or in-kind donations) for BGR projects. Dāna pāramitā is the Perfection in Giving" or 'Liberality'. It is the first practice or quality-alms-giving-that when developed purportedly leads to Buddhahood as illustrated in many of the former birth stories of the Buddha. The BGR website, presumably composed by Bhikkhu Bodhi, is eloquent when discussing this virtue. Better to let him speak (and teach) for the organization!

> The most tangible expression of our sense of human solidarity is the act of giving. Through giving, we break down the psychological barriers that separate us from others and affirm our fundamental unity. Through giving, we let the water of compassion flow through our own hearts and into the hearts of others. The practice of generosity ennobles and dignifies our character; at the same time, it helps those in need find a base of security that will support their efforts to provide for themselves and their families. Most importantly, giving demonstrates to others that they do not walk alone; that there are people far away, never seen by them, who care for them and share their suffering; that there are those who earnestly wish to help.

With such thoughts, we invite everyone who empathizes with our mission to contribute to our work by making a donation. A large number of small gifts can combine to create a mass of funds that can be fruitfully used to aid those in need. The Buddha said that to give food is to give the recipients life, health, beauty, happiness, and mental clarity. By giving these, the donor in turn acquires a store of merit, of wholesome *karma*, that will eventually ripen in these five benefits.[24]

A BGR Walk to Feed the Hungry took place in west central Florida in March 2015. It was the first of its kind in the area and was very successful despite the small and disparate Buddhist convert population in the Tampa Bay area where I reside. About thirty Americans, led by two young Sri Lankan *bhikkhus* of the Mahamevnawa Meditation Center, joined the Walk one beautiful spring morning and raised just under $3000; not bad for the first event of an unknown charity in a conservative Christian community! Ven. Bodhi was ill and could not attend the Florida Walk but he sent a message of gratitude that was read to the gathering. According to Bhikkhu Bodhi, the Walk inspires such a generous response because it

> ...evokes the deep seed of goodness always present in the human heart, and it does this through BGR's mission: to help disadvantaged communities around the world escape the trap of chronic hunger and malnutrition....We help people at the grassroots develop small-scale ecologically sustainable agricultural projects, with emphasis on making them independent and self-sustaining. We help girls and poor students attend school.... We help women start small cottage industries or learn better methods of crop cultivation to feed their families and sell surplus on the market....
>
> I feel that the walk not only helps the poor and hungry but it also helps us. For we also suffer from hunger: hunger for a deeper meaning and higher purpose in our lives. Sadly, in today's materialist culture the market reigns supreme, reducing all other values to naked dollars and cents. Every drop of meaning and purpose is squeezed dry by a worldview that asks

> us to look at everything in terms of its exchange value. The market has become a despot and his words are really scary.... The quality I believe we need most to push the world in... is what I call 'conscientious compassion'. We often think of compassion as a soft and gentle emotion, even a passive one—and a tendency to passivity is indeed a weak spot among us Buddhists. Gentleness and patience are admirable, but the kind of compassion we need today has to merge the softness of the meditative mind with courage and conviction and even fierceness. It must be driven by a fervent sense of conscience, by an urge to bring the imperatives of moral insight down into the real world. This is a compassion actively committed to promoting justice in the world, at multiple levels: social justice, economic justice, political justice, and legal justice. It must move us to redeem people from misery and help them rediscover their own inner dignity.[25]

Bhikkhu Bodhi's call for a dynamic 'conscientious compassion' to strive for social, economic, political and legal justice in society is an appeal for Buddhists to integrate with the non-Buddhist world. A sense of what is just and unjust is widely shared by people of different backgrounds and religions. It is inevitable that as Buddhists in the West act more prominently as reputable public charities and reveal a "a new social face"[26] that is demonstrably concerned for others, they will be recognized and become more influential. They will be closer to keeping the '*bodhisattva* vow' of saving all beings. One wonders when the term '*bodhisattva*' will enter common vocabulary like 'Zen', '*karma*', '*nirvana*' and '*guru*'. It will take time to shake the self-absorbed stereotype the "hirsute guru dwelling in a mountaintop cave" especially in locales where Buddhists are few and opposition to foreign faiths strong but there will be gradual but steady improvement if media accounts remain favorable.

It may be difficult in the beginning for Euro-American Buddhists to find their voice as a mass movement. Venerable Bodhi's call however, is a call to the individual, to follow their own "fervent sense of conscience and the imperatives of moral insight down into the real world...to merge the softness of the meditative mind with courage and conviction and even fierceness." Failure to express public confidence in Buddhist teachings by remaining passive when other religions or ideologies dominate all social institutions is failure to be true to the teachings and Buddha's example of lifelong, generous service to all beings.

Google searches for the phrase 'socially-engaged Buddhism' brings up 285,000 results or the phrase 'compassion and Buddhism' 1,190,000 results, and 'community service and Buddhism' about 2,930,000 results at the end of August 2014. Notwithstanding many repetitive entries and faulty robotic-generated links, these results are a virtual cornucopia of delights for the activist-scholar but impossible to summarize or do justice to the many dedicated individuals and organizations that are listed on-line, not to mention the people and groups who are not represented in cyber-space (in English only!). To pre-emptively fend off the trauma of intellectual paralysis of not knowing where to begin or how to sort out this avalanche of information, I will attempt to outline my own modest experience in 'Buddhist compassionate service' with reference to other good folk whom I have had the good fortune to have encountered over years in Asia where I have lived and visited and the state of Florida in the United States since 2001.

In the brief bio I submitted to the Uberoi Foundation, I called myself a "socially-engaged participant/observer of Buddhism." Spiritual unease at home on Long Island, New York, led to some years seeking wisdom vicariously in academic religious studies and anthropology in the US and Britain. I eventually pursued Buddhist studies at an advanced level in South Korea, with many research and study trips to other parts of Asia and a few lecture tours. I have met and studied with a number of great teachers over the years but I have been a mediocre student to them all. What little I have learned about religious transformation and the Buddha *dharma* I have had the temerity to share teaching and mentoring in a wide variety of settings, including universities, churches, retirement homes, trailer parks, jails, prisons, hospitals, hospices, the streets and animal refuges.

TALES FROM TWO PENINSULAS

South Korea

I may be the first Western Buddhist to study and write about death and dying formally in South Korea, although it was not my intention when I first went to Korea as a Peace Corps volunteer on leave from a doctoral program in anthropology at the University of Pennsylvania in 1980. As a Hansen's Disease (leprosy) control worker working out of a rural public health clinic, I had occasion to learn first-hand about stigmatized populations, trauma and depression, emergency medical relief, chronic disease care and end-of-life concerns in a rapidly developing country. I documented a traditional Korean funeral service and burial of a middle-aged man, a beloved husband and father. I shared in the grief of the family and village[27] and my heart broke open to the culture. This experience led me to explore more deeply how death in all its varieties across the population is handled in a traditional Confucian-Buddhist-shamanist culture with recent widespread conversion to Christianity.

I learned about the severe oppression of the Korean people during the bitter thirty-five year Japanese colonial period (1910 45) during which provincial crematoria were erected for the disposal of the dead. This abrupt superimposed foreign cultural innovation disrupted traditional Confucian burial practice and prolonged mourning rituals. I also vicariously experienced the suffering of the Korean people during the Korean civil war decades before when millions died and streets were said to become rivers of blood. One of my Peace Corps colleagues had been a US Marine during the war and he vividly described what the intense fighting was like with deep chagrin. Certain parts of Seoul where the fighting was fiercest were to become slums ('moon villages') for the poorest citizens because they were thought (and sensed) to be inhabited by sad and angry ghosts. I had to pass through one of these infamous neighborhoods within the decade after my Peace Corps stint to visit Buddhist temples where I lived, practiced, studied and raised a family. I learned about Korean Buddhist attitudes toward death and funeral rituals and prayers 'on the ground' as it were. Little did I know that this experience would prepare me to render Buddhist 'compassionate service' during later years in Korea.

When I was considering death and dying as a general area for doctoral dissertation research at Dongguk University, Korea's largest Buddhist university, 'death found me', or should I say, an uncanny number of friends, colleagues and acquaintances began to die around me for unrelated reasons. Inoperable and undiagnosed sudden onset liver disease in a young mother of two (a friend's dear wife), a tragic unexplained accident or possible suicide of a happy new father on an overseas business trip (a friend a close colleague at UNESCO), the death of a great Buddhist scholar and mentor in his prime, a university colleague in his 30s who studied at both UC Berkeley and U Penn when I was there, the self-immolation of a monk protesting the national financial crisis, etc. These unhappy events actually obliged me to attend Korean funerals and customary family gatherings and 'just be there' as a compassionate listener, very rare foreign presence in a thoroughly Korean environment.

When someone dies in traditional Korea, the family usually cares for the body, arranges for the viewing of the funerary tablet that sits before the closed casket, and attends to the burial or cremation. Those in mourning are very rarely left alone. Family members and friends, if they can, drop everything and join the bereaved twenty-four hours a day for at least three days. In the cases of my colleagues, all office work but the most pressing stopped. Everyone went to be with the aggrieved wife, husband or parents, sleeping on cardboard in basements or garages to always be nearby if there was no room at the residence of the deceased. Like funerals in other cultures, a makeshift banquet of delicious food is voluntarily offered, lots of drinking, lots of reminiscing about the dead, laughing and crying. Compassionate concern or fear may arise to prevent suicide of the young bereaved. This is not so uncommon in Korea which has the highest suicide rate in the world. For Buddhists I would attend the traditional devotional services every seven days until the culminating forty-ninth day temple service. This ceremony could be very long, elaborate and expensive with the offerings of dāna to the officiating monks and nuns and specially printed books like the *Diamond Skūtra* to participating laity.

My uncommon exposure to the rituals associated with dying and death in Korea as a non-medically trained foreigner who was not a Christian missionary in a way prepared me for voluntary compassionate response with bereaved families when two terrible tragedies with multiple deaths occurred in Seoul. One of the many bridges across the Han River in Seoul collapsed into the water early one rush hour morning in the fall of 1994. Thirty-two people died including many children on a bus going to school.[28] The abbot of the main Jogye Order headquarters temple in Seoul, Jogyesa, responded to his congregants immediately and prepared the main Dharma Hall for a collective funeral service for the victims. I was able to visit the temple to observe how the four-fold *sangha* served the victims' families. I was told that just by being there (as the sole Caucasian) and chanting and prostrating with the hundreds of other mourners gave the Korean Buddhist attendees consolation and rare encouragement. Perhaps a white Buddhist was a fortunate omen?

Eight months later a much more terrible accident occurred, the infamous Sampoong Department Store collapse during a very busy late afternoon shopping hour. Five hundred and two people died and over nine hundred were injured. This accident was a national tragedy and disgrace since it exposed dishonesty, a lack of adherence to safety standards, bribery at many levels, disregard for human life in pursuit of profit and general criminal negligence.[29] This was the largest peacetime disaster in Korean history. Local hospitals were overwhelmed by the dead bodies and injured that were immediately found. The accident site was huge, complicated and dangerous and victims were continually being retrieved even seventeen days after the collapse. Families and friends rushed to the site to reach their loved ones but had to be held back from entering the wreckage by police because of the danger and total confusion. A nearby university auditorium became a large waiting hall for the missing victims' families as the casualties were slowly discovered in the rubble.

Identifying the dead was challenging because of the devastative power of the massive collapse and the very hot weather. I joined a team of Jogye Order volunteers to do what I could to help the thousands of distraught, traumatized family members over the weeks. There was great chaos but the compassionate response of the public was also amazing. Many generous offers to the victims' families were made such as covering all funeral expenses, Cadillac limousine hearse service (a first in Korea!), hometown transportation costs, etc. Demonstrators also demanded justice from officialdom. Visitors to the family refuge site had to be reminded to register and provide names, photos and descriptions of the clothing the presumed victims were wearing at the time of the accident. Hundreds of albums of photos of articles found in the rubble had to be compiled and passed around the auditorium so that family members could identify them accurately if possible. Buddhists constructed makeshift funeral altars outside the auditorium so that mourners and the desperate hopeful could pray. Religious volunteers, individually, in partners or small groups sat with the bereaved to offer comfort, distribute water bottles, coffee, food, towels, clothing, pillows to enhance rest and sleeping and run errands for the elderly and the lost. Chair massage and hand acupressure/acupuncture to elevate mood as freely given. Many volunteers and rescue workers worked around the clock as did the media and clergy serving the distressed families.

Like with the recent Saewol-ho Ferry sinking that put the nation in mourning, Korea and especially Seoul residents went into a sullen period of deep, self-reflective rumination attempting to determine what could have caused this unexpected misfortune to so many innocent people. Most of the shoppers who died were rather affluent, too. The department store was a trendy, expensive one and in a ritzy part of Seoul. Why did some survive and others die? Even now, almost twenty years afterwards, it is a hard subject to discuss with many of those who remember it. Undigested grief accumulates and many people customarily drink alcohol to self-medicate. 'Compassion fatigue' affected thousands and many simply blocked off thinking or speaking about the tragedy.

Disturbed and Disturbing Spirits, Living and Dead

I was working on a doctoral thesis concerning the high rate of abortion among Korean Buddhist women at the time of the Sampoong Department Store collapse in late June 1995. Dread of misfortune was common in the literature, popular media and interviews with clergy who provided religious services for women who had many abortions. Women and sometimes men who were responsible for the aborted child would report nightmares, premonitions and uncanny occurrences. Sometimes shamans who communicated with the dead reported that the spirits of the aborted babies were greatly distressed and screaming. These disembodied spirits or fragments of floating consciousness were in frightful, searing pain in the 'between' state or some 'pre-birth bardo' because they were physically and emotionally traumatized by being deprived of their rightful human birth against their will. These spirits would rub against the living in strange ways at inopportune times to get the attention of their mothers or fathers. Their spiritual interference to gain attention caused misfortunes such as accidents, business failures and bankruptcies, marital discord and divorce, failure to pass university entrance exams or get into a desirable school, inexplicable untreatable illnesses and wounds that did not heal among other troubles in general. Sometimes fearsome other worldly auditory and visual visitations or hallucinations were reported. Even scientifically-minded or so-called rational university students, Christians, too, opined that the millions of unhappy spirits of aborted fetuses may have caused the terrible accidents the nation was subject to. This was a prevalent opinion back in the 1990s.

Abortions in Korea were very common during the country's intense industrial development phase that began in the 1970s. They were practically considered good female hygiene or 'cleansing'; especially if the baby was female. The country was became urbanized very rapidly and the rural agricultural way of life was all but abandoned. Rice paddies near urban centers could be sold for huge profit and shrewd families became rich overnight. The traditional large family of parents and six children was expensive to maintain in cities, affordable apartments in housing blocks were small and inconvenient and young children were a burden to men and women who had to work long hours, sometimes seven days a week, to get the much vaunted 'good things' in life. Educating children well became very expensive, too. Better to spend more on one or two kids rather than many. Lacking effective forms of birth control in a male-dominated conservative Confucian society, women were pressured into or chose to have abortions. Up-to-date, medically advanced and cheap abortions were and remain a quick and easy family planning method in Korea. Abortion clinics remain common even though the procedure is technically illegal. The annual abortion rate was as high in Korea as in United States with a population of about a fourth, around two million per year. Women who had three to six abortions or more were not uncommon during the period of my research.

Although abortion is clearly a violation of the first Buddhist precept of non-killing in the scriptures, an abortion survey conducted by the Korean Institute of Criminology in 1990 found that Buddhists had as high or higher an abortion rate as the rest of the population (in the Seoul sample survey) and that the highest number of repetitive abortions (three or more) were among Buddhists. Among these Buddhists a rapidly growing number began expressing their unease and guilt about their abortions and sought out Buddhist clergy to perform special purification and belated funeral ceremonies for the babies whose lives they felt they had discarded. They sought forgiveness from the children they had intentionally killed. Besides mail correspondence, personal consultations and telephone counseling, certain monks and nuns created lengthy 'auspicious rebirth ceremonies' (nak t'ae-a ch'ondo-jae) to assuage the deceased fetuses and provide relief for the worried mothers. I participated and observed many of these services as part of my dissertation research. These rituals entailed honoring the dead over forty-nine days with about three hours of traditional chanting, thousands of prostrations, quiet meditation and personal prayer, offerings of baby foods and treats on the altar and attending *dharma* talks that were like classes on the afterlife, female biology, pregnancy, gestation and observance of precepts with periods spent for discussion, ventilating anger and grief. Some monks and nuns required ceremony sponsors to perform volunteer work at orphanages and childcare centers to aid children in general.[30]

The senior biguni (P. bhikkhunī) Venerable Seongdeok who initiated the compassionate service Buddhist Volunteer Association (Bulgyo jawonbongsa yeonhaphoe) also pioneered the Buddhist Fetal Life Protection campaign to educate the Buddhist public about the value of life and "our rare opportunity as humans to attain enlightenment and render compassionate service to others." The Korean Buddhist Volunteer Association applies the *bodhisattva* "spirit of compassion at the grassroots level. BVA has reinforced the presence of Buddhist sensibilities in Korea by initiating free hospice volunteer and funeral ritual education courses, home caretaker training programs, soup kitchens, clothes distribution drives for the poor and elderly and wild animal feeding and reforestation projects during times of extreme weather and forest fires.[31]

No sooner had I finished writing my doctoral dissertation at Dongguk University than very late in the evening in the spring of 1996 three ancient Buddhist temples within pleasant walking from my home on the northern boundary of Seoul exploded in flames. Because the fires all broke out within minutes of one another and the temples were difficult to access down unpaved roads leading into the forested hills, fire trucks arrived too late to save all the wooden buildings. Residents of the temples themselves and their few neighbors had to do most of the firefighting. Ornately-painted *dharma* halls were thickly covered in soot, bell towers and the instruments were destroyed and in one temple nearest my home, a beautiful wooden shrine housing five hundred intricately hand-carved wooden statues of the early arhats were incinerated. Other buildings were severely damaged. What happened?

To make a long story short, upon investigation police confirmed what the general public suspected, that extremist and/or mentally unbalanced 'Christians' were responsible for the attacks. The temples had been leafleted with hellfire and damnation; Biblical tracts decrying idolatry and false gods for months earlier. Other Buddhist sites in Seoul and around the country had decades-long histories of Christian-wrought vandalism and desecrations. There were frequent demonstrations in the streets and at temple entrances denouncing Buddhists and other heathens with strident zealotry. Christian ministers were videotaped and filmed by TV crews threatening and encouraging extreme actions against unbelievers. Although provincial temple abbots and Jogye Order headquarters were aware of the violence, very little was done to address the problem. Temples were attacked "in my own backyard" where I had gone on retreats, collected fresh water from mountain springs and where I taught our young daughter to bow to Buddha. I was 'fired up'! The doctoral thesis now out of the way, I threw myself into the task to see what could be done to bring a peaceful resolution to this one-way conflict. First I needed to do some background research.

There is no record of Buddhists retaliating against Christian aggression in Korea. It turned out that neither the ordained clergy nor the lay congregation publically exposed the violations of their temples' sanctity. They left responsibility for identifying the perpetrators up to the police. I was told repeatedly that Buddhists were afraid of the power and influence of Christians in Korea and did not want to make protests of any kind that might lead to unforeseen repercussions. I interviewed prominent Christian leaders who decried the arsonists as crazed extremists who did not act in the spirit of Christ. However, they did not want to make waves either. They took no responsibility for brethren of other denominations or independent mavericks. The abbots of the temples that were attacked in my area did join together to commiserate with one another and hold services extending loving-kindness, compassion and forgiveness to the stealthy arsonists and their supporters. Many of the lay people were angry and wanted some sort of revenge but the monks were able to diffuse their wrath with admonitions against ill-will and negative actions. Rather the four-fold *sangha* became inspired to do more ardent fundraising and rebuild their edifices as quickly as possible almost to spite the aggressors. They were quite successful renovating the old buildings but using concrete and steel rather than combustible wood. Some buildings and Dharma Halls still have residue of the smoke and soot eighteen years later.

Goaded on by the late Professor David Chappell of the Society of Buddhist Christian Studies, I wrote up my findings in an academic article for the association's journal[32] and organized a panel of important Korean Buddhist clergy and Korean theologians for the upcoming Chicago Conference to discuss inter-religious tension and harmony in Korea. Approached by English language and European news stringers in Seoul and the Internet, violent Christian aggression against Buddhism in Korea became international news. Learning about bad press overseas in the U.S., Australia, Great Britain, France, Germany, Switzerland including the World Council of Churches and all of Asia the Korean national Ministry of Culture sponsored meetings of Buddhist and Christian leaders to bring about some sort of amicable rapprochement.

Social pressure seemed to still the actions of the extremists by embarrassing elders of the churches. Buddhist leaders were unimpressed by Christian lip service, though, and except for some joint concerts by Catholic and Buddhist nuns including Won Buddhists and temple visits by very liberal graduate theology classes to learn Seon (Zen) meditation, there is little mutual spiritual growth between most Christians and Buddhists in Korea. I felt I had to do something to ameliorate religious relations in Korea. Many Koreans thanked me for my voluntary efforts that seemed to lessen some angst among temple dwellers and lovers of traditional Korean arts and architecture. Nevertheless trouble-making Biblical literalists remain unpredictable. Random attacks on Buddhist temples in Korea continue today. It is not enough that

Buddhists continue to live in fear of attacks, burying their heads in the sand, praying and hoping for the best, forgiving their tormentors. They must act. They have to engage the perpetrators or their controllers vigorously by means of continuous communication, break down walls of suspicion, changing minds and changing society.

Florida

Distressing calls from my mother in Florida became more and more dire at the end of 2000. In her eighties, she lived alone since my father's death on their forty-third anniversary in 1988. As the eldest child and only son, my wife and I decided that I must heed the call of filial piety and love for my mother and return to my parents' home to live, by mid-summer 2001. I had lived overseas fifteen years by then, pilgrimaged a bit in India and elsewhere, finally earned a Ph.D., become a Buddhist teacher, earned some notoriety for engaged Buddhist publications, married a great Korean woman, became a father. Enough. Now be a son.

Around the world, mention of the American state of Florida often conjures up images of a relaxed, tropical vacation land of sunshine and sandy beaches, Mickey Mouse at Orlando's Disney World or perhaps the romance and glamour of Miami. Yet amidst the vacationers, aging retirees, mosquitoes and alligators are pockets of sincere *Dharma* practitioners from the major traditions of Buddhism. Immigrant communities from Vietnam, Laos, Cambodia, Sri Lanka and Thailand have established their respective temples all over the state. Immigrants from Taiwan, Korea and Japan are smaller in number, their congregations small and consequently their temples very few.[33] Most ethnic groups have a resident monk or nun or two to provide teaching. While American converts to Buddhism are small in number and widespread throughout the state, in the last two decades they have become very active and have established Theravada, Zen, Tibetan Vajrayana and mindfulness (*vipassanā*) centers in most population centers. The foci of these centers are beginning meditation and basic teachings befitting newcomers to *Buddhadharma*. Membership is small and transient and financing activities is a constant challenge. Except for the Japanese-led Nichiren sect Soka Gakkai (SGI)[34], white Caucasians dominate most convert groups of all traditions. Unlike the culturally rich temple life of ethnic groups that follow traditional Buddhist calendrical rituals from their native countries, convert American Buddhists have a short Buddhist history, and few emotional associations with Buddhist holiday activities that include their entire families. Rarely do American Buddhist parents and their children engage in Buddhist practice or simple family fun together.[35]

Karma being what it is, there are few Koreans in Pinellas County, a peninsula within a peninsula, and those few are strong Christians or indifferent to Buddhism. The one Korean temple in Florida is a five-hour drive away. Among the handful of Korean Buddhists in the next county across the Tampa Bay was one devout and knowledgeable bosallim (Korean Buddhist female devotee) who we knew for a short while before I performed her funeral service. As a consequence of abruptly relocating from a land where I was practically a full-time lay Buddhist social advocate to an anonymous mother's son in a very strange land, conservative Christian Florida, I was in culture re-entry shock. It has taken time to find my bearings and feet in Buddhist activism again. I had to make my way amongst strangers without a supportive *sangha* at first. I took refuge with the Unitarian Universalists (UU). They are well-educated, charming conversationalists, very socially responsible, environmentally conscious, accept everyone, tolerate Buddhists. The coffee was good I formed a branch of the UU Buddhist Fellowship, wrote for its national newsletter, led a sixteen-week course to discuss the Dalai Lama's brilliant *Ethics for the New Millennium* using the Dalai Lama Foundation Guidebook and gave to many UU causes.

The challenge of obtaining 'right livelihood' in Florida as a vicarious 'social drop-in' from Korea has allowed me freedom to pursue engaged Buddhist work and compassionate service. I often remember my recently deceased Ph.D. advisor and founder of the first Korean lay Buddhist Dhamma Teachers' Association who stressed 'bosal haeng' above all—'*bodhisattva* action' meaning service to all beings. He had faith in this old hippie, socially engaged, American Buddhist ethical anthro-Dharmologist when other faculty members rolled their scholarly eyes. The *Dharma* wheel turns in the academy and out.

Identifying myself as a Buddhist in Florida has often been to my advantage as a volunteer chaplain in hospices and hospitals, prisons and the regional Tampa International Airport. Oddity sometimes has advantages if you can roll with it. Most local residents are surprised to meet a white, Italian American, New York-accented Buddhist in heavily Southern Baptist country and are either incredulous or bemused. Some are rather curious, and barrage me with numerous questions. They are seekers for something meaningful they haven't found yet in their churches. A few worry about my salvation (Thank you! Om). Some clergy are threatened lest I become too popular with the younger generation that has positive regard for charismatic Buddhists like the Dalai Lama and Richard Gere. *Dharma* teaching about peace, joy and inner freedom without guilt and damnation has immediate appeal. Buddhism seems fresh and new and it not associated with the sordid financial and sexual scandals of the established churches (yet). This is all good news because the only way Buddhists will be able to integrate with their contemporaries, like Śākyamuni and the early arhats did, is by mingling with common, everyday people and 'learning their language', penetrating their hearts and ultimate concerns. Intelligent rapport and kindly presence usually works, even with hostile folk. I ask myself when I find myself in awkward social situations, with a Robin Williams grin, "What would Buddha do?" or more wittily, 'WWSD?'[36] It does not require a Harvard Law degree to respond with a kind heart and show appreciative interest for others' cares, concerns and opinions, especially when serving prison populations, the homeless or the dying. But the prestige could have helped me on occasion, asupāyakauśalya, to get things done for the poor disadvantaged more effectively!

Initially volunteering as a Buddhist chaplain and meditation teacher in the county jail at a female inmate's request and later in state prisons has been a wonderful and sometimes painful education. There is a rich Buddhist prison literature and some informative websites that do not need review here. Penal institutions are numerous and diverse. Housing convicted criminals, security in prison is the highest priority. The second highest priority is security. Guess what the third priority is? Prisons are hard, authoritarian and cold. Regulations are inflexible and can change inexplicably without notice. Sometimes the salaried prison chaplains and wardens are helpful; often they are not. Although Buddhism and other Indian faiths and practices like yoga were introduced to American prisons decades ago, their acceptance throughout the differing state systems has been uneven and sporadic. The three Florida state prisons I have taught in have had relatively stable inmate *sanghas* for the last few years thanks to the dedicated efforts of the Southern Palm Zen Center. Inmates are allowed to gather for group study and meditation at least once a week and are usually led by the inmates themselves but monitored by volunteer chaplains who may or may not feel they are adequately trained to teach Buddhism but they have the minimal qualifications to satisfy the state authorities.

I am usually honored as a special teacher when I visit these inmate *sanghas*. I give very short *Dharma* talks and leave the floor open for the many questions that always come up. Inmates read a lot of everything and argue among themselves about minutiae of doctrine and practices all the time. Most often I cut through that with emphasis on compassion for themselves and others, selfless service in mind and action and self-forgiveness. My meditations are often on visualizing themselves as beings with dignity and inner strength and character. Inmates who have settled into or accepted their identities or routines as prisoners-'long-timers'-crave self-respect and acceptance as good people just serving time away from normal society, paying off their debt for contravening society's rules, depending on the gravity of their crimes.

County jail is where inmates wait for trial after they have been arrested or wait for sentencing after they have been found guilty in court. Some of the inmates I have met in my local county jail have the most poignant stories. Books could be written about them to do them justice. One Vietnamese Buddhist whom I saw in jail frequently and who became a friend was released after being found 'not guilty' of second degree murder after three years of incarceration waiting for a trial by jury. As I got to know him well discussing Buddhism and meditating together, I concluded that he was really innocent, inadvertently caught in a struggle between two Vietnamese gangs. After a year and a half wait, a court date was set. I sat through the trial beside his wife and two very young sons wearing my Buddhist robes in full gaze of the jury. The government brought in many so-called 'witnesses' and lots of police testimony but the material evidence was faulty as was the obvious prejudice of the police. Chung's tiny female Cuban immigrant attorney jumped all over them. The proceedings lasted four days and the sequestered jury argued all night until early morning when they came in with a unanimous decision of 'not guilty'. Chung's mother had flown in from Vietnam for the trial and spoke no English. Because of the trial's delays she had to fly back to Vietnam just before the trial began. She literally had 'sold the farm' or some parcels to pay for her son's lawyer. Chung's dutiful wife, a manicurist, had waited three years for this decision and brought their sleeping sons home before her husband stepped out of jail a free man. I met him at the gate. The first thing he did was call his mother in Vietnam collect from an outdoor pay phone on the sidewalk. His possessions bag was mostly full of Buddhist books I gave him over the years and a change of clothes. Before going home to his wife and children, he asked me to drive him to the nearest Vietnamese Buddhist temple so he could bow to the Buddha and then cross the street so he could bow to a huge crucifix in front of the church there. Then we went to his home so he could hold his second son for the first time. The child was born when his father was in the local jail a few miles away.

Other tales of Buddhist prisoners are not so happy. Teenage men convicted of second degree and first degree murder, going off to state prison to serve sixteen year sentences or two life terms. One young man had me sit silently on a cold metal seat in the noisy visitor's cubicle of one wing of the pod so he could chant in Pā li to me as if I were a *bhikkhu,* or better yet, a Buddha. He had practiced as a novitiate in a Laotian temple for three summers before becoming involved in a drive-by gang killing.

Another teen wanted to learn *Buddhadharma* and meditation from me so he could teach the *Dharma* to his mother by mail. He was going away for the rest of his life and wanted to do something good for his mother who lived for her only son. I met with this inmate in the psychiatric ward when he was on suicide watch. He had killed an eighty-four year old man while struggling to steal his cheap old car on a whim.

We are all subject to the First Noble Truth (*dukkha*) of life-birth, aging, sickness and inevitable death. We all crave (*taṇha*) satisfaction of our desires and are displeased when we don't get what we want or experience what we don't want. We all want to be free or end our suffering (*nirodha*) and we all can benefit following the guidelines of the Eightfold Path (*marga*). We have a lot in common with our fellow beings. The Buddha's fundamental teachings derive from observation of universal human experience and can be acknowledged as true by believers in other faiths, non-believers, atheists and agnostics, anyone subject to the 'full catastrophe' of human life, as Kazantzakis says in *Zorba the Greek*, employed by Jon Kabat-Zinn to illustrate the fullness of life:

> There is not one person on the planet who does not have his or her own version of the full catastrophe.
>
> *Catastrophe* here does not mean disaster. Rather it means the poignant enormity of our life experience. It includes crises and disaster but also all the little things that go wrong and that add up. The phrase reminds us that life is always in flux, that everything we think is permanent is actually only temporary and constantly changing. This includes our ideas, our opinions, our relationships, our jobs, our possessions, our creations, our bodies, everything.[37]

Buddha's expertise in analyzing *dukkha*—the 'full catastrophe' of human life—leads me to conclude that there are no better places to study and apply the comprehensive 'remedy' of the Four Noble Truths than where the transitions of life and death can be observed directly. In the Buddha's lifetime, the painful transitions of life could be readily observed everywhere outside the 'gated community' of his palace grounds. Yet for even closer intimacy with death, early followers of the Awakened One were assigned to sleep and meditate in charnel grounds where bodies could be seen in various stages of decomposition, bloated feasts for scavengers, maggots and worms.

Today most of us experiencing the comforts of developed nations must seek out hospitals and hospices to observe repulsive physical infirmities and inexorable death. Unless you are a medical professional or policeman, or when you yourself or a relative is gravely ill under hospice care, it is rare to encounter human death except obliquely in the news and entertainment. The dead have become invisible in modern Western society, handled by professionals for a fee. Our dead (perhaps not very beloved!) have become the responsibility and profit of corporate entities. The sights, smells and terrors of animal slaughter for food are hidden away lest people become disgusted of the cruel manner animals are killed for cheap meat and choose to become vegetarian or vegan. Unwanted pet euthanasia, too, is performed in secret but hunting and fishing of innocent sentient beings is glorified as 'sport' or 'manly'. Of course, fear of death is universal and it is the norm to avoid any encounter with it. More advanced Buddhist practice, however, seeks out death in order to understand impermanence, our close friend *anicca,* more deeply.[38]

Certain regions of the world and higher social classes remain in relative peace, free from the spectacle of daily violence, starvation and widespread disease. There hospice experience, the propinquity of death and the observation and analysis of emotions associated with our final transition should be part of an educational service for children, even a prerequisite for coming-of-age Three Jewel Refuge ceremony and definitely a requirement for other religious or monastic vows. The boundaries of your heart, your self-obsession, must break open again and again to make space for others' suffering. Our dharmic service is to be with the dying as a wise, empathic presence. Everyone's death is your own. It is quite amazing how the generation of *mettā* (loving-kindness) and *karunā* can, with concentrated attention, transform a dark and fearful death-bed scenario into one of peace, if not, joy.[39]

The last thirty years or so has seen a flowering of Buddhist "compassionate caring work for others" in the West. Besides very active propagation and support of prisoners who show interest in Buddhist meditation and *Dharma* study, American Buddhist converts have begun to integrate into the mainstream of American life through the establishment of Buddhist chaplaincy training programs and pastoral work. A recent volume on Buddhist chaplaincy and ministry lists thirteen websites of specific training programs for Buddhist chaplains and ministers so that they may satisfy official or stipulated requirements for paid employment in most hospices and medical institutions as well as government positions including prisons and the military.[40]

It is not only in normal deaths but also exceptionally sudden and unexpected end-of-life crises that Buddhists can assist the dying, their families and loved ones. We have witnessed the devastating 2004 Indian Ocean tsunami, the Japanese tsunami devastation and Fukushima nuclear radiation debacle and the as yet mysterious disappearance of the Malaysia Air flight 370 with 239 people onboard. The sight of the waiting, bereaved Asian families on CNN-TV raised great pathos across the U.S. I forwarded a *Tricycle* magazine article about Tzu Chi Buddhist volunteers who travelled to Beijing to console the distraught families with their empathic presence to my Christian chaplain colleagues at the Tampa Airport Interfaith Chaplaincy. It was encouraging to share Christian and Buddhist solidarity in *bodhisattva* action.[41]

I would like to conclude with an outline of some of the compassionate service activities initiated by a small Buddhist charity we established in Florida, True Dharma International Buddhist Mission, to encourage other Buddhist organizations in the area by example:

Volunteer on-call hospital and interfaith hospice spiritual support at Suncoast Hospice Advance Care Planning certification-informed discussion groups Jail and prison Dharma instruction and guided meditation practice; volunteer chaplaincy. Correspondence with inmates throughout Florida and around the U.S.

Animal rescue and adoption via SPCA, Humane Society, private parties Road kill retrieval, burial and blessings; creation of wildlife cemetery.

Cemetery blessed by FPMT Maitreya Project Heart Shrine Relic Tour relic collection Adopt-A-Mile Keep County Beautiful program-2 miles of roadside litter cleanup quarterly Telephone talk line for end-of-life questions.

Suicide referrals-networking with suicide prevention organizations and agencies Ex-inmate social re-entry facilitation.

Ex-cult victim counseling and support Compassion fatigue training and meditation.

Free Buddhist books for distribution thanks to FPMT, Corporate Body of the Buddha Educational Foundation and others.

Networking with ethnic Buddhist groups-Vietnamese, Laotian, Thai, Cambodian, Sri Lanka, Taiwanese.

Community garden produce distribution to food pantries-Eckerd College student garden Organic sustainable gardening-free seeds and advice.

Vegetarian cooking and education-Florida Voices for Animals event support.

Support of farm animal sanctuaries like Darlynn's Darlins Rescue Ranch, Polk City, Fl. Homeless information networking and emergency financial support.

Support of Buddhist Peace Fellowship actions protesting military incursions in Iraq, etc.

Tampa Bay-BPF mailing list.

Annual Change Your Mind Day presentations in cooperation with the Tampa Bay Buddhist Peace Fellowship Membership in St. Petersburg Interfaith Clergy Association Cooperation with

Florida Council of Churches Tampa International Airport Interfaith Chaplaincy.

Buddha's Birthday and Vesak teachings on compassion annually Organizer of FPMT Heart Shrine Relic Tour, UU Clearwater, Florida 2008.

NOTES

1. Malaysia Air Flight 370, a Boeing 777, left for Beijing from Kuala Lumpur on March 8, 2014, and disappeared less than an hour after takeoff with 239 people on board. International teams of search and rescue experts had yet to find or identify any wreckage of the plane or any human remains as of Summer 2015. Malaysia Air Flight 17 over Ukraine. Ebola virus outbreak in west Africa. Demonstrations of outrage over unarmed teenager police killing in Missouri.
2. See Intergovernmental Panel on Climate Change, www.ipcc.ch
3. "Although surveys of the health of adults in the developing world carried out in the 1980s suggested that many people between the ages of 20 and 50 were still suffering mainly from diseases of poverty, many countries have now gone through an epidemiological transition such that the global pattern of disease will change dramatically by 2020, with cardiorespiratory disease, depression, and the results of accidents replacing communicable disease as their major health problems." http://www.ncbi.nlm.nih.gov/books/NBK11740/.
4. Derek F. Maher, "Response to Aubrey de Grey from the Perspective of Buddhism," in James W. Haag, G.R. Peterson and M.M.L. Spezio, eds. *The Routledge Companion to Religion and Science* (London: Routledge Taylor and Francis Group, 2012), 540-48.
5. "Countries undergoing the epidemiological transition are increasingly caught between the two worlds of malnutrition and infectious disease on the one hand and the diseases of industrial countries, particularly cardiac disease, obesity, and diabetes, on the other. The increasing epidemic of tobacco-related diseases in developing countries exacerbates this problem. The global epidemic of obesity and type 2 diabetes is a prime example of this problem. An estimated 150 million people are affected with diabetes worldwide, and that number is expected to double by 2025. Furthermore, diabetes is associated with greatly increased risk of cardiovascular disease and hypertension; in some developing

countries the rate of stroke is already four to five times that in industrial countries. These frightening figures raise the questions whether, when developing countries have gone through the epidemiological transition, they may face the same pattern of diseases that are affecting industrial countries and whether such diseases may occur much more frequently and be more difficult to control." http://www.ncbi.nlm.nih.gov/books/NBK11740/.

6. Ch. 1 Twin Verses Yamako Vaggo
   (1) All that we are is the result of what we have thought: it is founded on our thoughts, it is made up of our thoughts.
   If a man speaks or acts with an evil thought, pain follows him, as the wheel follows the foot of the ox that draws the carriage.
   (2) All that we are is the result of what we have thought: it is founded on our thoughts, it is made up of our thoughts.
   If a man speaks or acts with a pure thought, happiness follows him, like a shadow that never leaves him. Müller, F. Max. *The Dhammapada* (*Sacred Books of the East*, Vol. X) (Oxford University Press, 1881).
7. Adrienne Howley, *The Naked Buddha* (New York: Marlowe and Company, 2002) 70-71.
8. Robert E. Buswell, Jr. and Lopez, Donald S. Jr. *The Princeton Dictionary of Buddhism* (Princeton: Princeton University Press, 2014), 424.
9. Paradukkhe sati sādhūnan hadayakampanan karoti iti karuṇā; kiātivāparadukkhan, hiṣsatiāvin setiāitiākaruṇā; kiriyatiāvdukkhiteṣu, pharaṇavasena pasḶriyati iti karuṇā. *Visuddhimagga of BuddhaghosḶcariya*, Harvard Oriental Series, Vol. 41, ed. Henry Clarke Warren, revised Dharmananda Kosambi (Cambridge: Harvard University Press, 1950), chapter IX, verse 92, p. 263, as cited by Stephen Jenkins, "Do Bodhisattvas Relieve Poverty?," in *Action Dharma: New Studies in Engaged Buddhism*, Christopher S. Queen, Charles Prebish and Damien Keown eds. (London: RoutledgeCurzon, 2003), 41.
10. His Holiness The Dalai Lama. *Ethics for the New Millennium* (New York: Riverhead Books, 1999), 74-75.
11. Kenneth Kraft, ed., Inner Peace, *World Peace: Essays on Buddhism and Nonviolence,* (Albany: SUNY Press,1992)18.
12. Arnold Kotler, "Breathing and Smiling: Traveling with Thich Nhat Hanh," *BPF Newsletter* 11:2 (Summer 1989), 22.

13. Thich Nhat Hanh, *The Miracle of Mindfulness!* (Boston: Beacon Press, 1975), 75.
14. Philip Russell Brown, 2004. "Socially Engaged Buddhism: A Buddhist Practice for the West." *Buddhanet*. Accessed from http://www.buddhanetz.org/texte/brown.htm.
15. http://nalanda.org.my/e-library/community/communityv2i3/a4.php.
16. http://nalanda.org.my/e-library/community/communityv2i3/a4.php.
17. See http://buddhism-dict.net/cgi-bin/xpr-db.pl?q=%E4%B8%8A%E6%B1%82%E8%8F%A9%E6%8F%90%E4%B8%8B%E5%8C%96%E8% A1%86%E7%94%9F.
18. http://www.buddhistglobalrelief.org/active/guideposts.html.
19. http://www.thebuddhadharma.com/web-archive/2007/9/1/a-challenge-to-buddhists.html.
20. http://www.thebuddhadharma.com/web-archive/2007/9/1/a-challenge-to-buddhists.html.
21. http://www.buddhistglobalrelief.org/active/ourHistory.html.
22. http://www.buddhistglobalrelief.org/active/financialInfo.html.
23. http://www.buddhistglobalrelief.org/active/guideposts.html.
24. http://www.buddhistglobalrelief.org/active/donation.php.
25. Ven. Bhikkhu Bodhi, 2013. Message to BGR Walks to Feed the Hungry. Email document file.
26. Received March 15, 2014.
27. The phrase 'new social face' is lifted from the title of Ken Jones' important contribution to Buddhist social activism, *The New Social Face of Buddhism: A Call to Action* (Boston: Wisdom Publications, 2003).
28. Frank Tedesco, "Dying in Modern Korea" in David W. Chappell and Karma Lekshe Tsomo, eds., *Living and Dying in Buddhist Cultures* (Manoa: Buddhist Studies Program, University of Hawai'i, 1994), 115-19.
29. For scanty data, see http://en.wikipedia.org/wiki/Seongsu_Bridge
30. http://en.wikipedia.org/wiki Sampoong_Department_Store_collapse. This article includes photos. 29 Tedesco, Frank M. 'Abortion in Korea' in Damien Keown, ed., *Buddhism and Abortion* (Honolulu: University of Hawai'i Press, 1999), Chapter 7, 121 55.
31. Frank M. Tedesco, "Social Engagement in South Korean Buddhism" in *Action Buddhism: New Studies in Engaged Buddhism*, Christopher

Queen, Charles Prebish and Damien Keown eds. (London: RoutledgeCurzon, 2003), 176-77.

32. Franla Tedesco, "Questions for Buddhist and Christian Cooperation in Korea," Buddhist-Christian Studies, 17, 1997, 179-95.
33. For mostly convert Buddhist groups in Florida, see http://www.smiling-buddha.com/fldharma/
34. David W. Chappell, "Racial Diversity in the Soka Gakkai" in Queen, Christopher S., ed. *Engaged Buddhism in the West* (Boston: Wisdom, 2000), 184-87.
35. Sumi Loundon Kim, "Family Programming in Buddhist Community" in Giles, Cheryl A. and Miller, Willa B. *The Arts of Contemplative Care* (Boston: Wisdom, 2012), 315-23.
36. "What Would Sid Do? http://www.huffingtonpost.com/lodro-rinzler/.
37. Kabat-Zinn, Jon, *Full Catastrophe Living: Using the Wisdom of Your Body and Mind to Face Stress, Pain, and Illness* (New York: Delta, 1990), 5-6.
38. "While the dominant orientation of Western culture toward death is avoidance, for over 2,500 years Buddhists have studied the question of how one can best live in the presence of death. In a sense, a life-threatening injury or disease makes Buddhists of us all, waking us from the illusion of immortality, suddenly and from that time forth. From the moment of diagnosis, death becomes the bell that won't stop ringing." Ira Byock, M.D., Foreword to Joan Halifax. *Being with Dying: Cultivating Compassion and Fearlessness in the Presence of Death* (Boston: Shambhala, 2008), xi.
39. One of the most popular Buddhist books in the West for dealing with death is the classic by an affable Tibetan lama, Sogyal Rinpoche, *The Tibetan Book of Living and Dying* (New York: Harper San Francisco, 1992). There are a plethora of compassionate end-of-life books on the market now. Elisabeth Kubler-Ross's books are among the classics. Buddhist translations and modern handbooks for healing and dying abound.
40. Cheryl A. Giles and Willa B. Miller, *The Arts of Contemplative Care* (Boston: Wisdom, 2012), 325.
41. Max Zahn, Buddhist volunteers comfort families of those lost on Flight 370. March 27, 2014, http://www.tricycle.com/blog/buddhist-volunteers-comfort-families-those-lost-flight-370.